KANE

A Castle Sin Novel

Book Three

Linzi Basset

A Dark BDSM Suspense Novel

By

Linzi Basset

Linzi Basset

KANE - CASTLE SIN #3

Copyright © 2019 Linzi Basset
Edited by: Kristen Breanne
Proofreaders: Marie Vayer, Melanie Marnell, Kemberlee
Snelling, Charlotte Strickland
Published & Cover Design by: Linzi Basset
ISBN: 9781709594250

use of the information contained in this book.

Contents

Author's Note

Dear Reader,

Castle Sin
Seven dungeons
Seven Masters
Seven times the kink.

An exclusive BDSM club offering memberships only to selected Dominants. Submissives and slaves were available for every taste.

Personally, trained by each of the Castle Masters.

In Kane, book 3, we meet Kane Sinclair or Master Bear and Rose Lovett. A story of deceit, despair, and vengeance.
"It is said that a woman who has found her true Master has no control over the command he has over her inner submissive." His voice lowered an octave. *"Just like yours just did."*

Altered by a cruel twist of fate, his life was forever changed. Could he ever learn to love again?

Kane Sinclair, or Master Bear at Castle Sin, was tired of Hollywood. It was time to move on from being an actor and living in the past. Even after sixteen years of self-castigation and guilt due to the loss of the only woman he'd ever loved, moving on from her had never been in the cards ... but he could move on from Hollywood. Especially when the slightly plump and bratty Rose Lovett arrived at Castle Sin's training academy to offer him a distraction. He couldn't deny the chemistry between them or the unexplained magnetic pull he simply couldn't resist.

"So, that's what the sprinkling of silver at your temples means. You do know loss of memory is a sure sign of dotage."

She was haunted by the lies of her past and the love of the man she could never forget.

Rose's arrival as sub RL at Castle Sin came in the wake of a double-edged promise. One, she soon realized, wouldn't be as easy to fulfill. For the first five months, she managed to avoid the powerful Master Bear. He unsettled her, but the moment she came under his radar, she knew exactly what she had done. He had the ability to twist her body and her mind in ways she could never have imagined. Though she tried to keep her distance, what woman wouldn't stand queue for the attention of the "*pass-*

out-fucking-machine," Master Bear?

Under his unwavering scrutiny, Rose couldn't hide the secrets she had possessed for so long, and when Master Bear discovered them, his fury unleashed the demon inside him.

Their lives had been cruelly twisted by fate.

She could have been his future ...

If only the lies shrouded in the ghosts of their past would allow him to forgive and forget ...

Editor Note:

This just tugs on your heartstrings, and so many other parts. A slight veer off the normal paved path, this story takes you on a ride (don't we all wish literally) of mental, emotional, and physical stimulation that will have you wishing Master Bear would pay you a visit. Sprinkle that with the nostalgia of their past and the prayer for their future, and you won't be able to put this book down...unless you pass out.

I trust you will enjoy this story as much as I did creating it.

Warm regards,
Linzi Basset

Linzi Basset

Chapter One

"The answer is no, Cleopatra. I've had my fun and I'm going to bed."

He sighed. He could be a bastard ... at times. Something he readily admitted to himself. That in itself wasn't a big deal but there were times that he deliberately fed the dark demons inside his soul. Then he didn't give a fuck who was on the receiving end of those beasts demanding relief from the emptiness inside his soul—that dark void. A never-ending swirling vortex that consumed everything, left him feeling nothing. Desolate. Sweet fuck all to subside in his hollow soul that crept in the shadows.

Lately, he'd been drawing back from people more and more because its emptiness had become so all-consuming it threatened to drown him.

"But Master Bear, I have so much energy left." Cleopatra slid closer to the brooding man at the bar. She had been left breathless after the devastating scene with him in The Dungeon of Sin, and still now, long since his aftercare had finished, her entire body sizzled. He, on the other hand, had smiled at her, patted her chin and walked away. Like he hadn't just fucked her until she passed out. Her loins throbbed for more, and tonight, she wasn't allowing him to deny her like he had done with every sub who begged to spend the night with him.

It was a known fact that many of the full-time employed submissives had tried to get under the elusive older Master's skin. He exuded confidence and a high-octane power that acted like a magnet. The fact that he was mountain-man rough and attractive, not to mention he fucked like a stallion, made him even more alluring to women of all ages.

"I can make your bed less lonely, Master Bear. I'd love to repay you for the earth-shattering climax you just gave me," she cooed in his ear as she pressed against his side. Her hand stole over his stomach, inching towards the bulge in his leathers.

"Did I give you permission to touch me, sub?"

Cleopatra froze as his dark voice timbered through her. She glanced at him as she retracted her hand which started to tremble from the glacial look in his eyes. She'd forgotten about his cast in steel rule—never to touch without permission—in her eagerness to prove she'd be the one to win him over. Master Bear was known as one of the easygoing cousins of the seven owners of Castle Sin, an exclusive BDSM club on the privately-owned, The Seven Keys Island, in Key West—until you rubbed him the wrong way.

"I apologize, Master Bear. I never meant to be disrespectful," she murmured with lowered eyes and stood in the Castle Sin present position with her hands behind her back, feet spread apart, and her shoulders straight with tits pushed forward.

Kane Sinclair felt listless. The demonstration he just had with Cleopatra had been intense and ended in an explosive climax. Not that it mattered. He still felt charged. His cock at half-mast was an indication that yet again, he hadn't achieved the mind-blowing climaxes he used to with …

"Fuck," he cursed the unwanted memory searing through his mind, like a burning ember that just wouldn't die no matter how hard he had tried over the past sixteen years. He turned his gaze to the petite blonde submissive, waiting on his wrath.

"What's your position here at Castle Sin, Cleopatra?" His voice slashed like the cutting edge of a knife through the air. She visibly trembled and licked her lips nervously.

"I'm an employed submissive, Master Bear."

"Yes, and that means you're here to serve whom?"

Her chin lowered an inch more, her voice into a whisper. "The paying members of Castle Sin, Master Bear."

"Then I suggest you go back to The Dungeon of Sin and do just that."

Kane didn't feel anything at the surprise that flashed in her eyes. He didn't appreciate manipulative submissives, those who tried to top from the bottom, like Cleopatra subtly attempted.

Sometimes getting old was a fucking nuisance. Every submissive and trainee was careful not to sass him and Shane, the oldest two of the seven Sinclair, aka Rothman, cousins as they were known in Tinsel town as actors. Probably because they had the reputation of dishing out harsh punishments.

That was part of the bullshit listlessness he felt. He loved brats, cheeky subs who weren't scared to push his boundaries, willing to take a chance, no matter the repercussions. That was the kind of challenge he missed. Training the Doms and submissives fulfilled him to an extent but on a personal level, he had yet to hit the mark.

Like Stone and Hawk had with the two cousins, Peyton and Savannah, whom they'd fallen in love with. Cheeky as they come and challenging their mighty Masters fearlessly.

"Do you mean … aren't you going to punish me, Master Bear?" Cleopatra asked with a mixture of fear and excitement in her voice.

"No, I'm not, but if you insist, I'll ask Master Fox to take care of it in my stead."

Cleopatra's wary gaze flickered to Shane Sinclair, the oldest of the cousins, who sauntered closer. She retreated a couple of steps. Master Fox was the one Dom she walked circles around. His reputation of wielding two whips simultaneously in both hands was well known.

"That won't be necessary, Master Bear. Thank you for choosing me for the demonstration. I had a lot of fun."

Kane didn't respond. She quickly made herself scarce as Shane reached the bar and slipped onto the barstool next to him. He didn't look at Shane as he sipped on the rich, dark flavor of the single malt McMillan whiskey he'd been nursing for a while.

"Where's your mind at, Kane?" Shane studied him for a moment. He didn't miss the rigid line of his jaw or the impassive expression. "Even during the scene, you made the sub fly, but I got the impression that you weren't in it. Not like you're supposed to be."

"You're right. I shouldn't have done the demonstration." His eyes drifted to the couple to his right. Peyton Jackson, Stone's sub, faced off against him, her foot tapping in frustration as she stabbed a stiff finger against his chest.

Stone's deep rumble reached their ears. "Ah, Petals, I love it when your bratty mouth lands you smack in the middle of punishment."

"I guess I'm tired of floating between subs." Kane shrugged as he turned his attention back to Shane. "Since Stone and Hawk found their proverbial birds of a feather, I've felt myself searching." He glanced at Shane. "I want what they have, Shane, and not just any permanent sub, the kind of woman they found—cheeky, bratty and challenging. That's what I'm after." He sighed. "Besides, I can't allow the past to keep haunting me. I'm fucking tired of walking the path alone."

"I've waited over sixteen years to hear you say that." Shane squeezed his shoulder. "Neither of us ..." Shane swallowed visibly as he found his mind floundering into chambers that had been off limits for an equal number of years. "We're too fucking old to compete with these young studs."

"Old, my ass. In case you haven't noticed, we're the only Masters every sub here, no matter their age, tries to lure to their bed for the night."

"There's much to be said for experience." Shane chuckled. "Is that what Cleopatra was after?"

"What else?" Kane swallowed the last of his drink. "You know what's the worst of it, Shane? Of becoming so entrenched with our acting careers, fame, and fortune?" He tapped his finger on the counter, indicating a refill before he looked at Shane. "Being fatherless. I've always wanted children, a daughter and a son ... for that we're too fucking old. No woman over forty will be willing to have a baby and I'm not interested in younger women ... not as a wife."

"It's the same void I feel. A wife and children." Shane's voice sounded whimsical. He accepted the drink the bartender handed him and took a sip. "You know we only have ourselves to blame. Instead of using the time between movie productions to find someone, we buried ourselves in the war zones accepting covert black ops."

"It was the only way I could cope ... and forget." Kane's eyes filled with sadness. "I suppose it was watching that bastard, Decker Cooper, who caused Savannah so much pain, burn to death that unchained the memories and this feeling of … I don't know … need."

"It had to be done. He'd have found a way to avoid jail again and he would've continued tormenting Hawk and Savannah," Shane said silently.

As the oldest cousins of the family, they took protecting and caring for them and their loved ones very seriously. No one had been there for them all those years ago and they'd sworn to keep their family safe. Decker Cooper was the scum of the earth who had enriched himself with human trafficking. It was at his hands that Savannah Thorne, Hawk's sub, had ended up as a sex slave for a year to the feared leader of the Russian Bratva. He had to pay and they made sure he'd never hurt anyone again. Neither of them felt any remorse for the horrid death they'd bestowed on the man. It had been deserved.

Kane nursed his drink between his hands. "But it was too quick. He should've died a slow torturous death."

"At least he suffered until his dying breath." Shane hesitated briefly, knowing why torching and watching the bastard burn alive had been haunting Kane. "Have you ever visited her grave?"

For a moment, the question hung heavy between them.

"For what? It's not as if that's where her body is buried. It's an empty fucking coffin, Shane. No. I didn't attend the funeral and I'll never go to the grave." Kane got up. His expression turned somber. "And let's not fool ourselves. We didn't go searching for a woman because we never got over losing the ones we had."

"In my case, I was the fool." Shane got up and caught Kane's eyes with an earnest look. "Narine would never have wanted you to be alone for this long. It's about time, Kane. Way past time."

"I'm done for the night. I'm going to—"

"Oh, hell no. You're coming to the dungeon with me. Who knows, there might be one of the trainees or subs we've overlooked that might be perfect for either of us."

"Who are you trying to fool, Shane? You want to check if Stone's PA is playing tonight." Kane chuckled and forced the tiredness off his shoulders as they walked toward The Dungeon of Sin.

"You can't deny Alexa looks rather scrumptious on a Saint Andrew's Cross." Shane's eyes glimmered. "I have a feeling about that one, Kane. She tickles something inside me that I haven't felt in a long time."

"So, go for it."

"Soon ... for now, I'm enjoying playing cat and mouse too much."

Kane laughed as they entered the Torture Chamber and he found his eyes searching the room. He was startled when he realized what he was doing.

"Fuck me," he grunted.

"What?" Shane looked around and followed his gaze that was riveted on a scene in the far corner. "Sub RL? What's ... ah! I see," he smiled. "So, you already found what you sought."

"I only just realized that I search for her every time I walk into one of the dungeons. It's like my eyes automatically zoom in on her, like my mind connects with her before I know where she is."

"She's a beautiful woman, and if I recall correctly, mid-forties? Perfect age for you."

"Hmm … problem is, the moment I walk into a room or approach her, she clamps shut and runs in the opposite direction. She hardly ever looks directly at me and I get the impression she deliberately avoids getting close to me."

"Well, unfortunately for her, as of tomorrow, she won't have a choice. She'll be up close and personal in your training dungeon for a month."

"Perfect timing, I'd say," Kane chuckled. "You find your little mouse, Shane. I'm going to mosey over there and see what the fuss is all about."

Eyes turned to watch Kane as he strolled through the Torture Chamber. A regular occurrence, as the subs were magnetically drawn to the powerful Master who exuded confidence by his mere presence. He was the perfect portrayal of the bear totem, his spiritual animal. Always equanimous, he reflected qualities of emotional strength and fearlessness. Everyone was in awe of the subtle way he projected it to others. He had become a grounding force for many subs over the years as he guided them to find their inner submissive, embrace it, and become the best they could be.

"Just what gave you the right, sub? No wait, you're not a submissive of the club, you're still a trainee, according to the red band on your wrist." The irate voice of a Dom Kane didn't recognize, grated in his ears as he approached. His eyes narrowed as sub RL slammed her fists on her hips and tossed back her hair.

Blatant disrespect, sub RL? You should know better by now.

His gaze followed the luxurious curtain of chestnut tresses tumbling down her back. She was the kind of woman that other females of all ages loved to hate. She was forty-four, if memory served him correctly, but she had the exuberance of youth enhanced by her poise and a sexy strut that exuded confidence. She was tall, probably five-foot-seven, and a little on the plump side but with a perfectly curved body and gorgeously rounded hips that he'd witnessed made many Doms stop in their tracks and stare. He halted a couple of steps behind her, accessing her profile as she turned her head to the Dom scowling at her. His fingers itched to trace the line of her high cheekbones, to feel if her skin was as smooth and silky as it looked in its flawless perfection. Apart from the small laugh lines around her eyes, she didn't show any signs of her age. Her breathtaking beauty was enhanced by the intelligence and confidence she always radiated, which was the conduit of his attraction to her.

Her rosy lips glistened as she licked them once, pursed the fullness into a pout and took a deep breath.

"I might be a trainee here but I've been a submissive for a long time and I'm not an idiot."

Kane's ears pricked as she openly sassed the angry Dom. Her voice had a scratchy roughness that caused his cock to twitch delightfully. His instincts about Rose Lovett had been spot on. This was the kind of woman he'd been searching for.

"You are indeed if you think I'm going to stand for a sub talking to me like that," the Dom sneered.

"I don't care but I'll not stand by and allow this scene to continue."

"Really?" The Dom turned to the small gathering of people behind him. "Did someone hear this sub use her safeword? No, she didn't and—"

"Because she's in too much pain to even think! Anyone can see that sub is in distress." Rose pointed furiously toward a woman on a spanking bench, crying pitifully. Her naked buttocks were covered in vicious red streaks.

Kane's curse exploded into the atmosphere as his gaze found the target of her stiff finger. All attention centered on him. He rushed forward and with two economic yanks, the sub was loose. He assisted her upright and held her shivering form against his chest.

"I'm sorry, Master Bear, I should've used my safeword but I couldn't get out a word. I was too shocked and in so much pain." She gulped back a sob. "We agreed on a medium flogging not … not what he did."

"It's over, Violet. I've got you." His deep voice soothed even the people who had gathered once the spectacle began.

"Master Bear, is it? Well, I demand to punish this trainee for interrupting my scene, not to mention her blatant disrespect toward me."

Kane turned to face the fuming man, his expression stoic as he stared at him. The Dom puffed up his chest and straightened his bulky form as he met Kane's brown eyes that glimmered like sunlight shining through whiskey.

"You don't deserve respect," Rose all but spat in his direction. Her eyes fell to the floor the moment Kane's head turned in her direction.

"We'll discuss this matter in my office." Kane looked around in search of Dom Evans, one of the senior Doms and training managers at Castle Sin Training Academy. He gestured to him. "Dom Evans, please take care of Violet. I'll be back to check on her in a bit."

Kane brushed the tears from her cheeks and smiled encouragingly at her. "Dom Evans will rub some arnica and the Castle's special soothing gel on to give you some relief." He frowned in thought. Violet had been an employed submissive at the Castle for the past ten months. She was well liked and had five years of experience behind her. "Was anyone present when you discussed the scene, Violet?"

"Yes, Master Bear. I requested Dom Danton to be there, seeing as I don't know this Dom and I felt I needed some reassurance."

"Good girl. Now, go with Dom Evans." Kane turned to the irate man who steamed angrily as he watched Evans pick Violet up and carry her toward the aftercare area. "I don't believe we've met?" The distrust gathered like clouds before a thunderstorm in Kane's eyes as he stared at him unflinchingly.

They were very strict about visitors. Only an exclusive member could request to sponsor a guest. Even then, they were first screened and a background check ran before permission was given.

"I'm Dom Gunther Locke from Tampa." His nose inched higher to indicate he deemed himself to be a man of importance.

"Who is your sponsor, Dom Gunther?" Kane's voice grated darkly from his lips. He didn't appreciate people riding high on personally induced self-importance.

Kane's hand snaked out to catch Rose's arm as she tried to edge unobtrusively away from the scene. She froze as his fingers wrapped around her elbow. Her surprised gasp floated toward him. It was a musical melody that offered him immense pleasure. Sub RL wasn't as unmoved by his presence as he'd believed. He dragged her against his side.

"Senator Martin," Dom Gunther crowed with another flash of blustering opinionism.

"Shall we go?" Kane started to walk. His hand tightened around Rose's arm as she hung back. He flicked a warning glance over his shoulder. "Is there a problem, sub RL?"

"No, Master Bear. I just don't see why I need to accompany you."

"Then you're in bigger trouble than you could imagine," he rasped.

"Me? Why the devil am I in trouble? I'm not the one who—"

Rose all but swallowed her tongue as he turned on her and she walked slam bang into his hard chest. Her hands spread out to push away from him. Her breathing faltered, her muscles locked, and she couldn't move, no matter how hard her brain screamed at her to.

Damn, he's so warm. How can he be this warm all over?

Kane held out his hand and clicked his fingers. Jenna, a club coordinator, placed a thin chain in his palm. She always served him when he was in attendance at the member dungeons.

"Hands behind your back, sub RL and make sure they stay there." He clipped one end of the chain into the O-ring of the red leather collar all trainees wore. The other end he attached to a loop of his pants. It irritated him that she didn't look at him but kept her gaze centered on his chest. "Keep up, my pet, and I suggest your mouth stay shut unless I specifically ask you question. Is that understood?"

"Yes, *Sir*," Rose snapped to attention, her eyes flared as she clamped her hands behind her.

Crack! Crack!

"Freaking hell ... oww," she wailed as his huge paw connected with her ass. She had no idea how he even managed to reach seeing as he stood facing her.

"What did you call me, sub RL?"

Her cheeks bloomed red and she couldn't even pretend it had been a slip of the tongue. It had been deliberate. An attempt to …

What? An attempt to make a complete ass of yourself, Rose? Not to mention a freaking scorching ass as reward!

"I'm sorry! I meant Master Bear," she squealed and stepped out of reach as his hand rose threateningly when she didn't respond quick enough.

"What's the hold-up?" Gunther Locke sneered behind Kane. "I came here to play and—"

Kane took off, ignoring the complaining man, with Rose tagging along behind him, muttering all the way about his inconsideration for not shortening his steps.

"You're ratcheting up the punishments, sub. I suggest you zip your lips and quickly."

Kane stopped next to Stone where he was overseeing a whipping demonstration by one of the assistant training Doms.

"I have a situation with a visiting Dom. Apparently, Senator Martin is his sponsor. Know anything about it?"

Stone's eyes flicked to the man approaching. "Yes, but the condition was that he had to be accompanied by Senator Martin at all times. Do you need me to take care of this?"

"No, I'll handle it. Please ask Senator Martin and Danton to join us in my office." He looked around. "Find out who the Dungeon Monitor on duty in this section is, Stone. If he had been doing his job, this wouldn't have gone as far as it did."

"I agree. I'll take care of it."

Kane continued toward his office, leaving Rose no choice but to jog to keep up with his long strides. He sat down behind the desk and tugged on the chain.

"Down. On your knees next to my chair, please."

Her eyes widened as he pointed to a spot next to him. He noticed that she still managed to keep from looking directly at him when she said in an indignant sputter, "You expect me to sit on the floor like a ... like a ..."

"A well-behaved pet." His voice sounded as smooth as silk. "Yes, sub RL, I do." The wicked smile quirking his lips was in reaction to her delightful brattiness, exactly what he'd been missing from other subs and trainees of Castle Sin.

To Rose, it was anything but a pleasant smile and it promised all kinds of *Dom* retribution. Just thinking of the punishment scenes she'd witnessed from him, made her legs crumble and she plopped onto her knees without any attempt at grace.

"It's a good thing you're in my training dungeon as from tomorrow. It seems you have a lot to learn about decorum and elegance."

She opened her mouth to snap at him but the timely arrival of Dom Gunther saved her from plunging herself deeper into trouble.

Chapter Two

"Please take a seat, Mr. Locke."

Gunther Locke sat down. He shifted uncomfortably under Kane's intense regard and looked around the room. In Rose's opinion, it was to avoid the cold, unflinching stare from the formidable Master Bear. She'd witnessed many submissives edging out of harm's way when he was on the warpath.

Kane's eyes were bewitching; it was as if their roasted-coffee-bean rim had diffused into a cream hued iris—mixing until it was the color of sun-dried beechwood. She'd noticed them change hues in tandem with his moods. His direct gaze was a sign of the confidence that oozed from his persona.

Rose turned her head slightly and darted an unobtrusive look at Kane. His mahogany hair had a tousled look that she loved so much. She'd seen him drag his hands through it often enough to know it was how the devil-may-care style was born. Usually brushed back, the locks now fell over his broad forehead, which tapered into a square, sculpted jaw and high cheekbones.

Gawd, he's so attractive. Just being near him makes me all hot and bothered.

Rose fisted her hands and tightened the muscles in her thighs to contain the rush of heat that shot south and settled in a spicy bouquet between her legs even *she* could detect. She wished she could clamp her knees together because as an all-powerful Master, Kane would have no problem sniffing her arousal. She discarded that thought at birth. On your knees in Castle Sin meant shuffle into the Nadu position and stay there. She had no intention of eliciting punishment from him. Not from Master Bear ... she couldn't afford to. The further she stayed away from him, the better.

"Well? Let's get this over with, shall we? I wish to get back to my scene," Gunther snapped. He crossed his arms over his chest.

Rose was hard pressed not to laugh at the subconscious act of raising a barrier from Kane's continued regard. She dared a more direct look this time.

His aquiline nose tilted regally, which sat above a full, very kissable mouth amid a neat stubble beard that gave him a rugged look—like an uncut diamond—a very desirable one.

It's such a pity he's off limits to me.

She suppressed the thought as it pierced through years of ironclad control into the deepest chambers of her heart. Pain sliced through her body.

Don't open that door, Rose. Do. Not. Open. It!

She pressed her lips together and forced her mind back to the present as Kane's deep voice flowed through her, calming and imparting a glow inside her. She latched onto the feeling like a starved animal.

"We're waiting on your sponsor and the Dom who was present during the negotiation of the scene with sub Violet," Kane said colloquially.

"What the fuck for? I thought we were here to discuss the attitude of this disrespectful trainee," Gunther exploded.

Rose stiffened, nibbling worriedly on her bottom lip. She had been hugely disrespectful, but she couldn't stand by and watch how he disregarded Violet's obvious distress and continued to flog her with cruel enjoyment.

She glanced at Kane to assess his mood but got sidetracked as her gaze found the crows' feet at his temples and the lines under his eyes that told of laughter, of warm smiles and affection. Another pain seared through her heart. *Focus, Rose!* She wished she could trace the deep vertical lines that edged between his brows and drew his face into a permanent frown. It stemmed from more than advancement in age but painted a picture of some hardship in his life. The few lines on his forehead didn't diminish the energy and power he exuded. If she didn't know he was inching toward fifty-two, she'd have thought him to be in his mid-forties.

"Be assured that I'll personally address sub RL's disrespect ... and no," Kane continued when Gunther opened his mouth to protest, "I don't need you to elaborate. I arrived at the time and was privy to the entire conversation."

Rose cringed at the dark edge that crept into Kane's voice. She lowered her eyes quickly as he slanted a sideways look at her. She had disregarded one of the main rules of the member's dungeons—to immediately call the Dungeon Monitor or one of the Masters.

Danton Hill walked in after a brief knock on the door. He was the security director of The Seven Keys Island and Be Secure Enterprises, the Global security company the seven Sinclair cousins owned. He was also the senior training Dom of the training academy. Senator Martin followed close on his heels. They sat down at Kane's prodding.

"Senator Martin, you were awarded permission to sponsor a guest this evening with the specific provision that he accompanies you at all times inside the dungeon," Kane said through thin lips. Although his body and posture were completely relaxed, his eyes shot daggers between the two men.

"I'm not a child that needs to be kept on a leash," Gunther snapped.

Eckard Martin slanted an annoyed look at his sister's brother-in-law. He should've followed his gut instinct and said no. He never liked Gunther Locke and he trusted him even less.

"I suspect you don't understand, Mr. Locke. You're here as a concession only because Senator Martin is a member of good standing at Castle Sin. This isn't an open club. We keep it exclusive and by invitation only for a reason and have very strict rules for any visitors."

"My apologies, Master Bear. I went for something to drink from the bar and got stuck in a conversation with a friend. The intention wasn't to be gone long, but ..." another annoyed look at Gunter, "I told him to wait at the reception area until I was back. What happened?"

"Dom Danton, please explain what agreement Dom Gunther made with sub Violet." Kane sat back in his chair, the chain of the leash slithered to the floor as he unclipped it from his belt. He placed his hand at the back of Rose's neck, caressing the softness of her skin with small circling motions. It pleased him to feel her stiffening under his touch, even more so when an uncontrolled shiver trailed through her frame.

"Violet agreed to an erotic, medium impact flogging over a spanking bench. She also insisted to be untied," Danton said.

Kane straightened. His gaze bore into Gunther who once again shifted uncomfortably. "So, you totally disregarded the agreed scene, Mr. Locke," Kane gruffed.

"Dom Gunther," he snapped.

"A Dom in Castle Sin takes care of the submissive he scenes with and he honors the agreement he made with her. You, sir, did neither. Violet was tied down so tightly she couldn't move and to make matters worse, you went beyond a *hard* impact flogging to brutal. That isn't the action of a *Dominant.*"

"Now, look here—"

"I suggest you shut up, Gunther." Eckard's acerbic tone cut him short. "Violet is a sweet young sub and I'm sorry she had to suffer because of his brutality. How is she?" A concerned frown marred his forehead.

"She'll be fine. We're taking care of her. Needless to say, Senator, the sponsorship for Mr. Locke is herewith withdrawn. He won't be allowed back inside Castle Sin's dungeons or on The Seven Keys Island." Kane leaned his elbows on the desk. His eyes darkened warningly. "I'm sorry it cuts your evening short but I want him off the island immediately."

"I understand." Eckard got up. He glowered at Gunther. "Get up. We're leaving."

"I'm not going anywhere. I came here to ... Hey! Let me go."

Gunther was caught off guard by Kane who yanked him out of the chair by the neck of his shirt. He'd moved around the desk so fast, Gunther didn't have time to get out of the furious man's way.

Kane pushed him toward the door.

"I didn't ask or give you a fucking choice. You're not welcome here." Kane pressed his face into Gunther's. "Let me give you a fair warning, Gunther

Locke. Say one word about this club, any of us or the patrons, and I'll make your life utter hell. Do you understand?"

Gunther stumbled as Kane dragged him down the hallway, across the enormous entrance hall and pushed him through the front door. "Yes, I understand," he mumbled as Eckard jabbed him in the side.

"I'm sorry for the unpleasantness, Master Bear. Be assured, I'll think twice before I sponsor family again."

Kane nodded and watched the two men leave with a morose expression on his face. He hated Doms who took advantage of the trust a submissive placed in them by offering her subjugation. The Gunthers of the world weren't Dominants, they weren't even men; they were fucking cowards.

He turned back toward his office. A movement at the top of the majestic staircase caught his eye.

"Freeze, sub RL." He didn't raise his voice and he wasn't even sure she heard him, but she turned into a statue, her hand resting on the balustrade.

All trainees were robbed of their identity during the training period and called by their initials. It was done specifically to draw the line of them developing expectations from any of the training Masters or Doms. They'd learned their lesson early on when Castle Sin's Training Academy was launched.

"Get back down here." The order was given in the same even tone. His lips twitched as Rose's chin dropped in dejection. He waited patiently until she turned and started to descend. "On your knees, please."

She shot a disbelieving look at him. Her mouth opened but when Danton, who leaned negligently against a wide arch leading into the Gathering Hall, cleared his throat in warning, she sank to her knees. Her low grumbling complaint floated toward them.

"Speak up, trainee, I can't hear you if you mumble," Kane continued to taunt her.

"I said, Master Bear, crawling down a flight of stairs is a sure-fire way to break something," Rose clipped.

"Hm, I think the stairs are sturdy enough to withstand your slight weight as you go, sub RL, and should you manage to break one in the process, not to worry, we'll fix it."

Her head snapped up. "When did you morph into the court jester, Master Bear? I assure you, I don't find your remark humorous in the least." She shot a chilled look Danton's way when he barked a short laugh.

"Speed it up, sub, you're wasting my time. On the other hand, don't. It's a rather sexy sight watching your ass jiggle as you descend."

"Jiggle! Are you saying I'm fat, Master Bear?"

Kane frowned as he detected a tinge of self-castigation tremble in her voice. She wasn't model thin and perhaps had a layer of added padding, but she was in no way fat. The black mini skirt paired with a tight sapphire blue corset, which pushed her gorgeous breasts upward for an enticing view, emphasized every sensual curve of her body. She was seduction, pure and simple, from the bottom of her feet to the top of her head but her reaction warned him that she was sensitive over her weight. His face darkened. It was something he'd put an end to ... and quickly.

"Did you hear me say that, Dom Danton?" He kept his eyes on hers, detecting the red blush blooming bright over her cheeks as she reached the bottom of the stairs. He pointed to a spot in front of his feet. Her lips thinned but she dutifully crawled closer.

"Nope. Far as I recall, you said sexy and I have to concur; fucking hot, Master Bear."

Rose didn't take kindly to being discussed like she wasn't even there and didn't think twice about getting to her feet once she reached Kane. His voice grated a warning in her tender ears.

"Did I tell you to stand?"

"Freaking hell," she muttered and sank back onto her knees.

"Good girl."

She felt her ears heating with pleasure as his deep voice washed over her and she basked in his praise.

"Now, you may stand."

Before she could help herself, she slanted a furious look at him, intending to blast his ears with her discontent ... and froze as their gazes clashed.

Her legs turned to rubber and try as she might, she couldn't gather the strength to get to her feet. Kane stared at her with an expression akin to shocked surprise, which rapidly morphed to suspicious anger. She bit the inside of her cheek and quickly lowered her eyes. This time, he would have none of it. He pinched her chin between his fingers and forced her head backward but she adamantly kept her gaze locked on his chest.

"Eyes," he snapped. He could feel his skin tighten around his frame that felt like it was about to shudder into shreds. It didn't help to brace himself. The moment her eyelids drifted upward, he got hit with the same debilitating blast of shocked disbelief like moments before. He'd looked into these eyes before, many times and loved how they turned smoky just before she screamed out her climax. They were like a blue flame on water and encapsulated all the passion inside her in their crystallized, ice beauty.

"Fuck." He shook his head and closed his eyes to ban the vision of the auburn-haired woman from his mind. He cleared his throat that suddenly clogged up. He sounded hoarse as he spoke. "You have unusual eyes." His fingers traced the outline of her lower lid. "Do you have any siblings with similar color eyes?"

"I ... ahem." Rose struggled to breathe in the face of the torment she could read in the now stoic man's eyes. "No, Master Bear. I'm an only child and my cousins on my father's side take after their Latina mother. They have very dark eyes." She whimpered as his fingers tightened on her chin. "D-do you know someone with the same color eyes?" Her voice sounded breathy and she prayed that he didn't notice how badly she trembled. She sighed in relief when his hand fell and he turned away.

"No ... not anymore." The words were uttered so softly, Rose had difficulty hearing them.

"I'm sorry, Master Bear." She swallowed hard as she stared at his stiff back. Her mind raced to find a way to steer his thoughts from her eyes.

"For what?"

"I'm wearing colored contact lenses. I've got very dull gray eyes and ..." She shrugged and offered him a wry smile. "I apologize for bringing back memories you preferred to forget. I—oh!" she gasped as he spun around and wrapped his hand around her throat. He yanked her to her feet and up close.

Rose knew better than to claw at his hand and kept as still as possible in the face of his anger.

"You should be, sub RL. It's the kind of memories I ..." His nose tilted regally as he exhaled slowly. The instantaneous transformation was breathtaking. One moment he was lost in a sphere of a painful past and the next, she was faced with the fearsome Master Bear.

"It's time for your punishment," he clipped coldly.

"But I had justification for what I did! That man ..." Her voice dwindled and evaporated in her throat as his eyes narrowed. His fingers tightened, forcing her to go onto her toes. Her breath wheezed from her lips as the position pushed her breasts against his hard and so very hot chest. They immediately puckered into hard little nubs.

"What were you supposed to do, sub RL, the moment you realized something was amiss?"

"Call the Dungeon Monitor or one of the Castle Masters."

"Instead, you chose to allow his torment of Violet to continue until *you* gathered enough courage to intervene, am I correct?"

Rose stared at the immovable man, his words castigating her with a similar sharpness as that of a whip against her back. She licked her lips as she cast her mind back to the scene.

"Oh no, you're right. Had I gone to fetch someone sooner, she'd not be ... oh god, I'm so sorry," she whispered as realization struck.

"No, sub RL, not yet ... but you will be." His hand loosened from around her throat. He caught the chain that was still attached to the red collar and dangled between her breasts. He wrapped one end around his fist. His lips curved in a smirk as he glanced at the high stilettos she wore as he took off toward the Dungeon of Sin.

"Keep up, sub. I'm not stopping and if you stumble and fall with those ridiculous stilts you're wearing, you'll crawl the rest of the way."

"As if I have a say over what I wear to the damn members' dungeon," Rose muttered under her breath as she hastened to keep up with his long strides.

As trainees, they were expected to attend in the three member dungeons, either as coordinators, waiters, or assist the Masters with demonstrations. Castle Sin provided their outfits, not that she didn't like what was offered; it was in very good taste and expensive, but because she was tall, she never wore high heels. But Madam Cherrie hadn't paid her any mind when she tried to explain it to her the first time she'd selected Rose's outfit.

"High heels shout out sexy and fuck me silly and that, dear trainee, is your purpose as a submissive at Castle Sin. To entice, to be pleasing to the eye, and to make the Doms salivate."

Madam Cherrie had been at Castle Sin for the past six years and was employed as the fashionista who personally designed all the outfits. She had amazing talent and a good eye to fit each of the submissives and trainees to enhance their postures and bring out their best features. Pity she was also a shrew and the self-appointed overseer of the trainees when the Masters weren't around. Unfortunately for Rose, Madam Cherrie seemed to have her knife in for her and went out of her way to make her life miserable.

"Fat lot it'll help me to entice the Doms if I break a fucking ankle in the process."

She was so engrossed in her own thoughts that she didn't notice Master Bear come to a halt and bumped smack bang into his back.

Rose was mortified to be caught inattentive in the presence of a Master. She tried to step back from him, she really did, but her legs wouldn't move. Probably because her libido spiked to overdrive the minute she made contact with his hard, muscled physique and felt herself immersed by the heat emanating from him. It infused through her skin to spark an eruption of heat inside her loins she hadn't felt in many ... many years.

"Is this an attempt to seduce me into not punishing you, sub RL?"

"Would it work?" Rose cursed the little devil on her shoulder that poked its sharp tail at her and evoked the response from her lips. She shivered as he took a step forward, taking the heat she'd been basking in with him. He turned and slanted an amused look at her.

"It might, if not for the fact that I would expect you to turn tail and run." He leaned closer to tilt up her chin. "Like you've done every time I get close to you since you arrived here."

Rose was startled. She hadn't thought he would notice. Not with the large number of trainees presently at the academy.

"Of course, I noticed, Rose." He grinned as her eyes flared, surprised that he could read her mind so accurately.

Good lord, how could he make my name sound so sexy, almost like he was caressing it with his tongue.

She swallowed the drool forming in her mouth as the cogs in her brains scrambled to find a viable excuse for trying to avoid him around every nook and cranny of the Castle.

"I didn't think you'd remember my name," she lilted lamely, her eyes dropping from his intense regard. She bit back a groan as she found herself staring at his lips.

The coil inside her loins tightened. His lips made the light in the dungeon seem a little bit darker as it became her sole focus. The world tilted as he leaned in with a wicked promise scrawled on his cupid's bow. Her stomach turned over as her mind raced to that forgotten place deep inside her soul that had been locked away, encased inside a steel box for years.

"Your eyes are begging for it, sub RL, and if you ask nicely, I might concede." His breath brushed like a hot breeze over her lips. "Do you want me to kiss you, Rose?"

"I ..." Her eyes flicked briefly upward to clash with his. *No! Say no! You fucking say no, Rose!* Her tongue did a quick foray over her bottom lip. "Yes, Master Bear," she said in a breathy voice. *What the fuck, Rose? Are you completely out of your mind?*

Rose heard and agreed with every order her subconsciousness shouted at her but common sense refused to prevail as it lost the battle against the demand of her ovaries urging her on.

"Please kiss me, Master Bear." Her voice turned husky as she reached toward his face to touch the softness of his lips. She felt the effect of their warmth connect with her mind to send it swirling in a sensual state of intoxication.

His eyes flared and narrowed. Rose dragged in a painful gasp as she lowered her hand. Master Bear had one rule that had been made abundantly clear on the day of their arrival. Not to be touched, ever, unless he gave permission, which according to the permanent subs, he never did.

"I'm sorry, Master Bear," she said with obvious regret at the loss of the heat under her fingers, "I didn't intentionally disregard your rule, it's just … I couldn't resist."

"Hmm … so am I," he said caustically as he took a step back. "If not for that I might have given you what you asked for."

He pointed at the bondage chair on the raised platform in the center of the Torture Chamber. "If you behave and take your punishment like a good little sub, I still might." His eyebrow did what the subs referred to as the Rothman twitch, seeing as all seven cousins had perfected the sexy move. It crawled higher on his forehead, giving him a much younger and oh-so-badass-look.

"It's up to you, sub RL." He reined her in with the chain until she stood tits-to-chest with him. His eyes homed in on her lips, glistening from her tongue making a desperate attempt to alleviate their sudden dryness.

"Personally, I'd be very disappointed to lose out on tasting these pretty, rosebud lips."

His eyes clashed with hers, stealing her breath as she watched the lightness of his warm brown eyes darken with swirls of midnight blue specks.

"The eyes are the gateway to the soul, Rose, and the lips are the same thing for the body. They're softness, passion, and the promise of sweetness to come."

He brushed his finger over her bottom lip, softly, like the wings of a butterfly and then harder with a rough intensity that robbed her of any thought.

"Are you going to give me a peek into your passion and sweetness, little dove?"

"Yes, Master Bear," she said on a puff of breath. She found it difficult to breathe, his closeness too much for her frayed mind and overcharged libido. She needed space ... between their bodies so that she could start thinking straight and remember what she was doing there in the first place. She flicked a sideways look at the intimidating chair. "What's my punishment going to be?"

During their initiation week, all the dungeon equipment had been demonstrated. This was a high back bondage chair. The side arms had been removed which meant her hands would be cuffed overhead to the heavy O-ring on the back panel. The chair didn't have an actual seat. It consisted of two red leather padded sections upon which a sub's legs rested that could be moved sideways, giving the Dom access to any part of the sub's lower body. It also had a height adjustment, depending on what the devious Master had in store for her.

The fact that it was on a platform in the center of the vast room, boded ill for Rose. It could only mean that her punishment was going to be public. Of course, it would be, seeing as her action was in full view of everyone in the room. What worried her more was that in similar situations to this, it was customary to involve the other Masters in the execution.

"Ah, glad you asked, sub RL. Suffice it to say, after this, you would think twice before disregarding one of the key rules of the Castle Sin dungeons."

Chapter Three

Great, Rose, just fucking great.

She had managed to avoid being the focus of Master Bear for close to five months and individual punishment for as long ... now here she was. She'd landed both ... at the same time!

"I don't like repeating an instruction, sub RL."

Kane's brusque tone brought her attention back to reality and the frowning man who regarded her with dire warning flashing in his eyes. She had to hustle to climb the stairs to the raised platform and not fall flat on her face as he yanked on the chain to drag her closer. She struggled to keep her composure. She couldn't afford a faux pas, not this early and most assuredly not before she'd at least attempted to honor the promise she'd made.

Yeah, only it's easier said than done. I had no idea how devastating being close to him would be. It's been years ... why does he still affect me this much?

It wasn't just being close to him physically, it was the essence that his strong presence exuded. She felt his gaze like the searing heat of a scorching midday sun on her face, which threatened to expose the emotions she so desperately strived to hide. She held her breath as adrenaline surged through her, setting her pulse vibrating over every inch of her body. It was like this every time she felt his eyes on her, even over a distance ... and the reason she endeavored to stay out of his way.

The fear that he might recognize her ... the woman he used to know ... underneath the mask that was now Rose Lovett.

That had been the reason she never looked directly at him. Her eyes had an unusual blue shade of crystal ice, with a ring of jagged hazel surrounding the pupils and was as rare as hens' teeth. She regretted not wearing the gray color contacts she always did but she hated the way her eyes itched and she'd taken them out after the training session ended. She just prayed he believed the excuse she'd offered.

"Where is your mind, sub? It sure as hell isn't here, with me, in this moment."

"Well, what do you expect, Master Bear? Punishment isn't exactly the way I thought I'd end my night in the Dungeon of Sin."

Kane didn't bother to hide his mirth at her surly retort. The rich tones of his deep chuckle stirred to life the feelings she'd been fool enough to believe hadn't just been dormant but gone and forgotten.

Oh, fool be me. Goddammit! I should never have come here.

"I don't suppose it was, my pet. Unfortunately, as you're aware, in here, for every action there's a reaction, which usually doesn't end the way the sub intended." His lips twitched again. "As one of the older and experienced subs of the lifestyle, I'd have thought you knew that by now." He patted the padded leg rests of the chair. "I want you on the chair, sub RL, naked if you please."

Rose shifted her weight from one leg to the other. Her stomach rolled as she glanced everywhere but at him. She'd never resented piling on the additional pounds during the four months she'd mentally prepared herself for Castle Sin as much as she did at this moment. An emotional eater, she'd found solace in pastries and all the decadent dishes she usually avoided. She'd been naked during training and group punishments but it hadn't bothered her then. This was different. She'd be under his scrutiny. Every bulge and fold would be on display to his fastidious gaze. Kane Rothman had always been a man who appreciated beauty and perfection and she was anything but—not at this stage.

"Do I have to be naked, Master Bear?" she asked with a slight quiver in her voice.

Kane didn't miss the rose-colored blush blooming over her cheeks as he stared at her. He'd seen her naked a couple of times and she'd never appeared uncomfortable. He racked his mind to recall whether voyeurism was a limit for her. It wasn't, therefore her attitude annoyed him.

"I'm not the kind of man who wastes my breath by saying things I don't mean. Being naked in public has never bothered you before. Why the sudden resistance, sub?"

Rose knew better than to admit her soft, ample curves and jiggling buttocks, bared to his eyes, bothered her. Each of the Masters appreciated the beauty of the naked form, male or female and a little additional padding wasn't even noticed. He'd scoff at her, and for all she knew, punish her for having such thoughts.

"It's not that," she hedged, glancing away quickly when his brows drew together in a thunderous frown. "I was just trying to ascertain what the punishment entails."

Her gasp cut off at birth as he used the chain to drag her up against him. She had to go on her toes to alleviate the pressure from the collar tightening around her throat.

"Do I look like an imbecile to you, Rose?" The deep rumble of his voice didn't hide the warning in its depth as the gruff tenor trembled over her skin.

"No, of course not, Master Bear."

"I'm getting fucking tired of you hiding your eyes from me, sub. From now on you'll look at me unless I instruct you otherwise, is that clear?"

Rose exhaled slowly, forcing her rattling heart to settle before she lifted her eyes to clash with the rising anger in his.

He lowered his head to level his gaze to hers and grated through thin lips, "I don't appreciate being held for the fool, sub RL, best you remember that." He seared a long look up and down her trembling form as he took back a step. "You're a beautiful woman, little dove, every delightful inch of you. For your sake, your reluctance to get naked had better not have anything to do with your gorgeously ample curves."

Rose had been in the BDSM lifestyle and exposed to powerful Doms long enough to know acceding in certain circumstances was the only way to avoid additional punishment. The glint in Kane's eyes was enough to warn her it would be anything but pleasant. She could feel her fingers tremble as she unhooked the small buttons holding the corset together. His gaze didn't waver from hers and she prayed that none of her frayed emotions were on display to blazon out her secret.

Her eyes flickered sideways, searching for a place to put the piece of clothing. Inherently neat, it irked her to drop it to the floor. Apart from the bondage chair, there wasn't a table or chair in sight. Frustrated and spurred on by the rumbling growl from the demon Master when she didn't continue, she slapped the garment over his shoulder and inelegantly shimmied out of the mini skirt. Her glare spoke volumes as it too landed on his shoulder and her fists on her rounded hips, showing off a pair of deep blue satin bikini panties. She wasn't into wearing thongs. She hated the way they crept up between her ass cheeks, especially since she'd piled on the added pounds.

"I suppose you want me to keep on these fuck me silly heels?"

Kane regarded her with a twitch of his lips. No other sub or trainee would have the audacity to use him as their personal clothing armoire. He was becoming more intrigued by the sensual trainee by the minute.

"Normally, I'd say yes but for what I have in mind, no. Take them off. I'd like to watch the way your toes curl."

"Freaking hell," she muttered as realization hit. It could only mean one of two things. Forced or withheld climaxes.

As long as it's not edging. I fucking hate how vulnerable and needy that makes me feel.

She reached out to use Kane's shoulder as a brace to remove her shoes. She already had one of the offending stilettos in her hand when she sensed the tenseness of his muscled bicep under her hand.

"I'm sorry." She snatched her hand away and clutched the shoe between both hands.

Kane stared at her, surprised at his body's reaction, both times she'd laid a hand on him. He didn't allow any woman to touch him, not since ... *her.* Purely because every time they did, he felt nothing. It left him feeling cold and detached. As long as he had the control and the decision when and how to touch, his body accepted the lust it generated. With Rose ... his skin tingled, a streak of heat that started at the point of contact and shot straight to his loins. It felt fucking wonderful but it confused the hell out of him.

She stood with one bare foot over the other, still wearing the shoe. The way she clutched its mate in her hands made him think of a naughty little girl caught playing dress up. Only there was nothing little-girl-like about her voluptuous body. Her silky hair flowed like a sensual river to below her shoulders. Her striking ice blue eyes punctured his as they traveled up and down her softly curved body. He could feel the effect of her skin glistening with sensual sweat in the twitch of his cock.

Rose had a movie star look, not overly tall, with definition that gave her curves the perfect balance of seductiveness. She held her body straight with the confidence of a woman who knew the effect she had on men. Her bone structure was flawless, the marble-like skin of her face carried over her entire body and exuded passion from every pore. The perfect cupid pout of her mouth pursed irritably as his eyes moved over her features. He couldn't find one flaw; even her nose was perfectly pert and straight under the almond shape of her eyes.

His gaze moved over her breasts, sitting high on her chest, the ideal size for his large hands. Their coral tipped areolae were the perfect placement for her perky nipples. A small frown drew his eyes closer as he detected two small stretch marks on the left side of her belly. He racked his mind and recalled her application indicated she'd had one child.

"You never breastfed I assume?"

Rose instantly went pale and stumbled as she straightened, having forgotten she was still wearing one shoe. His hand around her elbow held her upright.

"Wherever did that remark come from?" Her voice sounded strained as she used the opportunity to avoid his sharp gaze and took off the other shoe.

His large hand cupped one of her perfectly rounded breasts.

"These are natural beauties, my pet and they're still firm and pert with no sign of sagging.

Rose cursed those natural beauties as they awarded Kane by tightening under his continued caress.

"No, I didn't breastfeed," she answered his earlier question.

Kane's nose tilted upward as he regarded her regally. "Where is your child, Rose? You applied for submissive employment for a year after the training. That means you'll be away from him or her for almost two years."

"I ..." She swallowed hard. "My son is in a boarding school in Massachusetts, therefore I only see him a couple of times a year. The contract indicated we're allowed vacation time and I intended to take mine to coincide with school breaks."

He relaxed visibly. Rose cringed as he plucked her corset and skirt from his shoulder.

"Somewhat audacious to use me as your personal closet, my pet." He flung the garments at her and watched with obvious enjoyment as she scrambled to catch them without dropping her shoes. Her breasts bounced enticingly.

Her gaze blistered over him. "Well, what am I supposed to do with them? It's not as if the dungeons accommodate us poor subs and trainees with clothing pegs against the walls."

"An oversight I'll be sure to bring under Master Eagle's attention. Place them on the bottom shelf over there." Kane pointed at the wall to their left as he stepped onto the platform. "You've wasted enough time. Oh, and no matter how much that piece of lingerie enhances the charm of your femininity; if you're still wearing them by the time you return, they'll end up in shreds on the floor."

Every muscle in Rose's body trembled when she got onto the bondage chair, every inch of her bare to his discerning gaze. Kane caressed her calves as he ran his hands toward her ankles and cuffed them to the chair.

"Remind me, sub RL, why are you being punished?"

"So, that's what the sprinkling of silver at your temples means. You do know loss of memory is a sure sign of dotage—oh!" Rose gulped as Kane pushed her legs wide open so quickly, she forgot to breathe. It was an automatic reaction to cover her gaping pussy with her hands.

Kane's eyes drifted slowly upward to clash with hers from where he sat on his haunches between her legs and locked the leg rests in place.

"What do you think you're doing?"

A becoming red blush covered her chest and crawled up to tint her cheeks. It was one of Castle Sin's undisputed rules. Never cover any part of your body a Master or Dom had unveiled for his pleasure. She moved her hands onto her thighs.

"It seems there's a lot I'll have to attend to this month in my dungeon," Kane said with an evil glimmer in his eyes. "Hands over your head, sub."

Rose obeyed blindly. She did her best to regulate her breathing as he cuffed her wrists to the large O-ring attached to the top end of the high back of the chair. It forced her torso to stretch and lifted her hips a tad higher. Her thighs complained at the added pull to her already tightly stretched muscles.

"Oh shit," Rose protested as he lifted the seat of the chair to the height of his waist, relieving the pressure on her arms.

"Hmm, you truly are a treasure, little one." He brushed his palm up and down the length of her labia. "Such a pretty pussy. All puffy and pink." His index finger dipped inside with the next pass. Rose's hiss thrummed through his veins. "So hot and wet too."

It felt surreal in the position above his head, to look down at him as he stared at her exposed sex.

"I've never been as tempted to give a pass on punishment."

The deep tenor of his voice, combined with the words, scrambled her mind as visions of what he could rather do filled her mind.

"I for one wouldn't mind at all, Master Bear," she dared to chirp. Her hips jerked as he brushed his thumb over her budding clitoris.

He chuckled and winked at her. Rose could only stare as memories assailed her of a younger Kane Rothman teasing her in a similar fashion. The same naughty boy look flashed over his face.

"Master Bear, sub Jenna said you needed our assistance with a punishment?"

Rose groaned as Master Eagle's deep voice floated towards her. She looked up to find Kane's six cousins standing in a half circle in front of them. The members who were already gathered, chittered excitedly. They loved to watch punishments or scenes where all the cousins took part.

"Indeed, Master Eagle. Sub RL, you were about to remind me of the reason for your punishment. Be sure to speak up so everyone can hear."

"I waited too long and didn't follow a main rule of the member dungeons to alert one of the Masters or the Dungeon Monitor of a sub in distress, instead of intervening myself."

Kane nodded and briefly explained the situation to the rest. His gaze flickered over Rose, hesitating a little longer on her widely spread open private parts. That one searing look was enough to trigger every nerve in her body to burn hot, smoldering and inflamed in molten plasma, heating the shell of her core.

"Although sub RL neglected to follow a rule, she did manage to end sub Violet's torment and therefore, I decided to be lenient with her punishment and cut the time in half."

The breath Rose released was one of relief as she waited for her fate to be announced. She prayed it wouldn't be climax control. Being this close to

Kane and to be on the receiving end of his full attention, had her all hot and bothered. There was no way she'd be able to keep back her orgasms.

"As it's a Castle Sin rule you disregarded, each Master will decide on the punishment he's going to give you during his five-minute period. If you fail to achieve what's expected of you, you'll be pussy whipped with this electric rotating whip. The Master will decide the time period for the additional punishment."

Rose gaped at the torture tool he held up for her inspection. Black, with a handle of approximately seven inches and eight thin straps of no more than three inches attached to a rotating unit at the top. He switched it on. She gulped as he increased the speed and she watched the eight straps morph into one black whirring stripe. She could feel the skin of her labia shrink just thinking of the type of sting it would give.

"As an erotic instrument, this whip can offer ecstasy unsurpassed because the shortness of the straps allows a Dom to create incredible sensations with pinpoint precision. It awakens all nerves under the skin to release vast amounts of pleasurable endorphins." He switched it off and the straps separated into eight individual streaks. "This time, however, the aim is a more lashing effect and harder for more intense stimulation ... or pain." He dragged the short strips of leather through his fingers. "As you can see, there are steel tips right at the end to ensure the end result I'd like to achieve."

Her wary gaze drifted to his. The glimmer that darkened his eyes warned her that Master Bear itched to use the tool from demon hell on her. She'd heard the rumors about him and Master Fox being the most sadistic insofar as punishments were concerned, especially because they always did the unexpected.

"Master Eagle, if you please," Kane stepped back in line with the other Masters to watch.

"Would it be a problem if Masters Hawk and Tiger join me, Master Bear? We'll combine our punishment for a total of fifteen minutes," Stone's voice droned ominously in Rose's ear as he circled the chair.

"Not at all, Master Eagle." Kane rocked back on his heels and pushed his hands into the pockets of his leathers. The smile that teased his lips told Rose whatever Master Eagle planned, would be no walk in the park for her. "I'll be the timekeeper; commence at your leisure."

Hawk and Parker joined Stone on the platform and fell in line to circle her slowly, watching and assessing every blink of her eyes, every puff of breath until she could feel her entire body start to tremble. Fear transposed itself in a slither of sweat that trickled down her spine.

Goddammit! Just begin already. She ground her teeth so as not to shout it out at them. She'd learned early on how adept the cousins were at mind fucking. Facing the formidable king of the castle and the training master at the same time was beyond intimidating. Add Master Eagle's younger brother to the mix and it left her trembling.

She jerked as a sharp crack sounded next to her ear. Masters Hawk and Tiger each slapped a short-tail flogger against their leathers.

"Oh, lord," she wailed as Master Eagle stepped closer and ran the edge of his stainless-steel cane on the inside of her left thigh.

"Are you ready, sub RL?" The sharp point of the cold steel toggled her clitoris, causing her to jump in reaction. She looked at him, on the verge of begging before they even began.

"No, Master Eagle but I deserve to be punished."

"For the first round, sub RL, Masters Hawk and Tiger are going to whip your tits and I'll—shall we say—tap your delightful pussy. It's not going to be erotic, my pet and believe me, it'll hurt like hell but just in case you're a masochist, you're not allowed to come, is that clear?"

"Yes, Master Eagle." Rose hardly recognized her voice as it croaked from her throat.

Crack! Crack!

"Fuck!" she cried at the unexpectedness of the strips of leather landing against her nipples. The sting of the pain seared through her mind but before she could take a calming breath, the next ones connected.

"Breathe, sub," Master Eagle's deep voice filtered through the sound of the floggers slapping against her breasts. She gulped in a breath and then screamed as he added the first three stinging *taps* with his cane across her labia.

"That's no freaking tap," she whimpered.

"It is for me, little one … for now."

"Fucking hell," she moaned at the ominous promise in his voice as the three men gave her a breather; a very short one before the next strikes landed.

"You're doing very well, sub RL, but you should know that we add various elements to punishment, especially public ones. It's not all about pain but it never is about pleasure either. At least not for the sub." Hawk's voice drew her attention to him. He was a formidable training master but she had the utmost respect for him. The smile he offered warmed her heart just before his flogger connected with the tip of her nipple.

"Sweet jayzus!" She panted as Master Tiger landed a similar strike to the other. Her breath wheezed from her throat. "Good lord, how much longer?" she cried.

"Another ten minutes to go, little one," Stone rasped deeply as he used the tip of his cane to once again toggle her clitoris. Her stomach rolled and she cursed the nub that began to throb in reaction.

Then the real pats started. The cane softly tap-tap-tapped against her clit while the harsh slashes of the floggers kept raining on her nipples.

"No! That's so not fair," Rose protested loudly which of course elicited a wicked chuckle from Master Eagle.

"Punishment never is, my pet."

The teasing taps were sensual and managed to make her forget about the pain exploding from her nipples. The conflicting sensations of pain versus pleasure completely floored her mind. Soon, all she could concentrate on was the flush of heat that the cold steel against her swollen nub caused to settle in her loins. The sensations that flooded through her were surreal. She had no way of controlling the lust that flushed her pussy.

At the start of the punishment, all she had to bear, was the pain and to suffer through it. Now, with the added element, she desperately fought against the climax that steadily etched closer. The pain from the lashes on her nipples became a conduit to the desire that caused her body to thrash and jerk uncontrollably in the cuffs.

"Remember what I said, sub RL, do not come," Master Eagle warned as he stepped between her legs, with the other two men encroaching on either side of her.

Three mouths locked onto three throbbing nubs. Her nipples still stung painfully and her clit from the arousing taps.

"Gawd, no!" She should've known the demon Masters intended something like this when they decided to team up. The employed subs had warned them that they exerted punishment where a sub's body and mind were completely at odds with each other.

Rose dug deep and used every trick in the submissive book to stave off the climax but the coil inside her turned tighter and tighter with every suck and nip of teeth on her vulnerable and super sensitive nubs. She managed to last a couple of minutes but when all three men sucked hard and then bit into them, the coil snapped. Her breath turned ragged; a scream split the room as she arched her body into the sucking mouths. She shuddered as spasm after spasm rolled through her. Her veins exploded with heat that left her gasping for breath. For a moment she froze until she had to heave oxygen into her lungs. She was completely unaware that the people watching applauded the result of the mastery of the three men.

Rose opened her eyes and her gaze was caught by Kane's smoldering one, glowing like cinders as it remained fixed on her. She cringed as the repercussion of the orgasm drove home when he strolled onto the platform, not breaking eye contact as he approached. The closer he came, the more she trembled as she sensed a different emotion emanating from him than earlier.

"Seeing as the rest of the Masters also elected to team up, your punishment for disobeying Master Eagle will stand over until we're done." Kane brushed his hand over her cheek. A vein pulsed in his temple as she leaned into his touch. "Apart from the climax, you're taking your punishment very well. I'm proud of you, sub RL."

"Thank you, Master Bear." It shook Rose how his praise soothed her soul.

"Your next set of punishment will take place on the rotating frame," Kane explained as he uncuffed her arms and legs, gently massaging her muscles until she relaxed. She gasped as he picked her up and carried her to the steel frame that had been bolted to the floor.

"Where did that come from?" Her voice sounded hoarse as she stared at the contraption.

"We set it in place during the fifteen minutes of your first set. Place your feet on the footrests please."

Rose obeyed and watched as he deftly secured her ankles and calves to the X-cross inner frame. Her legs were spread wide and slightly bent at the knees. Her arms were likewise secured to the opposite end. He tied her against the narrow round bars with a leather strap around her waist. She could feel the thin steel press against her legs, arms, and the center of her back. The X-cross was attached to a large square outer frame, keeping it suspended off the floor. She stared at it perplexed. The round bars of the X-cross were thin and allowed total access to every part of her body.

"This is called the SWF, the spin-whip-fuck frame. We set it to spin while we whip you with floggers as it spins ten times. A Master will then fuck your ass and so it will continue until the time is over. Of course, you're not allowed to come."

"Of course," she said in a small voice. Her insides quivered. Anal sex was her Achilles heel and would surely be her downfall in this round. She could withstand a harsh whipping but she had yet to hold back a climax while being fucked in the ass. She was likely to be whipped by that fucking electric rotating whip for an hour afterward!

She cannily watched Masters Leo, Fox, Dragon, and Bear circling her, each holding a long-tailed whip in his hand.

Freaking hell. Why didn't I just call one of them? This is going to be no fun at all, she wailed in her mind as Master Bear cracked his flogger in the air.

"Ready, my pet?"

"Hell no," she snapped. The breath exploded from her chest as he set the cross to spin. She'd barely had time to accept the swirling room around her when the strikes began. All over her body, nonstop and setting streaks of scorching fire on her skin. It felt like forever before the room around her settled when Master Ace stopped the cross. The crinkling of paper warned her what was coming.

"Ah, shit," she cried as she felt his lubricated cock prod her back entrance, seconds before he thrust inside her to the hilt.

"Breathe, sub RL, and then brace yourself," Master Ace gruffed in her ear.

Rose's hands curled into fists as he commenced to pound her ass, hard and in a rapidly increasing rhythm that sparked every nerve ending inside her to life.

She moaned as the pressure inside her began to build, her clit throbbed in reaction, demanding attention. She closed her eyes, desperately attempting to hold back the climax that approached like a galloping horse. Then he was gone, leaving her feeling bereft, especially as he didn't climax. She could feel her rosette clenching and releasing, lost at being empty, and wanting of the pleasure it created.

The fifteen minutes felt like an hour as one after the other Master fucked her ass between the spinning whippings. When Kane stepped against her and tortured her with a slow slide of his cock until he was settled, she began to shiver. Her skin felt cold while his shaft scorched her all the way into the depth of her bowels.

"I had begun to think I'd never have the pleasure of fucking your sweet ass, little dove. I can feel you're on the edge. Don't come, my pet."

The familiar dulcet-tones overwhelmed her defenses. It coaxed her submissive persona to immediate obedience. She clenched her teeth as he began to thrust, slow and easy at first and then with rapid, hard snaps of his hips. Try as she might, she couldn't stave off the climax. The warmth of his hard shaft drilling into her sparked a flame to ignite every nerve ending that clenched at his cock.

"Fuck-fuck-fu-uck," she wailed as the orgasm that washed over her was unlike anything she'd ever experienced. The wrenching intensity of it seemed to shatter her from the inside out.

"I see I'll have to make sure my electric whip is fully charged," Kane grunted as he pounded her a couple more times, tumbling her head first into another climax that left her gasping for breath. Her body shook as he pulled out and immediately set her to spin.

Her skin glowed red and felt like it was connected to an electric wire, intensified by the climax that made her body sizzle all over. It was becoming more and more difficult to cling to her sanity, to hold back from orgasming over and over but the bastard Masters knew. They stopped the pleasure seconds before she tipped over the edge and yanked her back with a painful reminder that it was a punishment.

The cross came to a halt once more and another hard body stepped against her. Rose stiffened. Her entire body went into an immediate spasm as she recognized who it was. It was eerie that she was able to sense the moment Master Bear stepped into a room without seeing him. It was like the neurons in her brain immediately latched onto his magnetic presence. She felt the tremors begin inside her as his hand curled around her buttocks. She shook her head.

"Not you. God, please, Master Bear. Not again. I won't be able to … not you." The first time Kane had buried his cock inside her ass, she'd lit up like a blazing fire. It had felt like she was about to combust and she still felt the climax all the way into her toes. Since then, even with the others fucking her, she'd not been able to forget the sensations he'd extracted from her, the heat of his hard shaft driving into her, the way his hands gripped her hips to keep her in place. She wouldn't survive another brief promise of pleasure, only to be left empty. It was the worst of the punishment, knowing that not one of them had taken their full pleasure. It made her feel like a failure.

"What's this, sub RL? Each Master had two turns at this delightful ass of yours. Why do you suddenly have a problem with it?

"It's not that. It's just … I can't! Not with you. Please, I—"

"So, it's my touch you can't stand. Is that what you're saying?"

"Master Bear, please, it's just with you, I can't … I just can't—"

"Choose. Either I fuck your ass or concede to thirty minutes punishment with the electric whip."

Rose cringed at the censure in his voice, the gruff edge castigated her with every word that grated from his throat.

"The whip. I choose the whip."

She closed her eyes as his body turned to stone against her. She could swear she felt the heat recede from his skin before he stepped back.

"The punishment is over." Kane threw the whip that he'd draped over his shoulder at Shane. "The secondary punishment is postponed until I'm sure she'll be able to feel every fucking bite of that whip." He stomped down the stairs of the platform. "One of you will have to do aftercare. Apparently, this trainee is appalled by my touch."

Rose stared after him. She shivered at the public rebuff in his voice.

"That's not what I meant," she whispered as she followed his path toward the exit. The anger emanated from every angle of his body.

"That's what we all heard, sub RL," Master Leo's voice chastised gravelly.

"It's not what I meant, Master Leo," she reiterated as she slumped into his arms as Masters Fox and Dragon untied her from the frame.

"Exactly what did you mean then?" Master Fox's steel gray eyes pierced through the armor she tried to keep in place. He always made her feel that he could see inside her soul. It totally unsettled her.

"It's just ... I ..." She heaved in a deep breath. It's not something she could discuss with any of the Masters. Not without looking like a complete idiot. They were men, they wouldn't understand that Kane Rothman was the one man who could flip her switch with no more than the briefest of touch.

"I didn't mean that I don't like his touch."

"If you didn't, I suggest you set things right with Master Bear. You don't want him as an enemy, sub RL, not in here." Rose watched Master Fox's eyebrow crawl upward. "Or did you forget that you're in his training dungeon for the next month?"

"Freaking hell," she muttered under her breath.

"Indeed." Shane pinned her in place with a sharp look. "Fix your mistake, my pet, before it's too late."

Rose didn't say anything and leaned into Master Leo as he carried her to the aftercare area.

It was already too late. Years too late.

Chapter Four

The warm humidity of the island air made her feel sticky and suffocated. Sweat rolled down her skin in thick, salty beads. Her heart thumped loudly inside her chest. It was so hot, her skin felt like it was roasting. She began bouncing slightly as she jogged, which wore her out quicker.

"Good lord, I'm unfit," Rose wheezed as her burning lungs gasped for air. Her legs were numb and unsteady, painfully sore and her throat so dry, it felt like she'd swallowed sand.

"No more," she moaned as she slowed down and stumbled a couple yards further, knowing she had to move the lactic acid out of her system if she didn't want to be as stiff as an ironing board the following day.

"Let that be a lesson, Rose Lovett. Keeping fit and trim is important for your health," she lectured as she stopped at a stack of boulders rising from the sea like giant fingers pointing to the sky. The beach was deserted and quiet this early as most of the trainees and subs were still sleeping. The sound of the waves was muted, nothing more than a rustling of water crawling toward shore. She tapped the Fitbit on her arm and snorted as she checked the number of steps. "Only two thousand!" She glanced back at the castle. "It feels like ten freaking thousand."

She stood with her hands on her knees, trying to slow her erratic breathing. It didn't surprise her that she tired so quickly. She'd hardly slept after the disastrous comment that had chased away Kane in a dreadful rage.

She straightened as her cell phone in her pocket began to vibrate. A frown marred her brow as she recognized the caller.

"Tucker? Is something wrong?" The concern in her voice broke through her still erratic breathing.

"And a bright and breezy good morning to you too, Mom."

Rose relaxed at the teasing tone of her son's voice, which had been growing gruff and deepened into a man's over the past couple of months; He was growing up so fast. Too fast, and definitely too clever and big for his boots.

"Morning, honey, but you can't blame me for being concerned. You're supposed to be at breakfast already! Besides, I'm only supposed to phone you on Wednesday."

"I know but I couldn't wait any longer." He hesitated for a moment. "So, what did he say?"

Rose cringed. She should've known he wouldn't be patient for too long. He was too much like his father. Once he'd set his mind on something, he wanted it done immediately.

"I told you to be patient, Tucker. It's not something I can rush into."

"Come on, Mom. You've been there almost five months already."

"I need to find the right time, honey. You have—"

"You don't want to tell him." His voice lowered dejectedly. "You never did. You lied to me, Mom. You went there to pacify me but you don't intend to tell him, do you?"

"Tucker, I made you a promise and I will keep it. I just need a little more time."

"Yeah, sure, like it's gonna take months to tell him that he's my father. Great."

Rose sighed heavily. Teenagers could be so demanding. Tucker had a very strong personality and the maturity of a twenty-year-old. Not to mention the tenacity of a bulldog. The day he'd found out who his father was, he'd made it clear that he wanted to meet him. That had been two-and-a-half years ago when he turned thirteen. Now, almost sixteen, he refused to let go of the notion, just like a dog fighting over a bone.

"I will tell him, honey, I promise."

"I'll believe that the day I meet him and he says; hi, son." She could hear his voice thickening. Her eyes filled with tears at the emotional distress he was experiencing. "I have to go or I'll get into trouble. Bye, Mom." Tucker ended the call before Rose could respond.

"So, there's a honey in your life."

"Oh!" Rose was so startled at the deep voice grating behind her that she dropped her phone. She spun around. "Was that really necessary? Creeping up on me? I nearly had a heart attack," she snapped at Kane to hide her discomfort.

How much did he hear? Her heart rate increased at the thought that he had overheard more of the conversation than she was comfortable with.

She glared at him suspiciously. "Did you listen in to my conversation?"

Kane stood relaxed, his feet braced far apart with his hands low on his hips. Rose chucked in a deep breath. He looked like a veritable Greek god with the blue ocean as a backdrop.

Good lord, how can a man his age look so freaking hot and sexy in running shorts and sneakers?

Tall, standing at a good six-foot-one in his socks, he was well-toned, his body muscular and perfectly proportioned. Rose supposed it was a necessity in the ever-increasing competitive world of acting where younger bodies were coveted. Still, she'd witnessed the women admiring and drooling over his physique. Even the younger Doms stared at him with envy when he was all dressed up in leather pants and vest. His skin gleamed with sweat. Her eyes moved over his broad chest to latch onto his drool dripping washboard stomach that she battled to draw her eyes from.

"I'm on my early morning run, sub RL, not looking around to skunk after someone who made it abundantly clear that she loathes my touch."

"I never said that," she denied vehemently. It took a colossal effort to drag her eyes from his spectacular musculature.

"It seems we have a different recollection of what happened." His eyes dropped to the cell phone lying on the sand in front of her. "I can't imagine that your *honey* is very happy about your desire to stay on the island for two years."

Rose quickly picked up her cell, dusted off the sand and dropped it in her shorts' pocket.

"Not that it's any of your business but that was my son."

"I see." His eyes did a slow gander up and down her body.

Rose stiffened. Because it was so early, she hadn't expected to run into anyone, and dressed in a pair of loose fitting shorts and a sports-bra camisole, she sucked in her stomach and prayed that her thighs weren't visibly quivering to make her look like a jelly blob out on a run.

"Your ... what was it again? Thirteen-year-old son?"

Rose searched her mind but couldn't remember that she'd told him Tucker's age. She shifted her weight, hating how his intense scrutiny unsettled her. Like he knew she was hiding something. Until she was ready to approach Tucker's father, it was better to keep details about him vague.

"Yes, he turned thirteen a month before I came here."

"Funny, I could've sworn your application stated he was twelve."

Shit-shit-shit! That's what comes from telling lies, Rose.

The cogs in her brain scrambled frantically for a viable explanation for her perfunctory slip-up.

"He was twelve at the time I completed the application," she puffed, relieved that he wouldn't be able to discount that as a lie. She had submitted her application two months before her arrival on The Seven Keys Island.

Castle Sin didn't advertise the Training Academy or the employment possibilities. Recruits were sourced by Hunter Sutton, the owner of Club Sensation in Miami, which she'd learned recently was the main location of many more spread out all over the States. Lucky for Rose, she'd already been a member at the club and had the added benefit of a previously employed submissive of Castle Sin to guide her on how to get noticed and approached by the formidable Master.

"Hmm," Kane grunted and began to walk around her in a slow circle. She spun around and glared at him.

"Stop that," she snapped, crossing her arms low over her belly and pinching her legs together to make them look thinner. Out here in the bright sunshine, she felt even more exposed and ... *fat* under his brooding eyes. If she could, she'd bury herself under a layer of sand.

His eyes narrowed and he prowled closer, so close she could feel the heat emanating from his body, but not enough to touch.

"Drop your arms, Rose." His voice sounded brusque, irritated and as angry as the flash of gold in his eyes.

She cringed, knowing he was too astute not to read the signs of her embarrassment accurately. The Masters of Castle Sin hated women not embracing their bodies, no matter the shape or size.

"No. This is our free space. You don't get to order me around out here. Not this early and not outside of the Castle." Her nose tipped an inch higher as she stood her ground against the intimidating mastery of the Dom in front of her.

Dammit! Does he have to do that freaking eyebrow twitch, she complained silently as his left brow crawled upward in a suave slide.

"I don't?" The deliberate brogue he added to his voice engulfed her in its entirety and she could feel the inner submissive inside her react immediately. She fought it with all her might.

"No," she said morosely but the little voice inside her ordering her to drop her arms wouldn't keep its freaking mouth shut, and completely disregarding the instruction from her brain, they dropped to her sides.

"Good girl." His voice darkened. "Now, your legs."

"Kane, please, I don't—freaking hell." She simmered as her legs obeyed his instruction and completely ignored hers.

He didn't move back or say a word but continued to study her eyes silently.

"It is said that a submissive who has found her true Master has no control over the command he has over her inner subjugation." His voice lowered an octave. "Just like yours just did."

"I ... ahem, I've never heard of that," she hedged and shifted her weight from one leg to the other.

"No? Hmm ... I wonder ..." He circled her once again. "Don't move," he rasped as she attempted to turn along with him. "It seems we have a problem, Rose."

Stop calling me Rose! she screamed inside her mind. She managed to cope when he used sub RL. It was impersonal but the way he rolled the syllables around his tongue when he said her name, stirred to life every nerve ending and left her entire body tingling with anticipated lust.

"We do?" she managed to say.

"You have an unhealthy hang up over your body, Rose, and it stops, right now, right here."

"That's easier said than done," she muttered. She glanced at him as he stopped in front of her again. Standing close but not touching. She felt a shiver of desire trail down her spine. Just the thought of pressing against his hardness left her breathless.

"Explain."

Rose sighed heavily. She gestured at her body. "I've never been this fat and—"

"You're not fat. You are curvy and very nicely rounded."

"For me, this is being fat. I'm an emotional eater and before I came here, I had a couple of stressful months during which the pounds just piled up. I had to buy an entire new wardrobe for heaven's sake. None of my clothes looked or fit comfortably anymore. I'm still a good eighteen pounds over my usual weight, so I'm sorry, but feeling self-conscious and embarrassed about how I currently look, isn't going to change."

"Still? Meaning you've already lost some?"

"Yes, seven pounds since I arrived on the island. It's slow going but I've been jogging regularly and gone back to my regular exercise regimen." She was surprised he hadn't noticed, but then again, she'd been avoiding him like the plague. Her brow furrowed. "Only problem is the chef isn't helping by producing all those mouthwatering dishes."

"And what if I tell you I like you just the way you are and don't want you to lose any more weight?"

Rose gaped at him. He'd never dated a woman who wasn't perfect in every way, including model thin and super sexy.

"I'd wonder why," she lilted. At his questioning look, she elaborated, "I've seen the tabloids. Your taste in women, like your cousins, is well known. You all prefer sexy, hot, and perfect by your side."

"For dating and putting up a show for the sake of the producers, maybe, but personally ... I find you extremely sensual, gorgeously proportioned, and perfectly padded to withstand being fucked by me."

"I ... you ... ehm," she stammered and clamped her mouth shut. She sounded like a blubbering schoolgirl for heaven's sake. She could feel her face heating up at the vision his words evoked in her mind. "I've seen you fuck many subs and trainees, most of which are thinner than me. To be honest, it never seemed to be a problem."

"Maybe not for them, but I always hold myself back." He leaned his face closer. His breath teased her lips, he was that close. "With you, with these lovely curves, I won't have to." He smiled that wicked smile that gave him a badass look. "I'd like to fuck you, Rose, so hard and so rough that you'll pass out and when you come to, I'll still be fucking you. Who knows, I might fuck you through a couple of unconscious moments the day I get around to burying my cock deep inside your cunt."

He straightened and took a step back. "Pity though, isn't it?"

"What?" Her voice puffed from her lips in a breathless whisper.

"That you can't stand my touch." He started sauntering away. "Which means I don't get to fuck you." He stopped and turned to regard her with a thoughtful look. "Know what?"

"What?" Rose felt like kicking herself for sounding like a broken record, but try as she might, she couldn't get him fucking her like a heathen from her mind.

"If I can't have the pleasure of your orgasms, no one else will either. You, included."

"What?" *Dammit Rose! You have a vast vocabulary, use it!*

"From this moment, you don't get to climax, Rose, not even if a Master or Dom gives you permission. Your body, little dove, is going to starve itself, waiting to be satiated by mine and mine alone and that won't happen until you beg me to fuck you."

Rose was still staring after him with her mouth agape when he disappeared between the trees at the edge of the stretch of the beach. She shook her head to clear her mind and looked around. His words echoed inside her brain.

"Gmpf," she snorted. "Like that's ever gonna happen. These Masters know just how to spike a woman's arousal. There's no way I won't climax if they tell me to come. No way in hell."

Her phone vibrated again. This time, her stomach clenched. She didn't recognize the number. It was just after seven am and she really didn't have the strength to speak to strangers. She sighed, realizing she had no choice. What if something happened to Tucker? She swiped her finger over the screen.

"Yes, Rose speaking," she said in a breathy voice.

"Narine, darling ... I've been searching for you for a long time."

Rose turned to stone. The grating voice had been haunting her for over sixteen years. She'd never forget the sound of the man she hated more than life itself.

"What? No pleasant good morning? Not enjoying your little foray into salacious training?"

Rose felt cold all of a sudden. "What do you want?"

"Did I catch you sleeping?"

"Look, say what you phoned for and get it over with. I'm not in the mood for a cordial chit-chat."

"Still as feisty as ever. Very well, but I don't suppose I have to tell you why I phoned. You didn't call me with an update like you were ordered via email. Once a week, remember? It's been two weeks and I've yet to hear from you."

"You? You're the one blackmailing me? Jesus! Don't you ever stop?" Rose's stomach heaved as she battled to draw a proper breath into her lungs. It felt like a vice clamped around her body.

"I'm an entrepreneur of note, my dear. I use all the resources I need to get what I want. And you, darling, are in the perfect place to give it to me. Imagine my surprise when I saw your picture on the report my contact emailed me. It was sublime.

Together again. You and I … after almost seventeen years."

"You can go to hell. I'm not doing jack shit for you."

"Oh, you will, and I don't believe for one second you haven't already snapped a couple of pics for me. I know you, Narine Bosch, very well, and you can't say no to a challenge. Not knowing is a challenge in itself, so give it to me."

"I don't know what you expect from me but if you think I'm going to take photos of any of the people here, you're delusional." She frowned as a thought flashed through her mind. Castle Sin was a secret club and training academy. From what Rose had been able to ascertain since her arrival, the cousins still kept their lifestyle separate and secret from their public lives. They had to, especially to ensure the confidentiality of their members. She didn't believe for one minute that they would've told this asshole about it. "Where exactly do you think I am, Summers? I'm not exactly the groupie kind to follow a celebrity around."

"Come now, you should know by now that I'm a highly resourceful man. I know you've joined a

BDSM training academy and that the Rothmans run it, so don't try and bullshit me. You're right in the center of the action and *you* are the perfect solution to give me the ammunition I need to sway Kane's decision."

Rose didn't bother to prod him to find out how and where he got his information. She knew from previous experience that Roy had shady associations and didn't hesitate to use them. She relaxed a little as she realized that he didn't mention knowing the exact location of the training academy. She searched her mind to recall the details of his email. She'd scoffed at it before, not believing that Kane would ever walk away from Hollywood.

Now, hearing the thin undertone in Summers' voice, it seemed he had finally had enough. She cringed at the pain that seared through her heart.

"I'm a trainee here. Nothing I say is going to make him change his decision. If Kane Rothman made up his mind that he's done with acting, nothing and no one is going to change his mind."

"Really? You did once … remember?"

Rose froze at the coldness in the voice echoing in her ear. Her legs gave way and she flopped onto the sand.

"Yes, Narine, he lost you once and it was all he needed to get his mindset back to where we needed it to be and ensuring his cousins were just as invested in *their* acting careers. We're not ready to see them disappear from the big screen, not until we've got a contingency plan for a replacement locked tight. I sure as hell am not losing seven actors in one fell swoop."

"He loved me then. He doesn't know who I am now, and I have *no* intention of telling him." Rose didn't recognize the hoarse rasping voice coming from her lips.

"He doesn't have to, darling. He can't lose what he doesn't know he has, but you on the other hand ..."

"What do you mean?"

"Kane Rothman is a strong man and he has survived many of the dangerous covert ops he's been on over the years. Another thing that has to stop. We can't afford him and Shane getting killed chasing after some fucking terrorist. Nothing gets Kane under. Not even the death of his only true love. We both knew that. You knew he stood at the beginning of something big almost seventeen years ago, which is why you agreed to die in that explosion. To give him the opportunity to continue and succeed when he was ready to throw it away and marry you." He grunted loudly. "I don't know why or how you got to be there, Narine, but if you think Kane is going to forgive you for pretending to be dead all these years, you're a fool. I need the Rothmans to commit to another series with Marvel and you're gonna give me what I need to make it happen."

"Me pretend to be dead? You didn't give me a fucking choice, you asshole! You're the one … I almost died because you fucked up." She heaved in a breath. "Or did you? Over the years I've often wondered if the bomb didn't explode earlier with the aim to kill me. Is that it? You didn't just want me out of the way, you wanted me dead!"

"Melodramatic too. Another trait you haven't lost. I'm not a murderer, Narine. Besides, I had no reason to kill you. You readily accepted the three million dollars to disappear. Ah," he chuckled. "Is that it? You're holding out for money? I suppose that private boarding school must've emptied your bank account."

"I don't want your money and you're not listening to me," Rose yelled into the phone. "He hardly knows I exist! He sure as hell isn't attracted to an overweight forty-something woman. There are too many perky young ones vying for his attention. I. CAN'T. HELP. YOU."

"You underestimate the natural allure you have, darling. Irrespective of the years gone by and the hundreds of hours under constructive surgery to fix your scarred face, you're still the woman he loved. *You* are the *only* one who can help me."

"I once lost the one thing that meant the world to me and I gave it up because I truly believed it was what was best for him. I'm not going to be your puppet again."

"Really? That's not completely true though, is it? Not at this stage. I wonder if you'd survive the loss of your only son—Kane's flesh and blood—the one he doesn't even know exists."

"You fucking bastard!"

Fear owned Rose in that moment. She'd been so careful. Roy Summers had been the Rothman cousins' agent since the beginning and he had arranged for a new identity for her to start her life over. As an only child, she couldn't leave her parents behind and they'd been aware of the situation. They had tried to talk her out of it, but she had truly believed she was doing the right thing. They had sold their house in California and told everyone they were going to spend the rest of their time traveling the world before moving with Rose to Massachusetts where they assumed new identities.

She'd changed her name before Tucker's birth, a second time, specifically because she didn't want to be found. Not by him or his then partner, Leon Salvino, who was just as sleazy and now was Vice President of Marvel Studios. She'd moved to Miami when Tucker had turned thirteen in a further attempt to ensure he would be safe and not tracked through her. She just didn't trust those bastards. Tucker was happy at Phillips Academy, which had been the reason she'd moved there in the first place. She only saw him at her parents' place in

Massachusetts during school breaks. No one was supposed to know she'd fallen pregnant on that fateful night. It was the reason she lived far from home. She had always feared the day might come that Summers and Salvino wanted to silence her. It seemed her fears hadn't been in vain.

"How did you find out about him?" she asked in a hoarse voice.

"I've got many experts at my disposal, darling. It's a necessity in my world. The moment I recognized your picture as the woman you became, I put them to work. I know everything about you. Where you live, your parents and every little detail about your son, Tucker Kane Lovett. Now *that* I thought was so sweet. That you gave him his father's name."

"You leave my son alone. Do you hear me?!"

Hysteria etched closer and she started to tremble.

"If you do what I ask, I won't need to go near him. The choice is yours, Narine ... or no, it's Rose Lovett now, isn't it?"

"Go fuck yourself!" Rose ended the call. She pulled up her knees and clutched her legs close against her chest. The eyes that cast its gaze over the azure ocean were empty, desolate, and filled with painful memories that finally fought their way to the surface.

"Again, please babe." Her husky voice floated through the quiet, sultry night.

The deep chuckle from the man by her side reached deep inside her and clamped around her heart, so hard, she couldn't breathe.

"Your insatiable tonight, my fiery little sub. I might have a healthy libido but five times in a row … I need a breather, love." He rose over her and kissed her softly on the lips. *"And that juicy little cunt of yours too. It's probably already fucked raw."*

"Ah, my robust Master. you have such a way with words."

"How about these … I love you, Narine Bosch, more than I can express in words." He brushed his hand over her cheek and smiled tenderly as he wiped the tears from her eyes. *"No tears, my love. And no more fighting. Not tonight. Tonight, we celebrate the beginning of our lives together."*

"Kane?"

Her eyes widened as he reached into the drawer of the bedside table. He sat up and pulled her between his legs onto her knees.

The soft glow of the lamp basked the room in a golden hue that encased them like a floating cocoon. Narine felt the lump in her throat grow bigger by the second as he took her hand.

"I've reached a stage in my life where I need fulfillment. Of the kind celebrity status and all the money in the world can't offer me. You, my lovely submissive, are what I need to make me whole. I want to wake up every morning with you in my arms. I want you to be the mother of my children. Will you marry me, Narine Bosch, and make me one helluva happy man?"

"Kane, I love you with all my heart. Yes! Of course, I'll marry you."

Her eyes were in contest with the glimmering blue diamond ring he placed on her finger. He cupped her cheeks and smiled.

"So, it shall be. We are to be wed."

Her peeling laughter at his cheesy comment was cut short as he kissed her with such tenderness that the sorrow inside her exploded and left her raw and devastated. If only things could be different. If only Kane didn't intend to stop acting … then they could have their happy ever after. Roy Summers, the Rothman cousins' agent, was right. If Kane walked away from his acting career now, he'd come to resent her as he watched his cousins continue and flourish as a team. There was no other way. She had to disappear. She kept silent and clung to him, knowing this would be their last kiss.

"Let's take a refreshing dip in the ocean, my love, and then my little brat, you better be ready for me. Once I catch my second breath, there'll be no stopping until sunrise."

"I like the sound of that," she lilted and slipped from the bed. Her naked skin glowed like marble as she walked toward the bathroom. "You go, babe. I need to pee. I'll catch up with you."

"Don't dally, honey. I have yet to make love to you with the waves breaking around us."

Narine felt devastation take over. She turned to watch him leave the room and trotted to the window. Tears blinded her as her gaze followed him jogging across the lawn towards the beach. She picked up her cell phone and dialed Roy's number.

"It's time."

"Good. You've got ten minutes."

Narine had just finished dressing and slipped on sneakers when the explosion rocked the front of the house

"It's too soon!" she cried. She stood frozen for a moment. Her scream was cut short as she got sucked in by the backlash and flung against the wall. She struggled to breathe and through watery eyes stared at the flames surrounding her, growing bigger and crawling closer and closer. The heat was excruciating, she couldn't breathe but she managed to crawl to the latch in the closet that Roy had secretly installed as her escape hatch.

"No!" she cried as she struggled to lift the latch and felt the lick of the flames at her back. Her hair caught fire and she frantically slapped at the heat scorching their ends. She finally managed to open the latch. A loud whoosh drew her attention. She looked up, horrified at the rolling orange ball of fire hurtling toward her. She jumped through the narrow opening … but not before the flames engulfed her face. Her

screams were horrific in their agony, as was the ruthless heat that melted her skin.

Then, thankfully, she lost all sense of being as the claws of unconsciousness wrapped around her.

Rose started back to the present as a wave crashed to shore and doused her, leaving her completely soaked. She shook off the memories and got to her feet.

Kane would never forgive her for deceiving him, but the one thing their last night had given her was the miracle of their son, Tucker. That she hadn't had a miscarriage through the painful months of reconstructive surgery that followed was a miracle by itself. For that, she would be forever grateful.

She had done her best to keep the identity of Tucker's father from him but he'd come across old photos Kane had given her of him as a teenager. Because he was the mirror image of a younger Kane, it was easy to put two and two together. Now, Tucker only had one desire driving his every waking moment. To meet his father.

"Kane might hate me once he finds out the truth, but both of them deserve to find each other."

Rose made her way back to the castle. Her shoulders were slumped as she shuffled over the sand, looking and feeling like an old woman.

She dreaded what Kane would do when he found out about her deceit. Worse, that she'd kept his son from him for sixteen years.

Her mind spun in circles. For her son's sake, she'd committed to confessing her secret to Kane. Tucker kept putting pressure on her, and now, out of the blue, Roy Summers arrived on the horizon. How could one person be forced to suffer the same nightmare twice?

"How am I going to satisfy everyone in this completely fucked up scenario? Better yet, how am I going to get out of it?"

Chapter Five

"You're in a much better mood this morning than last night. Did something happen?" Shane studied Kane while dishing up his breakfast.

Kane shrugged as he loaded his plate with bacon, eggs, onions and mushrooms. "I'll have two pieces of toast, thanks," he said to the server operating the toaster. He glanced sideways at Shane. "Just feeling refreshed after my morning run and looking forward to start training with a new group in my dungeon today."

"Even though sub RL is among them?"

"Especially because of that." Kane smirked as they sat down at the far end of one of the long tables in the Great Dining Hall that, according to the subs, was a close rendition to the one in the Harry Potter movies.

"Do you have to be so mysterious? Come on, out with it. Something happened after you left the dungeon last night."

"I happened onto sub RL on my morning run on the beach." Kane frowned. "I had a suspicion last night, but she confirmed it this morning. She has a huge hang-up over her weight. Did any of you pick up on it during her training to date?"

"Hawk did, but he nipped it in the bud immediately. Since then she seemed to be comfortable with her body." Shane sipped his coffee. His eyes searched for the woman under discussion and latched onto her as she walked into the Great Dining Hall wearing the usual white training tunic all the trainees were given to wear. "Hmm, I think I get it. First, she didn't want you to fuck her last night and when in your presence, she's self-conscious about her weight. Seems to me, sub RL has a thing for you, Master Bear."

"Ms. Rose Lovett made a Freudian slip last night, I dare say." Kane chewed his food as he followed Rose's path to the buffet.

"Meaning?"

"I'm still trying to figure out her actual reason for giving me the cold shoulder last night, but her eyes and body gave her away on the beach earlier. Not to mention the spicy bouquet that teased my nostrils the entire time. She's up to something, Shane, and I'm going to find out what. If she thinks she's going to play me like a fiddle, she's in for a huge surprise."

"Did you notice the color of her eyes? I was quite taken aback when she looked at me. It was like looking into—"

"Color contacts," Kane cut in grimly. "She wore them again this morning." He searched for her among the trainees, watching her for a couple of moments. "It's fucking disturbing. In here, I want to see the real sub not a pretend one." He sat back in the chair. "She was on the phone when I found her and rather upset thinking I'd overheard the conversation."

"It is rather strange. Why go out all the way to the beach for a phone call?" Shane pondered.

"That's what triggered my suspicion. We still don't know who the person is that has been feeding intimate details about us to outsiders."

"And it started around the time she arrived on the island with Peyton's group." Shane stared at her over the distance. She seemed at ease and chatted amicably with the other women. "She's well-liked by everyone, and I noticed she's very protective over the younger trainees and employed submissives. I'm hard pressed to believe she's a snitch, Kane."

"One thing I've learned over the past couple of months, is not to trust anyone. Rose Lovett falls in that category. Do me a favor and ask Zeke to dig into her background. All the way into the dark and deep web if need be. Something is off."

Zeke, Shane's younger brother, along with Stone's younger brother, Parker, were the IT gurus of BSE, two key enablers in offering a full portfolio from software to hands on safety. Stone, Hawk, Parker, and Ace had been running the company on a full-time basis between movie productions. Kane and Shane had only become involved recently, although all of them owned shares in the business since Stone and Hawk started it years ago.

"Will do."

"In the meantime, I'm going to see just how far the delectable Ms. Rose Lovett is prepared to take the farce of shunning my touch."

"I know you well enough to realize you have something up your sleeve. Just don't fucking fall in love with the twit until we know for sure she is who she says she is. I don't want to see you get hurt again."

Kane laughed. "I'm too old for something as trivial as falling in love, Shane. I've learned not to allow my heart to make decisions. My dick and my mind are in tune with each other and the two of them know exactly what I want and need from a woman."

"Famous last words of many men."

"Relax, Shane. I might be intrigued by the woman and lust after the sub, but at this stage, that's all I'm willing to explore. Yeah, I admit that I want to search for my happy ever after, but I'm not going to fall over my feet and rush into something disastrous."

"Good to know."

"Any news from Salvino on the script changes you sent him?" Kane finished his coffee and sat forward, leaning his elbows on the table as he gazed over the dining hall. The sound of female chattering and laughter overpowered the low drone of the men. It soothed him. This was home. The one place where he felt he belonged. Where he could forget the dark memories of the past and maybe, just maybe, find happiness in the future. There were times that he preferred to stay at his private estate on Key Largo, a couple of blocks from where Hawk owned property, but lately, the loneliness had caught up with him and he preferred to live on The Seven Keys Island.

"Strangely, no. He's usually very quick to come back to me on suggested changes. You saw how stressed he was when we met him in Miami to discuss the final script."

"Yeah, he's unhappy that we're not interested to sign an extension for the Space Riders Marvel series or for a brand new one. He tried to sell it to me afterwards that they'd been working on a different angle with the series that'll mean a definite Oscar for the movie and for some of us."

"The gold statue doesn't have the same appeal as it did early in our careers. We both have six in our studies along with many Emmy Awards. The rest of the guys all have at least one or two. That's not going to change our minds." Shane pushed back his empty plate. He glanced at Kane. "Have you ever been sorry you allowed me to talk you into joining me in that war movie twenty-seven years ago?"

Kane smiled warmly. Shane was more like his twin than his cousin. They'd been close since birth, seeing as their families were neighbors and their fathers in the military together. Kane and Shane had only been eight years old when they were both killed in Vietnam during the fall of Saigon in 1975. It had left them devastated but it had also been the tragedy that had forced them to mature emotionally and take on the roles as the men of their homes. The bond between them had strengthened because of their grief and became solid in the years since.

"No. In fact, I believe it came at the perfect time in my life. I qualified in the financial field, not because it was something I wanted to do, but because my mother kept pushing me into a *safe* direction. If you recall, my father was a qualified CA and intended to start a consultancy firm after they returned from Saigon. It was supposed to be his final tour." Kane shook his head as it triggered a memory of the day they received the news of his father's death. "She was devastated when I joined the military after school and did everything in her power to steer me in a different direction. Every time we left on a tour, she firmly believed I wouldn't return."

"Are you saying you regret resigning from the military?"

"No, Shane, it was time. We both decided to join to honor our fathers and I believe the six years showed me why they loved it so much. Why they were so passionate about keeping the country safe; that's also why I had to get out—before I became like them—hardened military men who only lived for the next tour, the next challenge, and the thrill of being out there on the frontline." Kane sighed and stretched out his legs. "At the same time, I wasn't all too inspired to work in some bank or financial institution, locked in a square box, eight to ten hours a day. I became suffocated just thinking about it. The opportunity to act was a godsend and something I'll never regret."

"I'm glad. You're the one who kept all of us grounded, especially after Narine's death." Shane inhaled loudly. "Sorry, I know you don't want to hear her name."

Kane didn't respond at first. "Yeah, I've conditioned myself not to think of her. It's become easier over the years, but it sure as hell didn't help to bury the guilt I feel every day of my life for not saving her."

"Jesus, Kane! It's been sixteen, no, almost seventeen years. Don't tell me it's been hounding you all this time? There was nothing you could do. The explosion obliterated the entire front section of the house and the flames engulfed the rest of it within minutes."

"I heard her screams of terror and agony as I ran back to the house, Shane ... I still do ... they never fade." Kane sighed and shrugged before he got up. "Enough of this. We digressed. I'll give Salvino a call later today. If he's not prepared to adapt the script, he better have an alternative we're all happy with. Walk with me."

Shane fell in beside him. "I might be ready to lay down the reins as far as the Space Riders are concerned and be full time involved with Be Secure, but I'm not ready to walk away from acting completely. It's become a part of who and what I am. I'll still do a movie now and then but I'll be a lot more selective." He nudged Shane in the side. "And make sure it's something fitting my age."

Shane chuckled. "I'm with you and that's exactly how I feel. It's a relief, really. Doing a big Marvel production every eighteen months and others in between isn't something I wish to continue doing either. One movie every four or five years will satisfy the actor in me."

"I agree. Apart from Castle Sin, we've become the fucking old timers the young ones call us. Between chasing a successful acting career and the ghosts in our souls, we forgot how to have fun."

"It's never too late to start," Shane said as they walked down the stairs leading into the seven training dungeons. "See you later. I aim to have some fun with the trainees today."

"Ah, you mean mindfucking." Kane laughed with Shane as each headed toward their individual training dungeons.

His two assistant training Doms, Michael and Brad, were already waiting on him. A couple of the trainees had started filtering in and were standing around chatting and giggling. This group consisted only of the latest trainees that arrived five months ago.

"Morning Petals. Stone told me you'd be joining us this morning." Kane smiled warmly at Peyton, who had managed to capture Stone's heart even though he hadn't trusted her at first.

"Morning, Master Bear." She returned his smile.

He was one of Stone's cousins that her Master mostly involved in scenes where he watched them fuck her. It had brought them closer and she'd become rather fond of the older man. Her smile slipped a little. At first, she hadn't minded being fucked by other Masters because she had needed to please Stone. She still did, but it was becoming more and more difficult to fully enjoy the scenes where he aroused her until she was so senseless with lust, she begged to be fucked ... by whoever he chose. She loved Stone, deeply and she knew he felt the same about her. He was the only one she wanted and needed to be intimate with. It hurt that he didn't feel the same.

Kane tipped back her chin with his thumb; she blinked up at him.

"It's up to you, Petals, remember that. You're the one who holds his heart."

"I don't ..." Peyton stuttered as she searched his gaze, wondering once again how the deuce all these Masters managed to read their minds so well. She smiled ruefully as his one eyebrow arched in an acerbic reproach.

"Is it, Master Bear? He's made it clear it's not something that's going to change, and I love him too much to take the chance of losing him by refusing. Don't get me wrong, I've enjoyed every encounter ... it's just ..."

"You want only him."

She nodded, feeling rather miserable.

"He hasn't fucked any other woman since he committed to you, Peyton. You know that, right?" At her nod, he traced her cheek with a comforting palm. "I'm not going to say more than just this … your relationship is still in the early stages. All of your experiences and scenes together are part of the foundation you're setting for your future together. Soon, you'll know exactly what it is your Master is truly seeking from you."

"Complete submission. I already know that."

"There's more to complete submission than subjugating to his every command." He patted her pursed lips. "Be patient, little one. Soon, you'll understand. All you need to do is pay attention and learn your Master's tells. Once you look past what your perception of your submission means to him, you'll find the key and truly become the sub he knows you are. That's why he chose you, Petals. You have the strength he needs in a woman to tame the beast inside him."

"I think I'm going to attend the entire month of your classes. Something tells me I have much to learn from you."

Kane chuckled. "It'll be a pleasure having you around, my pet, as long as you've cleared it with your Master first."

"I'll discuss it with him tonight."

"It looks like everyone's here. Please join the trainees, so we can begin."

Peyton dared to go on her toes and planted a whacking kiss on his cheek. "Thank you, Master Bear." She giggled as he frowned at her. "Tsk, that wasn't touching you. I kissed you and that's something completely different."

"You're too much of a brat for your own good. Get your cute little ass in one of the chairs," Kane ordered with an indulgent smile.

Chapter Six

Rose chatted amicably with the trainees around the breakfast table. Inside, she was a raging mess. Just the thought at the audacity of Roy Summers to blackmail her infuriated her. Hadn't he done enough to destroy her life? Now he waltzed back in like it was his god given right to demand that she adhere to his demands.

Fucking asshole! I hope you burn in hell one day.

If she was ever lucky enough to chance upon him at the bottom of a well, she'd gaily just leave him there to rot, or better yet, throw a mountain of rocks on his head. Unfortunately for Rose, it was nothing more than a daydream. Like a bad penny, he'd shown up because he needed something from her—again. She couldn't believe he'd think she'd betray Kane a second time around. Because no matter how many times she'd told herself over the years what she had done was for his own good, in the end, it had been a betrayal—pure and simple.

"It's time, trainees."

Rose finished the last of her tea at the warning from Dom Michael, an assistant training Dom to Master Bear.

Drawing Kane's attention couldn't have come at a worse time. She came here to honor the promise she'd made to Tucker but needed to ingrain herself as one of the trainees first. Demonstrate to the Rothmans that she could be trusted. On the other hand, she couldn't delay the discussion she needed to have with him indefinitely. The sooner she told him about being a father, the quicker she could leave.

She just hadn't realized how difficult it would be to gather the courage to expose her deceit to him. She wasn't ready to see hate flash in his eyes. Over the years she dreamed of him, of finding him and telling him the truth. In those realms of make believe, it had always ended in blissful love and happiness. In reality, Rose knew it would be completely different. Kane would resent her for not trusting his choices in life, for making him suffer, believing she was dead. Knowing how desperately he'd wanted to have children then already, she knew it was the one thing he'd never be able to forgive her for—keeping his son from him for sixteen years.

Her legs felt rubbery as she silently followed the trainees down the stairs to Master Bear's training dungeon. She had no idea what to expect from Kane, especially after her slip up last night. The wicked promise of retribution she'd seen in his eyes on the beach earlier, kept flashing through her mind. He had something up his sleeve and she suspected the month in his dungeon was going to be anything but fun ... for her at least. She took a seat in the back row of the informal classroom area with the hope to be as inconspicuous as possible.

"Cheer up, Rose. Everyone says Master Bear's training is the best of all."

Rose smiled at Cora Dunnings, a petite redhead who was a newbie to the lifestyle and well-liked by the women and Doms alike.

"Oh, I forgot. He punished you last night." She rolled her eyes. "It was intense. I don't know how you survived it. I wouldn't have been able to."

"I've had some experience with intense punishments," Rose said. She turned her attention to the notepad in front of her and scribbled her name at the top. Cora got the unspoken message that she wasn't up for chit-chat and turned away. She locked out the animated chattering of the women around her as her mind drifted once again.

She'd made the promise to Tucker in a moment of weakness and had wanted to retract it the second it had left her mouth. He had been so excited, she couldn't find it in her heart to disappoint him. It happened at a time she'd been the most vulnerable, like every year on the anniversary of her supposed death. It wasn't the explosion or the thought that she was about to die that she remembered of the day. No, the memories that kept playing through her mind like a movie on replay was the moment Kane had asked her to marry him. In that moment, she'd forgotten the deceit about to occur. Instead, she'd soaked up his love and the thought of having her happy ever after with the man she loved.

A miscalculation of time had ended that dream forever. She had been forced to accept her fate. A new identity and a new face meant there would never be a chance at reconciliation, but she was punished every day of her life with the sweet memories of the year they had together. Always obliterated by the echo of Kane's agonized cries she still heard in her dreams, screaming her name through the roar of flames just before she'd passed out.

A warm tingle ran up her spine. She didn't have to look toward the entrance to know Kane had arrived. It had been like this from the first day she'd set foot on the island. It was as if her body had an electric connection to him that ignited the moment he was near. It was disconcerting and kept her unsettled all the time.

She cast a surreptitious glance at him and then couldn't drag her eyes from his musculature.

He looked fresh and relaxed in navy board shorts with checkered Vans on his feet. The red t-shirt molded to his broad chest and rippling muscles. His tousled hair and stubble beard added to his nonchalant but rough-around-the-edges look. No doubt the reason for all the trainees drooling over him. Even the young girls couldn't keep their eyes off him.

He's old enough to be your father for fuck's sake. Drool over Dom Michael or Brad if you have to. Leave him alone. Rose groaned as she listened to the voice in her head. She sounded like a jealous wife.

To exacerbate matters, she had to watch him tenderly brush Peyton's cheek and caress her lips. Rose had witnessed Kane fuck many subs in the dungeon during demonstrations and scenes but the ones that always sliced through her heart was when he fucked Peyton. His entire demeanor changed with her. He became gentle, tender and the way he touched her showed that he genuinely cared for her. Like he used to so long ago with her.

She grunted as Peyton went on her toes and kissed Kane's cheek. He didn't berate her for touching him, contrary to the cold look he'd given her for laying her hand on him the previous night.

"Seems that rule excludes Petals," she mumbled sotto voce but scolded herself immediately. Peyton was a lovely woman, cheeky with all the Masters and so in love with Master Eagle, Rose had no doubt it meant nothing.

"Okay if I sit with you, Rose?" Peyton smiled at her as she slinked into the chair beside her.

"Of course. It might just help to make him go easy on me."

Peyton smiled gently. "I've learned one thing in here and that's once punishment is over, it's done and forgiven." She frowned at the wry expression on Rose's face. "Or is there something else that happened we don't know about?"

Kane's deep voice saved Rose from having to respond. "Morning trainees."

Kane moved to stand in front of the row of desks and chairs where the women were sitting. It was imperative that trainees understood the depth and do's and don'ts of every action in the BDSM lifestyle, therefore each training dungeon had a 'schoolroom' type of area for theoretical discussions prior to moving deeper into the dungeon for practical.

"Welcome to the Bear's Dungeon. This is the fifth month of your training which could also be the turning point in your time here. Apart from the training you'll receive, there is also your mid-training evaluation."

"What does that comprise of, Master Bear?" Sub CD asked eagerly.

"Firstly, continuous evaluation throughout on how you're utilizing the training received to date. Secondly, an impact tool assessment to establish your understanding of the submissive being the one with the power. Lastly, a scene that will be aimed at challenging and pushing your darkest boundaries. You won't be forewarned on either of these, so it's important to use the skills you've learned to date to the best of your ability at all times."

"That sounds intense," Peyton said softly.

"Freaking intense," Rose agreed.

"Today you're going to learn the value of being able to assume a particular slave or submissive position from a single command. By a show of hands, how many of you wish to end up in a long term or permanent Dom/sub relationship?"

His gaze moved over the ten women who collectively raised their hands. Rose lifted hers but kept her eyes lowered to the desk in front of her.

"I'm glad all of you are dedicated to the Lifestyle to desire such a commitment. However, in the interim, you may also wish to have relationships that are based around play with different Dominants. As a submissive, the key aim is to please and to show willingness, to make it easier all round, no matter the Dom, so today, you'll be learning about submissive positions."

"Are you referring to Gorean slave positions, Master Bear?" A pretty blond in the front row asked.

"No, sub TV, that we'll get to later. Today, it's all about the basic positions a Dom might expect you to know. Obviously, there will be slight variations to each which your Dom will easily tweak and adapt to their own particular preference."

Rose felt the deep tones of his voice find resonance inside her. It was with Herculean effort that she managed to avoid looking at him. She didn't want to see the mocking glimmer in his eyes. She stiffened as his voice floated toward her again.

"Sub RL, as the most experienced sub here, please join me up front. I'd like you to demonstrate each position as I name and describe them."

There was no mistaking the glare Rose awarded Kane but other than make a scene, she had no choice but to join him. He ignored her as she approached and stood stiffly by his side.

"Does anyone have an idea how many basic positions there are?"

"Four?" Peyton said, holding her fingers in the air, which immediately elicited numerous call outs for different numbers.

"Settle down," Kane snapped at their unruly behavior. "I do not tolerate disruption during my training sessions. I expect you to act with proper decorum."

"Yes, Master Bear," they said in unison.

"There are nine different positions. Remember, we're dealing with the key ones only today. Once we move on to the more difficult Gorean moves, it'll blow your mind. The ones I'm teaching you today will be used by the Masters and the Dom members here or wherever you may go, so I suggest you pay attention. You'll be tested on these at the end of the week. I don't suppose I need to explain the penalty for failing tests in Castle Sin?"

"No, Master Bear."

"Very well. Sub RL, to ensure everyone can see the proper form, please remove your tunic."

"Why? It's thin and ... fine, I'll take it off," she mumbled in response to the sharp look he shot at her.

The tunics were made from thin white cotton with spaghetti straps holding it in place. Of course, they weren't allowed underwear, which meant Rose was naked underneath. She had no doubt he deliberately chose her because of what had happened earlier on the beach. She yanked the dress over her head and with two economic moves, folded it neatly and placed it on the desk in front of her.

She felt goose pimples raise the fine hairs on her arms as Kane insolently appraised her naked form. She was hard pressed not to fold her arms over her waist to hide the slight bulge of her tummy. She couldn't help the way she felt. When they'd been together, she'd been trim, firm and didn't have an ounce of fat on her body.

"Ready?"

"Yes, Master Bear," Rose said without looking at him.

"On the raised platform, please, sub RL, where everyone can see." Kane led the way onto the platform as he spoke. He seemed impressed that she followed him without protest.

One up for you, Rose, she silently applauded herself.

"We'll start with the easiest one. Sit."

Rose sat down with her legs crossed, back straight, and eyes cast down with her hands on her thighs.

"Perfect. You'll note her shoulders are drawn back which gives her a proud bearing." He traced the tip of the crop he had in his hand from the edge of one shoulder to the other.

Rose couldn't suppress the shiver that followed its path, which she had no doubt didn't go unnoticed.

"Part of perfecting these positions is the smooth and sensual transition from one to the next." He tapped her on the shoulder with the crop. "Kneel."

Rose effortlessly and gracefully turned into a kneeling position with her legs together. Her hands were crossed behind her with a straight back, breasts pushed out and eyes down.

"Be sure to make notes of the perfect posture because that's what Doms look for and the test is based on," Kane said to the group. "Down."

Rose would've been even more impressed with herself had she known how entranced Kane was by her sensuality during each transition. Every move was seamless, effortless and with such feminine grace, he had difficulty keeping his arousal constrained.

"In this position, you're expected to lie flat on the floor, face down. Your legs should be spread wide with hands behind your back," Kane explained as he dragged the tip of the crop over each body part he mentioned.

Rose trembled visibly.

Kane smiled wickedly.

"Next one, sub RL, bend."

Rose got up without assistance and stood with legs spread wide apart. She glanced at him briefly before she completed the position.

"As you can see, your pretty knees must be locked and your hands can either be on your knees or ankles. This is the position we use in Castle Sin for full body inspection. Next one, fours."

Rose straightened, her breathing was shallow, all too aware of the close proximity of Master Bear. So close, she felt his heat against her skin. He leaned in; his breath warm against her earlobe.

"Do I need to explain this one, my pet?"

"No, Master Bear," she lilted and dropped to the floor on all fours.

"This is the doggie style with elbows locked and knees together. Your head should always be tilted up." Kane tapped the crop under her chin. "Higher, sub RL. Perfect. The next one is one of my personal favorites. Arse."

This time it took Rose even longer to move into position, knowing what view he'd have from where he stood behind her. She remained in the same doggie style but pressed her cheek to the floor.

"Ouch!" she cried out as the crop cracked against the back of her thighs.

"Your knees must be wide apart. Wider, sub RL."

Rose shuffled her knees further apart, horrifyingly aware that Kane must be staring at her spread open pussy, wobbly ass, and thighs. She jerked as the edge of the crop teased the tender folds of her labia.

"Perfect. In this position, your palms must be flat on the surface and out in front of you." Kane glanced among the trainees who were scribbling feverishly in their notebooks and watching with animated expressions. "Any questions?"

"No, Master Bear, but I have to say, sub RL does these moves with such sensuality, it's got me all hot and bothered," Peyton said. All the trainees affirmed her statement.

"Indeed, she does," he said, dragging the edge of the crop over the length of her spine, between the crack of her ass to tap a lazy rhythm against her labia and clit.

Rose bit into her lip and planted her knees firmly into the floor to keep her hips from swaying back and forth in an invitation for more. The damn man was dragging this out deliberately, testing her and mocking her for the lie she'd spurted the previous night when she'd denied him. Every time he touched her with the impersonal edge of the crop, it was anything but. It felt warm, like it was his finger trailing over her skin, his hand tapping against her labia.

"Wait, sub RL."

Rose sighed in relief and straightened to kneel up on widespread thighs with her hands crossed behind her head and her breasts pushed out. Her breath hissed through her teeth as Kane brushed the clapper over the soft undercurve of her breasts and over the top. With soft teasing taps against her nipples, the lust she so desperately tried to ignore, sparked to life.

"Present." Kane's tenor wrapped itself around her loins and twisted and turned it until every nerve ending came to life. She was helpless against the flush of pheromones that rushed through her and filled her pussy with a spicy fragrance even she could smell.

"Is there a problem, my pet?"

She shook her head as Kane's dark voice moved her to action. She stretched out on her back with head straight and arms above her head, her palms facing up. She moaned as she reluctantly spread her legs wide open.

Kane stared at Rose, having given up on curtailing his arousal as he watched her seductive movements. In the present position, he felt like *her* Master looking down at her, ready to inspect every inch of her beautiful body.

"These last two positions are what most Doms expect from his sub during inspection."

"Inspect, sub RL."

Rose got up and stood with her legs opened wide. She clasped her hands behind her neck, pushed her chest out, and exhaled slowly before she raised her eyes to lock gazes with Kane. His look scorched her as it slowly moved over her body and back.

"Perfect form, my pet."

"Thank you, Master Bear." Rose cursed the croak that escaped from her throat. Here she was, trying to appear unmoved, not only to keep him at a distance but to persevere her own sanity, and what does she do? She stood there, basking in his praise with her juices dripping from her pussy.

His eyes didn't miss the glistening proof of her arousal on her puffy lips. He tapped the clapper of the crop against her labia. "What do we have here, my pet?"

Rose clamped her lips together and was tempted to do the same with her legs but knew better than to break form. Peyton offered the respite she was desperately seeking with a well-timed question.

"Master Bear, why does Castle Sin use *bend* for inspection and not this one?" Peyton's fingers rat-a-tatted on the desk. Kane's smile indicated he knew it was because she recalled that Stone made all his cousins inspect her intimately upon arrival for being bratty.

"Because it's the most effective for the short period of time we allocate to it upon arrival of new trainees. Some of us prefer to combine *bend* with *inspection* but remember what I said, each Dom or Master will still have his personal preference."

"Like with *present*? For us *present* means standing not lying down."

"Exactly, Petals. In here, we expect you to present your body to us at all times and because it's not always practical to do so lying down, we've adapted the Castle Sin present position."

His eyes trailed insolently over Rose's body. A glint was the only warning of his wicked intent. "Fours."

Her inner submissive reacted immediately and she dropped to her knees.

"Arse."

Rose moaned but moved into position and pressed her cheek against the floor and shuffled her knees far apart, ass presented high in the air. She had no desire to feel the sting of the crop against her thighs again.

She felt the glow spread over every inch of her exposed skin as Kane circled her. The crop slapped against an ass cheek here, caressed her spine there, and tapped against her labia and clit in between.

"Don't move, sub. You don't wish this training session to turn into a punishment, now do you?" he warned brusquely as she wiggled her hips in an effort to escape the snap of the cracker.

"Trainees, on the carpet in groups of three to practice these moves. One group in the far corner with Dom Michael and the second in this corner with Dom Brad. The third group is with me in front of the platform."

Kane tapped the crop against Rose's lower back. "Turn to face the other way, please."

Rose lifted her head. If she did, it meant that her gaping private parts would be in his face as he took the trainees through their practice.

Crack! Crack!

"Fuck! Oww!" she cried as he rewarded her with two punishing strikes against her pussy.

"Did I give you permission to lift your head?"

"No. I'm sorry, Master Bear, but why do you wish me to turn? I can assist with the practice," she said, watching him with her cheek back in place against the floor.

"Because I said so and because I wish to feast my eyes on your rosy pink, swollen and wet pussy, dripping juices on the floor. Care to take a guess what's going to happen if you make a mess on the platform, sub RL?"

Rose's eyes flickered.

I'd rather not, thank you very much.

She opened her mouth to protest but at the expectant flash of anticipation in his eyes, she snapped it closed. The one-eighty-degree turn was more like the plop of a large puppy than a graceful move.

Her ears turned red at his low chuckle that stirred all kinds of emotions deep inside her. She firmly pushed them aside.

I'll fucking drip all over this stupid platform. See if I don't!

If Kane Rothman thought for one moment she'd be waiting around after the class was finished to be punished for something he was the sole cause of, he had a surprise coming.

He's gonna be mighty pissed if you run off without permission, Rose.

Well, tough titties. He doesn't scare me ... too much.

Ha! Famous last words.

She blithely ignored the soliloquy with her mind and pressed her face against the floor. The next hour tested her ability to remain submissive to the limits. Her entire body was on fire, courtesy of feeling his scorching eyes blaze over her sex the entire time. The juices he'd referred to, played right along to taunt her and filled her pussy with liquid heat after every pass of his eyes. She was so wired and aroused, she'd climax from pressing her legs together, for heaven's sake!

Her muscles bunched in readiness when she heard Kane end the morning lesson. The moment the trainees were released, Rose was up and jumped off the platform, grabbed her tunic and pulled it on as she ran toward the exit.

"Sub RL, get back here!"

Rose ran faster at Kane's booming command. She ignored the warning from Peyton as she passed her. She knew she was in deep shit, but she had to get away from him before she crumbled from a climax ripping through her should he touch her with that damn crop again. She'd be punished for running from him for sure but rather that than failing the test he'd set out for her.

It wasn't a damn test, Rose. He's mocking you for denying him last night. She snorted at the voice in her head as she reached the stairs. The sound of his voice calling after her once again, alerted her that he was highly pissed off at her.

She'd worry about that later. For now ... she didn't give a rat's ass.

Chapter Seven

Kane glanced at his watch for the umpteenth time. He'd already been irritated when Leon Salvino insisted to personally meet with him instead of discussing the script telephonically. Leon was over thirty minutes late for the appointment which exacerbated his annoyance. If there was one thing he abhorred, it was tardiness. He always ensured he arrived on time for a meeting and expected the same courtesy from others.

"Especially since he chose the fucking time."

He breathed in the salty ocean breeze as he stepped onto the wrap around porch of his home on Key Largo. The house was built on a slight incline leading from the beach and had a gorgeous view of the ocean.

Salvino claimed he'd been in Miami on business but Kane wasn't in the mood for the city and had suggested meeting at his house. No one associated with their acting careers knew about Castle Sin or The Seven Keys Island. It was a decision all seven cousins had unanimously agreed upon. They were strict about keeping their private lives separate from their celebrity status in the public eye. Not only for their own safety and security but also for their members, the trainees, and employed submissives. Confidentiality was key in running an exclusive BDSM club, especially as they catered to many high society senators, businessmen, celebrities, and those in high level federal positions.

For that reason, they kept it from Roy Summers as well, who had been with them since the beginning of their acting careers. He was their agent and they had no reason not to trust him, but to ensure their privacy remained intact, he was only privy to limited personal information on all seven cousins.

Now that Kane had made a decision it was time to ease out of his acting career, he was driven by a need to walk away as quickly as possible, especially from big productions. He gregariously admitted that Rose Lovett's presence had much to do with his desire to remain at Castle Sin for the remainder of her training period instead of spending months in Hawaii on a movie production set.

"About time," he grumbled as the melodious chime of the doorbell floated through the open sliding doors.

He smiled broadly when he opened the door to find Shane and Hawk standing there. "Thanks for coming, even though I only asked you this morning to join the meeting. For some reason I feel uncomfortable meeting Salvino alone."

"That's why we're here," Shane said as they followed Kane to the bar in the great open room.

"This is a delaying tactic at best," Hawk said as he sat down on a barstool next to Shane. He was a registered attorney and the one who ensured the cousins were legally protected at all times. He also managed all BSE and Castle Sin's legal issues. It was why Kane had decided to ask him to join them.

"I agree. There's no reason to discuss the script. With the changes in the plot and certain scenes we already agreed upon, it's not only the perfect ending to the Space Riders series, it'll be one of the best movies we've ever made." Shane leaned on his elbows on the bar. "A cold beer will go down well, Kane."

"I have a suspicion there's more to this than meets the eye. I know we've worked with Salvino for close to eighteen years, and you and I even longer with Roy, but their attitudes lately are anything but professional." Kane handed them each a cold beer. "And he's now three quarters of an hour late. I'm getting pissed off."

"If Salvino finds another reason not to come to a resolution today, I suggest we set up a meeting with Marvel's President, Alan Bradley," Hawk said as he swallowed his first sip.

"I agree. I'd prefer to end the series on a high note, but if they continue trying to push us into a box, I won't think twice about walking away. They're very close to breaking the contract as it is." Kane took a swig of his beer. "That must be him." He strode to the front door with the gentle chimes dissipating in the atmosphere.

"My apologies for being late. My previous meeting went on longer than anticipated," Leon said the moment Kane opened the door.

"Apology accepted. Next time, please have the courtesy to phone and inform me you'll be late," Kane said curtly. He held open the door, surprised to find Roy Summers lurking behind Leon. "Roy," he acknowledged with a nod and a brief quirk of his lips. Clearly, Salvino had brought him along to team up against Kane. Proof of that was in the grim twist of his lips when he noticed Shane and Hawk at the bar.

After serving them drinks, they settled in the den.

"I agreed to this meeting, Leon, although I didn't see the need for it. At the last discussion, all parties agreed to the script changes and that it would represent the final movie in the Space Riders series," Kane said without preamble.

His sharp gaze pierced the tall, lanky man in place. Leon shifted in the chair and took a long sip of his beer.

"I know, but it's my duty to the company and your fans to try and convince you otherwise. This series is one of the most popular we've ever produced and it still has another couple of years' life in it. The fans demanding more is testimony to that."

"We offered you the alternative to bring in a younger, new cast as a secondary storyline in this movie, specifically so you could continue with the series." Kane's gaze didn't falter or soften. He was irritated. They'd gone over this issue numerous times and it was becoming tedious.

Leon sat forward and looked between the three cousins.

"I know, Kane, but let's be honest, Space Riders is you—the Rothman cousins. The fans won't be amenable to a new cast and it'll kill the series." He sat down the beer on the coffee table. "We can't do anything about Hawk and Stone insisting on being killed off in this movie because they didn't sign the renewal contract and had been courteous to still appear in the previous one but—"

"But nothing. The contract the rest of us signed was only for an additional two movies in the series. This is the last one for us, Leon. It ran its course and quite frankly, we're all tired of it. It was a good run but eighteen years is enough. Apart from Hawk and Stone, Ace and Parker indicated they're done with acting after this movie. Even Zeke has had enough. Shane and I? We've been lucky to be very successful in Hollywood but our priorities have changed. We'll do the odd movie every couple of years, but it'll be ones we choose because it would have meaning to us."

"Kane, you have to at least consider the consequences of just dropping out of the Hollywood scene," Roy said earnestly. "No one is going to come searching for you to offer you a blockbuster role."

"Nor do we expect anyone to," Shane said dryly. "Acting came as a bonus all those years ago to Kane and me but it took away so much more than we ever anticipated." Shane looked at Kane, remembering their conversation about family and children. "We're done. It's time for us to embark on a journey to build a future we hadn't been able to pursue till now."

"Look, Shane, I understand. You made sacrifices, but so does every actor out there willing to go the distance for their career and—"

"Don't talk to me about fucking sacrifices, Leon. You've got no goddamn clue just what we've ..." Kane heaved in a deep breath. His expression turned esoteric. "We had very successful careers. We have more Oscars and Emmys than we ever thought we'd receive. There's no further achievement we're after. We're done and so is this discussion. Sign off on that script. If we don't start filming in three months, there won't be a final movie."

"Kane! Calm down. There's no need to—"

"That'll be a breach of contract, Kane," Leon cut Roy short. "You definitely don't want to end your career in a public standoff with a big production studio such as Marvel," Leon said with a Cheshire grin on his face.

Kane's eyes narrowed. It was clear Salvino believed he had the upper hand. He looked at Hawk and nodded.

"I suggest you familiarize yourself again with the contract we signed for this movie before you threaten us, Leon." Hawk lazily finished his beer and leaned back in the chair.

"What do you mean?" Leon shifted uncomfortably under the collective scrutiny of the three men.

"The only one in breach is going to be Marvel, so I suggest you take Kane's warning to heart. Either we receive confirmation of the production schedule within ten days, or I'll personally take this matter to legal resolution."

The glance between Leon and Roy was filled with frustration but Kane detected a sense of desperation flashing between them. A niggling suspicion sparked to life, not for the first time in his association with the two men. There was more to this than attempting to convince them not to retire. His sixth sense warned him it had nothing to do with movie production.

"Guys, I've been your agent for over twenty years and the rest of the Rothmans for eighteen. Have I ever led you wrong? Forced you into a direction you weren't ready for or interested in?" It was a rhetorical question and Roy continued. "Trust me when I tell you, you'll be making a huge mistake to retire now. The two of you, because you're in the top ten most sought-after actors in the U.S. and the rest, equally for their skill and popularity with the public. No one who has ever walked away like this has ever made a comeback, Kane. Don't make the same mistake."

"Look, Roy," Kane sighed heavily, digging deep to remain patient, "I understand it would be a blow to your business to lose seven actors at once, but you're one of the best agents in the industry with a myriad of big acting names in your portfolio. It's not a decision we made lightly, nor is it one that's going to change. The Rothman cousins are officially retiring after this Space Riders movie."

"Yes, and if we're considered for parts in the future, we'll be happy. If not, I for one won't shed a tear about it," Shane said. "I came to the realization very recently that I should've walked away much earlier, like Kane intended to do all those years ago."

"But he didn't and if he had, he would've missed out on the tremendous success that brought fame and fortune along with it."

"I'm sorry to burst your bubble, Leon, but none of us were exactly destitute at that time. We'd already reached the top by then and amassed a fortune, not only from acting but through wise investments. I was ready to move on, to start a new chapter in my life. The only reason I stayed was to keep my mind occupied, to forget about ..." Kane heaved in a breath. His eyes flashed as he noticed Leon's cheeks turn red. "None of it matters. Yes, you were both good for us and we're grateful but we don't owe you anything. You, too, amassed fame and fortune in the wake of our success. We'd prefer our association to end amicably."

"Bottom line, gentlemen," Hawk interjected gruffly, "we honored our commitments to Marvel and to you Roy. The contracts won't be renewed. There's no reason to have this constant debate. After all the years of mutual respect and partnership, we'd appreciate your understanding and accept our decision."

"Not if we believe you're making a mistake. Shane, please," Leon once again tried to reach out to the one man he believed might be swayed. "Could you at least try—

"This is going nowhere," Kane cut him short. He got up and looked at them over the length of his nose. "This meeting is over."

Everyone followed Kane who briskly stomped toward the door to let them out. Leon shook his hand as he stood aside at the open door. His expression was grim.

"I'm not going to give up, Kane. The Rothmans' time isn't done. Not for many years to come and I'll make sure you realize it too."

"I'm with Leon, Kane. You have no idea the repercussions to us if ..." Roy's voice dissipated at the warning glare from Leon. "We'll talk soon. Thanks for meeting with us."

The cousins watched them drive off, each pensive.

"Why do I get the impression this goes beyond Hollywood?" Hawk asked.

"Because you could be right. I've often questioned their motives, especially when we're discussing expenses and profits during productions. There were numerous times the numbers didn't add up and they were quick to correct them when I picked up on it." Kane rubbed his stubble beard. "Makes me wonder how honest they've been over the years. Not just in respect of money but about what drives them so viciously to keep us."

"They definitely have a separate agenda. They seem almost driven by an underlying fear." Shane opened another round of beers and passed them around. "Do you think they've been skimming off the profits and pocketing it?"

"Maybe, but my gut tells me it's more involved than that. I think it'll be worthwhile to have Parker do a background check on both of them. Can you arrange it, Hawk?"

"Will do." Hawk took out his phone and made the call.

"Tell him to dig deep. If possible, see if he can find a way to trace their movements during the production of the last Marvel movie. That's the one thing I found strange. The need for both of them to be part of the crew on every movie. Roy sure as hell never shows his face on any of the other movie productions." Kane frowned as he took a sip of beer. "Check into their financials, any offshore accounts, even family members, friends, colleagues. Anyone who looks suspicious and who they're connecting with regularly."

"Especially during the Marvel movie productions," Shane reiterated.

Hawk relayed the instructions to Parker and ended with, "While you're at it, see if you can hack into their cell phones. I want a list of anyone they contacted more than once over the past three months. Start with recent calls and work backwards. If anything jumps out at you, let me know stat."

"Good call," Kane said once Hawk ended the connection. "They're definitely walking on a hot tin roof. They appeared stressed. If there's someone else involved, the calls should bring them to the surface."

He finished his beer. "I marinated some steaks to barbecue on the porch. How about it. Are you going to stay for lunch?"

"For your famous juicy steak and buttery jacket potatoes? Hell yes." Shane rubbed his belly.

"No question about it. I told Stone we might be back late, so he'll ensure our trainees are taken care of," Hawk said as they walked out onto the porch.

"What the fuck are we going to do?" Roy whined as he pulled away from the curb in front of Kane's house. "We have no other route to take, Leon, and we already committed to the next fucking series."

"Do you think I don't know that? Goddamn it! I believed we'd be able to convince Kane, but I expected him to be alone. It seims he's more in favor of ending his acting career than the rest of them." Leon snorted in memory of the failed meeting.

"And that surprises you? You know as well as I do, he would've walked away years before."

"Yes. We stopped him then and we sure as hell are going to stop him again. We have to. The Space Riders is the biggest production of Marvel Studios. It's made both of us rich and I'm not ready to stop. Fuck! I should've seen it coming and made contingency plans." Leon slammed his fist on the dashboard. He glanced at Roy. "Have you made any headway with Narine Bosch, or what is she calling herself these days?"

"Rose Lovett. I'm working on it. I've made contact but she's being hardheaded. It might take a week or two to convince her to play along."

"We don't have time to waste. The sooner we can convince, or fucking blackmail Kane if all else fail, to sign an extended contract, the better. Then it'll be easy to persuade the other four to follow suit. I can't postpone giving feedback to the president much longer. Alan is already questioning the delay, not to mention Zikri Malik."

"I'll push her harder."

"Offer her money. What did we give her to disappear before?"

"Three million, but she's adamant money isn't going to sway her."

Leon barked out a laugh. "You're still so naïve, Roy. Everyone has a tipping point. Even the innocent sounding little Ms. Lovett. Money talks, my friend. She's a single mother with a teenage son in a private school. Soon he's going to college. Believe me, offer her the right amount and she'll bite."

Chapter Eight

Rose was offered a respite for three days. To her relief, Kane had to leave the island for a meeting the day she ran out of his training dungeon. Doms Brad and Michael took care of their training the balance of that day. The past three days had been group training, concentrating on submissive decorum and indulging in some fun sex games during which none of the Masters of the Castle had been present.

When she walked into the Great Dining Hall on the fourth morning, a tingle at the back of her neck warned her that her luck had run out. A burst of deep, guttural laughter was all she needed to know that the Masters had returned ... in all their humongous glory.

He was there too. She felt him in the warmth that rushed through her veins like a heatwave through the desert. She kept her gaze riveted on the breakfast buffet and walked toward it faster, expecting at any minute to hear the deep rumble of his voice calling her over. She could hear the chords rattle the cogs in her mind as he rolled the name over his tongue, *sub RL.*

Get a grip, Rose, before you make a total ass of yourself.

"You seem flustered. Are you feeling sick, Rose?"

Rose started at the husky voice by her side. She glanced sideways and smiled at Alexa Silver—Stone's PA as well as a permanent sub at Castle Sin. She was liked by everyone, Masters, Doms, trainees, and subs, purely because she didn't think twice to put herself between a Dom and a sub if she thought intervening was necessary.

"No, I'm fine." She smiled as she dished up fruit, muesli, and yogurt. Her stomach rumbled at the mouthwatering smell of crisp bacon, eggs, and hash browns. Watching Alexa loading her plate with blueberry pancakes and syrup didn't help.

"Is that all you're having?" Alexa eyed the small helping in Rose's plate. "I'd starve if that's all I had to eat." Her nose wrinkled as she looked at the delicacies on her plate. "This is pure indulgence today. I need an energy boost. I usually eat very healthy, but once a month, I allow myself to pig out."

"And today is piggy day?" Rose laughed as they sat down juxtapose each other at one of the long dining room tables.

Alexa looked around surreptitiously. "As long as the seven Masters don't see me." A wicked smile played around her lips. "The amount of unhealthy fat, carbs, and meat those men consume every day ..." A visible shudder shook her frame. "I constantly keep reminding them and the hard-of-hearing chef to eat healthy, but do they listen?"

"Ah, so if they saw you eating what you deny them ..."

"You get the drift," Alexa said as she took a bite of syrup drenched pancake.

Rose drooled and had a hard time dragging her eyes to her own plate. She scooped a spoonful of yogurt drenched muesli into her mouth and quickly took a sip of her tea to help wash it down. She never liked the papery tasting cereal, but desperate times called for desperate measures. She was adamant to shake off the weight and if it meant she had to force food down her throat she hated ... so be it.

"Morning, ladies. Mind if we join you?"

"The more the merrier, I say," Alexa said with a wave of a hand at Peyton and Savannah.

"Not to be rude, but aren't the two of you supposed to be joining your respective other halves?" Rose asked with a glance at the opposite side of the room where the seven cousins were having breakfast.

"Pfft, my respective *other* half can stand on his head and whistle Tweedle Dee Tweedle Dum out of his asshole for all I care." Peyton tossed her long hair over her shoulder and hitched her nose in the air at the narrowed glance Stone cast her way.

"Yeah, and his high and mighty cousin can join him in a duet," Savannah, Hawk's fiancée quipped. She too rebuffed the silent eye command from her Master to join him.

"I have to say, the two of you are like a fresh breath of air in the Castle. I can't recall when last I'd seen Stone and Hawk smile and laugh as much as they do since you arrived." Alexa smiled gently. "Thank you."

"For what?" Peyton asked around a mouthful of bacon and eggs.

Oh, for fuck's sake! Why can't they be fat like me and live on water? Rose bemoaned her fate as she struggled to swallow the tasteless cereal while she salivated over the food on her companions' plates.

"For loving them. For opening their hearts to allow the men they're meant to be to be released from the bonds that had kept them chained to their past."

"Dammit, Alexa, do you have to go and spoil our aggravation with those louts to make us go all mushy inside?" Peyton grumbled.

"Don't get us wrong, we love them, but sometimes they're just ... just too freaking *Mastery.*"

Savannah bit into buttery toast and took a sip of coffee. "And lo and behold if we dare defy them."

"They should learn to chill and not go all huffed up at a little back chatting," Peyton muttered.

"You're riled up." Rose glanced between them. "What did they do?"

"Oh, we were supposedly cheeky last night. They put us, bent over in a stockade facing the wall with our bared asses and pussies toward the entrance of The Royal Dungeon, with a box of sex toys at our feet. As if that wasn't enough, they put a poster, inviting everyone entering or leaving the freaking place, to use one of the toys on us," Peyton relayed between bites of food.

"Yes, and this at opening time. You know how many members there were last night. They left us there for two hours," Savannah huffed in a thin voice.

"I suppose you weren't allowed to come?" Rose bit into a succulent strawberry.

"What do you think? I'd like to find the man who first came up with the idea of withholding climaxes and personally castrate him with a freaking blunt knife." Peyton slashed her knife through the air.

Their laughter filtered through the atmosphere, tingling their mirth all the way to the cousins, who were openly eyeing them.

Alexa looked at Rose. "What about Rose over here, ladies? Don't you agree that she might be perfect for one of the Masters?"

Rose looked at her and shook her head as she noticed the excited glimmer in her eyes. "Me? Nope, I'm not, so don't even think of playing cupid."

"You know, Alexa, you might just have something there. I've seen how she and Master Bear look at each other."

"Forget it," Rose urged, desperate to draw the attention away from her. "After the other night's disaster with my punishment, I'm not in favor with any of them."

"Aha! And therein lies the truth, doesn't it, Rose?" Alexa slapped her palm on the table. "Come on, spill. Why didn't you want Master Bear to fuck you at that specific point? I mean, let's be real, no one fucks like him, and there's not one sub in this castle that doesn't wish to be chosen by him."

"True, I can attest to that," Peyton said. "I love my Master but even he can't wrap my body into a pretzel like Master Bear can."

"Me too, even though it was punishment at the time, I passed out it was that intense," Savannah concurred.

"It's his trademark and the reason all the subs go gaga over him," Alexa said as she finished the last of her pancakes.

"What?" Rose asked with a deep frown which led to the three women smiling in delight. She noticed and huffed irritably, "WHAT?"

Oh, for fuck's sake, Rose ... ban that freaking word from your vocabulary.

Alexa stabbed a finger in the air at her. "You're jealous."

"Me? Don't be ridiculous."

"Question is, what made the green monster appear on her shoulder?" Savannah tapped her fingers on the table, watching her speculatively.

"Hmm ... you have a point, cuz. Is it because you haven't been fucked by him?" Peyton smiled as Rose's cheeks reddened.

"Or maybe, she realizes he's fucked all three of us and not her," Savannah said tongue in cheek. She jabbed Alexa in the side as Rose's cheeks darkened.

"Could also be she just realized that at this stage of the training, including the employed subs, she has close to seventy women to compete with."

"You're being ridiculous, all three of you. Believe me, even if I offered myself on a platter to the pass-out-fucking-machine that is Master Bear, he wouldn't be interested."

"Interesting statement, sub RL."

The haughty tenor thrilled through her so unexpectedly, the sip of tea she'd just taken went the wrong way and she choked. She heaved in a breath and gratefully took the water Alexa offered. It helped to ease the discomfort but her throat refused to open and she coughed. The lout behind her offered a hand by thumping her on the back until she twisted around in the seat to glare at his chest; habit kept her from looking directly at him.

"Enough! Are you trying to break my neck with that huge paw of yours?"

"Just being helpful," he grinned as she grunted and proffered her stiff back in response. She bit into a piece of fruit, thereby effectively discarding him.

Rose's fervent wishing him away was in vain as he came to stand next to her at the head of the table. She stoically ignored him.

"Let's discuss your desire to offer yourself on a platter to me, sub RL."

"That is *not* what I said," she spat indignantly through thin lips and stabbed viciously at a strawberry on her plate.

She noticed him crossing his arms over his chest from her peripheral vision but she refused to look at him.

"It seems you say a lot of things you claim not to have said." The censure rang clearly in the dark baroque tones that unraveled a flutter deep inside her chest. "Remind me what I said about keeping your eyes from me, sub."

Rose cursed under her breath. She heaved in a deep breath before she cast her eyes to his. It took a mammoth effort not to scamper back and hide behind Peyton who sat next to her at the vicious anger that flashed in his eyes.

"No!" she cried and bore back as he grabbed her arm and yanked her out of the bunk seat to drag her closer.

"Go to your room and take them out, Rose. Don't let me *ever* see you wear those fucking contacts again, is that understood?"

"Yes, Sir,"

Crack! Crack!

"Fuck! Master … Yes, *Master Bear*," she quickly puffed around a painful breath at the searing slaps he landed on her outer thigh. She stumbled to find her feet as he pushed her away from him and stomped off back to his table.

"The class starts in five minutes, sub RL. I'm warning you … don't be late." His voice floating over his shoulder spurred her into action.

"Freaking asshole," she muttered, rubbing her flaming leg as she ran upstairs to find the gray contact lenses to hide the ice blue color of her eyes.

"Well, well, well," Alexa said speculatively as they stared after the disappearing woman. "It seems I was right."

"You definitely were, and lemme tell you, that wasn't a normal sexual spark between them, that was pure, unadulterated lustful chemistry."

"And then some," Savannah agreed.

"Now ... if only I could figure out what the delightful Rose Lovett is hiding from the formidable Master Bear."

Peyton and Savannah looked at Alexa questioningly.

"What makes you say that?" Peyton leaned forward.

"It's clear as the light of day, ladies. Every time Kane comes near her, she tenses up and scurries off in the opposite direction. It must be hell. To be so drawn to a man only to run from him in what exactly … fear?" She got up and stretched lazily. "I think we need to make sure they don't pass each other like ships in the night. Those two light up like a wildfire around each other. It's something we can't allow to go to waste."

"We agree and we're in. Just let us know how we can help." Peyton finished her coffee.

"I'm going in for the big fat and carb fill up. Anyone joining me?" Alexa nodded toward the still laden tables in the front of the room.

"I started with that but I won't say no to some of those scrumptious pancakes you had." Savannah got up and followed Alexa to the buffet. Peyton just shook her head as she watched them fill their plates.

"We need to talk, Petals." She started at the harsh voice behind her.

She snorted softly. *Not, 'Can we talk, Peyton' or 'Honey, we have something to discuss'. Oh, no! The high and mighty King of the castle went straight for the jugular and turned all Dom on her and demanded her immediate subjugation by using her sub name.*

Suck it up, Sinclair. If you think I'm going to go all gooey after you made me suffer for two hours, then refused last night AND this morning to take care of my lustful needs, you don't know me very well.

Of course, she didn't dare say it out loud but showed her vexation by racking her back as straight as an ironing board. She took a sip from her coffee with a regal tilt of her chin.

"Do not ignore me, sub."

Peyton glanced this way and that, then shook her head as if she'd mistaken the growl behind her and leisurely buttered the piece of toast on her plate. She didn't miss the wide-eyed looks with which the trainees and subs openly stared at her. They expected Master Eagle to explode.

For that matter, so did Peyton but she awaited it with heat flowing through her veins and her clit tingling in expectation. She chose to ignore the tensing of her buttocks. Something had to suffer collateral damage and if it was her tender ass cheeks, so be it. She was after a climax and she intended to get one, come hell or high water.

"Morning, Stone. Lovely day, isn't it?" Alexa said in a chirpy voice as she and Savannah sat back down. He responded with a grunt. She glanced at Savannah, who rolled her eyes, knowing what her cousin was up to.

"Petals, I said we need to talk." His tenor deepened, the warning in his voice painted like a canvas of red hot flames in the atmosphere.

Peyton slapped at her hair and tossed it back.

Savannah suppressed her mirth with difficulty. Peyton had more guts than any sub she knew, but if she'd seen the gathering thunderclouds in her Master's eyes, she'd jump at his command.

"Something bothering you, Peyton?" she asked tongue in cheek.

"Yes," Peyton lilted in a sugar sweet voice. "There's a pesky fly buzzing around my head."

"That fucking does it."

"Hey!" Peyton flailed and kicked her legs as Stone summarily yanked her out of the bunk seat and plonked her over his shoulder. Her breath whooshed from her lips as her stomach impacted with his unyielding strength. "Put me down, you big lout! Now! I said … OWW! she screamed unnecessarily loud as two sharp slaps landed on her behind.

"Rather overdramatic, wouldn't you say, Petals," he ridiculed as he stomped toward the informal seating area in the far corner.

"Your overgrown Neanderthal! Bully! Miscreant! Put. Me. Down!"

Peyton boxed his back, smiling gleefully as he grunted, then yelped as he pushed her further over his shoulder, holding onto her ankles. She had to grab onto his belt in fear that her head would thump on the ground.

"You're an asshole, Stone Sinclair. I hope you know that," she snapped between gulping breaths from being mishandled.

"And you, my little spitfire, are a spoiled and recalcitrant brat."

"I am not ... oomph," she huffed out a breath as he unceremoniously dumped her on one of the sofas, "... spoiled," she ended suppressing a grin at his narrow-eyed look. She tried to scramble out of the way as he got hold of one sneakered foot and in one economic flurry of hands, relieved her of the pair of shorts and panties. "What the devil do you think you're doing?" she whispered loudly. "Everyone is having breakfast." She flicked a glance past him and moaned. "Were having breakfast. Now, they're just watching us." She crossed her hands to cover her womanly bits and shot a fierce glare at him. "Give me back my clothes."

"After," he said with an amused grin.

"After what?"

He laughed at the eager expression on her face. The freaking beast outright laughed at her! She scooted hands and feet onto the seat as he came closer, looking like a tiger ready to strike. He caught her hand and before she realized his intent, he sat down and yanked her face down over his legs. He pushed her forward until she was balanced precariously over his thighs. She grabbed onto his legs for support.

"After I imprint in your mind via the heat of my palm on your cute little ass that deliberate disrespect such as you just displayed in public will not be tolerated."

"You don't need to imprint anything on my ass. If you hadn't … *oww*," she screamed as four successive blows cracked on her tender behind. "Stop that!"

Of course, he didn't. He continued until her angry shrieks and insults stopped and were replaced by whimpers and soft pleas for him to end the punishment. He did but to add insult to the injury, he rubbed the scorching heat deeper into her sensitive skin.

"Open your legs, Petals."

"Like hell I will," she gasped and then screamed furiously at him when he commenced spanking her scorching ass.

"Damn you, Stone Sinclair," she wailed, doing her best not to burst into tears. Every crack felt like lava splashing onto her skin.

"No, my pet, this is all your own doing. Until you do as I say, I'll continue whacking your ass."

Peyton lasted three more slaps of his humongous paw and then gave in with a furious growl. Her legs fell open.

"That's more like it, Petals."

The deep timbre of his voice didn't soothe her as it usually did. This time it brought a cringe, knowing what he intended.

Crack! Crack! Crack! Crack! Crack!

"Fucking hell!" she gasped, and her hips jerked as he landed the punishing strikes over her pussy and clit. She whimpered as he brushed his hands over the punished folds, mortified but not all too surprised at the flush of arousal it elicited in her loins. His spankings, even punishing ones, always had that effect on her.

"Shall I continue, Petals, or do you have something to say to me?"

Peyton was tempted to keep her lips clamped shut. Another couple of those against her clit and she'd combust like a waterfall. She sighed regretfully. She'd learned not to try and manipulate Stone. He was too astute and would surely find another way to keep her from climaxing.

"I'm sorry, Master Eagle, for openly disrespecting you."

"Hmm," he grunted as he gently rubbed the blooming red cheeks lovingly. "Are you ready to talk now, Peyton?"

Peyton struggled and twisted until he released his hold on her. She pushed off his lap, grabbed her shorts and shimmied into them. She planted her fists on her hip and her toe tap-tap-tapped on the floor. Her still naked breasts wiggled enticingly.

"*Now* you ask me if I wanna talk, not demand like you did earlier?" She shook a stiff finger at his head. "You're a—"

"Careful, baby ... my hand isn't even smarting. I can continue for hours if need be."

"Gmph, typical Dom," she sniped and pivoted on her heel.

"Maybe I should just marry you."

Peyton froze, her one foot dangling in the air as his words registered. She stomped it down onto the floor when she realized she must look like an imbecile and spun around.

"What did you say?"

"Maybe then you'd be less inclined to defy me around every nook and cranny."

"Well, I never ... if you think ... you're such a ... you should just ..." She clamped her mouth shut as she listened to her own stammering. Why he had the uncanny ability to make her sound like an illiterate monkey, she had no idea. She heaved in a breath and pinned him in place with a blazing violet stare. "It's no wonder my eggs refuse to allow your rowdy, wiggling, spermy ... *doodles* entry. If that's how you propose, Stone Sinclair, I hope you're ready to be married to a ... a *toad* one day!"

Peyton stomped off, ignoring his wicked grin and the outburst of laughter from the people who had remained seated to enjoy the show. She would've been delighted to hear Stone's murmur as she disappeared under the arched entryway.

"God, I love that woman."

Chapter Nine

"Up front with me, sub RL."

Rose sighed as she walked into Kane's training dungeon and his dark orotund order rang in her ears. She'd done so well in the first five months to avoid being noticed by him—all undone in one night. She dragged her feet as she forced her body to obey his order. The reminder that she was still due punishment from him, kept ringing through her mind every time he was in close proximity. She expected him to take out that electric whip at any time.

"Eyes," he snapped as she stopped next to him.

She glared at him through the gray lenses, irritation rife in her expression. Did he honestly think she'd defy him and taunt him in his own dungeon by disobeying?

He leaned closer, his breath hot on her skin.

"I'm beginning to think you hadn't bothered to read the Castle's rules for trainees and subs. Continue glaring at me, my pet, and you'll end up with your ass trussed in the air to be fucked and whipped the rest of the day."

Her eyes flickered but she quickly lowered her gaze. She remembered him as a kind and caring Dom. A Master who treated her like a princess and punished her only when she really overstepped his rules. She had basked in his Domination and he in her submission. A combination she'd failed to find in the intervening years, no matter how hard she'd searched.

It seemed he had changed and took pleasure in dishing out punishment, or more accurately, threatening her with it.

Kane wasn't ignorant of the turmoil raging through her. It was there in the tenseness of her body, the expectant flicker in her eyes, waiting to be punished. He didn't bother to wonder about his desire to inflict pain and suffering on her. He knew where it stemmed from.

He wanted her, lusted after her with increasing desire he had no means of controlling. That she'd snuffed him openly grated at him but that wasn't the reason for making her suffer. He hated lies and Rose Lovett told the biggest fib ever when she claimed she'd choose punishment over being fucked by him.

That was the reason he would continue taunting her, chipping away at her denial until she broke down and begged him to fuck her. Until such time, he intended to make her realize the foolery of her claim. He was going to spike her desire bit by bit until she was ready to combust ... all without laying a hand on her.

His lips twitched into an evil grin.

Yes, Ms. Rose Lovett is going to beg me, a lot sooner than even she realizes.

He chuckled and reveled in watching her body tense. He had no intention of touching or fucking her but that didn't mean he wouldn't elicit the help of others in her fall from grace.

Kane was confident in the effect he had over Rose to know the claim he'd made on the beach wasn't just boasting. He had every intention to make her realize that as well. No matter who gave her permission to come, until he was the one fucking her, her body would refuse to comply.

"What's so funny, Master Bear," Rose chipped out through thin lips.

"Just thinking of how much fun it's going to be."

She flashed an annoyed look at him. He got the impression she was tempted to plant her fists on her hips to illustrate how irked she was.

"Let me guess. The *fun* you're referring to is me."

"Ah yes, my pet, your suffering is going to be such a pleasure to watch."

Kane ignored her indignant stutter and turned to face the trainees watching their interaction with animated interest.

"Morning, trainees. I've decided to deviate a little from the planned schedule today."

"Sorry we're late, Master Bear, but our Masters insist that we attend this class today," Peyton said as she and Savannah rushed inside and took seats in the back row.

"I'll excuse you this time. You both know the time classes commence in the morning. No," he held up his hand when they started protesting simultaneously. "I'm not interested. If you are to attend, you're on time or you leave. No exceptions. Is that understood, Petals and Tulip?"

"Yes, Master Bear," they said in unison. Their expressions spoke volumes. If he chased them out for being late, they'd be punished by their Masters for not following their instructions.

"Our training today is going to be outside."

The trainees shifted uncomfortably as the assistant training Doms chuckled. Their eyes glimmered in anticipated pleasure as Kane's cousin, Ace, Danton Hill, and Evans Carter arrived.

"Master Leo and Doms Danton and Evans are kind enough to assist with the training seeing as it requires one Dom to pair up with two trainees. Follow me, ladies."

A dark blush stained Rose's cheeks as Kane clipped a leading chain into the O-ring of her red leather collar. He hooked the other end into a loop of his cargo shorts.

"Why am I the only one chained?" she puffed stiffly.

Kane shrugged and started walking. Rose was forced to rush after him as he made no effort to shorten his strides to accommodate her much shorter legs.

"Master Bear, I asked you a question."

He slanted an amused look over his shoulder and said tonelessly. "I don't need a reason nor do I need to offer an explanation for anything I choose to do in my training sessions, sub RL, but seeing as you insist." He smiled broadly. "Because I can."

He ushered her into the passenger seat of one of the four beach buggies standing in front of the castle. "Petals and Tulip, you ride with me," he said as he cranked the engine. "Hold on ladies, we're heading up the hill to the top."

The four buggies drove in a convoy around the castle and followed a winding road up the hill behind it. The trainees chatted gaily with the Doms, relaxed and happy to be outside during training time.

Their attitude changed as they arrived at their destination and they realized the area they entered, enclosed by palm trees, shrubs, and large willows, was set up for either training or scenes.

"Relax, subs. This is a training session, but as you also know, you're trained in all aspects of submission and not all of it is pleasant. Today, however, it's in your hands how pleasurable or punishing it's going to be."

He smiled at the trainees standing in a neat row facing him, except for Rose who was forced to take place next to him, courtesy of the short length of the chain.

"This session is going to be two hours long. After that, I've arranged with the chef to set up lunch for us on the beach." He chuckled at their shouts of joy. "And yes, you'll have the afternoon off." He glanced at Rose. "At least, most of you will."

Kane glanced at the assistant training Doms. "All ready?"

"Yes, Master Bear," said Dom Brad.

"Trainees, we're going to play some games this morning. You'll be given instructions on what to do as well as the repercussions if you fail to adhere to the rules of each game." His lips quirked. "Yes, you guessed it, that's where the punishments come in. Some of them will be easy, others not so much and are solely based on how badly you fail at each game." He looked at each woman. "Any questions? No? Good, then let's get you ready. Remove your tunics, please and hand them to Master Leo. Even though we are mainly in the shade, the Doms will assist you to cover your delicate skin with suntan lotion."

Rose attempted to follow the women's example but got hoodwinked by the chain around her neck.

"Master Bear."

Kane turned his head sideways. He noticed how Rose's fingers clenched around the material she held bundled against her stomach.

"Yes?"

Rose exhaled slowly and bit back the sharp retort springing to her lips. The dratted man could see her dilemma but chose to pretend he didn't.

"I can't remove mine unless you unclip the chain," she bit out shortly as his eyes took a leisurely gander up and down her body.

"I imagine that is a challenge, yes."

Her eyes narrowed. He was deliberately goading her. He wanted her to snap at him. No doubt to pile on more punishment! Her fingers loosened and the dress dropped back in place.

Well, tough titties, I'm not giving you the satisfaction. She took a calming breath. "Does that mean I'm not included in the game training?"

"Whatever gave you that idea?" His gaze dropped to the collar around her neck. "I'm willing to assist in you removing your tunic … but it's going to cost you."

"Cost *me*? Why must I offer anything in exchange for an order *you* gave? It's not my fault you clapped this stupid chain on my neck."

"Isn't it? I suppose that's a matter of opinion, my dear sub RL." He looked around. "I see everyone is almost ready. I expect you to be too, so I suggest you get to it otherwise your game is off to a dour beginning."

"What do you want in exchange to assist me to remove my tunic, Master Bear?" Rose stood as straight as a lamppost, her sneaker tapping on the grass.

"Hm, let me see. You loathe my touch—"

"I *never* said that!"

He ignored her indignant protest and continued, "But I don't happen to mind yours, so in exchange for me unclipping the chain, I require a loving kiss." He waited until she stepped closer and went on her toes, aiming for his lips. "On my dick."

"On your ..." Rose swallowed the word and try as she might, she couldn't keep from glaring at him.

"Well, that just cost you more than a loving kiss, sub RL. Now, you'll give junior a French kiss."

"The trainees are ready, Master Bear." Ace's amused voice was the conduit that made her reach for Kane's cargo shorts. He was clearly out to get her. She'd be damned if she gave him any more ammunition to turn the *loving kiss* into a full-blown throat fuck.

"No need to remove my shorts, my pet. Just take junior out through the zipper opening." He offered her his naughty boy smile that made her stop and stare. "I'm commando, so it won't be too difficult.

Of freaking course he's commando, she snapped in her mind and fumbled with the zipper. *Anything to make it easy for the women flocking around him in hopes to be the next one he fucks until she passes out.*

The moment her fingers encountered the hard and hot heat of his cock, her breath wheezed through her lips and the jealous irritation dissipated. It was the one thing of Kane she could never forget. How hot he always felt. To the touch of her fingers, her lips, and her very needy pussy, which chose that moment to clench and flush with liquid heat she could feel trickling from her slit.

"I want a kiss, sub RL, not a caress. Get to it, you're wasting everyone's time." Kane's voice thickened but the warning was undeniable in his tone.

Rose bent over and wrapped her lips around his blunt cockhead. She closed her eyes as memories assailed her at the familiar feel and taste of him inside her mouth. Her tongue flicked out to trace the opening at the top, licking up the precum that trickled out at her ministrations. She rolled her tongue around the mushroom shaped tip and sucked, like she was enjoying a lollipop. He grew harder, bigger with every flick of her tongue, every seductive suck until her lips were stretched wide to accommodate him.

"Enough."

Rose heard the order but continued the *kiss* until she felt the hard edge of something below her chin forcing her up. She reluctantly released his cock with a loud pop and watched it swing in a perpendicular arch.

"Oww," she protested as another sharp prod under her chin brought her upright and within a hair's breadth from Kane's face. His eyes darkened, as did the expression on his face.

"Why is it, Rose, that every time you touch me, it feels so familiar?" He didn't miss her eyes flicker. "So, the next question is, where and when were we intimate?" His eyes slitted. "I've been very careful in choosing sexual partners my entire life. I made a point of never fucking a groupie and you ... I would've remembered you." He traced her cheek with the object in his hand. "This beautiful face would've been ingrained in my memory bank." His chest rose as she shifted her weight. A spark flashed in his gaze as another suspicion was confirmed in that split second before she looked away.

"Another secret." He tapped the clapper of the crop in his hand against her chin to bring her gaze back to his. She had no idea where it came from because he didn't have it with him on the trip there. His eyes were narrowed, rigid, cold, and hard as he released the chain clip.

Rose quickly shimmied out of the tunic as she struggled to compose herself, completely flayed bare by the burning and impenetrable stare that brutally reduced her effort to appear moderately innocent.

"No, not a secret ... a lie. How many more am I going to uncover, I wonder?" He clipped the chain into the O-ring of her collar. "Trust is a fickle thing, sub RL. There are many who talk the talk, but only those who *walk* the talk gain my trust, my unconditional faith. Do you know why?"

His voice thrilled in a deep tenor all the way inside her heart. She couldn't get out a word and shook her head. This time, Kane allowed it to pass.

"Because the language of truth, and love for that matter, isn't spoken but lived. I don't listen to what you say, Rose. I watch what you do, how you act." He straightened and took back a step. His chin tilted regally. "Best you remember that."

He turned to the group waiting patiently for his attention, leaving Rose in a state of confusion. Did he in so many words, albeit hidden within a threat, say that there could be love between them? The cogs in her brain floundered about to dissect every word until reality gave her a resounding wake up slap.

I am keeping secrets from him and lying on top of that. Not a little white lie, a gross and painful one. No matter what he might say now, once he knows the truth, it won't matter. He'll never forgive me.

His gruff voice yanked her back to the surroundings.

"The first game is a group one, and even though it's going to be fun, this is training, therefore each game has an objective. For this one, it's to teach you to concentrate on your end goal irrespective of restrictions placed on you."

A collective groan echoed around them as the trainees realized the restrictions would be anything but fun for them.

"Each of you will be adorned with a nipple and clit Y-shaped chain. The alligator clamps will be nice and tight to ensure it won't slip off during the game. If you do manage to get yours off, it'll be tightened. So, the clamps are your restrictions." He smiled as Ace waved at him where they'd set up the play area. "You're going to play a match of volleyball, trainees."

"Volleyball? Wearing clamps? That's torture, Master Bear," Peyton immediately protested.

Kane ignored her.

"There will be three periods of five minutes each. The winner of each set has the choice of either removing their clit or nipple clamps or adding a restriction to their opponents. The losing team will each receive a punishment from us individually." He gestured toward the net. "We're not complete ogres and lowered the net so you won't need to jump ... except if your opponents play to win, that is."

The women groaned. The demonic Master's aim was clear. He was setting them up against each other. No one enjoyed punishment and he knew it. They were going to play to win and that meant suffering the pain *and* arousal the three clamps would add to the play.

"Right, Petals and Tulip, you're on opposing sides. While the clamps are being attached, please select your teams."

"Sub RL," Peyton immediately called her name. She was tall and would definitely be an asset to the team.

"Sub CB," Savannah followed.

Kane unclipped the chain. Rose kept her gaze rooted on the center of his chest, only noticing for the first time how tight the t-shirt molded his muscled chest. Her stomach clenched, her loins tightened, and her pussy tingled.

"Go to Master Leo, so he can rub suntan lotion on. We don't want this silky skin burned, now do we?" He ran the edge of the crop between her breasts and over their sensitive under curve before tapping it lightly against her nipples.

"Of course, Master Bear," she mumbled and quickly trotted to where the Doms were securing the clamps on the trainees. She felt miserable, having realized as he ran the crop over her skin that apart from yanking her out of her seat at breakfast, he hadn't touched her since that night in the dungeon.

Her heavy sigh floated on the slight breeze as heavy as thick, rolling fog. "When are you going to realize it doesn't matter, Rose," she said sotto voce. "There's no future for you with Kane. You fucked up when you chose to believe you knew what was best for him. For that alone, he'd never forgive you, and once he finds out about Tucker he'd—" She gulped back the word. He definitely would hate her but it was an unbearable thought she refused to say out loud.

The little soliloquy didn't help to ease the growing arousal though, especially since she could feel Kane's eyes on her no matter where she went. Her legs felt rubbery as she approached Master Leo; the tingling down her spine told her Master Bear's gaze followed her. It was with mammoth effort that she kept her hands by her side and didn't give in to the desire to cover her jiggling butt from his gaze.

"Why so glum, sub RL?" Master Leo said as he lathered his hands with a generous amount of suntan lotion.

Rose crossed her arms over her round belly and shifted her weight under his appreciative stare. She couldn't help it, but every time one of the Masters looked at her like that, she cringed because she imagined what they saw was the same as she did in the mirror every morning. Overly rounded hips, heavy thighs and a tummy that bulged too much.

"Drop your arms, sub RL, or do I need to remind you of the position you're supposed to present yourself in at all times?"

Master Leo was known for his strictness. He had no compunction to correct an errant trainee with the rubber paddle that was always clipped to the loop of his pants. It had hard steel studs on the broad edge for that extra painful nip. She'd felt its sting once, which was much worse than that of a leather one, not to mention how the sound of rubber against skin made her tense before the pain registered.

"No, Master Leo." Rose reluctantly clasped her hands behind her back.

"I asked you a question, trainee. Why so glum?"

Of course, it was too much to hope for that he'd forget the question. Rose peeked at him as he stepped closer and rubbed the lotion over her arms and shoulders.

"I'm not overly comfortable being naked in the open, Master Leo."

His gaze did a thorough inventory of her body that made her squirm as she noticed the heat in his eyes.

"With a body like yours, you should be naked all the time." Ace's eyes narrowed as she shifted her weight and appeared visibly uncomfortable under his exploratory gaze. "What is this, sub? Don't tell me you think there's something wrong with you?"

Rose couldn't help the tiny snort that escaped her lips. "You need to have your eyes tested, Master Leo." She looked at her body briefly. "I'm fat and everything jiggles when I walk."

Ace clasped her chin between his fingers and tilted back her head. His gaze glinted warningly.

"You're anything but fat. You have a little added padding, but fuck if it's not gorgeous on you. Haven't you noticed when you're in the member's dungeon how every Dom stops and stares when you walk past?"

Rose hissed as he rubbed the lotion over her chest and breasts, paying special attention to her nipples. The damn traitors, of course, had to jump to attention and turned into stabbing soldiers in his palms. His lips twitched into an appreciative smile.

"You're the kind of woman every Dom wants to fuck, sub RL, not only because of your generous curves but because you carry your sensuality like a siren all over your body. It oozes from every inch of your skin and spikes testosterone of every hot-blooded man close to you through the roof." He quickly finished lathering her body and walked around her, examining her critically. His grin leered at her. "Myself included."

Crack!

"Oww!" Rose jumped at the painful slap on her ass. She looked at him with a hurtful expression. "What was that for?"

"For the enticing and arousing view of your ass *jiggling* under the impact of my hand." He quickly put on the clamps, ignoring her protest as he pulled on the Y-chain, tugging her nipples down to fit the one on her clit in place. He chuckled at her expression. "You better join your team before I decide to add a couple more swats on your delectable butt."

Rose didn't need a second invitation.

Chapter Ten

"I'm sure most of you know the rules of volleyball but let me reiterate them briefly." Kane sat on the referee chair next to the net and looked from left to right, ensuring all trainees were paying attention to him.

Rose realized the court was a permanent fixture and not a temporary setup like they'd speculated while taking their places on either side of the net. Kane's brisk tone forced her attention back to him.

"Each side is allowed a maximum of three hits. Points are made on every serve for the winning team. A player may not hit the ball twice in succession but you're allowed to make contact with the ball with any part of your body. No catching, holding, or throwing the ball. You're allowed to play a ball off the net during a volley or serve. If it hits a boundary line, it's in." He glanced around again. "Any questions?"

"To win a round you have to be two points ahead in a match or doesn't that matter at the end of five minutes?" Rose asked. She was the tallest of the women there and she winced every time she moved at how the short Y-chain caused the clamps on her nipples and clit to pull and pinch her nubs.

"Whoever is ahead when the siren goes off, wins the round, except in the final round. To give each team a fair chance, to win, you need to be two points ahead and win two sets." He took a sip of water. "Your clamps will be removed during the two-minute rest period to offer you some relief." He looked at his demon helpers standing around the court. "Everyone ready?"

"Let the fun begin, Master Bear." Ace laughed at the twelve glares shooting daggers at him. "Peyton's team won the coin flip and elected to receive."

"One more thing, seeing as each period is so short, no time outs are allowed. Tulip, is your team ready to serve?" Kane glanced at her as he set his stopwatch.

"I don't suppose no is the correct answer," Savannah lilted and smiled as the men laughed. "We're ready, Master Bear."

Kane tapped his watch to start the count-off and barked, "Play."

It was evident from the get-go that each team played to win. The points remained neck and neck throughout. All went well for the women during the first three minutes but then the effect of the tight alligator clamps on their girly bits started to take their toll. Mistakes were made. Moans floated to the sky more often as stretching to hit the ball became painful.

"Time."

Rose's team yelled gleefully as the period ended with them one point ahead. She went down onto her haunches to alleviate the pressure on the clamps. She groaned as Kane's voice rang out over the twitter of the women, "Petals and sub RL, you're with me."

"Come, Rose, let's get these fucking clamps off," Peyton yanked her by the hand. She straightened and reluctantly followed her toward Kane where he waited for them next to the referee chair.

"Off! Get them off," Peyton demanded as she stopped in front of Kane. "Thanks, Dom Evans," she cooed as he handed her a bottle of cold water.

Rose just smiled as he handed hers and thirstily gulped down a couple of sips. She watched Kane gently pinch Peyton's nipples before releasing the clamp and then eased the pressure from around her abused nub. Peyton hissed in relief as he did the same with her clit.

"Sub RL," Kane called her closer. His gaze zoomed in on her reddened nipples. She felt the heat bubble in her veins as his eyebrow did that sexy forehead crawl. "We have a conundrum, my pet," he murmured and used the crop to stroke the pinched edges of the sensitive nubs. "I'd love to offer you the same courtesy as Petals to reduce the pain and discomfort upon removal of the clamps but seeing as you abhor my touch ..."

"Fu-uck!" Rose's wail echoed skyward and dissipated in an echo around them as he released the nipple clamps without further warning or any aid to alleviate the painful rush of blood filling the abused vessels. She was still struggling to breathe when he took off the clit clamp. This time her torment sounded tearful as her legs gave in and she crumbled to the ground. She hugged her knees and rocked back and forth, cursing the dratted devil in her mind as she willed the burning torture away.

"Breathe through the pain, Rose," Kane ordered sharply and watched as she heaved in deep, broken breaths. "Good girl."

Wouldn't you know it—instead of telling him to go to blazes, she fucking basked in his praise.

Stupid, stupid, stupid woman! You better wake up and smell the roses, Rose and quickly, otherwise you're setting yourself up for the kind of hurt you won't be able to recover from—not again.

"Seriously, Rose, fix this misunderstanding with Master Bear," Peyton said as Kane walked over to join the other men. "If only to save your own hide. There's one thing I learned about these Masters and that's once they believe something, nothing will sway them until the truth comes out."

"To be honest, Peyton, in the long run, it'll be better for my hide if he keeps believing I hate his hands on me."

"I don't understand." Peyton tilted her head sideways and regarded her curiously. The investigative journalist inside her stirred to life. It was time to find an assignment to feed the need for the adrenaline rush inside her. Stone said she could continue working, so there was nothing preventing her from contacting her editor, Cyril Douglas, to find her a job—one that wouldn't keep her away from home too long. Excitement burst to life to manifest itself in the brilliant smile on her face. "On the other hand, don't tell me. It's my job to dig out secrets, so I'm making you my next assignment."

Rose struggled to keep the horror from her expression. That was the last thing she needed. It was already difficult enough to keep her composure around Kane. She couldn't cope with a journalist nosing around her as well. She forced a dry laugh from her lips.

"Believe me, you'll be wasting your time. There's no deep, dark secret to uncover. To be honest, I live a rather boring life." She frowned at the truth of it. A wry smile split over her face. "I'm a painter and seeing as my son is in boarding school, I've kinda become a hermit."

"You? Unsociable? Come on, Rose, you don't expect me to believe that."

"Time to get ready for period two, trainees," Master Leo's guttural voice interrupted any further questions from Peyton, much to Rose's relief.

"Well, let's get these freaking claws fitted. My poor nipples are cringing just thinking about those damn clamps." Peyton complained as they approached Master Bear. She pushed a reluctant Rose ahead to be first, flashing her a broad smile as she glared at her.

Kane tapped the crop against Rose's nipples to tease them erect and then placed the clamps in place. She bit her lip as the pain seemed worse than the first time.

"Okay, little one?" He asked as he flicked the edge of the crop back and forth over her clit. Rose nodded. She was beginning to resent the freaking tool. She was so immersed in her thoughts she didn't realize he clamped her clit until pain seared through her. A raw cry burst from her lips.

"Easy, sub, breathe in slowly. Again. That's better." Kane searched her expression and only turned to Peyton once he assured himself Rose was breathing normally.

It angered her how his care over her, albeit from a distance and without touching her, toggled loose the natural submissive inside her. How it pleased her, worse, how she craved to please him just as much, no matter that she knew nothing could ever come of it.

She didn't stand around for Peyton to be fitted but elected to wait on court. Anything to get away from Kane's magnetic presence. She'd forgotten how potent his powerful Domination and confidence was and how it affected her both physically and emotionally. She barely managed to cope with the constant surging lust in his presence; to hide her feelings was becoming exceedingly more difficult with each passing day.

"Before we begin, the winning team still needs to decide what advantage they wish to take for this period. Petals? Have you discussed it?"

Peyton looked between her team members. They nodded in unity, albeit some of them groaned. "We have, Master Bear. We decided not to punish Tulip's team, nor are we going to take the offer of losing some of our clamps. If we're gonna win this, it'll be fair and square."

Kane's respect for this group of trainees rose exponentially. It seldom happened that one team didn't jump at the chance of gaining an advantage over the other.

"Well played, ladies. We salute your sportsmanship." The five men taking their places around the court confirmed Kane's praise with a round of applause.

"Freaking brilliant idea, Rose. Now, if we lose this set, the other team would be obliged to do the same so as not to lose face," Peyton beamed as they took their places.

"Ready?" Kane checked with the teams. "Play!"

This time it was clear from the first hit that Savannah's team was out to win and it turned into a grueling match of playing off each point. With a couple of seconds on the clock, the teams were equal, then Savannah clipped the ball from low down and it flew over the heads of Peyton's team. Rose fell back and jumped, only to crumble to the ground with a shriek of pain as the clamp around her clit ripped off from the pressure on the chain. The ball landed in play but no one cared as they all rushed to Rose where she was curled into a ball of pain.

Kane reached her first and gently picked her up. He carried her to a chaise lounge under the trees and laid her down carefully.

"Get off the nipple clamps, Ace," he said roughly as he straightened Rose's legs and prodded her throbbing clitoris.

She moaned but hardly registered Master Leo gently removing the clamps from her nipples; she was too aware of Kane's warm fingers examining her clit. She was mortified at the arousal that set her loins tingling with every brush of his finger.

"It's very red and swollen but the skin isn't torn." He sat back on his haunches and studied her teary eyes. "No more clamps for you on this precious little nub. How do you feel, Rose?"

The tender care in his deep voice trembled through her mind and squeezed through the cracks of the wall she'd built around her heart in an effort to forget him over the years. A wall that steadfastly crumbled the longer she stayed on the island. It was useless to deny it. She still loved Kane, even after almost seventeen years of separation.

"I'm okay, Master Bear. The worst is over, I think."

His lips twisted in a regretful grimace. "My apologies for laying my hands on you, sub RL." He ignored her crestfallen expression and stood up. "Master Leo, please rub some of the Castle's soothing gel on her clit." He looked to the trainees standing around the chair. "This break is two minutes longer, everyone, to allow sub RL recovery time. Rehydrate, please."

Rose covertly watched him walk away, drooling over the Gluteus Maximus rippling in his tight buns with every step he took. It was unfair that a man his age looked so sexy and hot. Something she noticed with annoyance many of the trainees agreed with if their expressions staring at him were anything to go by.

I suppose they're all hoping to be chosen to be fucked into oblivion by the mighty sexual prowess of Master Bear.

"Stop glaring at everyone, Rose. You don't want them to know how you feel, do you?" Peyton lilted softly in her ear.

"Forget about the women, it's the men you need to be careful about. If those cousins got drift you're all gaga over him ... ah, Rose, I'm afraid, then they'll team up and you won't stand a chance."

"Lord, no. That's the last thing I need." Rose struggled to sit up. She peeked at the two women who seemed adamant to become besties with her. "Just so you know, I don't *feel* anything, except lust and who can blame me? He's got a yummy ass."

"There's no denying that, girlfriend but there's appreciating a sexy butt and there's being possessive over the man who carries said butt." Peyton's knowing smile mocked Rose's effort to push them off track.

"Yep, and that glare of yours, dear Rose, screamed out, hands off! He's mine."

"You're being ridiculous," Rose muttered as she gulped down half of the bottled water.

"Time," Kane's voice rippled on the breeze toward them. Rose got up and moaned.

"Are you sure you can continue, Rose? Shouldn't you sit this period out?" Peyton asked in concern.

"The final period? No way. I'm part of the team and I'll see it through." She ushered them toward the Doms to get fitted with the clamps. She hissed when Master Leo clamped her nipples and spread her legs for the one on her clit.

Ace shook his head. "You heard Master Bear. This little nub isn't getting another clamp."

"That's not fair to the other players, Master Leo. I'll have an advantage." She shook her head. "Either you clamp my clit or remove everyone else's." She straightened and waited, holding her breath.

"Sub RL is right." She started as Kane's deep voice rumbled behind her. "Remove everyone's clit clamps but add weights to the nipple chains."

The trainees didn't even complain about that, too relieved that they were losing the clit clamps. They even giggled excitedly as they took their places on the court.

"It's the final round. Remember, the winning team must be two points ahead. The period will continue until that is achieved. Ready?" Kane looked around the court. "Play!"

If the first rounds were grueling, this one turned into a massacre of equal measure on both sides. Each team played to win. They ground their teeth as the weights swinging from their nipples, weren't just pinching and uncomfortable, but aided in raising their libido. The demon Doms chuckled, as after each point, many trainees clenched their legs together and hunched over, moaning and cursing their fate. The tantalizing aroma of their spicy juices infiltrated the air.

Kane stopped play after seven minutes. The points continued to play seesaw as neither team was ready to be defeated.

"I'm very impressed, trainees. You're definitely achieving the purpose of this training exercise. Focusing on the end goal, no matter the obstacles. Rehydrate please and then we'll continue."

Five grueling minutes later, the scores were still tied. Rose sat on her haunches, struggling to find her breath after a long and constant battle for a point.

"This is useless, Master Bear. I don't think there's going to be a winner in this match," she puffed gasping for breath,

"I have to admit, it's the first time we've had such an evenly matched group. There is one option, trainees. If a team forfeits, the other wins. The forfeit team, however, will be punished."

"That's hardly fair," Rose mumbled. She looked at Savannah. "What if both teams forfeit at the same time?"

"Then you're all punished."

"We forfeit!" All the women shouted out in a choir. If their nipples were as painful as hers, Rose didn't blame them.

The Doms immediately started removing clamps and sighs of relief drifted to the sky as the men awarded them with a gentle rubbing of their breasts. Rose was lucky enough to be on the receiving end of Master Leo's ministrations and purred like a cat receiving a bowl of milk. She was more than aware of Kane's eyes on her as she sat down on a chaise lounge and accepted a plate of fruit from Dom Danton.

"Well played, sub RL," he said with a broad grin. "At least now all of us can join in the fun." He laughed at her expression and with a naughty wink moved on.

"Damn Doms," Peyton complained, having overheard his comment as she and Savannah joined her.

"Yeah, and it doesn't take a genius to figure out the kind of punishment they have in mind." Savannah gestured to her breasts. "We didn't jump around with those damn clamps for nothing. They freaking knew how aroused it'd make us."

"No! Not climax control. I fucking hate that," Peyton railed. She popped a strawberry into her mouth. "Hmm, at least the luscious fruit makes up for what's coming."

Rose didn't look forward to the punishment for a different reason. Kane had made it clear he wouldn't be touching her again with the apology he'd offered after the incident with the clit clamp. Peyton would most probably get all the benefit from his warm hands and soft lips, where she would have to be satisfied with the impersonal teasing of his crop.

Life is just so unfucking fair, she complained in her mind.

Maybe, but you know it's for the best if he keeps his distance.

But I don't want him to, she negated her subconscious mind.

God, yes, it was true. She craved to feel his hands caress her, tease her and bring her to heights that always blew her mind. His skills had obviously been honed to precision, based on the reaction of all the subs toward him.

"Your body, little dove, is going to starve itself, waiting to be satiated by mine and mine alone and that won't happen until you beg me to fuck you."

The prediction Kane had made on the beach had sounded cocky and she'd shunned it at the time but the dratted man had known. Somehow, he knew he had an effect over her that she was unable to control. Her loins were tied in knots from the need to climax. The sex games they'd played with the assistant training Doms in his absence had been torture for her. It didn't matter that the Doms gave her permission to come or how hard she'd tried or how close she was to an orgasm, it never happened. Not even when she tried to masturbate or used her dependable magic wand. The clamps had exacerbated her lust, so much so that she could feel her loins throb incessantly, demandingly and left her trembling in need.

Then so be it. If I have to beg him, that's what I'll do. I can't go on like this. It feels like I'm going to tear apart from the pressure inside me.

Not to mention that she was wet ... all the goddamn time!

"Trainees, please report to your allocated Doms. Tulip, please swap places with sub RL." Kane met her startled gaze with an impassive look as he approached them. "No need to make you suffer more than you already did. At least Master Leo will have the pleasure of feeling your silky skin under his hands."

"Master Bear, this is silly. I never actually said—"

"And I told you it's your actions that speak the loudest, sub. You might not have said it but your choice at the time did. Stop wasting time. I'm sure everyone will like to get this over with so we can all relax on the beach and enjoy lunch."

"Yes, Sir," she snapped, jumped up and charged past him to find Master Leo. "Fucking OWW!" she cried as two searing strikes cracked on her ass. She spun around, nursing her burning cheeks and belatedly realized her mistake as she stared at the crop in his hand. Her snippy mouth reacted too fast again. "Master! I meant Master. I apologize for my disrespect."

"Don't let it happen again, sub. You're treading on thin ice where I'm concerned."

Rose thought it best not to respond and quickly trotted off. She joined Master Leo and Cora under a large willow tree a couple of yards further.

"Ah, sub RL, I'm delighted Master Bear entrusted you to me. I'm sure you're keen to get to the beach and cool off in the ocean, so let's start. Because the volleyball match took so long, Master Bear shortened your punishment periods to five minutes each. Today's training is all about focusing on your goal no matter the restrictions placed on you, correct?"

"Yes, Master Leo," they chorused.

"As a team, you mastered it beautifully. Now, I'm going to test your individual ability to stay focused. Sub RL, while I attend to sub CD's evaluation, you can relax." He picked up a bright purple dildo from the table and held it up. "Just to make sure you don't feel neglected while I feast on sub CD, this hedgehog bearded vibrator will keep you company."

"You're not serious!" Rose stared at the dildo in horror. It had what she hoped was a silicone cover with numerous, *hedgehog beards*, all around the shaft and bulbous head.

"Relax, my pet. The entire thing is made from silicone and is not as daunting as it looks. It's soft but it gives that added pleasure as it vibrates and twirls inside your tight little cunt."

He pointed at the chaise lounge. "On your back, little one and spread your legs." Rose grumbled under her breath but did as instructed. She jerked as Master Leo ran his finger over labia and dipped the tip inside. "I see I don't even have to lubricate the Hedgehog."

Rose felt the heat rush from her chest to color her cheeks but refrained from making a snarky remark. She bit her lip as he prodded her slit with the silicone monster sex toy, as she preferred to call it.

"This can be as easy or as difficult as you make it, my pet. Relax your muscles." Master Leo gave her a sharp look. "Sub RL, do as your told."

"I'm trying but that thing looks like it's gonna poke holes in my pussy!" she protested. "Owww! Fucking hell, Master Leo!' she shrieked as he slapped her hard on her thighs and without giving her time to realize that she'd relaxed her inner muscles in the process, pushed the dildo all the way inside.

"There, see? All the fuss about nothing."

He smiled as he switched on the remote and Rose jerked in reaction to the strong vibration of the toy. He pressed another button and she groaned, gripping the side of the chair as the damn thing began to twist to and fro inside her, stimulating every nerve ending inside her vagina. The silicone *beards* doing a fantastic job to shoot her arousal sky-high in less than thirty seconds. She was horrified at the immediate flush of juices filling her channel but elated simultaneously. Maybe this would give her the climax she desperately needed.

"One rule, sub, and I don't suppose I need to tell you what that is?" Master Leo's eyebrow lifted in a question mark.

"No, you don't. I'm not allowed to come."

"Brilliant." He turned to Cora who had been watching wide eyed. "On the table, sub CD, and drop your legs over the sides. I'm going to feast on your delectable pussy and you don't move or climax, understood?"

"Yes, Master Leo," Cora said and scrambled into position.

Rose watched Master Leo's lips latch onto Cora's clit, she heard her moans and moments later, noticed her body thrashing. Her low moans and pleas sounded far off as Rose felt herself etching closer to the edge. She could swear her clit sizzled in tune with the vibrator inside her. She moaned as stabs of heat, like volcanic needlepoints started in her loins, filled her pussy. She arched her back and then ... his blasted voice boomed in her mind.

"*... that won't happen until you beg me to fuck you.*"

"No!" she wailed softly as the climax receded into an insistent throb of her clit and pussy that clenched and released around the dildo. She twisted her torso and looked back to find Kane's head buried between Savannah's thighs. The way she thrashed and jerked in his hands was a sign of his expertise. Cora's high-pitched cry as she climaxed, yanked Rose's attention back to the couple next to her

Fuck, all of them had the ability to turn a woman into a blob of quivering need. I need to come! Why can't I come?

But Rose knew why as it was proven twice more in the remaining time where she teetered on the edge, desperate to climax and then ... she flatlined. It didn't matter that she closed her mind to her surroundings or Kane in the background, she couldn't tip over. She'd heard of this phenomenon before, but she'd always believed the subs exaggerated. That it was impossible not to come when you're so over-stimulated, you feel ready to combust.

Now that she was on the receiving end, she wished she'd paid more attention to find out how they'd managed to cope with it. Because no matter how badly she wanted to come, she had to stay away from Kane—at least until she told him about Tucker.

"Enjoying the hedgehog, sub RL?" Master Leo mocked her back to the present. "I'm impressed that you managed not to come but I see you thoroughly enjoyed playing with him. You're lying in a pool of your own juices." He smacked his lips. "And I get to benefit." He chuckled as her pussy wouldn't release its grip from around the toy when he pulled it out. "On the table, please and, sub CD, your turn with this red hedgehog."

He ignored Cora's protests, who struggled to stand after his ruthless ministrations and quickly pushed it inside her pussy. His grin was wicked. "Now you may come as often as you'd like, my pet."

He approached Rose who lay trembling on the iron table. "Hm ... this is going to be so much fun." He ran his hand over her stomach, her thighs and finally toggled her clit. Her hips surged upward. A sharp slap on her clit elicited a cry from her. "You don't move, sub, no matter what I do, is that understood?"

"Yes, Master Leo," Rose whispered. She closed her eyes, trying to mentally prepare herself for his onslaught. Nothing could have prepared her for his hot lips closing around her clit, or the strong sucking motion that catapulted her right back to the edge of the abyss. She hooked her ankles around the legs of the table and anchored her hips flat on the table, knowing there was no way she'd be able to keep still otherwise.

She had no intention of keeping back her climax. If Master Leo managed to push her over, she was fucking falling, even if it meant she came crashing back to punishment.

The tight coil in her loins demanded it.

Her clit throbbing like a pressure valve insisted upon it.

And her pussy begged for it.

"Such a juicy cunt you have, my pet," Master Leo murmured against her labia and then he plunged his tongue inside, licking, sucking and nibbling like a starved nomad. His fingers pinched and rolled her clit with merciless evocation.

Yes! Oh, fucking glorious, yes!

No! No-no-no-no!

The jubilant cry as she felt herself pitching over the edge turned into a wail of denial as once again, *his* invisible hand yanked her back, to leave her suffering with the pressure inside her reaching a point of explosive combustion.

"Amazing control, sub RL. I'm impressed," Master Leo said as he finally lifted his head from between her thighs. He caressed her quivering stomach, "Easy, sub. Try and relax, breathe in slowly," he coached her as he noticed her shuddering frame and struggle to draw a proper breath. "Do you need to come, Rose?"

"Yes, god yes!" she cried passionately.

He slicked his tongue over her clit. "Then come, my pet."

But no matter that he buried his fingers deep inside her and toggled the nub of nerves in the front wall of her vagina, sucked and bit her clit, she just couldn't.

"Stop wasting your time, Master Leo. Sub RL can't come. I made sure of that."

Kane's dry voice penetrated Rose's frayed mind. She whimpered as Master Leo stopped his effort and straightened. Her eyes opened and clashed with a gaze that pierced all the way into her soul. His expression remained impassive but she noticed the flash of Dominant satisfaction in his eyes.

"You're a monster," she croaked.

Kane shrugged and started strolling toward the beach buggy. His response floated over his shoulder back to her. "That's a matter of opinion, my pet. One that many subs and trainees would deny. Hurry up, sub RL, you're keeping everyone from lunch."

Master Leo assisted Rose from the table. He caught her in his arms when her legs gave in. She clung to him, pressing her face into his chest as one shudder after the other racked her body.

"Jesus, Rose, what the hell?" He forced up her chin and stared into her eyes that were swirling with the desperate demands from her body. "Just what the hell did he mean by that? That he made sure you can't climax?"

"H-he said that I won't be able to c-come until he's the one f-fucking me and only after I b-begged him." She moaned. "And he's right. It's been four days and no matter how hard I try ... I ... I c-can't come!"

"Hmm, I guess you didn't take Master Fox's and my warning to heart to fix the misunderstanding. I'm afraid there's nothing any of us can do to help you, sub RL. You're solely at the mercy of Master Bear." He tapped her on the nose. "Your fate is in your own hands, my pet. Own up to it or continue to suffer." He lifted her in his arms. "Come, I'll carry you to the buggy."

Rose didn't bother to protest. She was only too happy to lean against his strong body and wallow in his hard arms wrapped protectively around her.

Chapter Eleven

"Master Bear, you need to come with me. Something is wrong with sub RL." Cora stood wringing her hands next to the large wingback chair where Kane sat, enjoying a bourbon with his cousins after dinner.

Kane looked at her. He hadn't seen Rose at dinner but hadn't thought much about it, seeing as he'd arrived late and many of the trainees had already left the Great Dining Hall.

"Explain," he said and took a sip of the decadent elixir. He rolled it on his tongue, appreciating the rich smooth texture before he swallowed.

"She took a shower when we returned from the beach and went to lie on her bed. She hasn't moved since, except ..."

"Yes, sub CD, except what?" Kane prodded impatiently.

"Her entire body is shuddering, so badly the bed even shakes. I tried to talk to her but she can't get out a word the way her teeth are clattering. She looks feverish and her skin is clammy but she's not hot to the touch." Cora looked at him beseechingly. "Please, Master Bear, I don't know what to do to help her."

Seeing as Rose was currently a trainee in his dungeon, she was under his care and the reason why Cora sought him out.

"Thank you, sub CD. I'll be there momentarily." He finished his drink in one gulp as she nodded and rushed back to their room.

"Do you think it's sunstroke?" Stone's concern was evident in the frown calligraphed on his forehead.

Ace chuckled. "I hardly think so. If I had to hazard a guess, our little Rosebud's shudders are the result of lust eating at her loins."

"You don't say?" Shane sat forward and glanced at Kane who didn't seem in any hurry to rush to her side.

"It seems our esteemed Master Bear has a hold over the poor woman that surpasses Domination." Ace stretched out his legs.

"For fuck's sake, spit it out, Ace. Do you always have to be so mysterious about everything?" Parker exploded.

"Kane told her four days ago that she won't be able to climax, no matter that a Master gives her permission, nor if she tried to masturbate. Turns out, he was right, she can't. And you know the training the past four days involved spiking their arousal over and over. Other than the rest who have had numerous climaxes, poor Rose has had no relief. After this morning and the games on the beach afterward, I believe she's about to combust out of her skin."

"That's rather cruel, don't you think, Kane?" Hawk studied him as he sipped his drink.

"Especially as you usually make subs pass out from climaxing rather than withholding it."

"The situation called for drastic measures." Kane got up and stretched lazily. "I believe I'm about to pluck the fruit of my patience over the past four days."

"This is an interesting development," Stone mused. "Care to enlighten us how you knew you had such power over Rose?"

Kane shrugged, his expression enigmatic. "Instinct. There's something about the way her inner submissive responds to me that I can't resist." His eyes sparked angrily. "She had it coming by lying. Every time she looks at me, I can see the need in her eyes to feel my touch and yet she pushed me away. Tonight, I'm going to find out why."

He winked at Danton, who was more than a colleague, he was a good friend. "You might have to take over my classes for the next day or two, Danton. I have every intention of expunging every drop of regret from Ms. Rose Lovett's tight little cunt."

"And they call me the beast."

Kane ignored Stone's dry remark as he strolled through the roomy Reception Hall and upstairs to Rose's room that she shared with two other trainees. He felt no regret for making her suffer. He abhorred lies and secrets. He had learned his lesson in this respect the hard way when he had kept a big secret from the woman he loved.

The cousins were only known to the public as the Rothmans, purely to protect them and their family from invasive fans, paparazzi, and stalkers. He still regretted not divulging his true identity to Narine the moment he'd realized her love for him was true, but history had taught him to be careful and he had waited. If he hadn't, she might have understood why he'd decided to leave acting and not continued to put pressure on him to change his mind.

Maybe then they wouldn't have fought for days leading up to that fateful night. Because of the tension between them, he'd canceled the trip he'd planned to ask her to marry him. Instead, they had stayed at home, fighting over her not accepting his decision. It ended in earthshattering make up sex, but he had been living with the guilt ever since that she still hadn't known who he really was when she'd died.

If only he hadn't kept secrets from her, they wouldn't have been home and her death could've been prevented.

Kane shook off the morbid thoughts as he entered the room. Rose's roommates huddled next to her on the bed, doing their best to soothe her. He could see her body shuddering as he approached.

"Master Bear! Thank god," Cora cried as she noticed him. "She's getting worse. Please, you have to do something."

"I'll take care of her, Cora. Move out of the way, please."

Kane sat down on the bed as they vacated their spots. He brushed Rose's hair back from her brow, shocked at how hot she felt to the touch. Her eyes flickered open and flared wide as she recognized him through the haze he could see in her eyes. She caught his hand and clamped it between her breasts.

"P-please ... Kane, I b-beg you. I can't ... anymore."

Kane ignored the gasp of the trainees at her use of his name. He picked her up and straightened, his eyes glued on her feverish face.

"Yes, sweet Rose, I believe it's time." He smiled at the relief that made her tense body relax into his. He turned toward the door. "Thanks for alerting me, Cora. You can relax, she'll be fine."

"But she has a fever!"

"Sub CD, I appreciate you caring for her, but she is my responsibility and I'll ensure she's taken care of. Now, please get out of my way."

Cora belatedly realized she barred the almighty Master Bear's exit and jumped to the side. "I'm sorry, I'm just concerned. She seemed fine the entire day ... and suddenly ... this!" She gestured at Rose's trembling form.

"Sub RL will be fine in a day or two." He strode through the door, aware of the women's shocked expressions as he took the stairs to his private apartment.

He couldn't hide his own concern. Part of her ailment was no doubt driven by suppressed lust, but Rose had a fever, an extremely high one if the scorching heat infiltrating his skin was anything to go by. Stone's assumption that she perhaps had sunstroke might just be accurate.

He racked his mind for the symptoms of heatstroke. It had been hot but not scorching and they had made sure the trainees were well hydrated, even on the beach. For that reason, he doubted that her body's temperature control system had failed. He laid her on the bed.

"Relax, Rose, I'll be right back," he crooned in a gruff voice as she clung to his shirt. He rushed to the bathroom for the first aid kit and the thermoscan thermometer. If her core body temperature was greater than 104 degrees Fahrenheit, she might need to go to the hospital. She didn't show any signs of nausea, disorientation or any of the other symptoms, which put him a little at ease.

"Easy, little dove." His deep voice settled her restlessness as he quickly checked her temperature. He sagged with relief at the flashing number of 102 degrees. It was high but not dangerously so. He stroked her hair and smiled as her eyes flickered open. "You have a fever, Rose. I'm going to run a cool bath and give you some ibuprofen. You should be fine in a couple of hours."

"I don't need a cold bath or freaking p-pills," she snapped through clenched teeth. "You know what I need."

"Not before I'm satisfied that your body temperature is back to normal." Kane pried loose her fingers clutching at his shirt again and went to fill the tub with cold water. "Relax, little dove. I'll take care of you," he whispered in her ear upon his return as he gently undressed her, picked her up, and carried her to the bathroom.

"Deep breath, Rose, the coldness is going to be a shock to your body."

"Shit," she hissed as he lowered her into the tub. "It's too c-cold. Let me out," she demanded, attempting to get up.

"Not yet. Give it a moment." Kane used his hands to run the cold water over her arms, her chest, and shoulders. He used a wet cloth and tenderly wiped her face. "There, see. Already better."

Kane thwarted her every attempt to get out of the tub until he was satisfied that the feverish glow was dissipating from her skin. He lifted her out and with brisk rubbing movements, dried her shivering body before he carried her back to bed and placed her under the duvet.

"Stay here," he ordered as he walked out of the room to fix something for her to eat before she took the meds. She'd skipped dinner and needed sustenance to build up her strength.

It might not be sunstroke but the fever definitely stemmed from more than the sexual tension that had been building to a fever pitch over the past four days. He scoffed at the thought that maybe he shouldn't have instructed the assistant training Doms to keep feeding her arousal as much as they did.

"She had it coming. Maybe now, she'll be honest about her true desires."

As he reflected over the past couple of days, he couldn't shake the feeling that there was more to Rose Lovett than met the eye. He recalled the phone call she had on the beach. His brows straight-lined.

"She said her son is in boarding school in Massachusetts, which meant he should've been having breakfast at that time." He knew how strict the rules were in dormitories. His gaze sharpened as he dished up the heated lasagna. "She lied about that too."

The suspicion that she might be the betrayer in their midst returned with a vengeance. There were just too many questions around her stories, too many inconsistencies. He had learned over the years not to trust easily, that it was safer to maintain an emotional distance. It shook him that he stood on the edge of losing that ability to keep Rose at bay, irrespective of not completely trusting her.

"What the fuck is it about her that draws me like a magnet?"

He picked up the tray and slowly returned to the room. His mind had been made up ... months ago upon her arrival at Castle Sin. He was going to fuck her tonight, pound her cunt until she couldn't breathe and passed out. Then continue until she had no defenses left and bared it all to him. He was going to ruin her for all other men. After him, she'd always crave his possession, his domination ... which he may or may not offer once he got to the truth.

"Yes, little dove, you can't hide from me. Not your lies and sure as hell not your lust."

Rose wrestled with the frustration at war against the fever she could still feel simmering on her skin. Since the explosion, she was prone to such a reaction after a long day in the sun and heat. It had never affected her this bad before.

"Because it's exacerbated by the fever of lust and suppressed passion, Rose. And it's your own fucking fault."

She snorted at the hoarse croak floating in the atmosphere. She struggled upright and looked around. Her eyes flared at the subtle beauty of the decorations in the roomy bedroom. The bedding was a soft dove gray, as were the brocade curtains with swirls of dark red. The softly draped material was caught to the sides to leave the wall-to-ceiling windows open, allowing the bright bluish beams of the moon to slither through. The same dark red as the curtains was contrasted in scattered cushions on the charcoal wingback chairs facing the window. The furniture consisted of heavy, dark wood pieces—a perfect match for the Master of the room.

"Oh, my god," she gasped and scrambled from the bed to stumble on wobbly legs to the writing desk against the far wall, her eyes glued on the framed photograph. Tears burned behind her eyelids as she traced Kane's loving face, his hair windblown on the backdrop of the beach as he stared with a tender smile at the auburn haired woman in his arms. The love in his gaze tore at her heart as did regret and loss as she stared at the face of Narine Bosch, the woman she used to be. The woman who had died within six hours after this picture had been taken. A woman who was no more, would never be again, no matter how she'd long to be over the years. She'd never been able to regain the same energy, liveliness, and passion for life like she'd had in those days. Today, she was an empty shell, not even a speck of the woman she used to be left. Not on the outside and sure as hell not on the inside.

Rose had nothing to give. Not love or passion to any man. God knew she'd tried over the years, desperate to move on, to forget and in some way began to live again. She'd failed. Every single time she'd become involved with a man. Guilt always interfered. She knew it was ridiculous, but it had always felt that she was cheating on Kane until she finally gave up trying. The love for him refused to be locked into a corner of her mind. It surged to the surface every time to mock her efforts to forget him. She finally submitted to the force of his memory, the unconditional love he'd offered her, and poured all the emotions and feelings she had into loving and caring for their son. She'd accepted that she'd grow old alone.

"God, Tucker, I can't do this. I can't tear open all those memories." She swallowed back the sob threatening to choke her. "I lost him once. I did it because I believed it was for the best. I did it all knowing how empty my life would be, but I can't … I just can't stand watching the hate in his eyes when I tell him—"

"What are you doing out of bed?"

"I ... ehm, I needed to stretch my legs." She brushed the tears from her cheeks that she hadn't realized had fallen as she stared at the picture.

"Come, you need to eat."

Rose did her best to compose herself and appear normal as she trotted back to bed and slipped under the covers. She pulled the duvet over her breasts and clamped it under her arms. Being naked at this moment in his presence left her feeling completely bare and vulnerable in ways she couldn't comprehend.

Kane settled the tray over her legs. The aroma of the lasagna and hot ciabatta bread filled her nostrils. Her growling stomach attested to the fact that she'd not had anything substantial to eat since breakfast.

"I guess I'm hungrier than I realized," she lamented to excuse the rumbling she was sure he could hear.

"Hm." He studied her intently. "Come to think of it, I can't recall that I saw you eating at lunch on the beach." A dark look encroached on his expression. "Don't tell me you're starving yourself to lose weight, Rose."

Rose could feel the heated blush bloom over her cheeks. She peeked at him as she bit into the buttered piece of bread. "No, I like food too much, but at the time ..." She felt the telltale tightening of her loins clenching as the coil once again began to build inside her.

"Yes?"

"The hunger I had then had nothing to do with food." She ate in silence for a couple of minutes until the thought of taking another bite became smothered under the insistent throbbing in her lower body. Heat surged through her veins as the lust that needed to be satisfied took over. She felt hot all over and knew he noticed the rosy glow covering her skin when he frowned and laid his palm against her forehead.

"You're burning up again. Finish up, Rose, so you can take the ibuprofen."

She grabbed the tray, got off the bed and with long strides stomped to the writing desk and sat it down with a loud clatter. Her eyes seared into his over the short distance. She heaved in a deep breath and slowly walked back to the bed, unaware of how sensually seductive the gentle sway of her hips was to the gaze of the man riveted on her approaching form.

"Ibuprofen isn't going to help for the fever I have, Master Bear, and you know it. You made sure I'd suffer. You wanted me to and I can understand why but you punished me for the wrong reasons."

"Is that so?"

Kane leaned against the headboard and crossed his long legs, drawing Rose's feverish gaze to the rippling muscles in his thighs, his broad chest and his overall animal grace that made her mouth go dry.

"Yes, the reason I chose the punishment wasn't because I can't stand your touch."

"You could've fooled me, my pet." His eyes darkened as Rose kneeled on the bed at his feet and started to crawl closer over his legs.

She stopped at the warning flash in his eyes, reminding her about his no touch rule, but she refused to be intimidated and kept her eyes locked on his. There was no anger in his as he watched her and she realized she still wore the color contact lenses.

"I couldn't allow you to fuck me, Master Bear, not again. I was on the verge of combusting and you … the first time you thrust inside me, it shattered me. I never came as hard as I did when you pounded into my ass. I'd already failed twice, I couldn't a third time, and I knew I'd climax the moment your cock found its way inside my ass again."

Kane didn't say anything, just continued to regard her with an impenetrable stare. Rose tried to withstand the silence but the coil inside her kept demanding action. She lowered her torso until the tips of her nipples teased the skin on his knees.

"May I touch you, Master Bear."

"No."

She struggled to keep her composure under the darkly uttered syllable.

"Just no?"

"One thing you have to understand from the start, my pet, is that I don't like to be touched. I do the touching, always, and unless I lay your hand on my body giving you permission to do so, doing it will result in dire consequences for you."

She straightened her arms. "So, if I touched you now, instead of fucking me like I so desperately need you to, you'll punish me?"

"No, Rose, I'll send you back to your room."

"That would be worse than whipping my ass," she mumbled.

"I don't play games and I never appreciate a sub attempting to top me from the bottom. I don't fall for seductive lures, no matter how enticing, so don't bother to try. This is the deal, Rose. In a sexual relationship, I *will* be your Master, always. I'll never allow you to seduce me or to manipulate what I do to you in any way. If that's a problem, you better leave because if you decide to stay, know this; you'll submit to my sexual demands when, where, and how I decide. You'll follow my orders blindly. Break any of my rules and you'll be severely punished."

Rose sat back on her haunches. She blinked in confusion. Did she hear him correctly?

"Are you … is this your way of asking me to be your submissive?"

"I can't recall asking anything. I told you how it is. It's your decision whether or not it's what you need."

"And if I don't?"

"Then you go back to your room immediately."

"You're not serious. You've got to be kidding me." She stared at him flabbergasted. Here she was, baring her soul to him by admitting the sexual effect he had over her and he had no compunction to send her away.

"I think you came to know me well enough over the past couple of months to realize I'm not the joking kind of man."

Rose's loins reminded her of her dire need by clenching so tight it felt like a vice was clamped around it and tightened more and more with each passing second. She felt the tremor start deep in her core to present itself in shudders trembling through her frame. She wrapped her arms around her waist in an attempt to stay the flush of pheromones that heated her veins and shot her libido to a feverish pitch in all but two seconds. There was no need to think about it. She needed him, craved his possession and yearned for his Domination. That was the bottom line and she stood defenseless in the power of the magnetic pull he presented.

"No, you're not, but I never thought you to be cruel either."

Don't do it, Rose. Stay strong. You know it's for the best to stay away from him. For your own survival. It won't last. Once the truth comes out, he's going to cast you aside, hate you even.

Rose couldn't deny the thoughts that ran through her mind, but they paled in comparison to the lust that raged through her body. It took over and scrambled any attempt to think clearly.

I want him too much. I need him. God, the years without him have been torture. He's here within my grasp to give me what I need. What only he has ever been able to give me. Complete sexual pleasure while controlling every aspect of my need.

"Cruelty has nothing to do with it, little dove. I've had my share of sexual encounters over the years to know what I want, what drives my need, and gives me the utmost satisfaction. I'll never abuse the honor of the Domination a submissive allows me to have, but I'll always be the decision maker because I know exactly what a sub needs before she does." He straightened and regarded her with a sharp glimmer in his eyes. The expression on his face indicative of having made up his mind. "I'm not getting any younger. I've been searching for someone with enough inner strength to be the partner I need in a Dom/sub relationship. I believe I found that in you. The question is, Rose, do you know what it is you've been searching for?"

"Yes, Master Bear, I do."

"And?"

"It's you. I want you."

Kane remained still. Rose squirmed under his unblinking stare.

"As what? What exactly do you want from me?"

"All of you. Your Domination, your attention … whatever you're willing to give." Rose declared defeat and ignored the warning voices in her head shouting at her to leave. To get out of the room, fuck, to leave the island, but she refused to budge. She loved Kane, always had and that would never change. She took a leap of faith and although it was ludicrous at best, she hoped that once he knew the entire story, he might come to forgive her one day.

"I'll give you all that, but ..." He hesitated briefly. "I've known love once. The kind of deep, gut wrenching love that only comes across our paths once in a lifetime. Don't expect me to fall in love with you, Rose. I'd offer you my commitment in a Dom/sub relationship and if it develops into something stronger over time, maybe more but love will never be part of it."

Rose had to swallow a couple of times before she could respond.

"I understand and accept that." She ran her hands over her thighs. "I have to ask ... this is rather sudden, Master Bear. I've been here for five months but we never really had any interactions till recently. Why me and why now?"

"Far be it for me to remind you that you're the one constantly running in the opposite direction when I enter a room, Rose. If anything, I should be the one asking you that question, but as far as I'm concerned, it's simple. I'll be fifty-two in a couple of months and I decided I want someone in my life. I want a woman to share special moments with, to laugh and build new experiences and memories with. Living in the past ... well, it doesn't make for a warm, soft body to wake up to in the morning." His eyes took a gander over her curvy body. "Why you? You intrigue me. I am drawn to you and I'd be fucked if I understand why but I'm old and wise enough not to fight the kind of chemistry between us. I believe you'll be a match for me, Rose. In more ways than one."

"Then I accept, Master Bear, but please, can we stop talking now? The fire inside me is burning me alive and raging higher as we speak, tightening my core to such pressure it's painful. I can't stand it anymore. Please, I beg you. Fuck me."

Chapter Twelve

Rose felt like a virgin when Kane leaned forward and dragged her toward him by the shoulders. She went willingly, gasping for breath as she landed on his hard and warm chest. Her hands curled into fists as she forced them not to flatten and caress the solid wall of muscle buffering her soft curves.

"Good girl," he praised, catching her by surprise as with a mighty twist, he toppled her onto her back and settled between her thighs. He dragged her hands over her head and before she realized his intent, she heard the sharp click of cuffs locking around them before she felt the teasing of fur-lined steel handcuffs.

"There's a question in your eyes, Rose," he said as he traced the rounded curve of her jaw.

"It's said that you never invite any of the trainees or subs to your private apartment and yet ... the cuffs, attached to the bed frame ..."

"Ah, yes and they're correct. I never had another woman in this bed but I knew you were going to end up here, so I made a few, shall we say ... adjustments."

"There's ... oh," she gasped as he lowered his head and placed hard, open-mouth kisses along the side of her throat, nibbling and sucking as he went. "There's more," she managed to say on a puff of breath.

"A couple, yes, and trust me, little dove, before you leave this room, you're going to be introduced to all of them."

Rose couldn't keep the thought of his hard cock, currently pressed against her stomach, penetrating the soft folds of her pussy from entering her mind. It rapidly turned into a chant that overwhelmed her senses. The carnal thought broke through to rid her of the disjunction of suppressed lust that had plagued her mind and body for days.

"Oh, sweet lord." The husky moan reverberated deep within her throat, racing up but choked off as she clenched her jaw. Her neck arched as she gave herself over to the flash of heat that surged through her stomach as Kane probed a thick finger deep inside her pussy.

"Fuck, Rose, you're like a furnace and wet, so gorgeously soaked." His eyes darkened as he watched her struggle to find something to cling to, her fingers searched the air aimlessly before they finally caught onto the wooden slats of the headboard. The chain attached to the cuffs rattled. "You really are on edge, aren't you, baby?"

"Yes," she cried, surrendering in a staccato of moans as he lazily swirled his fingers inside her, teasingly tapping the nub of nerves on the inside of her vaginal wall.

"Please, no more," she gasped as he twisted his hand to brush his thumb over her clit in tandem with his teasing fingers on the inside. The combined stimulation triggered a series of jagged tremors that tore through and shook loose the bonds of her starved sexuality.

She opened her eyes. "No foreplay, I beg you, Master Bear. I can't stand it anymore. These last couple of days ... it's been torture and I don't know how you did it but I have to ... I *need* to come. Please, just fuck me. I want to feel your hard cock pound my pussy. Now, fuck me, now."

Her passionate plea didn't have the immediate effect she'd hoped for. Her frustration spiked at the satisfied male grin on his lips as he continued to stroke the satiny walls of her vagina.

"Patience, little dove. You know the saying; all good things come to those who wait."

"Fuck good things! I want an orgasm. That's it. Full stop! Don't make me ... ahhh! Gaawd!" she screamed as he suddenly thrust hilt deep into her, stretching her pussy to the extreme to accommodate his wide girth. He moved sensually, rolling his hips, grinding his crotch against her clit. Rose gasped as she felt the hard pressure teasing her cervix. She'd forgotten how big he was.

"I can't hold ... ohshitohshit ... back," she wailed as she felt the telltale pricks of heat stab at her loins in preparation of a release that had been building for days.

"You don't have to, my pet."

Kane's voice came to her as if from afar as she thrashed and jagged under him, desperate for him to move. To give her that small nudge she needed to fall over and drown in the depths of bliss. Then he did and thrust his thick veiny shaft in and out, to the hilt with every plunge, stroking and flexing against the silky warm folds that gave way against his hard but welcome trespass.

"Oh, yes ... lord, it feels good," she croaked and lifted her legs to wrap them around his waist.

"No."

The harsh order penetrated and with a moan of regret, she lowered them. She bent her knees and dug her heels into the bed, pushing her hips up, forcing him deeper as he pounded into her. The desperation to tumble into the abyss was etched on her face, in the grimace of her open lips and a glazed look in her eyes. Her desperate jerks and slapping her hips into his as he thrust forward didn't help. She couldn't tip over.

Kane stared at her in amazed wonder, realizing how strong the hold was that his domination had over her inner submissive. His smile was one of utter male satisfaction.

"Let go, my pet. Come for me, Rose."

It was all she needed to erupt in a gush of liquid—her hoarse cry carried through the room like a drowning sailor crying for help as she writhed and jerked against Kane's still thrusting shaft. His crotch was soaked in her essence and awakened the demon in him to wring every ounce of passion she had to give from her. She arched her neck as the spasms of the orgasm pierced through her body.

"Beautiful, little dove, but you have more to give." Kane closed a strong hand around her waist, he pushed her one leg up and clamped it against the bed next to her body. She whimpered as he guided her hips in a teetering dance, then he reached for her swollen clit.

"I'm going to strum this little piece of hungry flesh to play another verse for me. Give me an encore, little dove. Come for me again, Rose."

"Shit! It's too much! Sensitive ... sweet holy *fuck*," she wailed as she jerked against his firm touch, torturing and exciting her simultaneously.

"Please," she begged him for release but this time, he refused to be rushed. He enjoyed the combination of pleasure and desperation that played a canvas of harmonious lust across her face too much. He eased the thrusts of his hips into a slow, deep rhythm.

"Damn you, Master Bear. I need to come." Rose blinked up at him as he chuckled. "You're a demon," she hissed, canting against his hand and hips in a desperate attempt to clinch the rush toward another climax. He countered with a well-aimed swipe of his thumb over her clitoris. Her hips jerked. "Please, Kane, make me come ... aww!"

Crack! Crack! Crack! Crack!

"Fucking hell," she screamed as the hard and punishing slaps seared a burning streak against her nipples.

"Did I give you permission to use my name?"

"I'm sorry," she barely managed the apology as the pain morphed into a slither of hot lava from her nipples to her loins, triggering the release to rush to culmination.

Kane powered into her. His hips snapped hard and sharp in a rhythm to the like of pistons of a runaway train. Rose felt like she became the conduit of heat, her skin glowed from the blood rushing through her veins and her pussy ... *fucking praying mantis!* ... became an incinerator from the heat his driving cock generated.

"Yes, Rose, that's the look I was after. The one shouting at me to push you to the limit, to fuck you harder ... like this," he growled through hard lips as he caught both legs and pushed them back, tilting her hips up to angle them in position so he could drill into her.

"Too much," she stammered as she struggled against the feeling like the hooves of racing horses, galloping faster and faster pushing her closer to the edge. She gasped, struggling to breathe as her body solidified. Every muscle locked as her pussy became the maestro of every organ in her body. Clenching, releasing and repeating, spasming so hard that she flailed in her mind.

"Gaawwwd," she cried in desperation as darkness encroached on her from afar until it slithered into a narrow needle the moment the climax ripped through her. It dragged her under and she slipped into a black void of unconsciousness, her body still jerking as Kane continued to pound her.

"Perfect, little rosebud," he grated as his cock swelled tauter against her silky walls. She twitched against him as she came to moments later. Her eyes snapped open and a raw cry echoed in his ears as he slammed into her, once again pushing her eager ovaries into overload.

"You have t-to stop. I can't ... it's too much," she begged on a whimper.

"Au contraire, my errant little dove. You can and you will. Do you know why?"

"Master Bear ... please, I need to ... I can't breathe," she begged fearfully, realizing this Kane wasn't the man she used to know. He had been powerful then, sexually demanding but this man ... *oh, fucking hell* ... he was so much more. He exuded power, confidence, and in his eyes flashed the promise of such unexpurgated lustful intent that she couldn't fathom surviving his onslaught.

His hand locked around her throat. He leaned closer, his fingers tightened as he clipped out against her cheek. "Do you know why, Rose?"

"N-no, Master Bear," she quailed, struggling to breathe from the tight grip he had on her.

"Because your body now belongs to me. You just gave it to me. It's mine to do with as I please, to mold and direct as I want. Yes, little dove, it'll follow every command I give even during the times you're passed out, it'll still respond to my touch, my voice."

Her eyes widened. She shook her head. Such power didn't exist. It couldn't. She wouldn't survive it. No woman could.

"No, it c-can't," she coughed as his fingers tightened again, forcing her to remain still.

"It already is, Rose, and nothing you say or do is going to change that. Shall I prove it to you?"

She didn't dare shake her head, in case he took it as an invitation to put more pressure around her throat. She could barely breathe as it was. He pulled out his throbbing cock, eliciting a forlorn whimper from her lips. His smile was pleased as much as it was wicked.

He lifted his body from hers, leaving her feeling bereft and cold without his weight and heat infiltrating her skin. The only contact he maintained, was the tight grip around her throat.

"Come, Rose. Come for your Master, little dove."

Rose stared at him, the thought that he had finally lost his marbles still forming in her mind, when she felt the hot prickles deep in her core. Her hips drifted upward, her clit sizzled, like it had just received a bolt of electricity.

"Ohlord-ohlord-ohlord," she chanted. Her back arched high as heat rippled over her, and like the slow early morning waves rolling to shore, she climaxed. Her body shuddered, flailed, and jagged in the claws of an orgasm that gained strength the longer it continued. "Stop ... help me, Master Bear ... make it stop," she begged as it felt like she was about to be ripped apart.

He eased the hold around her throat. His breath burned her lips as he leaned closer. "This is only the beginning, Rose. I need to know now ... can you handle it? Are you woman enough to give me all that I desire, submissive enough to drown in the need to please me in every demand I give?"

Rose shivered when he whispered in her ear, his voice deep and raw. Every nerve in her body burned hot and smoldered, fomented in molten plasma, heating the shell of her core. She struggled to breathe as her loins continued to clench and release, sending ripples of spasmodic pleasure-pain to keep her pussy in contraction.

Good lord, giving birth hadn't even been this intense!

The combination of pleasure, pain and discomfort completely fried her mind but her body continued the course its Master had set it upon. It felt unreal, like she floated in outer space, looking down onto them. She was lifted onto a maelstrom of quivering lustfulness at his words, hungry for every promised act. Her brain kicked against it, her common sense told her it was dangerous to give anyone such power over her but her body—the biggest traitor of all, demanded it.

She was too weak to resist.

"Yes, Master Bear. Ugh … please," she begged as her eyes lifted to meet his. "I am yours to do as you please."

He smiled briefly and breached the inch that separated their lips. "That's enough for now, my little rosebud."

Rose had no time to exult in the rippling climax receding like the backlash of the ocean, to leave behind pulsing and trembling muscles in her pussy as his lips claimed hers.

The kiss she had been craving for so long finally happened. It was as devastatingly familiar as it was new. His mouth was anything but gentle. It represented the man he was, hard and demanding. His tongue plunged into her mouth and with the first sweep, he turned her inside out with a kiss packed with lustful promise and unchecked hunger. The saturated color of her sensual groan spilled out between their meshed lips. She teetered then fell as he pushed his tongue deeper inside the recess of her mouth.

I love him so much. How am I going to survive if he chases me away once I tell him the truth? God, how am I going to carry on living *if I have to lose him a second time?*

She choked as his hand tightened threateningly, cutting off her ability to breathe. His head lifted and she gasped for breath. The chains rattled as she yanked in desperation on the cuffs.

She quieted as she met the furious warning in his eyes.

"Don't ever, and I mean *ever*, allow your mind to drift when you're with me. Do you understand me, Rose?"

For the first time in her life, she feared him. His cunning perception of the moment her mind had drifted scared the living daylights out of her. He looked like a demon, with red warning streaks flashing in the depths of his darkening brown eyes, his lips slashed into a straight line. His fingers tightened.

"I'm sorry," she squealed fearfully. "It won't happen again, Master Bear. Please, I promise."

His fingers relaxed; he lowered his body to settle on top of hers. Her breath wheezed from her lips as his heat seared all the way into her soul. Just like that, the fear dissolved and turned into flaming desire.

Good lord, help me. After fucking me once, suddenly I turn into a nymphomaniac!

"Oh ... my," she lilted as his lips traced the imprints his hold had left around her throat, kissing and soothing away the final of her fears. His gentleness assured her that no matter what he intended for her, he'd always take care of her afterward.

"Now, my pet, it's my turn." He tapped her on the lips as he slowly pushed his cock back inside her still pulsing pussy. She moaned at the excruciating slow entry as he savored every inch before he settled hilt deep. "And your hungry and eager little cunt doesn't get to come this time. Is that understood?"

"You're not—"

His sharp look from between narrowed eyelids cut off her protest.

"I'll try, Master Bear," she conceded.

"You'll do better than try, Rose. Don't think I've forgotten that you're still due punishment from my electric whip." His smile turned evil. "Now, there's your incentive. Come, and we'll add an additional fifteen minutes to your thirty-minute punishment, which we'll attend to in The Dungeon of Sin right after I'm done with you."

"I won't come," she said hurriedly.

The Cheshire grin on his lips didn't bode well for Rose. Somehow, Kane took her response as a challenge. Her clit cringed as she recalled the tiny steel tips at the end of the leather strips of the torture tool.

I won't fucking come. You just wait and see, buster.

Kane grunted as he drew back his cock slowly, awakening every nerve ending on its path. Their eyes met.

"Ready, Rose? This is for me and my pleasure. It's going to be hard, raw and so fucking rough the bed is going to dance around on the floor. Once I'm done, you won't know where I end and you begin. This, my pet, is going to be a good, hard fuck."

Before she could brace herself, he hooked his arms under her knees, lifted her hips and slammed back into her. He set a mind-blowing rhythm as he powered into her.

The boundaries that once circumscribed the limits of Kane's intimacy with the other subs were suddenly overrun by an emancipated lust. He exalted in every second of his frenzied possession, of every cry and scream he wrung from her in his race to find the sexual release and satisfaction he'd been searching and yearning for, for over sixteen years.

The familiar pricks of heat at the back of his loins, followed by a rush of euphoria washing over him urged him to speed up. His balls tightened and he was wracked by tempestuous spasms of ejaculate that left him ragged and twitching against her as he continued to thrust until he spilled every drop. He released her legs and leaned on his elbows over her, staring at her with a heated gaze that seared into her flushed face. Her haggard breathing and pleading eyes didn't penetrate his mind. He was too engulfed in the best sexual and satiated feeling he'd ever had to notice her need to climax.

Nothing had ever come close to the exhilarating rush that was created by the unleashing of massive amounts of coherent chemistry. Dumped unexpectedly into the convergence of an emotional and physical torrent that pullulated through him. He felt the ripple of sensation as her pussy tightened around his length. He became enveloped by the liquid-warm squeeze of flesh upon flesh in an erotic and cherished embrace that swept him up onto the face of a soporific wave. He reveled in the feeling, clasping it within his mind. It was the kind of aphrodisiac he could become addicted to and never wanted to come down from.

Kane Sinclair had finally met his match.

Chapter Thirteen

"Meet Zikri Malik, co-founder of the Hollywood production company, Blue Emerald Pictures. The one behind The Fox of Wall Street, MTV award movie, in 2013." Parker pointed to the picture of the Malaysian man on the large overhead screen. The seven cousins and Danton were meeting in the Be Secure boardroom in the underground, four-story bunker behind the castle.

"Hold on, wasn't he charged with suspicion of money-laundering of Malaysian state investment funds recently?" Kane sipped on the hot latte Alexa had just handed to him. "Nothing to eat this morning, little one?" he asked her as she headed for the door and his stomach rumbled, reminding him that he needed sustenance.

"It's just after eight-thirty in the morning. Didn't you have breakfast?" she asked cheekily.

"I daresay Master Bear had other things than food on his mind when he woke up this morning," Shane teased.

"Woke up? I haven't been to sleep yet, so—"

"No sleep? Poor little rosebud. She must've passed out the moment you left the room," Shane continued. He looked at Stone. "Maybe you should send Petals with some of the Castle soothing gel to his room. I'd hazard a guess that she might be a tad raw this morning."

"No need. I took care of it personally." Kane stretched his legs out, a satisfied smile curled his lips upward at the memory of Rose's mortification when he spread her legs and sensually soothed the gel all over her labia, clit, and on the inside of her vagina. He glanced at Alexa who stared at him wide-eyed. "Food, Alexa. I'm hungry and while you're at it, please make sure the chef did as I requested to deliver breakfast to Rose in my apartment."

"In your apartment? You ... she's in your—" She gulped back the rest of her words at his sharp glance. "Of course. Coming right up," she mumbled as she left the room.

"Shall we continue?" Kane cut off Shane as he started off again. "You interrupted my morning, Parker, and I'd like to get back to it before lunch, please."

"Looks like our cousin finally met his match. I can't remember the last time he gorged himself on a woman for days," Stone said with a happy smile on his face. Since he and Hawk had found love, he wanted to see all of them happy and settled.

Kane's snort was his only response. He tapped his fingers on the table. "Parker, time is ticking."

"Kane is right. Zikri Malik got charged four weeks ago with five counts of money laundering. The allegation is that he received $248 million in illicit money from Malaysia Development Bhd, or 1MDB, the state investment fund established by his stepfather, aka the disgraced former Malaysian prime minister, Amar Raja. According to Malaysian law, each of the five charges against him are punishable with a five-year prison term."

"And this is relevant to us, because?" Kane asked with raised eyebrows.

"You asked us to look into Roy Summers and Leon Salvino. Turns out the one thing the two of them have in common is one, Zikri Malik," Zeke, Shane's brother interjected. He swiped a finger over his iPad screen and various pictures of the three men in conversation and luncheon dates appeared on the screen.

"I fucking knew they were up to something." Kane glanced at Shane. "I just never believed they'd be involved with money laundering on such a large scale."

"How did you find this?" Shane straightened, his back taut with anger.

"We had to dig into the dark and deep web. You'd be amazed at everything we uncovered. Apparently, he used the money he stole to buy luxurious property all over the States and used some of it to finance the brief foray into the film production company. It lasted a good couple of years before it went bust but it had all been a front. He used it to get a foot into the industry and where he teamed up with Roy and Leon ... on the second Space Riders film."

"Now I remember," Ace's fingers rat-a-tatted on the table as he searched his memory. "Blue Emerald Pictures co-financed a large part of our movies. The past four years as far as I can remember, it's been a private financier backing the movies."

"Yes, and as a high-flying Hollywood production banner, Marvel had no reason to suspect anything, especially not since their vice-president vouched for them and also *sourced* the private financier," Parker continued.

"All with stolen money," Hawk sneered. "That's how they turned the money. What percentage of the profit or the proceeds of the movies did he get?"

"Malik was clever. He insisted on equal distribution rights and Marvel agreed, knowing the films would bring in billions and that way they didn't have to pour vast amounts of liquid cash upfront into one production," Zeke said. "After the film's release, Malik benefited from the deal by getting fifty percent share of profits made on box office sales."

"Meaning he made more than ten times the money he poured into each production," Parker said. "Of course, it wasn't the only money he's making backstabbing Marvel."

"Him and the bastards, Summers and Salvino," Kane sneered.

"Yeah, and at a guess, that must be why they're so desperate to sway our decision to pull out of the Marvel productions," Shane rasped and took a sip of his coffee.

"Exactly. Based on secret bank accounts we uncovered that they have in the Cayman Islands and Switzerland, I calculated that they roughly received in the vicinity of five million each per movie." Parker swiped a couple of spreadsheets onto the screens. "They built up huge balances on the sly over time, not just as Malik's lackeys but in utilizing black money to cover unaccounted production costs and even under-the-table actor fees. For which Malik rewarded them lavishly, of course. Marvel, and us for that matter, would have made millions more per movie produced if not for them shaving money off the bottom."

"Are they only involved in money laundering through Marvel?" Stone studied the reports in the file Parker had handed him before the meeting.

"So far, it appears to be the only one and only on the Space Riders films," Parker confirmed.

"And the agency fee from Summers? Could you find anything that he cuckolded Marvel and us over time?" Kane frowned as certain notations on the spreadsheet caught his attention. With a financial degree in his repertoire, he was relatively sharp to pick up inconsistencies, which was why he'd been suspicious for some time now.

"I haven't gotten so far as yet but I have made notes to check up on specific transactions that don't add up to the ones on the information you supplied." Parker closed the files as Alexa arrived with a tray stacked with a large steamy breakfast for Kane.

"Ahh ... smells delicious." He winked at her. "Thanks, you're a lifesaver."

"Gmph, if I was the one preparing it, you would've received a much healthier plate of food. Not these fat slathered sausages, bacon, and a dozen eggs."

"Blasphemy, woman! Don't curse my food, rather fill up our cups." Kane immediately started eating. He glanced at Parker and asked around a mouthful of eggs, "How did he get caught?"

"The proceedings against him followed a flurry of charges against Amar Raja and his inner circle. The former prime minister and his wife, Malik's mother, Aisha Bakir, are both facing dozens of money laundering and corruption charges. Meanwhile, Umar Rizi, Malik's friend and the alleged mastermind of the 1MDB scandal, is wanted by authorities in Malaysia, the U.S. and Singapore on various charges," Parker relayed between sips of his coffee."

"What a circle of fucktards," Ace grated.

"But Malik hasn't been caught yet," Zeke said. "He disappeared the minute the others were arrested. There are rumors that he's hiding in China. Zeke and I are following up on a couple of leads."

"Which means he's now a fugitive at large and probably desperate to have access to money," Parker interjected. "The U.S. Department of Justice alleges that over $4.5 billion was diverted from 1MDB by Malik, Raja, and their conspirators in Malaysia, Saudi Arabia, and the United Arab Emirates—making the case one of the biggest financial crimes ever."

"He's fucked," Shane said gruffly. "He won't be able to set foot in this country without being arrested on sight." He rubbed his scruffy beard in thought. "Makes me wonder what Summers and Salvino are up to and whether their actions are the results of demands from Malik."

"A man in his position is dangerous. It could very well be that he's already provided the cash influx for the next movie and is now desperate for the returns. He can't be happy that the filming hasn't even commenced," Kane mused. "Keep digging, Parker, and thanks, guys, you're doing a terrific job."

"Are you going to inform Marvel and DOJ about our findings? And that Summers and Salvino are involved?" Parker asked Stone.

Stone frowned as he pondered his response. "I don't think so. Let's play this by ear for now. I'd like to find out first how deeply entangled Summers and Salvino are. We need to be sure Marvel hasn't been using them as a front to keep their hands clean, so to speak. We need sufficient proof to sink those involved and have them locked up for a long time."

"Have any of you considered that seeing as Malik is hiding in China, another party might be involved? For that matter, be the brains behind the entire thing." Ace looked around the table.

"Are you alluding to the Triads? The Chinese Mafia?" Danton said.

"Ace could be onto something. There are many coalitions between Malaysia and the Chinese." Stone closed the file and pushed it out of the way to lean his elbows on the table. "Although the Triads have been more into drug and sex trafficking, they have been dipping their toes in money laundering now and then. Nothing on such a large scale though. Let's tackle that angle, Parker. It could very well be that the Triads expanded into the U.S. on the sly and silently became one of the main money launderers in the U.S. No one would suspect it, particularly if they do it under the guise of people like Malik."

"Agreed, especially in light of the fact that the movie production industry in China suddenly exploded and financially surpasses any other country," Shane said.

"If there's something in the cyber world, we'll find it," Zeke said.

"Have you had time to look into Rose's background, Parker?" Kane finished his meal and pushed back the plate.

"Still working on it. On the surface there's nothing. She lives a quiet life. Owns a quaint cottage in Miami and surprisingly, she's the sought-after artist, Rozi." Parker looked at Stone. "The pianist in red oil painting, upstairs in your penthouse, is hers."

"I remember. It cost a fortune but it was worth every penny."

"Which poses the question. What is a renowned artist doing hiding on a secluded island under the ruse of a submissive in training?" Kane said, deep in thought.

"We've only covered the basics so far, Kane. As soon as I uncover something substantial, I'll let you know."

"I have to admit, this entire situation with Summers and Salvino is leaving a bitter taste in my mouth. The thought of acting in another Space Riders movie isn't something I look forward to at this stage." Shane paged through the folder in front of him. "Hawk, what are the legal implications if we pull out now and is it possible to use this information as justification?"

"There's a lot of fine print in those contracts. I'll have to go through them with a fine-tooth comb. Give me a couple of days but unless we have solid proof of money laundering and that it negatively affected us financially, we won't have a foot to stand on."

"Losing out on the money isn't what bothers me," Shane tapped on the folder. "That these fuckers got away with it for so long, does."

"Agreed, but it would be the strongest point of contention." Hawk sighed heavily. "The law is a fickle thing and as there's currently no proof that

Marvel as a company benefited or was aware of what was going on, they can't be held accountable."

"Even if it's one of their top leaders at the head of it?" Danton said.

"Even then."

"That's fucked up," Zeke grated indignantly.

"Right, let's finish the last items on the agenda. I have a couple of trainee evaluation sessions to complete today," Stone brought the meeting to order.

The next hour was spent discussing new business and developments Parker and Zeke were working on.

"Do you have any fucking idea what'll happen to all of us if this movie is pulled?"

"Calm down, Zikri. We're working on a solution." Leon Salvino gestured wildly at Roy Summers and mouthed the question, "Has she contacted you?"

Roy shook his head which elicited a furious glare from his cohort.

"I can't believe the two of you are this fucking naïve. No one messes with Chan Ho. Don't you fuckin' get it? We're not dealing with the enforcer of the Chinese Mafia. Chan Ho is the goddamned leader of Sun Lee Fong Triads, the biggest and most feared of all the Triad groups in China."

"We're not idiots," Leon sneered, indignant at the insult. "We're well aware of the repercussions if this movie production doesn't start soon. As I said, we're working on a plan."

"Don't fuck with me, Salvino. I happen to know that you're the one holding back on the production schedule. All the actors are under a tight contract to finish the series, there's no reason for the delay in commencing with filming."

Leon shifted in his chair. Zikri Malik was shortsighted. There was a lot more at stake than this one movie. Unless he could get the Rothmans to extend their contract with Marvel, they were screwed. He had made a written commitment to the Triads to continue laundering money for them through the Marvel Studios. None of the other Marvel productions were as big and required as much financial backing as the ones the Rothmans were involved in. That was why he'd been able to hide the black money and the underhanded shady dealings he and Roy embarked on together. He already had a new series lined up that would be as big, if not bigger than Space Riders that he wanted to dangle as an enticement but that would only be a success if Shane and Kane played the leading roles. Their characters would make the film a hit, and because the cousins were so popular, the public loved them acting together. It was guaranteed to bring in billions.

"I'm thinking ahead, Zikri. Chan Ho made it clear he wanted to strengthen his footprint in the U.S. He's only been involved for the past two years and look how much black money we turned for him. Are you sure he'd be happy if I rushed to get this one movie done only to slam the door closed on any further opportunities with one of the biggest production houses in the U.S?"

"You're the one who doesn't understand, Salvino. You already made that commitment to him and he'll keep you to it. At this very moment, Chan Ho is only interested in the here and now. In what he can turn in the shortest amount of time. Yes, he walked into an established setup and we grasped at the opportunity because it doubled our income stream but as far as the Triads are concerned, they don't give a shit how you honor your commitment in the future. It's now and only now that matters." Zikri heaved in a heavy breath. "Stop fucking around with future deals. Chan Ho wants an answer, Salvino."

"And he'll get it, he only needs to be patient!"

"You seem to forget that the Sun Lee Fong Triads have branched out internationally, including to the U.S. If you believe you're too far to be concerned about his wrath, you better wake the fuck up."

"Look, Zikri, all I'm trying to do is ensure—"

"All you need to ensure is that the fucking production of the next Space Rider movie starts. Nothing else matters, Salvino. You better have a date for me to report to Chan Ho by the end of the week, or he's sending the local enforcer of the clan to make sure you understand that he's not playing games."

"Fuck!" Leon cursed and flung his cell phone onto the desk with a loud clattering as the connection was summarily cut.

"Now what?' Roy appeared jittery as he lifted his drink to his lips.

"Have you heard anything from that bitch?"

"No, and I haven't been able to get a hold of her either. She must've blocked my number and doesn't answer the calls from the burner phone I bought. My emails have been bouncing back as well."

Leon paced in front of the window of his luxurious office in the Frank G. Wells Building in Burbank, California. He didn't trust Zikri. He was being too pushy. He rubbed his thick beard as he pivoted to face Roy.

"Something is chasing Zikri and it's not the Triads. At a guess, it's the threat that's hanging over his head of being caught and dumped in jail."

"Yeah, and it scares the shit out of me too. Don't think for one minute he'll think twice to rat us out to save his own hide. He'll probably dump everything on our heads. We've got no collateral. He's the one in bed with the big shots of the Triads. It'll be easy as pie for him to lay all the blame on us." Roy gulped down his drink. "How sure are you we can't be connected with him and the shady dealings on the Space Riders productions?"

"Don't worry. I made sure our association with Malik is airtight and the shares received are bypassed via various banks and accounts before it ends in ours. The hacker I use is the best. She made sure there are no traces leading to us. Besides, we had nothing to do with where the charges against him originated." Leon grunted at the blank look from Roy.

"Don't you watch the news? Malik dipped into Malaysian state investment funds. That's where he got the money from to start the production company that triggered the first shift of funds of the Space Riders movie a couple of months later." He refilled their glasses and handed one to Roy. "But we do have a problem. The money Zikri *invested* in the film has already been utilized to pay location and hotel deposits and advances for the crew and cast, material, and sets. There's no way to give it back to them if this thing goes sour. Three quarters of that came from the Triads."

"Shit. That must be why Zikri is so invested in the production starting. The Triads are going to take their pound of flesh out of his hide."

"Ours too, Roy. Don't forget they know exactly who we are. Fuck, fuck, fuck! I have no other choice. I'm going to have to release the production schedule. Even Alan Bradley is on my back about the delay. He's not interested in worrying about locking the Rothmans into another contract at this stage."

"Why not? It's Marvel that's gonna lose out. They've been the biggest success ever."

"He knows it but he's under pressure as we're responsible for penalties to the Disney Studios on delays of movie releases. As it is, the film is already behind schedule. And that, my friend, isn't only going to cost us a couple of million each, it'll cost Zikri and the Triads close to a billion."

"Shit, I didn't think about that."

"Then it's time you do." Leon resumed his pacing. "It's time to tighten the noose around Narine's neck, Roy. Get pictures of her boy and send it to her with a clear threat of what'll happen to him. If push comes to shove and she doesn't comply, we put that threat into action. She's our best bet to have ammunition against the Rothmans and get Kane to sign and convince the others to follow his lead."

"How? I can try the burner but how do I know she'll even receive it. If she's set her phone to discard unknown numbers—"

"I'll send you the hacker's details. She'll be able to get your email delivered."

"I've got it." Roy brightened as a thought flashed through his mind. "If she can clone the school's email address, I can use that to send the email. She'll be sure to open it."

"Brilliant. Get it done and soon. In the meantime, I'll post the production schedule. At the very least, we should film the scenes killing off Stone and Hawk soon."

"I'll keep you updated."

Leon watched Roy leave with a pensive expression on his face. They were both in too deep to pull out now. He cursed himself for not creating an escape hatch right at the beginning. It was too late now to try and find a way to pin everything on Zikri and Roy. If he could get visual evidence of the Rothmans acting out their dirty kink, he'd be able to force Kane and Shane to sign a fixed contract for another series. If he could get their commitment, at the very least, he'd be assured of Zeke, and at a push Parker.

"I can work with that. I'll fucking have to if there's no other way."

Chapter Fourteen

"Why the devil do we have to wear these all of a sudden?" Rose held up the short and flowing mini dress made from sheer material. The standing rule at the Castle was no underwear. That meant every part of her body would be on display through the white gauze-like dress.

She was still trying to recover from the two days and nights she'd spent in Kane's bed. Her cheeks bloomed at the memories that assailed her. Kane had perfected the art of sex and he was an expert at twisting and turning a woman's body along with her mind until she was as weak as an overcooked noodle.

Through it all, he'd paid homage to her body, to every curve and bulge, scoffing at her embarrassment to be walking around naked in his apartment.

If only I could shed these extra pounds, then I wouldn't mind, but until then ...

Rose constantly worried that her thighs and ass jiggled when she walked in front of him. She kept her tummy pulled in so hard that at times she almost passed out from holding her breath. She knew it was ridiculous. She was a forty-four-year-old woman who always exuded confidence, even naked in the presence of the other Masters and Doms. All that flew out the door the moment Kane appeared and she wilted under insecurities. She knew why. He'd loved her body once ... the perfectly trim, firm and shapely form that could be molded into positions that would make a gymnast envious. Now, when he pushed her legs next to her ears, all she worried about was the fat pushing upward into unsightly bulging folds around her stomach.

None of which seemed to faze Kane. In fact, he loved to stroke her stomach and the curve of her rounded hips.

"Better hustle, Rose. I heard the twittering around the breakfast table that Master Bear is like a bear with a sore tooth this morning." Cora giggled. "How appropriate is that! Come on, put on the dress. You don't want to start your first day back in the dungeon on his wrong side, now do you?" Cora prodded her urgently.

Rose grumbled irritably but yanked the offending garment over her head and pushed her feet into white slip on sneakers. She wondered about Kane's mood as they made their way to the dungeon. She had breakfast very early and had returned to the room before he'd arrived, simply because she needed to compose herself before facing him again in the light of day. He had been in an amicable mood when he'd escorted her to the Great Dining Hall the previous night and told her to get to bed early. He even gave her a hard kiss that had curled her toes before they entered. From there he'd gone to join his cousins and she with Cora and the other trainees. She couldn't help but wonder what had changed in the hours in between.

"Take your seats, trainees. We have a lot to discuss today." Kane's voice boomed through the acoustics of the dungeon, leaving a gruff echo in the background.

Rose took her usual seat in the back row, noticing that Master Leo's group of trainees had joined them. The two cousins stood in front of the neat rows of tables and chairs waiting for them to settle.

"Today, we're discussing that which you are the custodian of—your body. It's *our* most valuable asset that *you* have the responsibility of treating properly and to communicate any issues regarding it's well-being to us, its rightful owners." Kane looked at the surprised faces staring at him. He smiled briefly at their confusion. "As a submissive, what is it that you offer a Dominant? Sub CD?"

"My body, and all the pleasure, pain and orgasms that come with it, for him to care and protect," she said. "Oh! I see," she exclaimed as her words registered.

"Exactly, sub CD," Kane praised. "Once you give your commitment as a submissive, your body no longer belongs to you and you have no right to do with it as you choose. *You* are not free to hide it from view. It's not yours to dislike or be critical of. It's a body, a vessel in which you live, but is owned by another. Currently it's owned by us. For as long as you're a trainee or a paid submissive of Castle Sin, your body belongs to the Castle Masters."

"You're here to learn the skills of a submissive, to understand what pleases a Dominant, and how to act to give him the ammunition to care for you in the way you crave to be. Pay attention today, trainees; this is one of the most important lessons you'll learn of your entire training," Ace said with a gentle smile. "We are your body's temporary custodians now but one day you'll find the Dominant who will desire to possess it long term."

"One can only hope," Cora chirped next to Rose.

"I daresay, you won't find it too difficult, sub CD," Kane rumbled. "You have quite a couple of endearing qualities … that is if you can learn to curb the brat that pops up now and then."

"But Master Bear, where's the fun in that?" she said tongue-in-cheek, eliciting chuckles from trainees, Masters, and training Doms alike.

"Let's get started. I'd like everyone to get up and stand next to each other in front of the stage." Kane pointed to the far side of the room, waiting as they quickly shuffled into place and as one, stood in the Castle present position. Legs spread shoulder width apart, hands clasped behind their backs, shoulders straight and breasts pushed forward. "Perfect form, trainees," he praised, sounding like a proud father.

"The purpose of today's training is for you to become comfortable with your body being on display, particularly the parts which are usually covered up. Your nipples, buttocks, and vulva. In the BDSM community, shame isn't tolerated, no matter your size, shape, or form. You need to embrace your body as the conduit to achieving the pleasure you crave and that a Dominant can offer you. To achieve that, from this point forward, when allowed, the clothes you'll wear will be made from the same sheer material as the dress you received this morning."

"Excuse me, Master Bear, what do you mean by *when* allowed," Rose asked with trepidation.

"You've had five months of easing into training, sub RL, and we noticed there are some of you who still struggle with nudity, therefore the sessions are going to be more intense going forward. Clothes aren't a necessity during the training period, therefore, you'll be naked except the days when you'll be issued an outfit to wear."

"Even during meals and off times?" Rose could hear the panic in her voice. Kane's lips flattened and his eyes flashed as he noticed her discomfort.

"At all times, sub RL."

"That sucks," she muttered under her breath. Kane chose to ignore her.

"To start, please remove the dresses and hand them to Madam Cherrie."

Kane noticed Rose's reluctance, but a peek at him was enough to spur her to action and she yanked it over her head. Once she'd handed the garment over, her hands fluttered to cross over her stomach, a gesture he'd seen her do numerous times over the past two days that she'd spent with him. Every time he'd slapped her hands away but to no avail. He studied her critically. She was a beautiful woman and the added padding to her gorgeously curvy form gave her that added sensuality that drew him like a beacon on a misty night. Why she couldn't see it annoyed him.

"Position, sub RL," he snapped. He grunted when she straightened and took the position with obvious reluctance.

"Before we continue, please select two items from the accessories table against the far wall," he said and pointed to where Dom Brad stood next to a table displaying all kinds of jewelry.

Rose didn't join in the excited chattering of the other trainees as they made their selection. For herself, she chose a silver rope necklace, and because she was the last to arrive at the table, she was forced to take the remaining nipple jewelry. It was a stylish crystal teardrop set and quite beautiful but not what she'd have chosen. It would only draw attention and that was the last thing she desired.

"Please dress yourself with your selection," Ace said in his gruff voice as he joined the training Doms to assist where necessary.

"Need help, sub RL?"

Rose started as Ace spoke next to her. She'd been struggling with the necklace and didn't see him approach. She smiled briefly. "I'd appreciate it, Master Leo." She lifted her hair and dutifully turned to offer her back.

"There, now the nipple jewelry."

"I'm sure I'll be able to ..." she bit back her protest as his eyebrow did the *Castle Master hitch*. "Very well," she sighed and handed over the jewelry.

"Let's just make sure these buds are properly prepared. We don't want you to lose your jewelry, now do we?"

"No, Master Leo," Rose said in a thin voice, mortified that her body reacted to his teasing caress.

"Perfect," Ace said as her nipples stood firm and hard against her breasts. He slipped the soft silicone cinch over a nub and tugged on it until it was snug around her nipple and then repeated the process with the other. He tapped his fingers against the teardrops hanging from a link chain. "Beautiful, sub RL."

"Thank you, Master Leo," she said and took her place next to Cora. She groaned as the gems wiggled with every movement she made. It offered a feeling of sensuality, stimulation, and to her chagrin, arousal. The cinch wasn't tight around her nipple, which meant she'd probably have to wear them the entire day.

It's going to be a long, torturously arousing day, she bemoaned her fate silently.

"You look enticing, ladies." Kane looked at the twenty trainees with a pleased smile. "For this morning, your task is to learn to accept that you are the carrier of your body for the pleasure of others. You do not feel embarrassed to be adorned in jewelry alone, or uncomfortable being completely naked. Most of all, you'll embrace the pleasure of acceptance by the Masters your body now belongs to."

He noticed a couple of the trainees shuffling with uncertainty and recognized them as the ones with insecurity issues. Rose was among them.

"Initially, you might struggle wearing so little outside of the dungeon but remind yourself that you're on display for the pleasure of the Castle Sin Masters and Doms. A Dominant is excited and appreciates the beauty of the human body and the confidence of pure submission offered freely. Embrace it and you'll be comfortable and relaxed." He headed to the arch entrance. "Follow me, trainees."

He stopped outside the Great Gathering Hall from where the sound of deep male voices and tinkling laughter of women floated toward them. Too many to consist of only the Castle Masters and Training Doms. Rose could feel her stomach cramping at the thought of walking around with her naked bulges on display in front of strangers ... in broad daylight.

"Once every couple of months we invite members for a day of fun and relaxation. They are spoiled with food, drink, and any kind of sport they'd like to enjoy. Swimming, golf, deep sea diving or ... some play outside the dungeon." Ace smiled as their eyes widened. "Yes, you heard me. The Gathering Hall has been changed into an informal dungeon. All scenes any of them are interested in, happens here."

"It's the perfect setting for you to learn to be comfortable being on display. The members are aware that you're all trainees and they won't approach you for a scene. However, you are to be friendly and accommodating should they approach you and talk to you or wish to appreciate your nakedness with some caresses. Understood?" Kane waited for confirmation from them all before he continued. "You will remain in the present position the entire time, thereby ensuring that every part of *our* body is available for viewing. I expect you to mingle throughout the room, smile and chat with the members, and thank them if they choose to appreciate *our* body. If I catch anyone's hands moving to cover any part of *our* body, they'll be cuffed behind your back for the remainder of the morning."

"You're welcome to enjoy snacks, water, and juice but no liquor. Always remember to keep every aspect of our body on display, even while eating. Any questions?" Ace asked but apart from a low murmur from the group, no one spoke up. "Good."

Kane and Ace stepped aside and gestured to the high arch leading into the massive hall.

"Proceed."

Rose heaved in a deep breath and followed the others. She made a point of avoiding Kane's eyes that seared into her like two bursts of fire. He appeared aloof toward her, like the past two days never happened. Like he hadn't fucked her nonstop until she begged him to stop and still he continued, regardless. It was no small wonder that she could feel muscles pulling where she didn't even know she had any.

The chill emanating from him as she passed him, hurt. More than she cared to admit. She squared her shoulders and kept her gaze straight ahead, refusing to allow any of her thoughts to surface.

She couldn't afford to give him ammunition to hurt her. She knew Kane well enough to know that once he found out about her deceit and lies, he'd use it against her to lash back.

Rose immediately made a beeline towards the refreshment table where she spotted Alexa, Peyton, and Savannah.

"Oh, my, aren't these pretty?" Savannah tapped the teardrop gems of the nipple jewelry as she reached them.

Rose's hands loosened to reach forward and stop the swinging motion but remembered Kane's warning just in time and had to grind on her teeth until they settled.

"Not funny, Savannah. Do you have any idea how arousing these damn things are? They're not tight but just enough to make you aware and with every move I make, they swing, exacerbating it more."

Peyton glanced around, noticing all the trainees adorned in a similar fashion. "Don't tell me this is part of your training?"

Alexa laughed. "The two of you can be lucky you missed Kane's sessions. He's the one responsible for making us accept our bodies and be proud to put it on display." She looked at Rose. "It's the, *'it's our body,'* lesson, isn't it?"

"Yes, imagine that, and here I thought my entire life it belonged to me." Rose snickered.

Alexa briefly explained the purpose of the lesson at the other two women's confused expressions.

"So, you have to mingle and chat, in broad daylight, outside of the dungeon, among the members like this?" Savannah asked, releasing a small shudder, relieved Hawk hadn't insisted that she attend the class.

"As naked as a fucking jaybird, yes." Rose shifted her weight as a familiar tingle raced down her spine. "He's watching me, isn't he?"

"Oh, yes and by the look in his eyes, I'd say if you know what's good for you, you better start mingling and parade *their* body in front of the members," Alexa said with a smile.

"Ugh, I freaking hate this," Rose muttered, but with a wave, she trotted off in the opposite direction from where the demon Master Bear stood watching.

She slowed her steps as her nipples tightened from the gently swaying motion of the gems. Mustering enough courage, she did her best to make eye contact with some of the members. It disconcerted her to notice how the Doms, young and old, leered at her body as she walked past. Her reaction to pull in her stomach and squeeze her thighs together as she went, was an automatic reaction in an attempt to shrink the bulges, which she was sure jiggled with every step.

Of course, they can't miss that and must be wondering how I ended up here.

"Excuse me, trainee, a moment, please."

Rose reluctantly stopped as a brief touch on her elbow accompanied the deep voice behind her. She turned and bit back the groan as she came face to face with a group of four men. At a guess, they ranged from forty to fifty years of age.

"Good morning, Sirs," Rose said politely.

Her fingers tightened as she once again suffered under the hot gazes traveling up and down her body. In all the years she'd been a submissive, she'd loved dressing up in kink, some of it skimpy but everything was always covered. It had taken a couple of weeks to become used to being naked for certain training sessions in front of all the Masters and training Doms. Now, she was somewhat relaxed, except when Kane was near. She hated him seeing her overweight curves.

"What is your name?"

"Sub RL, Sir." Rose shifted uncomfortably as the bulkiest of the four addressed her. He ran his finger over her collar bone and smiled as her nipples perked. Being naked during a scene was one thing, but to be parading around naked in broad daylight to a mammoth number of scrutinizing eyes, completely unraveled her. To be touched on top of that and have nowhere to hide her body's reaction, discombobulated her totally.

"I'd love to know your real name, my pet," he drawled in a heavy Texan accent.

"As a trainee, it's the only name I'm allowed, Sir."

"Of course, and we don't want to see you punished to accommodate us."

His fingers trailed over her chest to tickle the tips of her hard nipples standing to attention.

"Such glorious beauty, don't you agree, boys?"

"Makes my mouth water, to be honest," the blonde among them crooned.

Rose felt goosebumps form on her skin as he brushed a large palm over the curve of her buttocks. His breath warmed her cheek as he said softly, "Do you feel that, little one?" His hands cupped her cheeks and he squeezed gently before he moved them over her hips to tease her stomach with the tips of his fingers. "The sensation of skin on skin, how it causes your nipples to tighten and quiver without a touch?"

"Yes, Sir," she puffed, trying desperately to control the rush of heat that followed the path of his hands, but her body had a mind of its own and her nipples played along with every touch and slide of his hands.

"Are you allowed to play in the dungeon, trainee?" he husked in her ear.

"Only if my training Master gives his permission, Sir."

"And who is he?"

"Master Bear," she managed to croak as his fingers teasingly fondled the soft skin just above her clit.

"I hope he says yes and that you'll be allowed to attend the festivities in the dungeon tonight." He cupped her breasts and jiggled them. "We'll be looking for you, sub RL."

Rose's legs wobbled as she stumbled away, mortified that her body reacted so lasciviously to a stranger's touch, and *that* after the sexual overindulgence of the past two days.

"How did it make you feel when they touched you, sub RL?"

Rose stumbled to a halt at the dark voice that trembled through her. She dropped her chin to her chest, praying for strength. Experiencing it was confusing enough, having to talk about it on top of that ... didn't the man ever stop? Or was he deliberately tormenting her?

She exhaled and turned to face him, standing in the perfect present position. "It's difficult to explain. Usually, in a scene, I know exactly what I want and what to expect. This was … unsettling."

"Why?" Kane crossed his arms over his chest, enjoying the rosy blush heating her cheeks. It was so easy to goad her and watch her react. Not only to his questions but to his presence. He took a step closer, encroaching on her space, so close her nipples brushed against the white cotton shirt he wore. He suppressed the smile as her breath puffed loudly from her lips.

She frowned as she struggled to compose herself and formulate a coherent response, which with his closeness was exceedingly difficult. "I felt sensations … I'm not sure how to explain it … I think because I didn't invite it, it wasn't mine … it was almost like it was the sensations they experienced touching me that I felt reverberate through me."

"Bravo, little dove. You already latched onto our afternoon lesson. I'm elated you could recognize it for what it was."

Rose stared at him, remembering his first touch so many years ago and how it had burned through her mind all the way into her soul. She could never understand the intensity of her feelings at the time ... until now.

"I've been a submissive for twenty years, why has no one ever told me this?"

"Because it's not something submissives are taught in usual club-based training. Here, we aim to give every submissive all the tools, skills, and understanding of what it takes to be the best sub they can be."

"How is it possible to distinguish between a normal touch and one that forces a sub to feel what a Dom wants her to feel?'

"It's more than what he wants you to feel, Rose. This afternoon you'll learn the kind of mindfulness which will help you to experience feelings that are *intended* for you, rather than the ones you would naturally direct."

"I'm not sure I understand."

Kane brushed his hands over her arms and squeezed her hands. "That made you feel relaxed and safe, correct?"

"Yes, Master Bear."

He retraced the same path and continued to massage her shoulders and gently circled her throat, tilting back her chin with his thumb.

"This makes you tingle with expectation, correct?"

Rose nodded, too overwhelmed by the arousal his touch evoked to get out a word. He smiled. His one hand shifted to grip her throat firmly. Her eyes widened and she went on her toes. Her breath wheezed out of her chest as he placed his spread open hand low over her stomach, dragging it in slow circles, now and then pushing his fingers firmly into her softness. Rose felt faint, unable to compute the rush of sensations that thrilled down her legs from where he touched her to crawl back up to set her clit throbbing. His fingers tightened lightly around her throat, his hand on her stomach closed around the slight bulge and he squeezed ... hard.

"Fuck! I'm ... coming," she squealed and clawed at his arms as her knees threatened to buckle when the world began to tilt around her as a climax rolled over her. It was so unexpected she couldn't breathe; her gaze was caught by the intensity of his the entire time. His hand on her stomach relaxed, just a little, his fingers caressed the side of her neck and the climax, in the middle of gaining momentum, receded, like the slow backlash of the surf.

"Oh, my god," she gasped; for the first time in her life, she was insecure in her own sexuality. Her breath caught as his fist suddenly clamped closed again and the orgasm inside her erupted. The wail that echoed through her mind was already evaporating when she realized it had come from her lips.

"And that, my sweet Rose, is me projecting the sensations I feel coursing through me, into you."

"I don't ... how is it even possible?" she gasped, still clutching him as her pussy continued to spasm.

"What just happened was you allowing me to channel the feelings I wanted you to experience, using your body as the medium. It's not always for pleasure, my pet, it's equally effective for pain. The sensations you just experienced, arrived from the part of your body I touched but it was channeled to you directly from me. Ultimately, what you felt wasn't about or for you but about me, what I wanted to feel and experience." He brushed his lips against hers. "Your mind was locked into the moment, your inner submissive completely under my control, which allowed you to experience my needs, my desires."

"God, that sounds unbelievable and if I hadn't experienced it myself, I wouldn't have believed it was possible." she croaked as she finally managed to find her breath.

"You'll be surprised. Using mindfulness, you can explore those dark desires inside you that you fear and believe is something you wouldn't be able to tolerate. An experienced Dom can channel it and convert it into something you desire immensely." He smiled gently. "Once you understand that submitting your body means giving up control of what it experiences and the way it experiences it, then you have mastered the highest skill of submission."

"I always believed I knew what it meant, but this is on a totally different level." She blinked and her eyes fluttered. "I'm not sure I'll be able to cope with that all the time."

Kane chuckled, a deep, rich sound that infiltrated every nerve ending in her body to slither all the way into her heart and find residence there ... where it belonged.

"You won't know when it's about to happen, my pet, nor will you be able to control it. Once you're inner submissive has mastered the skill of mindfulness, it'll be an unconscious switch, especially in the presence of your true Dom. With him, you'll yearn to experience it more often than not. Do you know why, little dove?"

"No, Master Bear."

"Because it gives you power of such magnitude over him, he'll become your slave."

She snorted a laugh. "I find that difficult to believe, Master Bear."

Kane didn't respond right away, just stared at her with an enigmatic expression.

"It's through mindfulness that a Dom learns the true needs of his submissive, Rose. To know her deepest, darkest desires and to ensure he gives her what she's too afraid to ask for."

He loosened the hold he had on her throat, which to Rose's surprise, she hadn't even noticed he still had. He patted her on the nose.

"I've tapped into yours, little dove, and I'm going to make sure you experience every one of them before you leave here." His laugh was pure evil, like the rise of Hades from hell himself.

"You won't escape me, Rose. Just thinking of your dark needs has been driving me insane. Soon ... soon you *will* be mine ... in every sense of the word."

Rose watched him leave. Her heart beat like a drum solo against her chest. She couldn't breathe. It felt like the Great Gathering Hall had shrunk and was threatening to squeeze her into a pulp.

"He couldn't have. I never ever spoke about it. Oh, freaking hell, if he knows, I'm doomed. I'll be completely and utterly doomed." Rose listened to the hoarse fear trembling like a shrill soprano in her voice. She threw caution to the wind and wrapped her arms around her as a cold chill cloaked her in a cocoon of fear ... but not fear as if she were scared.

Fear that Kane would find out the truth about her before he did as he promised.

"To be his again, in every sense of the word … Lord, I'll give anything for that, if only for a short period. It'll be enough to last me a lifetime."

Chapter Fifteen

"This must be the information about next year's boarding fees," Rose muttered as she checked her emails after dinner the following day. She tapped to open the mail from Phillips Academy. Her skin turned pasty as she skimmed over the words.

"How the fuck did he manage to do this?"

Her voice slammed against the wall of the room and echoed its hoarse and angry tones back at her. She couldn't believe that the bastards were so desperate that they'd hack into the school's computer system.

"Oh, my god," she whimpered as she read the message a second time and the threat sunk in.

Time for playing games is over. We've arranged a visit to Phillips Academy tomorrow to give a talk at their Career Day open house. We are specifically going to talk about two icons in the movie industry, Kane and Shane Rothman. I'm looking forward to meeting your son. We can't wait to take him out to ... shall we say ... dinner?

You have ten hours to change my mind with some positive development. Do what I expect, or you lose another man in your life.

Rose couldn't move as she felt the world around her evaporate into nothingness. She'd been naïve, all those years ago, to believe them. She should've listened to her heart and to Kane instead of two money hungry bastards.

"A second time. Kane wants out again and they still can't let go. Why? There are hundreds of up and coming fantastic actors to mold. Why can't they allow him to lead the life he desires?"

A dry sob broke from her lips. She listened to its echo in the quiet room. Her roommates were still in the Great Dining Hall, relaxing before attending to their duties in The Royal Dungeon a little later.

"How did they even find me here?" She frowned. Everything involving Castle Sin and The Seven Keys Island was done in secret. There was no way he could've gained information about the identities of the women, except...

"Someone on the island is double crossing them. It has to be. A trusted employee, Dom or sub ... it could be anyone."

Her eyes caught the date of the email. She went cold. Two days ago. The ten-hour window he'd given her had passed.

"Oh no, Tucker!"

Her fingers trembled as she searched for the folder on her iPad with the school activity schedules. For all she knew, it was just another trick to scare her into following their bidding. She turned to a frozen icicle as she found the entry for Career Day. It had been the day before.

"I have to talk with him." She grabbed her phone and ran downstairs, blind to the questioning looks that followed her as she tore through the

Reception Hall and out the front door. She didn't stop until she reached the beach. Her breathing was haggard as she dialed Tucker's number. She paced back and forth, blind to the purple and orange glow of the sunset over the sea.

"Hey, Mom."

"Tucker! Thank god."

"What's the matter? You sound out of breath." His young voice rose and fell in deep and light tones, a sign of becoming a man.

"I'm fine. I just had a sudden desire to talk to you." She detected a drone of voices in the background with a melody of smooth jazz as the undertone.

"Where are you?"

"You won't believe what happened yesterday. The vice president of Marvel Studios and a Hollywood agent came to talk to us on career day. It was absolutely epic! And guess what? Because him and his cousins are the biggest stars at the moment, they told us everything about my dad. I'm so stoked!"

Rose's legs crumbled and she wilted to the sand. Tears trickled over her cheeks.

"Where are you, Tucker?"

"Oh, Dave, Johnathan and I are having dinner with the school headmaster, Mr. Salvino and Mr. Summers, the vice president and agent. The headmaster invited us because we asked the most questions during the session and he's a personal friend of Mr. Salvino. I can't begin to tell you how exciting this is. Mom, can you believe it?"

"Tucker, I need you to listen to me very carefully. Please, darling, I need you to phone a cab, right now, get into it and go back to the dorm."

"Why? We haven't even had our main course yet and what about my friends? I can't just leave—"

"Tucker! Just do as I say. I beg you, please. I promise I'll explain later. Don't tell them you're leaving. Just go!"

"Is this because you're scared I'll tell them Kane Rothman is my father? That's it, isn't it? You still don't plan on telling him about me and now you're taking away the only opportunity I have of hearing stories about him ... no, Mom. I'm not going anywhere. At least I'm getting to know a little something about my father."

"Darling, you … god, Tucker. They're not to be trusted. Just do as I say."

"I'm sorry, Mother, but I want to know everything there is about my father." He dragged in a deep breath. "I love you, but you've had sixteen years to tell him about me. You've been promising me for over two years that you will and now that you have the opportunity, you still don't. I'm sorry, Mom, but if this is a way for me to meet him, I'm going to take it."

"Tucker! No!" Rose covered her mouth to stifle the sobs as he cut the connection. She redialed but it went to voicemail. Her shoulders slumped dejectedly. "I have to get Tucker away from them!"

She frantically dialed her parents' landline. It rang a couple of times before it went through to the answering machine. She ended the call and tried their cell phones. Both went to voicemail.

"Dammit, they're on the seven-day cruise," she croaked, remembering the phone call she'd had with her mother a couple of weeks ago. She'd assured them it was fine to take the trip. The school always contacted Rose directly if needed and she didn't believe anything could happen in such a short time. She had no reason to … then.

Tucker was so desperate to meet Kane, he'd fall for any story or promises Roy and Leon made.

"Please, Tucker, please don't go anywhere with them. Remember the lessons about strangers. Please don't trust them!"

Rose attempted a final desperate call to the dormitory father but apart from ensuring her Tucker was in safe hands with the headmaster, he had no further information to offer.

"I'm not happy that my son has been taken off school premises to meet strangers without my permission, Mr. Nicker. I suggest you inform Mr. Greenhorn about that and I expect a phone call from him in explanation as to why he didn't contact me beforehand."

"I believe he did, Ms. Lovett, but all he got was your voicemail. As far as I know, he did leave a couple of messages. Look, all the other boys' parents gave permission and Tucker assured Mr. Greenhorn you'd be fine with it. You really don't need to be concerned. Mr. Greenhorn would never let anything happen to any of the kids or let them leave with anyone you hadn't approved. Rest assured, I'll personally make sure Tucker is safe and sound in his room tonight."

It didn't help to ease Rose's concern but knowing there was nothing further she could do, she returned to the castle, just in time to meet Cora and Diane as they walked out of the Great Dining Room.

"It seems Master Bear was serious about our dress code," Diane grumbled. She pointed to the sheer frock she wore. "We have two options for attire tonight in The Royal Dungeon. This and barefoot or naked with heels."

"You're not serious?" Rose responded automatically. She was too concerned to have any desire to join them in the dungeon but apart from claiming to be sick, she had no choice. Especially if she wished to avoid further distrust to widen the gap between her and Kane.

"I'm afraid she is," Cora said. "I've been drooling over those sexy corset leather and lace dresses Madam Cherrie showed us, but I guess we'll only get to wear them after we graduate from the academy."

Rose sighed elaborately. "I guess it's this for me then but I need to take a shower first. I feel sticky from the heat and walking on the beach."

"Good idea. We might not be wearing sexy clothes but nothing stops us from doing our hair and faces. At least it'll perk me up a little," Cora lilted as they ascended the stairs.

I shouldn't have spoken to Mom that way. She doesn't deserve to be treated like that."

Tucker castigated himself as he weaved his way back to the table where his best friends, Dave Flint and Johnathan Douglas, were chatting animatedly with the impressionable men from Hollywood.

His steps slowed as he noticed Leon Salvino's face turn into an impatient smirk as Dave asked him yet another question. He glanced at his watch and looked around. Tucker instinctively ducked behind a large plant, his mother's words rising from the back of his mind.

"They're not to be trusted."

He frowned as he continued to study the two men. His mom wasn't prone to overreact. At times she was very protective but never without reason. He'd grown up learning to trust his instincts and it was from her that he'd learned to never make harsh decisions. Perhaps that was why he was more mature than most of his friends and why they always looked up to him for advice and guidance.

"I've always trusted her to lead me in the right direction. I shouldn't judge or doubt her now."

He listened to his whispered words. His dark brown eyes glimmered with silver sparks as he noticed the Marvel vice president nudge the podgy man by his side and gestured toward the restroom, where Tucker had gone just before his mother phoned.

"Why is he so invested in my presence? Come to think of it, they ignored Dave and Jonathan the entire time."

He cast his mind back to the myriad of questions they'd fired at him from the moment they'd picked them up in a grand limousine from the dormitory.

"Every question they asked was about mom and her past. Why are they so interested in her? What is it they're after?" He exhaled loudly as a thought came to him. "They know! That's why mom is so upset."

Excitement surged through him. It felt like the adrenaline rush just before he ran out on the baseball field.

"If they know, maybe I can coerce them to tell me where to find him." He shrugged off the twinge of guilt at not trusting his mother to do as she'd promised. He wanted to meet Kane Rothman and he'd waited long enough. He nodded and squared his shoulders as he began to make his way back to the table, his mind made up.

"They're obviously after something. Maybe I can offer them a trade."

"Hey, bud, we were just about to come and find you. Did you get lost?" Dave asked as he pumped a fist against his shoulder as he slipped into the booth next to him.

"Naw, a bit of an upset stomach," Tucker said and patted his belly. He glanced around. "Maybe it's because they're taking so long with the food. Should I go and find out what's keeping them?"

"Ah, the appetite of growing boys," Leon laughed. "Patience, young man. This is a very popular restaurant, but I promise, the food is worth the wait."

The three-sixty switch of the two men from impatience to oozing with friendliness cemented Tucker's belief that their sudden visit to the school and subsequent invitation to dinner was no coincidence. They had come looking for him. He shifted uneasily in his chair. Maybe he should listen to his mother and get the hell away from them.

"What did you say your mother does again, Tucker?" Roy asked.

Tucker stuffed half of a fresh bread roll in his mouth and mumbled around it, "I didn't." He waved a hand in the air and chewed furiously, pretending to be a hungry teenager. "Forget about mothers and fathers, we want to know what it takes to become a Hollywood actor."

"Yeah! I'd give anything to play in a Marvel movie, like the Space Riders. Man! Those guys are dope!" Jonathan enthused and leaned forward expectantly.

Tucker found it almost amusing to watch the two grown men struggle to maintain their composure while he basked in their frustration at being manipulated by a teenager.

Ha! I guess that's what Mom meant by I'm a lot like Dad. Just the thought that he had some of his father's qualities, even though he'd never met him, caused another surge of excitement to race through him. The desire to finally come face to face with the man who gave him life, intensified by the moment.

He might agree with his mom that these men couldn't be trusted, but after her, they were his best bet to finally meet Kane Rothman.

Since she had left to join some training academy he and his cousins were involved in, Tucker had used his hacking skills—which were self-taught and no one knew about—to try and obtain information on where to find him, just in case his mother lost her nerve. But everything he tried dead-ended. For one, he couldn't find any acting academy that the Rothman cousins were involved in. In fact, the only information available anywhere on the web and the dark web was the same that was publicly known about the actors.

Sorry, Mom, I understand you need time but they might make meeting Dad happen a lot faster than you.

"That little shit is just as sharp as his father," Leon exploded the moment they pulled out of the school premises on the way back to the hotel.

"He's more than sharp, he's fucking clever. I don't know about you, but I got the impression he's onto us." Roy shifted in the seat. "Every time I looked into his eyes, I saw Kane staring at me with a directness that empties your soul and makes you squirm. Fucking nitwit! And just like his father, he knows just how to detract attention from a topic. He made me feel like I was the damn kid and he the grown up."

"This is turning into a fuckup, Roy. Have you been able to get the location where Narine is from your source? If she won't take photos, we need to get someone else to."

"No, he had no qualms about sharing the information after the ad I placed in the dark web, but he refuses to supply any further details or play along. Your hacker lady even tried to pin his location using his IP address but he's a clever bugger. It's redirected in a maze out there."

"If only we knew where she was, so we could get to her." Leon lit a cigar and breathed the calming tobacco into his lungs. "If our time wasn't running out, we could try using a PI to keep watch over Kane's property in Key Largo. If she's at a training academy he's involved in, surely we'd be able to have him followed there?"

"Maybe I'm a bit slow but how would finding her now help us with Kane's decision? You've already posted the production schedule and that at least gives us a little grace with the Triads."

"Think about it, Roy. If Kane finds out the love of his life is still alive, he'd do anything to get her back."

"Not if he knows she deliberately kept the fact that she survived the fire *and* the existence of his child from him for sixteen years."

"See, that's where we differ. I see the positive and you the negative. You should know Kane better than I do. You've been his agent longer than me. He might be angry at first, but if there's one thing I've learned over the years about Kane Rothman, it's that he, along with Shane, is fiercely protective over family and loved ones. Believe me, even though he might hate Narine for what she did, he'd do anything to keep the mother of his child safe from harm."

"Even agree to sign another ten-year fixed term contract with Marvel."

"Yes, my dear Roy, even that."

"Are you saying we're ditching using Tucker as bait to get Narine to do our bidding?"

"No, but it wouldn't hurt to have more than one route to pursue. We don't have a choice, Roy. If we don't have the volume of offset we committed to the Triads after this movie, we're shark bait. They'll use us for as long as we're of value to them. They don't leave witnesses behind and we know too much about their operation. We can't afford to lay slack, we have to get Kane's buy in and quickly."

"It's still a long shot, Leon. Fuck, why don't we just find a similar exciting cast as the Rothmans for the project you have in mind? At least that way we're not left at the mercy of a man who made it clear he's done with Marvel and largely with acting as a whole."

"Because, like Space Riders, it'll take at least two seasons to reach the same returns as they're currently at and that means, the Triads are going to lose money. I'm afraid we don't have much of a choice. It's at least five of the Rothmans or we're fucking dead."

"I checked the mail I sent Narine two days ago. She only read it earlier tonight. Once she talks to Tucker, she'll realize we mean business and send us the fucking photos and videos. Let's just hope he values their reputation enough to change his mind and sign."

"He'll change his mind, Roy, mark my words." Leon smiled slyly and pulled out a piece of paper from his pocket. "Tucker slipped this into my pocket as we left the restaurant."

I know you know. Seeing as you're so interested in my mother, maybe we can help each other. Phone me tomorrow after school. 617 467 3321.

"Slap me silly with a wet fish," Roy crowed as he read the note. "Are you seriously considering kidnapping him and holding him for ransom?"

"If by ransom you mean until Kane gives me at least five signed contracts, then yes."

Chapter Sixteen

Kane stood on a platform in the middle of the whipping chamber of The Royal Dungeon. A spotlight shone on the torture table behind him. He scanned the crowd with a dark flash of swirling emotion in his eyes.

"If your expression is any indication, there's a tornado brewing," Shane said as he joined him. "What's up?"

"I caught Rose taking a phone call on the beach again earlier."

"You don't believe she spoke to her son?"

"I was too far to hear but from the tone of her voice, no, I don't think so." He glanced at Shane.

"Besides, she ran out of the castle like she was being chased by a demon, which is why I followed her. And why does she need to go to the beach to talk with him? She has enough privacy in their room."

"You have a point. Have you asked Parker for the transcripts of her calls?"

"Stone put a stop to that. He feels it's an invasion of the subs' and trainees' privacy. We're only monitoring that they don't skip training to make or receive phone calls." He pushed his hands into the pockets of his leathers. "If it wasn't for the fact that we still don't know who is leaking information to the outside, I probably wouldn't give it the time of day."

Shane followed Kane's gaze that was riveted to the high arched entrance of the chamber. He studied Rose as she arrived with her roommates. "Do you honestly think she's a spy? And to what end? You heard Parker. They can't find anything shady in her background."

"Maybe so, but there's something Rose Lovett is hiding. I just have no idea what."

"Maybe Stone and I should have a chat with her. You never know, we might just uncover something valuable."

"Do it. That woman got under my skin, but I'm not letting her in until I'm a hundred percent certain I can trust her."

"I'm glad you're levelheaded about her, but don't let the past stand in the way of your future happiness, Kane. It's been long past time to move on."

"It's got nothing to do with memories of Narine. She's dead and nothing is going to bring her back. I'll never forget her or the love we shared, but that doesn't mean I'm going to settle for anything less than what I had with her."

"You believe Rose is the one to give you the same unconditional submission and love as she had?"

"I know she is. I just need to make sure she doesn't have a hidden or dark agenda."

"Yeah, when it comes to the Sinclairs, trust is a fucker." Shane's gaze dropped to the tool Kane twirled between his fingers. "I see our delightful sub RL is going to receive her long overdue punishment."

"Indeed." Kane called Jenna over and instructed her to fetch sub RL. "I decided to combine it with a demonstration."

"Meaning?"

"I promised her thirty minutes punishment but thirty minutes with this electric whip is going to tear that little clit of hers into shreds and seeing as I have every intention of fucking her later, I'm going to alternate the punishment with eroticism."

"That in itself is going to be punishment. I guess you're going to keep her on edge?"

"Of course. What better way to prepare her and then pluck the fruits of my labor later?"

"You summoned, Master Bear."

Kane's gaze settled on the pout of Rose's full lips as she stood below them in the present position.

"Eyes."

He suppressed a smile as her lips thinned but she dutifully lifted her gaze to his. Since the last time he'd ordered her to remove the color contacts, she hadn't dared wear them again. It pleased him.

He hated deceit and falseness, even on something that minute.

"Still sulking, sub RL?"

"I'm not sulking, nor have I been," she said curtly.

"No? Somehow I got the impression you were annoyed last night that I said no to play with our Texas members."

"I don't know what gave you that idea." Rose shifted her weight but tilted her chin a little higher.

Kane knew what she was irked about and it pleased him to no end. He'd used her for a demonstration twice the previous night, both times building her arousal to the point of exploding and then denying her a climax. She'd been on edge and keen to scene with the four Texans, but he had other plans and said as much. Rose had no way of knowing the plans he'd mentioned weren't intended for last night and gracefully accepted his decision. She had no compunction to slap her discontent on his head when he'd ordered her after an intense edging scene to go to bed, again denying her release a third time. Before he could say a word, she'd flounced off and had been avoiding him today.

His little rosebud needed to learn the benefit of patience. He loved teasing and taunting her with the uncontrolled lust he awakened inside her. He'd be damned if he allowed other Doms to reap the rewards.

"Are you sure?" He switched on the electric whip and her eyes shot to the tool in his hand at the soft swoosh sound.

"Ah, shit."

"Indeed. It's time for your much-delayed punishment, sub RL. Take off your slip and get on the punishment table, please." He switched off the whip as she hesitated. "Do I need to increase your punishment?"

Her eyes drifted from the torture tool to his face. She licked her lips. The glistening surface kickstarted his testosterone with a pleasing twitch to his cock.

"You're not seriously going to beat me for thirty minutes with that thing?"

"I'm not?"

"Why do Doms always make that response sound like a threat? It was a simple question, Master Bear, and requires a simple answer," she snipped but thought it best to scurry up the stairs at the darkening of his eyes. Thirty minutes were already frightening enough; she didn't need him to add to it, although it might just be what she needed to keep her mind off the latest development.

A development that forced her to make a decision she wasn't ready for. She had to protect Tucker and if that meant she had to spill the beans to Kane earlier than planned, so be it, but she refused to play any part in forcing his life in a direction he didn't want. Not again.

She had to face reality. It didn't matter when or how she told him, he would end up hating her and cast her off the island and out of his life.

Rose stiffened as she felt his heat pressed against her back. He circled her throat with his hand and pinned her in place by adding the slightest pressure when she tried to move away.

"You're a little snippy, sub RL. Did your short tête-à-tête on the beach not bring the results you were after?"

She glanced sideways at him, surprised at the flashes of anger in the depths of his eyes. His words penetrated and she realized he must have seen her hasty departure as she dashed through the Reception Hall earlier and obviously came to a wrong conclusion.

"It wasn't like that. I just ... went for a walk."

"Let's not waste time. Get into position." His gravelly voice was laced with a chilled tenor.

Rose wisely kept her mouth shut and got on the table.

Kane was disappointed. If she'd at least told him about the phone call, he'd be less inclined to mistrust her. Maybe he should stick with his gut instinct and stay away from her. She spelled trouble with a capital T.

He ignored the trembling in Rose's thighs as he spread her legs and dropped them over the side of the table to cuff her ankles in place.

"Sit up," he ordered curtly. Again, he ignored her confusion and dragged her arms behind her back. He deftly wrapped a rope around her elbows and with quick efficient movements, he bound her forearms together in a simple Shibari harness. He finished with a knot at her wrists before he fed the long length of remaining rope through a pulley chain hanging from the roof. He tightened the chain until she leaned backward at a forty-five-degree angle that pushed her breasts out wantonly.

His eyes flashed as he regarded her through slitted lids. "You will watch your punishment." His expression was enigmatic as her startled gaze met his. "I want you to see what I see when I use the whip on you. I want you to see each flash of the steel tips the second before it hits your flesh. I want to see the pain in your eyes the moment it connects and most of all, I want you to see your cunt weep for more."

"You're a demon." Rose struggled, but Kane had made sure there was no give. Not from her legs, nor from her arms. She was strapped up, helpless with nowhere to go. She closed her eyes.

"Open your eyes, sub, and keep them glued to where I use the whip. If you don't, I'll stick scotch tape on your eyelids to keep them open."

"What have I done to make you this angry? What changed since I spent time in your apartment?"

"Nothing changed, my pet. I gave you what you needed, sex, and I got what I wanted at the same time—a couple of days of good, hard fucking. I daresay, it's about to happen again tonight but don't make the mistake to believe it means anything more than that. You're here to be trained and this punishment is part of your training. Don't confuse that with the arrangement we discussed. Understood?"

"Oh, I understand, but you made one mistake, Master Bear," she clipped through thin lips. She'd never been this insulted.

"I did?" The amusement in his voice sparked her annoyance to full blown anger.

"Yes, you did. There will be no more *good, hard fucking*. At least not with me." She all but exploded when he laughed.

"Ah, little one, so predictable. Never fear, I won't make you beg this time. I have no intention of—"

"Is it your intention to bore me to death with all your talking or are you going to start the fucking punishment anytime soon?"

Rose was too angry to take heed of the gasps of the trainees and subs gathered below to watch. All she wanted to do was get it over with so she could disappear to her room and wallow in the pain searing through her heart. She'd been such a fool, a stupid, naïve idiot to think she'd be able to capture Kane's heart again. He had changed, in more ways than one. He was a more powerful Dom, yes, but he had lost the empathy he used to have for all subs and that filled her with the deepest sorrow of all.

The whirr of the electric whip caused her to jerk. She wished her mind could drift to a faraway place so that she could lose herself in her subconscious. Instead, she found herself mesmerized by the glow in Kane's eyes as he watched her.

"This is a punishment and I expect you to hold out for as long as you can, but if it becomes too much, what is the safeword I expect to hear?"

Rose was tempted not to respond but knew she'd already aggravated him with her cheeky response. The taut lines of his body attested to his silent anger. He caught her chin between his fingers and forced her eyes to his. She could feel his anger blast its power at her as he pushed his face closer.

"You just paved the road to your own pain, Rose, don't make it worse."

She trembled as realization struck. No Dom appreciated being pressured to punish a submissive. Her angry retort had forced his hand. Everyone present now expected him to retaliate. She trembled at the implication. He might have shown her some mercy ... now she knew he'd offer her none. Self-preservation won the day and she swallowed back the fear threatening to choke her.

"My safeword is King, Master Bear."

Kane turned to the crowd watching. Rose was mortified to notice all the Masters present as well.

"Sub RL is receiving the punishment that was pushed back a week ago. The original timespan would've been ten minutes but increased to thirty by her own choice. However, the steel tips on the leather strips will cause painful damage and that's not going to achieve the result I wish with this punishment. Therefore, I'm extending the time to an hour and amending it to include additional punishment for her disrespectful defiance just now. I'll use the electric whip on her for five minutes at every ten-minute interval. During that time, the subs of the Castle will use either their hands, mouths, or any of the toys in this box to tease her. It's their choice whether it'll be playful, sexual, or painful. Sub RL is free to climax but for every time she comes, the punishment is extended by five minutes."

Rose stared at him in horror. She'd seen the subs attending to a similar punishment before and remember cringing as she watched how expertly they manipulated the woman's body. She was screwed either way. She had never been able to withstand the contrast between pleasure and pain. There was no way she'd be able to keep from climaxing. An hour was already a haunting prospect and she cursed her wayward tongue and bruised ego for getting her into deeper shit.

Kane stepped against the table between her legs.

"I'm sorry," she whispered, genuinely contrite for speaking to him in such a derogatory fashion in view of everyone.

"I imagine you are. A little late, don't you think? And no, Rose, you're not nearly sorry enough, but believe me, you soon will be." He switched on the whip. "Keep your eyes on the area the whip strikes, sub. Every time you look away, I'll increase the speed and the strength of the hits." His eyes darkened as their eyes met. "Remember, *you* asked for this."

Rose realized that not all the strips of leather ended in steel tips but at least half did. Her body tried to bear back as he brought the tool closer. She tried to close her eyes but couldn't as she watched the silver tips flash in the lights as it rotated closer.

"Oww! Fucking hell," she cried out as the first lashes connected and then continued in a nonstop slapping motion all over her labia and on the tender inside of her gaping lips. Kane moved the tool the entire time, just a slit twist to ensure it landed on a different spot every time.

Rose heaved in a breath between her pitiful cries. Every inch of her pussy scorched where the steel tips hit, alternating with the strikes of the leather strips. Her clit throbbed incessantly, to her dismay, seeing as Kane hadn't even aimed at it yet. The thought came at the same time as he brought the tool closer and the intensity of the hits increased. She squealed in pain as the strips slapped against the inside of her pussy.

"God, please, Master Bear! Not so close. Oww!"

"You're doing well, sub RL. Just remember to breathe," he said in a low vibration, his gaze on the telltale wetness that glistened on her spread open labia.

"I can't ... stop. You have to ... OWWW!"

Her scream slammed against the walls as Kane increased the speed and then it was over. Rose was close to tears as she stared at her skin turning a darker shade of red. Her breathing was erratic. Shame heated her cheeks as Kane swiped his finger over the inside of her pussy.

"It seems I was right about you, sub RL. You have a masochist inside you," he taunted her and then sucked her juices from his finger.

Rose felt the pull of his lips in the tightening of her loins and the rush of heat flushing her veins.

Good god, how can I be aroused after ... no, while, I was in so much pain? Is he right? Am I a masochist?

"You may begin, Madam Cherrie."

Kane's voice yanked her back to the present. She watched with trepidation as the tall fashionista of the Castle approached. She had an excited glimmer in her eyes as she smiled at Kane. "Anything specific you'd like me to do, Master Bear?"

Rose felt like puking at the syrup that literally dribbled from every word. She stared at Kane, horrified that he seemed enamored by her obvious attempt at flattery. Even tied up like she was, Rose felt like ripping out the woman's eyes. How could Kane not see what she was doing?

"I'll leave it up to you to please me, Cherrie."

Oh lord, spare me, Rose sneered silently.

Unfortunately for Rose, Madam Cherrie chose the one thing that she'd hoped she wouldn't. Her hands ... to tease the still painful labia and with a wicked smile, flicked her nails over Rose's clitoris, over and over until she couldn't hold back the moans.

The dratted women obviously knew Kane had avoided her clit and aimed to use that against Rose.

"Let's see what you taste like, trainee," Madam Cherrie coed as she leaned over and sucked the swollen nub into her mouth.

If Rose could move, her hips would've soared high from the gentle and sensual sucking of the soft lips surrounding her nub. The coil inside her tightened with every pull on her vulnerable clit.

"No," Rose protested when two more subs joined Cherrie and latched onto her nipples. They had training sessions with Master Leo on pleasing women, and it was evident that these three knew just how to tease and arouse.

"Time."

The call came at the moment that Rose felt herself tip over the edge but the subs immediately stepped back and her soft wail of protest was met with a snicker from the members watching.

The climax drifted away to nestle deep inside her loins ... waiting.

She barely had time to recover when the first lashes of the electric whip fell. Her raw scream sounded like a plea for mercy to Rose. Her gaze was riveted on the rotating leather strips. They were moving so fast it looked like one strip hitting her pussy with merciless accuracy. Her breathing became fast, desperate as she struggled to drag oxygen into her lungs along with the uncontrolled screams and cries that escaped her lips.

"Motherfucker!" she screamed as Kane unexpectedly moved the whip and flogged her nipples. "Oww-oww-oww! Please nooo!" she cried and tried to move out of the way to no avail. She'd been whipped on her nipples before but never had it hurt so much. Her mind screamed at her to use her safeword but she couldn't get it past her lips. She refused to disappoint Kane any further. She could take more, even if it killed her.

Just when she thought she'd reached the end of her tether, he stopped.

Kane tipped her chin and studied her intently. "You're very brave, Rose. I'm proud of you, you're taking the punishment very well."

"Th-thank you, Master Bear," she puffed out as she struggled to find her composure, which was difficult with her nipples and pussy that throbbed painfully in tandem. It felt like someone had poured lava over her skin.

His fingers tightened on her chin. Her eyes fluttered open.

"Just remember, Rose," he said in a serious tone, "oww, isn't a safeword."

"I'm not a dimwit, Master Bear," she snapped and then hung her head. "I'm sorry, I don't know where that came from."

His eyes darkened. "I think you do, but know this, little dove, I won't allow you to push yourself past your limits. If I have to use the safeword to end the punishment, it won't end well for you. Then even begging for mercy isn't going to help you."

Rose was still trying to work through his words when three subs approached. "Fucking hell," she whimpered and groaned as they began rummaging through the toy box. She didn't know if she'd be able to take too much. Not with her vulva and nipples on fire.

But over the next two sets, Rose realized she'd misjudged the subs of Castle Sin. They had probably all been through something similar. Some licked and sucked her out and others teased her with G-spot vibrators, vibrating butt plugs, and suction cups on her clit. They avoided all the painful areas and spiked her arousal with obvious glee.

Rose had no defense left and by the time Kane called time for the fourth time, she'd climaxed five times. She felt like crying when he announced an additional twenty-five minutes to her punishment.

Every time Kane started the whip it hurt more, it seemed faster, harder, and Rose's screams grew louder and louder.

"Jesus Christ! OWW! Fuck-fuck-fuck!" Her wail sounded raw, like a hunted animal caught in the claws of death as the steel tips connected with her clit.

"Rose," Kane's voice was so low, she had no idea how she heard it but the warning filtered through her mind and she listened.

"King," she whimpered and then louder, "King!"

The whip had already stopped the first time she puffed out the word and within seconds, she was cut loose. Kane lifted her in his arms and carried her to the aftercare section in the Reception Hall of the dungeon.

"Good girl," he praised as he rocked her on his lap, stroking her hair as she sobbed in his arms. She didn't even protest when her legs were gently spread apart and fingers she knew couldn't be Kane's—because they were wrapped around her in a comforting hug cuddling her close—gently spread a soothing gel all over her scorching skin.

"I'm sorry, Master Bear," she lilted in a teary voice. "I'll never be disrespectful again."

Kane chuckled. "Somehow, I'm not so sure about that. You're too fiery for your own good."

"You say that as if it's a bad thing," she mumbled and snuggled closer as her eyelids grew heavy.

He responded with a kiss on her forehead, sighing heavily as she fell asleep.

He was immensely proud that she'd held out for as long as she did but struggled with the war raging inside him. On the one hand, he wanted to keep her safe and close to his heart. At the same time, he couldn't shake the feeling that she wasn't who she said she was. That she had secrets, deep dark secrets. Instinct told him it would affect his life in ways he'd never envisioned.

He stared at her beautiful face and tenderly wiped away the last remnants of her tears. He stilled as his fingers encountered a small scar just inside her hairline. Further investigation unearthed three more. The puzzle that was Rose Lovett intensified.

His voice sounded raw in the silence that surrounded the booth.

"You'll soon learn, Rose, that the malignancy of secrets is like a cancer in the soul."

Chapter Seventeen

Rose's eyelids fluttered lazily, as if reluctant to acknowledge the streaks of sunlight that penetrated and dissolved the blackness of sleep. She stretched and yawned as she moved onto her side with the grace of a feline. Her eyes opened, glazed over with the final remnants of a dream.

"Oh! I'm in your ..." She glanced around in confusion, recognizing the tastefully decorated room. Her gaze moved back to the man lying next to her, leaning on his hand as he watched her silently. "... room," she ended lamely.

"So you are."

"I ..." She frowned, desperate to shake the haze of sleep from her mind in an effort to form a coherent thought. She struggled upright and leaned against the headboard, dragging the sheet with, to cover her nakedness.

"No."

Rose shot an indignant look at him. It was bad enough that she was all groggy and probably looked bedraggled and as old as her age.

Oh fuck! I must have cockatoo hair!

It took a mammoth effort not to check her hair as she desperately clutched the sheet to her breasts. It was a wasted effort as Kane yanked it from her grasp with one hard tug.

"Now, tell me how you feel about your punishment last night."

Rose glared at him. How the devil was she supposed to concentrate and remember anything while lying naked and wrinkled under his watchful eye and ... *oh sweet freaking hell,* she gasped as she got an eyeful of his naked body and his big and already aroused cock. *Damn, he's got a gorgeous dick.* She licked her lips as she drooled over the perfectly mushroom-shaped tip, the blue veins that pulsed as he grew even harder under her gaze.

"Rose, pay attention and get your greedy eyes off my crown jewels."

She felt the blush bloom all the way from her toes to her cheeks. "Well, it's not my fault that you're flaunting them in my face. I mean a girl isn't made of steel, you know."

Kane chuckled. "I'll take that as a compliment." His expression turned serious. "I'm waiting."

"It hurt like the freaking hell come to earth," she said. "I never wish to see that damn whip again, and yet ..." she hesitated as she struggled to find the words to describe how the subs had made her feel, "the subs, good lord, I never believed I'd be able to get off being caressed, licked, and sucked by a woman." A small smile curved her lips. "I guess I was naïve. They ... *we* are women and know better than anyone how to tease and give the female form pleasure. That was what made the whipping that followed tolerable, that to my shock and horror caused me to become aroused, even while my brain screamed in pain. It proved to me just how much I can tolerate ... under the guidance of the right Master."

"Well said but I'm warning you now, Rose, don't let me ever catch you stretching yourself past your limits. Yes, I noticed it and I realized the moment you decided to hold out until the very end, even if it killed you. I will not stand for it, is that understood. That's why you have a safeword."

"Yes, and I'm sorry. I just didn't want to disappoint you."

His eyes moved over her face and continued a leisurely path further down. A scowl warned her hands out of the way that crawled upward to cover her stomach.

"I told you the last time you were here that I don't tolerate you hiding your body from me. I'll assume you're still half asleep and forgot about that."

"You know how I feel about parading around naked," she muttered. She clasped her hands into fists by her side, not sure what to do with them, because she had no doubt no matter where she placed them on her body, would constitute a crime in his eyes.

She pulled in her stomach and held her breath as he placed his hand on her. His scowl darkened.

"Don't do that."

"I'm not ... oww! Dammit, is that really necessary?" she complained and rubbed the spot where he'd slapped her breast. It stung but surprisingly wasn't as painful as she'd imagined it would be after her punishment the previous night. At his warning look, she puffed out her breath and relaxed her stomach, wincing as she watched his palm rise along with it.

"That's better. Who does this body belong to, Rose?" His gaze was sharp, cutting through her defenses.

"You, Master Bear."

"Kane."

Her eyes shot to his. She stared at him questioningly. "I don't understand."

"This is my apartment, Rose. Here, you aren't a trainee and until you recognize the switch to Dom, I am Kane."

"Okay." She felt a shiver of anticipation at the switch in their relationship course through her. A sharp reminder that she needed to check on Tucker couldn't even douse the pleasure that heated her heart.

Kane drew small circles on her stomach and around her belly button. "If this body belongs to me, who are you to criticize its beauty and sensuality, Rose?"

"I'm trying, but it's not easy to accept how much weight I've picked up. I haven't gotten used to the changes it brought to my body and I'm not sure I ever will."

"Hmm. That's going to pose a problem to the success of your training. A true submissive knows how to completely embrace the concept of her body and who it belongs to in its entirety. Unless you can conquer that, you're likely to fail."

Rose lowered her eyes. She felt like a miserable failure. All she'd wanted to do since she'd arrived on the island was to impress him with her complete submission, especially once he started paying attention to her. She might just as well blurt out the sordid tale of her deceit and lies and leave because he'd never be interested in a half-hearted submissive.

"Don't despair, Rose," he said in a smooth rumble that tickled at her heartstrings. "That's why I'm here. To guide you and show you just how beautiful and seductive your body is." He stroked a sensual trail from her knee to her hip. "Show me the parts you hate the most about yourself, little one. Is it there or is it here?" He continued to caress a path over her bulging stomach and around each breast. "I need to know, my rosebud," he said against her lips, his eyes seared into hers, "because then I'll know where to begin loving you first."

Rose's heart missed a beat as she stared into his eyes so close to hers. His words echoed over and over in her mind. He'd said before how beautiful he found her body but the way he just said it, alluding to love ... it confused her. Did he mean to break down the way she saw herself by loving her curves, or did he mean love ... of the heart?

"Kane, you're not playing fair."

"Nothing is ever fair ... when it comes to love, sweetie."

"Love?" Butterflies danced in her stomach as she stared at him, unbeknownst to her, with her heart in her eyes.

"Breathe, baby, it's kind of a necessity for survival," he teased as he brushed his lips over hers, softly, like the wings of a moth testing the breeze on its first flight.

"So soft and warm." His breath teased hers to puff from deep in her chest as she exhaled to merge in the space between their mouths. His lips glided over hers, disseminating a sensual softness doused in glorious heat. She trembled at his patience. Lord, she'd forgotten the patience with which he kissed when he aimed to break through defenses. It wasn't a dive into the depths. Oh, no, he had perfected moving with erotic precision, giving her the impression that he was memorizing the shape of her mouth, the feel of her lips. He circled one hand to cradle the back of her head and the other firmly wrapped around her neck. She was helpless, completely under his spell. Her body and her will no longer reacted to her commands, it all gravitated to the game he played with his mind over hers.

"I love your lips, Rose. I could spend hours nibbling and munching on them," he murmured, ignoring her moan, silently begging for more and continued to take his own sweet time possessing her mouth.

"But first, I need to pay homage to the softest, hottest and wettest part of your body." Rose gasped as he slithered lower, imparting a tantalizing foray of open-mouthed kisses down the center of her body until he reached his aim and flicked his tongue over her clitoris. "Not to mention the most sensual bouquet that drives me fucking insane with lust."

This was a different Kane than the one she'd come to know over the past couple of months. Rose became unsettled. Did he suspect something? She found no rhyme or reason to his sudden change of mood this morning from last night. It was as if he was a different person, switching from the cold, calculating Master who had punished her mercilessly to blistering hot in the blink of an eye.

Then she felt it, with the first erotic sweep of his tongue over her still slightly swollen labia. Within that one caress and the tenderness of his rough hands spreading her legs wide as he settled his broad shoulders between her thighs, peeked through the caring and loving Dom she fell in love with so many years ago.

"Ah, baby, already so wet for me," he purred as he found the treasure between her legs; pleased that her labia was already glistening with her honeyed juices.

Rose fisted her hands in the sheet as he slowly teased her nether lips apart. A finger dipped inside, wetting it and then he sensually spread the wetness around her clit.

"Oh, sweet lord!" She jerked as he immediately started to rub the little nub with quick, hard motions. It completely yanked her out of her comfort zone. The slight twinge of pain was a reminder of the whipping but it only added to the rush of pheromones that heated her blood. His touch wasn't tentative, it was perfect and aimed to get her off quickly.

"Come! I need to come," she managed to gasp the plea, ignorant to the starkness of Kane's gaze as he watched her writhe and jag in his hold.

"Come, Rose."

He pressed harder, rubbed quicker, and before she could comprehend the heat that flushed into her chest cavity, her body bowed in a perfect arch as a raw carnal scream echoed in the room.

"Oh god, oh god!" she whimpered, desperately trying to find her equilibrium that he'd shattered with no effort at all.

"So beautiful," he murmured, his gaze fixated on the grimace on her face as he ruthlessly fed the waves of pleasure, pinching and rolling the swollen nub that had her tumbling head first into another turbulent foray of spasms that rocked her entire body.

"Hold fast, little dove, it's my turn now and I get to taste and feast from my favorite meal," he growled against her stomach that quivered as she tried to come down to earth. Her eyes met his and she felt herself drowning in the murky depths of his warm brown eyes that had turned as dark as the decadent chocolate she loved so much.

"M-meal?" she stammered.

"Yes, my rosebud ... you."

Rose's breathing turned erratic and choppy as he tickled the soft skin with the tip of his tongue where the smooth puffy folds hid her treasure.

"Tell me first, baby, are you very sore?" He smiled at the catlike mewl that slipped from deep within her throat as he licked the top of her slit teasingly.

"Just a twinge, but no, I'm not sore." Her fingers clawed at the bedding in an attempt to keep from grasping his head and guiding his mouth and tongue where she needed it ... hard and delving deep inside her pussy.

"Please, Kane ... I need to touch you," she begged in a croaky whisper. She held her breath as she felt his body tense against her thighs. "I'm sorry. I shouldn't have asked."

His gaze remained warm as he stared at her. A barely there smile set her mind at ease. He took her hands and placed them on his shoulders.

"This is as much as I'm prepared to give. Keep them there, Rose. If they stray, it's over."

"Thank you." Rose rolled her eyes at her stupid response but Kane took it in stride.

"It's my pleasure, my pet."

"I ... am I supposed to call you Master now?" Rose was confused and too scared to do something wrong that would make him stop.

Kane lowered his head and stared at her spread open sex. He inhaled deeply and sighed in pleasure at the decadent bouquet that filled his nostrils.

"No, baby. This is all about pleasure. Yours and mine."

Rose relaxed and flattened her palms over his shoulders, drooling at the feel of his strength as she felt the ropey muscles flex and ripple as he leaned closer.

"Oh my," she moaned as he blew a breath of hot air against her gaping pussy and then shattered her circuits by licking a slow path up and down her slit, from top to bottom, ending with a few salacious flicks on her clit. He repeatedly teased her until she thrashed in helpless surrender against him. He finally relented and sucked her clit, drawing a primal groan of ecstasy from her as he twirled his tongue around the tip.

"And now ... I feast."

Kane pressed his mouth against the satiny folds, licking at the wetness with obvious enjoyment. Rose groaned as her loins flared with heat and jerked as he rubbed her clit with slow circular movements while lashing at the silky folds with his tongue. He tucked his face into her loins, triggering a rush of sensations to flush her pussy with a generous helping that he lapped up with a deep growl.

"Fuck, baby, I could become addicted to the taste of you. I want more and I know just how to get it from you."

Kane smiled in that bad boy, wicked way that left her defenseless and vulnerable, physically and emotionally. He slid two fingers inside her and began to pump. He twisted his hand, searching and finding the spongy pad of nerves inside her.

"Freaking ... good lord," she moaned as potent jolts of rapture hiked the pressure inside her, threatening to explode. "More," she begged for it, for that final push as she canted her hips against his face. Heat engulfed her chest and rushed toward her loins.

"Don't force it, little one," he said with a smile against her skin as he closed his teeth around her clitoris, biting down gently. Her moan raised an octave, her body spiraling higher and higher as she teetered on the edge. Kane clamped his teeth around the nub and shook his head.

"Ahhh … gaaawwd!" Rose graveled a low grunt. She jerked and then screamed as heat exploded all over her body with her essence gushing from her as she squirted into Kane's waiting mouth.

"Yes, little one. This is what I'm after," he rasped as he sucked at the onrush, slurping loudly, greedily at the juicy slithers of nectar that rolled off his lips and dribbled down his chin.

"Oh my god, I've never done that before," Rose wailed, completely mortified as she stared at his face buried between her thighs, battling to control the spasms that shook through her.

"Get used to it, Rose. I believe I just found my all-time favorite dish."

For once Rose didn't cringe when he ran an appreciative look over her body. She felt free from the chains of self-consciousness, of castigating herself over the choices she made in the past. A small voice in the back of her head cautioned her it was only a fleeting thing, that as soon as the shackles of euphoria loosened its hold on her, the guilt would come rearing back.

None of that mattered. Not at this moment when he stared at her with such hunger and greed etched on his face. It was there because he wanted her, Rose Lovett, the woman she had become, not the one she knew chained him to the past.

For now, she buried all the negative thoughts in the hope that bubbled to life inside her. She was right where she wanted to be. Here, with Kane, to love him and help him to see that she could be the submissive he was searching for. Maybe in time, he'd realize the love she offered was stronger than the pain she'd caused and grasp at how much more life had to offer.

Rose held her breath as she noticed the carnal light flare in his eyes when he caught her staring at him. She smiled tentatively and the dark look brightened. She dragged in a breath. A flash of hope. In his eyes and in her heart. It was like a bright star flickering in a hopelessly dark universe that shimmered invitingly at her.

He brushed his fingers over her cheek. "Rose …"

Her heart went out to him at the visual struggle he had with the conflict inside him. The past held onto a tightrope, refusing to let go. She flailed inside her mind, realizing for the first time how much he must have suffered believing she had died in the fire. The powerful Master Bear was a beast trapped inside the cage of his past, one that refused to release him to the future.

He shook his head, his eyes turned cold as the man she'd woken up to morphed right in front of her eyes, back into the unmovable, stoic Master Bear who had locked his heart and feelings from everyone, except his family.

"I was a fool," he muttered as he stared at her, the distrust he'd been harboring scathing with a vengeance at his insides. His heart was frozen. He'd believed he could love again but no matter how hard he tried, he couldn't unlock the iron fist that clamped around his ability to allow emotions to rule his mind.

"Kane, there's always hope," she whispered, desperate to reach the part of him that he'd opened to her for such a brief and wonderful moment.

"No," he snapped as he pushed her to the center of the bed, drilling his fingers inside her pussy with deep, firm strokes as he sucked wildly on her nipple.

"Kane, please let's …"

"Master Bear, sub. This is what I'm allowed, only this. I understand it, I've lived it for seventeen years. I don't fucking need anything more," he rasped in a raw voice.

Rose's breathing turned erratic as she struggled to overcome the disappointment and heartache for the man she loved with all her heart.

"Ahh, shit," she cried as he thrust inside her. His cock stretched her pussy with one hard plunge that punched her straight into a breathless tide and evacuated all thoughts from her mind.

"Master Bear!" she moaned as pleasure rippled through her even with his rough treatment.

Kane was deaf to her cry as he closed his mind to his surroundings and pounded into her with astounding and mind-blowing speed. His mind snapped as he let loose the demon inside him with a primal growl, a grimace of raw intensity on his face.

"This, little dove, is all that matters. Fucking your brains out. Don't expect anything else from me … ever."

His words registered, but Rose was too overwhelmed by the pressure gathering inside her loins. Her nails dug into his shoulders and then—he was gone.

"Noo! Damn you," she wailed at the loss. She gasped as he spread her legs wide and buried his face into her pussy, all in one suave move. He sucked and licked with harsh, uncouth and slurping sounds that caused her lust to spiral into overdrive. He tilted her hips higher and angled his face to allow for a deeper delving of her channel as he sucked up the juices she had no way of controlling.

"Yes, my pet and you fucking love every second of this, don't you?" With gleaming eyes, he pushed his finger to the hilt inside her anus, twirling and stretching it as he nibbled on her clit. He laughed at her scream that slammed against the walls at the unexpectedness and burning pain his rough action caused.

"Yes, Rose, tonight I'm going to take what you denied me the other night," he said in a deep voice, grunting as he watched her with a dark expression. "Yes, scream for me, sub," he taunted as another cry escaped her lips. He sat on his knees between her legs. "Again, my pet, let me hear that hoarse cry," he ordered as he pushed three fingers into her pussy, and commenced to fuck her both ways with fast deep plunges that destroyed Rose's ability to think. His lips quirked as she moaned and twitched uncontrollably.

Rose was lambasted by the sensations he created with his hands, ruthless as they were, with the only intent to take what he wanted. Her mind had struck a blank; she couldn't form a coherent thought let alone utter a word. Her body arched as heat began to flow toward her loins and then ... once again, he was gone.

"Damn you! Stop doing that," she wailed as her core tightened painfully.

He laughed in response and before she realized his intent, he once again yanked her legs apart and buried his face into her pussy. This time he plundered ruthlessly, his only aim to spike her lust higher to keep her on the edge.

"Such beauty in a swollen pink nub," he said as he teased her clit, causing her to jerk at how sensitive it was from all the bites and sucking. Even the ganglia deep inside her felt raw from all the rubbing. And oh lord, her back hole burned from the continued and merciless finger fucking. And still, he didn't let up.

He kept her on the edge with ruthless intent, pulling away every time she was on the verge of a climax, ignoring her pleas to let her come.

"You're exactly what I've been looking for, sub RL. A sub who has the stamina and the body to withstand everything I take from it.

Rose was in a vortex and his words didn't compute, but she locked them away to mull over later. She kept coiling higher and higher—yet he kept her from reaching the top. Her loins cramped and pulsed with the need to climax.

"Please, Master Bear, make me come. I beg you. I need to come!"

She gasped when Kane flipped her over on her stomach and yanked her onto her knees, flicking his thumb over her clit as he plunged his fingers deep inside her pussy.

"Just look at that. So, fucking needy and wet. Perfectly prepared for me."

She whimpered helplessly.

"Yes!" he growled as her screams filled the atmosphere as he thrust his cock into her anus without any warning. To the hilt in one hard thrust. "I love the sounds you make, sub," he taunted her with his breathing that sounded haggard in her ear as she sobbed against the burning pain.

Rose physically prepared herself for him to begin his pounding, her back bowing in a combination of submission and fear. But as he'd done since she'd woken up to his stare, he once again surprised her and his movements stilled.

"Fuck," he grunted. "Fuck and damnation." He brushed his hand over her tense back. "Dammit, Rose, how the fuck do you do this to me?" he grated through clenched teeth. The tension in his body spoke of his own lust, but he quieted the demon inside him as he slowly stroked her clit and pussy to awakening before he began to rock into her.

"I can't . . . I need to . . . ooh, fuck, that feels good," Rose moaned into the sheets. Her fingers clawed and bunched the material between her fingers.

Rose had been fucked in the ass many times. But never felt like this. The sensations he generated with the gentle sliding motions into her ass exploded in her loins—heated her body like she was on fire. She couldn't comprehend what was happening. It shot her into a maelstrom of confusion. It had never been like this—in the past—with him. He was so hot, scorching and every plunge awakened every nerve ending that surrounded his satiny shaft. Each thrust invited the coil to tighten inside her loins.

"You make me wish for so many things, sub."

His voice sounded far off, an echo of melancholy as he tugged on her nipples and brushed his fingers over her clit. Softly at first and then harder until she pleaded for more. With a grunt of pleasure at her complete subjugation, he finally pushed his fingers deep inside her pussy.

"Ohh ... yess," she hissed as he tapped against the ganglia of nerves deep inside her and simultaneously strummed the swollen nub of her clitoris with his thumb.

"Holy freaking ... helll!" she screamed as she exploded, drowning in the waves of pleasure rolling over her as Kane continued to thrust into her— deeper, faster—his fingers all the while not wavering in their quest to stimulate her to keep climaxing over and over.

"My god," she grunted. Her eyes rolled upward in their sockets as she felt the scorching heat of his semen fill her bowels. Her whimper sounded weak as the force of his ejaculate so deep inside her, triggered another orgasm of her own. Her knees gave way under the force of the spasms that continued to wreak havoc through her. She slumped on the bed as Kane withdrew, her body shuddering and her chest heaving from exertion.

Rose whimpered weakly as he flipped her over, his hands much gentler. She blinked and their eyes met. She couldn't read his expression. The stoic mask was back in place.

"I'm not going to apologize, Rose." He heaved in a deep sigh. It crackled in the atmosphere with the harmony of a forgotten melody—thin, tired and filled with hopelessness. "This is who I am and always will be. I had hoped ... believed it might be different ... with you."

Rose reached out and cupped his cheek. "Kane, let me—"

He moved, just an inch but it was enough to dislodge her hand. He caught it before she lowered it. He stared into her eyes for long, tense moments and then he placed a tender kiss in her palm.

"No, I have nothing to give. Let's leave it at that."

He got up and took one last look at her disheveled body, lying in a relaxed repose, completely satiated. She had never looked more beautiful.

"I can't promise that I'll stay away from you, Rose. You are too enticing and I can't resist the erotic pull that gravitates me to you. If you don't want me near you, you better add me as a hard limit on your file, otherwise, I'm going to continue gorging myself on your charming body. Heed my warning, sub, because I'll never offer you more."

Rose watched him disappear into the bathroom with a grieving heart. She had done this to him. She was the cause of the coldness that couldn't melt inside his heart. Tears began to flow as she jumped from the bed. She grabbed his shirt and, struggling into it, she ran from his apartment.

Rose had never known such despair, not even during that long year of struggling with the burn wounds, operations, and the desperation to keep the unborn baby inside her alive. At times it had been touch and go, but she and Tucker had both had the will to survive. If only she'd had the same strength later to have done the right thing and told Kane about his child sooner ... much sooner.

"I love him so much and I'm going to break his heart a second time. Oh god, how am I ever going to make it up to him?"

Chapter Eighteen

"What did you find, Parker?" Stone sat down at the head of the large oval table in the boardroom of BSE. "Alexa, please arrange with the chef to serve our breakfast here," he said as she headed toward the door after serving them coffee.

"Already done," she said in an affronted tone, like it was something he should know not to ask.

"Yes, and tell them to hurry, I'm starving."

Shane chuckled as he looked at Kane. "No reason to wonder what spiked your appetite."

Kane didn't spar in return as usual, just took a sip of his coffee, his expression morose and closed. After his shower the previous morning, he'd returned to an empty room, which in retrospect was better. He'd instructed Brad to take charge of the training and went to his house in Key Largo for the day. He'd spend the night and returned early this morning. He needed time to purge the memories that had surfaced from his mind. It had taken a sleepless night, but he'd managed to lock the door firmly once again. He ignored the concerned looks from Stone and Shane as he glanced at Parker. "Let's have it, Parker."

"Right. Ace's speculation was spot on. We uncovered a string of coded communication between Malik and Chan Ho, the assumed leader of the Sun Lee Fong Triads. From the ones we've been able to decode, it's evident that they have been involved in money laundering in the U.S. We found numerous properties the Triads purchased specifically in L.A., Washington, New York, and Miami. All registered to a corporation by the name of SLFT Enterprises."

"Jesus, that's ballsy. SLFT, aka Sun Lee Fong Triads, I assume?" Kane shook his head. "Criminals never cease to amaze me."

"There are also two global logistic companies, one in L.A. and the other in Miami. We can assume they're preparing for distribution in and out of the States without having to source transportation. They're setting up a complete network to run a full-fledged criminal organization in the United States." Zeke flicked through the information on his iPad as he talked.

"In the middle of mafia territory. I can already see the conflict and wars that's going to invite," Ace grated irritably.

"I'm still looking into a couple of properties mentioned in less prominent areas. Zeke and I are speculating it might be whorehouses or drug kitchens. One of the properties in Miami shows signs of life. There's a lot of traffic going in and out. It might be a cash drop-off point. We zoomed in on it last night using the GeoEye system. Guess who's hiding there?" Parker asked and continued, not expecting a response. He flicked an image onto the monitor. "Zikri Malik, in all his glory, and this man, who we can't link to any identity kit anywhere. For all we know, that's Chan Ho, because we can't find a photo of the very elusive Triad leader anywhere on the web."

"So, Malik isn't in China as speculated but hiding right under our noses." Kane mused as he stared at the images. "Is there a way you can get a drone close enough to listen in to what's going on in that house?"

Parker brought up the GeoEye system and studied the property. "Hmm, not sure it's possible. Zeke? What do you think?"

"It'll be risky. Security seems to be airtight. See there?" Zeke used a laser pen to point out various sensors around the house and fence perimeters. "Those sensors are top of the range and the latest technology only available currently in China. It sweeps not only the ground level but angles up at intervals as high as ten miles in the air."

"Yeah, and for our drones to pick up clear communication, it'll have to be as close as two to five miles max," Parker said.

"Seems they have a lot to hide." Stone leaned forward as he studied the house.

Kane made a mental note of the coordinates shown on the screen. A sideways glance at Shane confirmed they were on the same page. Malik made an error in judgment to come back to the U.S. If he ever left, for that matter.

"There's specific mention made in recent messages about eliminating the middleman who apparently is causing a delay in the turn of their investment, as they refer to it." Parker gestured to Zeke. "Zeke also found the channel on the dark web Malik uses to relay instructions to one Sam Jones, aka, Leon Salvino."

"Sam Jones?" Hawk queried.

"An assumed name. Most criminals use a different name on the dark web. The same goes for Malik and Chan Ho but we managed to crack the IP addresses and that's how we traced it to them."

"Anything of particular interest in the string of communication with Leon?" Kane tapped his fingers on the desk.

Parker shifted in his chair and cleared his throat. "You're the main topic in all of them."

"Me?" Kane stilled.

"It seems the Triads are annoyed about the delay in the production of the Space Riders movie. They want their money and are becoming impatient.

It seems that Leon has delayed it pending you committing to contracting all of us for another series."

"That's not going to happen and I made that clear more than once," Kane snapped. "He's a fucking asshole and naïve if he still believes after our meeting the other day that he can force me into anything."

Parker glanced at Stone. "There's a more immediate issue. We're concerned about an email received by one of the trainees. At first, we ignored it because it came from the school her son is at. As soon as she opened it, our nanoT tracking system flagged it as a cloned account. We checked it. The email came from an unknown location and IP we can't trace, not yet anyway."

Zeke swiped his finger over his iPad and the message flashed on the large monitor on the wall.

Time for playing games is over. We arranged a visit to Phillips Academy tomorrow to give a talk at their Career Day open house. We are specifically going to talk about two icons in

the movie industry, Kane and Shane Rothman. I'm looking forward to meeting your son. We can't wait to take him out to ... shall we say ... dinner?

You have ten hours to change my mind with some positive development. Do what I expect, or you lose another man in your life.

Kane felt a cold shiver race down his spine. "Who was it sent to?"

Parker rubbed his jaw. "Rose Lovett."

"So, someone is blackmailing Rose," Stone mused as he read the message. "I can't fathom with what. It's not as though we're dealing with any high-profile cases at the moment, and as far as I know, she's never been seen skulking around anywhere."

Kane's fingers tingled as he remembered tracing the tiny scars in Rose's hairline.

"It has to be Leon and Roy. Who else would have enough information about Shane and me to talk about us at a career day?" Kane shook his head. "But it doesn't make sense. The way it's worded alludes to either Shane or me having a connection with her son."

"He's not mine. I made fucking sure there are no Shane Juniors running around anywhere."

"Same here and I sure as hell know I never met Rose until she arrived at the island."

"It *was* them. I contacted the school and they confirmed that the vice president of Marvel Studios and a Hollywood agent visited the school on career day." Parker tapped his screen. "I checked Rose's phone register and she made some calls last night minutes after she read the email."

"The first call was to an unlisted number we can't trace, which we assume might be her son. It's not strange as many parents nowadays use it as a measure to keep their kids safe from pedophiles," Zeke said. "She tried three other numbers, one is a landline in Massachusetts and the other two cell phones. We traced it to her parents, Thomas and Rita Lovett, but none of those calls were answered. Lastly, she called the dormitory of the school."

"So, what are they after?" Ace interjected.

"The only thing I can think of is that they want to use her to blackmail us. Maybe record scenes or take photos. It'll be the perfect ammunition to have a hold over us. Don't get me wrong, I'm not ashamed of the lifestyle we live, but we all know how it'll impact our members. If they know about Castle Sin it's already placing them at risk. With the range of high profile and public clients we have, we can't afford to be exposed." Kane searched his mind but couldn't recall Rose ever acting suspicious in the training academy or the dungeons.

"I never noticed anything suspicious in her actions. She's never attempted to take any photos, that's for sure. In fact, she's one of the most committed trainees we've had in a long time," Stone said.

"Hence the threat. She's obviously not dancing to their tune." Shane stretched out his legs. He glanced at the door as it opened. Alexa and three servers arrived with their breakfast. "About time, little snip."

She snorted and tilted her nose but didn't respond. For once, she didn't offer her usual snide comments about their fat-and-carb-filled meal. As soon as she was satisfied each man received his food, she ushered the servers out.

"How was Rose recruited?" Hawk tapped his iPad and searched for her personal file.

"I checked it after our previous meeting," Stone said around a bite of bacon. "Hunter Sutton spotted her in Club Sensation as a fresh member. She fit the specs of older subs we asked for to a T. Apparently, she was invited by one of our earlier employed subs, Kathy Mulder, to join."

"I remember Kathy. Nice tits," Zeke interjected.

"And her reason for giving up a lucrative career as an artist for two years?" Hawk continued to prod.

"She claimed she needed a new challenge in her life. That she'd been in a slump and lost her inspiration to paint. She believed following her passion to be a true submissive might be what she needed to kickstart her artistic side again." Stone shrugged. "Shane and I found her to be open and honest during our initial meeting with her."

"So, it could mean that someone contacted her after she'd arrived on the island," Kane mused thoughtfully. He glanced at Shane, his food forgotten for the moment. "Have you and Stone chatted with her yet?"

"There's been no time, especially since you had her locked in your apartment for days on end."

"And you, Parker, did you uncover anything further in her past?"

"Nothing. She's as clean as a whistle ... except for one thing."

"One huge problem," Zeke snorted.

"Rose Lovett didn't exist until sixteen years ago," Parker said.

Kane felt his stomach lurch. "Exactly sixteen years?"

"Lemme check." Parker's fingers slid over the screen. "No, closer to fifteen-and-a-half."

Kane relaxed and cursed his wild imagination, but he couldn't shake the familiarity that intensified the more time he spent in Rose's presence. He sighed and said, "Make sure you keep a close eye on her on the CCTV recordings. Just in case we're missing something and she's cleverer than we think."

"We now have proof that Leon and Roy are in cahoots with Malik and the Triads. Did you find anything that indicates anyone else is involved from the Marvel Studios?" Shane finished eating and sat back.

"No, they are definitely working alone. I've dropped all the files and information on how they operate as well as the communication we've decoded so far in a secure network folder, named SLFT. You all have the security key to access it." Parker closed his iPad and started to eat.

"I think it's time to take this to the DOJ and Alan Bradley. I'll get Alexa to set up a meeting for us with Eckard Duke, the Attorney General of DOJ and Alan," Stone said and pressed the buzzer on the console in front of him.

"I suggest you get Homeland Security and the FBI involved as well. It's an opportunity to crack down on the Triads in the U.S. at the same time," Kane said and took the last bite of bacon. "Before they ingrain themselves too deep."

"Good idea." Stone's voice droned in the background as he gave the instructions to Alexa over the telecom.

"There's still one thing that bothers me. How did Leon and Roy find out about Castle Sin? It's not common knowledge and no one who had been trained here or worked for us would break our confidence. Of that, I'm pretty sure." Kane straightened. "It brings us back to the question of whether there's someone on the island playing a double role. This is the third time information only known by those on the island has been leaked to the outside."

"Zeke and I have scoured every person's background again. We can't find anything." Parker sounded just as frustrated as Kane.

"If you're looking for information that's not freely available and you're a criminal, where would you look for answers or information?" Hawk looked between Zeke and Parker.

"The deep and dark web," they responded in unison.

"Fuck! We've been so busy looking into these things, it never came to mind. You're right. We're gonna check if anyone reached out for information about any of us. If it's there, I'll fucking find it and we can finally strangle the fucker backstabbing us."

Shane didn't bother to hide the dark awakening of the devil inside him as he listened to the feedback. There was nothing he and Kane wouldn't do to protect their family and loved ones. Shane was livid that the men they'd come to trust attempted to blackmail Kane, who had suffered more than enough in his life. He didn't need this added aggravation.

"Let us know the moment you find something." Stone stood up. "Kane, Hawk, Shane, and I will attend the meeting with the DOJ. Ace, I need you to set a team in place to start ghosting Leon and Roy. I want to know what those bastards do before they think of it."

"We arranged a picnic at the paradise alcove for all the trainees. Let's join them there. I don't want them to become too complacent and start slacking in their training because our minds are elsewhere," Hawk said as they left the room.

"I trust this time all of them are properly clothed. I don't want a repeat of what happened to Rose that day they were naked on the beach."

"No need to worry, Kane, I gave very strict instructions. Shorts and t-shirts over their bathing suits. Lesson learned, cousin."

"What do you mean, is my son home?" Rose felt as if a vice tightened around her body, slowly squeezing the breath from her lungs. She gasped and sank down on her knees, hardly registering the heat of the sand against her shins. The gay laughter and shrieks from the Masters, trainees, and training Doms having fun on the other side of the alcove, dimmed in the background

"Are you saying he's not?"

Rose could hear the panic in the voice of the dormitory father.

"No! It's in the middle of the school term, what would he be doing home? What the devil is going on there, Mr. Nicker?" Rose's voice raised shrilly. She could hear the edge of hysteria creep through.

"I'm sure it's just a misunderstanding. I got the impression from Mr. Greenhorn that Mr. Salvino from Marvel Studios, obtained written permission from you yesterday to pick Tucker up from school."

"What?" Rose's voice croaked out so softly, it drifted off on the breeze.

"But he didn't return last night and he's still not back. I can't reach him on his cell phone, which is why I assumed he might have spent the night at home after they met you for dinner."

"I didn't have dinner with them. I'm not even in Massachusetts, Mr. Nicker!" Rose was fast losing the tenuous hold she had over the panic that gripped her heart. The possibility that Salvino and Summers kidnapped her son to force her hand, made her stomach heave.

"This is worrying. Look, Ms. Lovett, don't panic. Perhaps I should've spoken to Mr. Greenhorn first. Let me find out from him if he's heard from Mr. Salvino. I'll be in contact soon."

The connection died and Rose lowered the phone to her lap. She felt defeated, raw, and at the mercy of two cruel men who used a teenage boy in their demented power game.

She answered her phone immediately as it vibrated again.

"Yes?"

"I'm sorry, Ms. Lovett, but we can't get ahold of Mr. Salvino either. Mr. Greenhorn already contacted the police and reported Tucker as missing."

"You better pray they find my son, Mr. Nicker, otherwise you and Mr. Greenhorn will wish you were never born."

"Now, now, Ms. Lovett, there's no need for such threats. I'm sure Tucker is just a little tardy today."

"My son isn't the tardy type! I'm getting on a plane as soon as I can and I promise you, if you don't have answers for me by the time I get there, there'll be hell to pay."

Rose ended the call and struggled to her feet. She felt lost, and apart from the need to get to Massachusetts as soon as possible, she had no idea what to do to find Tucker. She refused to consider that those bastards kidnapped him.

"I can't believe that. I just can't, because if I do … God, what do I do? How do I find him? Kane! I have to tell him. He'll know what to do."

Rose began to run, not once giving thought to doing what she knew Roy wanted from her in return for Tucker's safe return.

"*If* they have him. I pray they don't," she murmured as she ran around the alcove. She refused to sink so low. She'd rather risk Kane's fury and hate than betray him a second time.

The shrill sound of an alarm sounding right next to her scared her so badly that she fell to her knees and covered her ears. The sound of Kane and Stone's deep voices penetrated. She lifted her head and scrambled to her feet as they came running toward her.

"The breach is just on the other side of the alcove," Kane said as they ran past her, hardly giving her a glance.

Rose turned and followed everyone chasing after them to see what had triggered the underwater perimeter alarm. They arrived just in time to see

Kane and Stone haul someone in diving gear from the surf. They pushed him toward the beach.

"Who the hell are you?" Kane barked as he yanked the oxygen tank from the perpetrator's back and threw it on the sand while Stone pulled the diving mask and the hood from his head.

"Oh my god," Rose's shrill cry echoed in the enclosed alcove, drawing Kane's gaze to see her legs crumble as she fainted.

"Rose!" He ran toward her, the culprit forgotten as he knelt beside her and tapped her cheeks. "Rose, wake up."

"Holy Mother of God!"

Shane's raw exclamation dragged Kane's attention back to the figure struggling against Stone's hard hold on his arm. Kane felt his entire body flush with heat, sparked by disbelief. He couldn't remember moving but the next moment he stood in front of the young boy that stood tall and boldly returned his intense stare.

"Who are you?" Kane didn't recognize his own voice as he struggled to compute the vision in front of him.

"Tucker ... and I'm your son."

Kane couldn't move, except for his eyes that couldn't get enough of the young face that didn't flinch under his inspection. He didn't question the authenticity of the claim. He couldn't, seeing as the boy was an exact replica of himself as a teenager.

"How old are you?" His voice was thick with emotion.

"I'll be sixteen next week."

"Rose! Are you okay? Don't tell me you've got a fever again?"

Peyton's concerned voice registered in Kane's mind. He turned to stone as once again he envisioned feeling the small ridges of scars under his fingertips when he'd caressed Rose's face. He spun around and obliterated her with a malignant stare.

Rose shivered as she looked into his eyes blazing with anger as he stomped closer. She lost all sense of time. The whole world around her stopped moving and came to a complete halt as he reached her and hauled her to her feet, ignoring her cry of pain at the tight hold he had on her arm. Distraught and disillusioned, and now hateful, past all caring and repair, he looked into her eyes.

"Take them out."

Rose didn't have to ask what he meant. It was obvious that one way or the other, he'd made the connection.

"Kane, I—"

"Now."

His voice didn't rise, he didn't shout but he could just as well have. The effect on her was devastating. In that one word, she felt her entire life fall apart. She felt the burn of tears behind her eyes. She choked back a scream that scratched at her throat to be released. Her gaze dropped, unable to look at the venomous hatred in his face again. She wished it could vanish in the blur of tears blinding her; such a consoling thought, if only evanescent. Colorless and silent.

If only ... but it was too late for that.

Her fingers trembled but she managed to remove the color contacts.

He clamped his hand under her chin and forced her gaze to his. His breath hissed from his chest as he read the guilt in her ice blue eyes.

"You fucking lying, deceitful bitch."

"Please let me explain."

"No, you can't. You're dead, remember? Burned to a cinder in an explosion that obliterated my house, that destroyed my life." He spoke in a soft voice but it carried so much strength and hate that Rose wanted to crawl into herself and vanish.

"Let go of my mother."

Rose whimpered as Tucker spoke behind Kane, his voice clear and sharp. She could envision him, standing ready in a Krav Maga position, to take on a man twice his size to protect her. She'd insisted that he take lessons from a young age and he'd achieved his junior black belt at the beginning of the year.

"Please, Kane. I beg you, not in front of Tucker."

Kane's hand dropped immediately, but his gaze promised hell and fury to be unleashed on her head. He took a step sideways and with a sob, Rose grabbed hold of Tucker and held on for dear life.

"How could you do this to me? I've been scared out of my mind when I heard you disappeared from school. I thought you'd been ..." Rose swallowed the words as she became aware of how enraptured everyone watching was by the drama unfolding.

"I'm sorry I made you worry, but I had to come," Tucker said into her hair.

"Back to the beach, everyone. The food just arrived, and you know how upset chef gets if it's wasted." Danton ushered everyone back to the other side of the alcove, leaving the cousins to deal with Rose and Tucker.

"Let me get this straight; are you saying that Rose is ... Narine?" Ace asked as shocked by the turn of events as the rest of the men staring at mother and son.

"Why don't we ask her?" Kane's voice clipped through thin lips. He couldn't take his eyes off his son, but at the same time, he struggled with the fury that threatened to choke him from the inside. "Well? Are you? Narine Bosch?"

Rose cringed at the question forming in Tucker's eyes. She had never told him the sordid tale. She never wanted him to know how cruel life could be if you made the wrong choices.

"Mom? I don't understand."

Rose licked her lips that suddenly felt cracked and dry. She squared her shoulders. Her secret was out in the open. Tucker was going to find out the truth sooner or later. It might as well be sooner.

"Narine Bosch died in that explosion," she said softly. "The bomb ... detonated too early. I couldn't get the latch open and ..." Her voice thinned as the horror of that night played out inside her mind. "My face ... a ball of fire engulfed me just as I dropped through the opening. I ... it took too many operations and reconstructive surgery to count to ... to turn me into Rose Lovett."

"You tried to kill Dad?" Tucker's disbelieving voice shocked through Rose.

"No! Oh god no! It wasn't like that ... it ... I ..." Rose faltered and raised pleading eyes to Kane. His body looked like it was carved out of stone. His eyes were almost black in his immeasurably expressionless face.

Shane was the one who took pity on her. "This isn't the time or the place. Why don't we introduce Tucker to everyone and get to know him?" He glanced at Kane who still hadn't moved. If he blinked, no one noticed. "Kane, you and Rose need privacy to talk. Let it go for now." He slung his arm around Tucker's shoulders. "I'm guessing you must be hungry?"

"Starving."

"Let's go eat."

Rose didn't move. She couldn't. Kane's fearsome gaze pierced through her and pinned her in place.

"Yes, we need to talk but I need to calm down first. If I'm alone with you now, I won't be responsible for my actions. Wrapping my hands around your throat and squeezing the life out of you sounds like a beautiful prospect at this moment."

"Kane, it's not—"

"Shut the fuck up. I don't want to hear it or look at your lying, deceitful face, even less." He stomped to the end of the alcove. "Danton!" he bellowed, ignoring her shivering form.

"Hey, Kane," Danton jogged closer. His gaze moved between them.

"Lock her in the cage in the punishment room in my dungeon. I leave her in your care. No visitors and she stays there until I come to fetch her."

"Kane, you're acting irrational. You're angry and—"

"I'm furious, Danton, but I'm thinking clearly and rationally for the first time in almost seventeen years." He flung a look of disgust over his shoulder at Rose. "Get this slut out of my sight."

Rose gasped at his crude insult and sank to her knees as she watched him stomp off. She had known this would happen, but she'd secretly hoped he'd be so happy to find out she was still alive that he'd at least try to listen and understand.

It seemed Kane had changed in more ways than she could ever have imagined.

"He'll cool off, Rose."

"I suppose he will, but that's not going to change how much he now hates me."

Chapter Nineteen

"You have to eat, Rose. This is the second day that you haven't touched your food." Danton scowled at her as he noticed the untouched plate of food next to the cage in the Bear's Dungeon.

"I'm not hungry."

"Do you want to stretch your legs?"

"And have him angry at you for disobeying his orders? No, thank you, I'm fine."

Rose pulled up her legs and clasped her arms around them. She didn't have the strength to complain or fight the conditions she had been forced to live in for the past two days. It was hot and humid in the punishing room and she could smell how she reeked of sweat. The t-shirt and shorts she'd worn to the beach stuck to her body and she was tempted to take them off. She leaned her head back against the steel bars. It was uncomfortable lodgings, to say the least. The solid steel puppy slave cage was high enough for her to sit up but too short for her to lie down and straighten her legs. At least Danton had placed a padded board at the bottom before he'd locked her in.

The worst of it was that she wasn't given the courtesy of toilet breaks. She had to use a bedpan, which was no easy task to get her shorts off and on in the limited space. It was beyond embarrassing when Danton fetched it to empty it.

"I don't care. Come, just five minutes." Danton unlocked the cage. Rose didn't move.

"No, Sir. I'm not going to get you into trouble. Thank you though." She smiled wanly. "I can't even blame him. I deserve to be treated like this. I still can't believe that he didn't chase me off the island immediately and ... and take my son away from me."

"He'll never do that, Rose. Kane might be angry now, but he's not a monster." Danton picked up the plate. "Can I at least bring you some fruit?"

He sighed as she shook her head. "Make sure you remain hydrated. Tonight, you'll eat. I don't want to start force feeding you, but I will if I have to."

Rose stared after him with dull eyes.

"So, now you're playing the martyr."

Rose startled at the deep timbre in the voice coming from the dark corner of the room. She squinted but couldn't make out anything.

"How long have you been there?"

"Long enough. I have to admit, watching and smelling your stinking body as you crawl around the cage doesn't give me the satisfaction I thought it would. I should've instructed Danton no amenities allowed. You would've looked a lot better covered in your own piss and shit."

Rose flinched at the violence that came along with the vile picture his words painted.

"If that'll make you feel better, go for it," she lilted as she tilted her head back against the steel bars again. "How is Tucker?"

"*My son* is well, thank you."

Rose didn't miss the hidden threat in how he worded and spat out the sentence. She searched the dark corner with concerned eyes.

"Where is he? Please don't tell me you brought him to the Castle! He's at an impressionable age, you can't … he's curious—"

"I may not have had the privilege of being a father for the first sixteen years of my son's life but I'm not a fucking idiot."

"I know and I'm sorry. That's not what I meant to imply. It's just—"

"Start eating, sub RL, or I'll instruct Danton to tie you to the cage and force feed you with a tube down your throat."

"Kane, please … I need to explain. Just let me—"

"No need. I get it. You realized you were pregnant and instead of just fucking telling me you don't want your child around a man like me, you pretended to be dead."

"That's not true! I didn't know I was pregnant, and at that point … I wasn't."

"What the fuck are you saying? Anyone can see Tucker is mine."

"He is … he was conceived … on that night."

She stared at him as he appeared like an apparition from hell. His eyes shot sparks of fire at her.

"I only realized I was pregnant when I was four months along. Up until then, I'd been under sedation most of the time. The operations, the skin grafts ..." She swallowed hard. "The moment the doctors detected the pregnancy I refused further medication. I was scared I'd lose him ... or that he might already have been affected by all the drugs. They had to stop my treatment and further reconstructive surgery had to wait until after he was born." She smiled. "I cried so much when I held him in my arms the first time. He was absolutely perfect, no defects and ... I always called him my miracle baby."

"Yes ... *you* held him in your arms. Who are you, exactly? Narine or Rose?"

Rose closed her eyes, realizing that Kane was still too angry to listen or even try to understand.

"Narine Bosch died in that explosion. Tucker never knew about her or what happened. To him, I've always been Rose."

"When did you tell him about me?"

431

Rose looked listlessly at him. Her smile felt painful. "I didn't. He found the picture you gave me that was taken on your sixteenth birthday. He recognized himself in you immediately. A couple of weeks later you and Shane appeared on a talk show. They showed pictures of you as teenagers. He put two and two together."

"You never told him." His voice grated raw in the atmosphere. "Let me guess. If he hadn't found out, you never would have."

Rose didn't respond. There was nothing she could say.

His boots scraped on the stone floor as he stomped off. His words floated over his shoulder as he disappeared through the door.

"Enjoy your accommodation, Rose Lovett. You'll be here for a long time."

"We've been compromised."

Zikri Malik looked up from the suspense novel he was reading. He wasn't much of a reader but sitting around doing nothing was getting to him. He missed being at the forefront of wheeling and dealing as the owner of various companies in the U.S. and Malaysia.

If it hadn't been for his stepfather's greed and love for luxury, none of this would've happened. The hate Zikri harbored for Amar Raja grew by leaps and bounds the longer he had to remain in hiding to avoid incarceration. He could only hope his legal team would find a way to have him absolved from all charges soon.

Then he'd pay the former prime minister a visit in jail. He was going to pay for ratting out his stepson. The only person, apart from Zikri's mother, who had stood by him when he was removed from the presidency.

He glanced at the wiry frame of the Chinese man pacing in front of the open sliding doors. Zikri knew from experience that his slender look was deceiving. He was as strong as a tiger and as fast as a fox. A master in more than one of the ancient combat fighting skills, he was feared by many and revered by the nation as the undefeatable champion of the Kung Fu World Championship since 2003.

Of course, they didn't know him as Chan Ho, the feared leader of the Sun Lee Fong Triads.

"What are you talking about?"

"One of my sources in the FBI just informed me that a meeting had been arranged with the DOJ."

"How does that affect us?"

"The topic of discussion is money laundering that involves Chinese Triads."

Zikri went cold. He didn't need to look into Chan Ho's eyes to know that he held him personally responsible for the information leaking out to the authorities. He simmered with anger. If it hadn't been for Salvino and Summers' greed they wouldn't be in this position. Him delaying the production of the Rothmans' final Space Riders movie must've triggered their suspicion to investigate further.

"Did your source say anything else? Who requested the meeting?"

"Be Secure Enterprises. Apparently, they're the CyberGhost in charge of protecting the data and offer overall security protocol to all the Government Institutions." Chan Ho continued to pace, puffing furiously on a thin black cigar.

Zikri's nose wrinkled at the potent and overly sweet smell of the tobacco permeating the air.

"Never heard of them."

"Neither have I." Chan Ho stopped and stood with his legs spread and his arms behind his back, staring at Zikri. "We have to convince them there is nothing to report to the DOJ."

"How are we supposed to do that?"

"Every man has a trigger; we just need to find theirs." He dragged long and hard on the cigar before he puffed out the smoke in perfectly round circles. He watched it float higher until they dissolved into slithers of nothingness. "We do have a problem."

"Which is?" Zikri shifted uncomfortably as the black eyes of the white-haired man pierced through him.

"We can't find any information on who owns the company or where their offices are. The company registration information is closed to the public. They don't operate on site at any of the Government buildings." Chan Ho remained motionless, his expression cold. "We have two options. Bribe someone at the County Recorder's Office for a copy of the original owner's certificate or we need a hacker to find where they operate from. Someone with the kind of skills to penetrate or avoid detection from the NanoT programs installed in the FBI and DOJ's operating systems. Someone who can use their own technology to find a backdoor leading back to them."

"NanoT? That kind of skill isn't available readily and it's not going to come cheap."

Chan Ho's face split into a brief sardonic smile. "That's your problem, Malik. I'm holding you personally accountable for the money I'm losing due to the delay in the release of the Space Riders film. I financed more than enough of your fuckups over the years. This is your responsibility, you will pay for it."

He turned to stare out of the window, his gaze followed the lazy fluttering of the sails of a boat at sea. The silence dragged and became thick and uncomfortable. Zikri's gaze locked onto the ribbon of smoke twisting and squirming like a garter snake in torment trying to escape until it dissolved into the atmosphere.

"Make it happen, Malik, and quick. If my operation in the U.S. is compromised ... I don't suppose I need to tell you what will happen then."

Zikri didn't respond but stomped out of the room. He might be a thieving criminal, but he wasn't a thug. He knew how to coerce in the business world. Bribing wasn't much different, but with a red cross on his back, he didn't dare set foot outside of the Miami mansion the Triads owned, especially not to waltz into a place where every angle was covered by CCTV cameras.

He had been surprised when Chan Ho had arrived two days ago. He never became personally involved in operational problems. That was why he paid Enforcers exorbitant amounts of money to ensure his instructions were followed. His reason for needing a vacation away from home didn't wash. Chan Ho didn't do anything without a purpose. Zikri had been on tenterhooks ever since.

"What's the rush?"

Zikri would've landed flat on his back if Li Jun, the massive bodyguard that had arrived with Chan Ho, didn't catch his arm as he ran into him turning into the hallway. He studied him speculatively. His black, beady eyes always made Zikri question his loyalty, but Chan Ho obviously trusted him. He never went anywhere without him.

"How would you like to make some extra cash?"

Li shifted and leaned his shoulder against the wall. He crossed his feet and licked his thick lips. Zikri held back the glee that his instinct had been spot on. Li was a money grabber.

"I'm always up for it." His heavy accent droned lazily over their heads.

"I need information from the County Recorder's Office. Be Secure Enterprises. I have their company registration number but the ownership information has been filed as closed, so it's not available to the public."

"And you need me to bribe the information out of some clerk? That's not my scene, Malik, and you should know that."

"I'll pay you double your daily rate," Zikri snapped. He knew only too well that Li strong armed people and those who didn't play along, he tortured or killed.

"I suppose I could deviate from my usual modus operandi." Li straightened. "When do you need it?"

"Today. The Florida County Recorder's Office is a fifteen-minute drive from here." Zikri glanced at his watch. "They close at four, so you have an hour."

"Exactly what is it you need?"

"A copy of the company registration documents. Make sure it includes the shareholder list detailing each person's name and address. Without that, it's worthless."

"Text me the County Office address as well as Be Secure's company registration number. Which department will I get the info from?"

"It's a closed file, which might mean you'd have to find the legal department, probably a manager or senior official."

Li tapped Zikri on his head as he passed him by. "Spot on. I'll get what you need. Make sure the money is transferred into my account by the time I return, otherwise you get shit." He walked away and called out an exorbitant amount over his shoulder that made Zikri glare after him.

"Jesus, that's more than what a middle-class family earns in a year," he muttered. On the other hand, no amount of money would be too much to keep his own ass alive.

"I'm afraid I'm totally lost," Li offered a shy smile that made him appear vulnerable and unsure, a feat that wasn't easy for a three-hundred-pound solid muscle, ex sumo wrestler champion that stood six-and-a-half feet in his shoes. Maybe because of that, his little boy smile appealed to people.

"What are you looking for?" the petite blonde woman asked. She took a step back to look up at him, visibly intimidated by his size.

"I need to file registration papers."

"Oh, the registration office is one level up to the left."

"I've been there but they say I need to obtain an affidavit for certain documentation." He smiled again. She relaxed. "They suggested I try begging someone in the legal department to assist me? You do have a Notary Public here I assume?"

She glanced around, seemingly uncomfortable.

"We do but it's not for public service. He only certifies company documentation."

"Please, won't he make an exception, just this once?" He glanced at his watch. He appeared professional, dressed in a crisp black suit with a pristine white cotton shirt and silver tie. His shoes had been polished until they shone like mirrors. He always took pride in his appearance. "Your office closes in thirty minutes. I'll never get back in time if I have to go across town to MPD." He added a panicked pitch to his voice. "I might even get fired if I don't file them today."

She shifted her weight and looked around. "Stay here. Let me see if Mr. Mello is available but I can't promise anything."

"That alone gives me hope."

Li watched her lithe body as she walked away. He moved a little further into the reception area and peeked down the hallway to catch her disappear into the last door on the right. He smiled and moved around the office, pretending to study the prints on the wall.

"I'm terribly sorry, sir. Mr. Mello said it's against our policy to assist clients." She glanced at the clock against the wall. "There's a Notary Public at banks and all the big ones are within a block from here. If you hurry, you'll make it in time."

"Thanks for the tip and for trying. You're a sweet lady."

Li smiled broadly and, whistling a happy tune, walked toward the stairs. Once he was out of sight, he slipped into an empty office and waited with the door slightly ajar. Moments later the click of high heels echoed through the hallway. He peeked through the opening and waited until the blonde he'd just walked away from, disappeared around the corner.

His tread was light for such a large man as he made his way back to the legal department. He didn't hesitate but walked directly to the office she'd gone into earlier.

The man behind the desk looked up sharply. His broad shoulders straightened as he stared at Li with obvious animosity.

"This office is already closed for the day."

"You're still here." Gone was the amicable guy that had charmed the receptionist. In his place, stood the cruel, emotionless strong-arm of the leader of the Chinese Triads. "And you're going to give me the information I want."

"There are procedures to follow to obtain information from this department. I'm sure you were already informed as much. Until that is done, I'm afraid I can't help ...ugh!"

The man's head snapped to the side as Li took a step closer and backhanded him. Blood spattered over the papers on his desk. He wailed and clutched his nose, looking like a grotesque question mark.

"I need this file." Li slapped a piece of paper on the desk. "Make sure to print the shareholder listing as well."

"Look," Mr. Mello attempted to reason with Li but held up his hand in surrender as he took a threatening step closer. "This is highly irregular. I can lose my job," he sniffed as blood continued to flow from his broken nose.

"What's a job worth if you're dead?"

Mello didn't protest any further. His bloodstained fingers trembled as he searched for the file on his computer. "Here it is."

"Print it out and make sure it's everything I need."

"I'm not an idiot," Mello snapped as the printer began to spit out the chosen documentation.

Li checked it briefly. He glanced at the man huddling forward in his chair, nursing his nose. He felt no regret or sympathy for the man. He exulted in it, as much as he thrived on cruelty. How else, it was in his DNA. He had naturally evolved into the life of a criminal after he'd given up wrestling. He viewed it as a different level of contact sport.

He breathed in and almost crooned at the smell of blood permeating the air. He became heady from the adrenaline rush that flooded his body. He smiled, knowing this was it. A decision he always made in a split second. No forward planning, no intention, just the need ... to kill. It was the rush of riding the demon inside him to new heights of barbarity. He thrived on the feeling of pleasure with every experience.

He placed the papers on the desk and slowly pulled out the thin wire he always carried in the inside pocket of his jacket. Excitement rushed through him as he reached around Mello and yanked the wire tight around his neck. If he didn't die from strangulation, he'd bleed to death from the cut slicing through skin and muscle. Li didn't concern himself that he'd lost sight of the main purpose; that this hadn't been what Malik had in mind.

"Such a rush," he growled at the hot flush of satisfaction as he felt Mello's body turn rigid, his voice gurgling in shock under Li's hands. Li yanked him back, eyes glimmering as he looked into his.

"Fuck, yes," he smiled as he watched him struggle in vain to breathe. "Ahh, such beauty," he crooned as, finally, the realization of death took hold of Mello, turning into a frenzy as he violently attempted to fight for his life. Li snapped the wire and twisted it, growling at the gush of blood that spurted all over the desk as it slashed through his carotid.

"Who would've thought I'd end my day with such a highlight?" Li released the wire and with meticulous concentration used Mello's sleeve to wipe it clean. Later, he'd go through the ritual of cleansing it properly.

His jaunty steps as he walked out of the building belied the violence and death he'd left behind.

Chapter Twenty

"Clean off her stench and make sure you reach every nook and cranny with those hoses."

Rose's humiliation was complete when she had to strip bare and stand in the large open shower stall in the corner of the punishment room, blasted by cold sprays of water from power hoses. All of this with Kane watching her squirm and fall to the floor as she slipped under the force of the water. She shrieked as it blasted into her anus and vagina, leaving her feeling lower than a dirty pig.

"You're a demon," she cried as she lay shivering on the cold marble tiles once Doms Brad and Michael switched off the hoses.

Kane didn't seem at all perturbed or insulted by her cry. In fact, he didn't seem to care about her feelings one way or the other.

Rose cringed as his rancorous gaze swept over her to further erode the final vestige of what was left of the love they used to share. She had to face reality and accept that there was no way to get it back or any way to restore it. It was all brinkmanship as they consistently pushed each other toward the edge, leaving her hurt and reeling.

"Take her to the public bathing area. There are subs waiting to sanitize and wash her."

"I can wash myself," she snapped as she struggled to her feet.

"You have no rights, slut." Kane's lips turned into an evil grin as she flinched, realizing she should've kept her mouth shut instead of provoking him. She wasn't a trainee anymore, she was the enemy. "Your body belongs to me and you do not have the right to touch it. Go, and tell them to hurry. I have people waiting for her."

"What do you mean?" Let me go," Rose struggled against Brad and Michael's hold, but they were too strong. "Kane! What are you going to do?" she screamed and strained her neck to look at him as the two men forced her up the stairs.

He laughed. "Don't worry, I have no intention of selling you into sex slavery. You are the mother of my son, after all, but I intend to have fun extracting my pound of flesh from you."

Kane didn't feel any pleasure from his actions. Quite the contrary, he hated seeing the fiery Rose on the verge of breaking down and turning into a willing punching bag. Her brief defiance just now offered some hope that she had become a stronger submissive than the one she used to be.

Be it as it may, he had no intention of backing down. He might not enjoy it, but at least it soothed the fury inside him that refused to simmer down. Rose Lovett had to suffer for the heartache and pain she'd caused him. He felt the rage bubbling higher as the thoughts rushed through his brain.

In the back of his mind, he knew there must be a darker story behind the explosion and he needed to know what it was. Meeting Tucker had changed his life as much as it had made him bitter. Whatever had driven Rose to pretend to be dead, he couldn't get over the fact that she'd kept his son, his own flesh and blood, from him for sixteen years.

For that, she would pay dearly.

"Don't you think you're being too hard on Rose, Kane?" Shane asked as he joined him in the torture chamber of The Dungeon of Sin. Even though it was mid-week, the club was packed.

Kane checked the chains hanging from the roof that he'd instructed Michael to set up on the platform meant for public humiliation.

"This is part of every sub's mid-training evaluation to assess how they've progressed. It's no more and no less than the rest of the group has to master."

"This may be, but what about what you have planned afterward?"

Kane glanced at him. His eyes glinted like shards of ice. "This scene is the easy part. Pain is a fleeting thing and Rose gets off on it, no matter how much she denies it." He tapped his head. "I'm going to fuck with her mind, Shane. Clear it of all her vicious lies and secrets. I'm going to do what any Dom worth his shoes would. I'm going to give her what she needs. It's one of her darkest desires, one she'll never voice aloud. I'm going to make sure once it's over, she suffers the ultimate humiliation. The one thing she hates. Maybe then ... I might be willing to listen to her explanation."

"If Stone allows it to go that far," Shane reminded him that their younger cousin had the ultimate power at Castle Sin. He could put an end to a scene as much as he could add to it.

Kane's lips flattened as he met Stone's gaze resting on him from the other side of the platform where he stood with Ace, Hawk, Savannah, and Peyton.

"He won't."

"Anger is our worst enemy, Kane, remember that. Don't alienate Rose to such an extent that you'd never be able to bridge the gap."

"You're quite the philosopher tonight, aren't you?" He smirked. "What makes you think I want to? After what she did to me? Forget it, Shane. I might have loved Narine, but this woman … I'm not a fool."

"You don't even know what happened or why. Are you even interested, or have you played judge and jury, found her guilty and are preparing to prosecute her, all in one? Come on, Kane, be honest with yourself. You want to know."

"What I want is for you to understand, even if it's to a minute degree, just how fucking hard the past seventeen years have been for me. Do you even know why I fucking never allow a woman to sleep in my bed? No, you don't because I don't allow anyone close once I fall asleep at night."

"Kane ..."

"Because more than half of every goddamn month since then I relive that night in my dreams. It never stopped. I don't want or need anyone's pity when I wake up screaming Narine's name as I claw at the sheets, in my dream desperately trying to get through the aluminum door frame that melted shut from the heat, ignoring the flames licking at my hands. The worst part is pitifully sobbing as I realized her terrified screams had stopped ... that she ... that she ... fuck!" Kane spat out the word. His hand clutched the crop he held so hard that his knuckles turned white. "Don't fucking tell me I'm too hard on her, Shane. She deserves everything I'm going to do to her."

"Jesus, why have you never told me? I could've helped you through this," Shane exclaimed, noticing, not for the first time, the wildly haunted look in Kane's eyes.

"Because it wouldn't have helped. Do you think I haven't tried? That I haven't gone from one psychologist to the next? I guess now I know why the dreams never stopped. It was the universe telling me she wasn't dead." He looked at Shane, his eyes cold and hard, completely void of emotion. "Now that I know she's not ... I fucking wish she was."

"You don't mean that."

Kane looked toward the entrance. His face turned stoic. "Don't I?"

Shane followed his gaze. Rose was naked and blindfolded. Danton led her by a chain linked into a broad leather collar around her neck. She hunched forward with a pained look on her face, courtesy of the nose to clit kneeling clamps connected to a tight chain in between. It was usually used on a sub in a kneeling position or on their backs but never standing. Walking with the tight pressure of the vice-like type of clamps on both her nose and clit must be excruciating.

Kane got onto the platform. The crop tap-tap-tapped against his leathers as he waited.

"Rose." Shane stepped in front of the trio. The sharp glance at the assisting Doms loosened their hold on her and they stepped aside. He placed his hand on her arm, both of which were cuffed behind her neck to the collar around her neck.

"Master Fox?" Her voice sounded small and forlorn, like she had accepted her fate and knew something inhumane was about to happen.

"Be strong, little one, you will get through this."

"I never meant to hurt him. I thought ... I believed them that it was for the best ... I never should've listened." She shuddered as emotions overcame her. "He'll never forgive me."

"He's angry, Rose, and acting irrationally because of it. Don't let what's about to happen destroy your belief in him, in what's still in your heart."

"He's more than angry, Shane." Rose leaned into his palm as he cupped her cheek, needing the comfort of a strong Master such as him. "He hates me."

"I don't believe that for a second." Shane was frustrated because he couldn't see her eyes but would never interfere in another Master's scene. "Rose, some of what's about to happen ... not many subs have such needs or desires. If it becomes too much, I want you to promise me you'll use your safeword."

"I deserve everything he does to me."

"Not in this environment. This is a BDSM club where safe, sane, and consensual rules. Don't ever forget that. I won't allow him to push you too far, neither will Stone. Don't be a martyr, Rose, and more importantly, don't lose the last of his respect by allowing him to turn this into public vengeance."

"What do you mean?"

"A Dom has more respect for a sub if she uses her safeword rather than suffer beyond her boundaries. It shows how strong and confident she is in her Dom's understanding and honoring the power she gave him over her."

"That's hardly relevant in this case." Her mouth flattened stubbornly.

Shane sighed. Rose had already decided she'd bow to Kane's rage and submit to his will, no matter how demented it might become.

"Do you know what he intends to do?" Her voice sounded as brittle as she looked.

"He said something about your deepest, darkest need that you'll never voice." His gaze sharpened as she turned pale under the edge of the spotlight that shone directly on her face. "Rose?"

"I … it's … how can he know about it?" She suddenly remembered Kane mentioning it once before.

"He has tapped into the true submissive deep inside you … Kane is one of the most perceptive Doms I've ever met. He sees what a sub feels before she experiences it. He knows, Rose, and if it's something you don't have the strength for, do *not* agree to this scene."

"Master Fox, is this tête-à-tête going to continue much longer? You are holding up sub RL's evaluation."

Kane's brusque tenor rippled over Rose that triggered a shudder to chase down her spine. She thought she detected a dichotomous tone in his voice. Maybe it was wishful thinking but she latched onto it. It offered her a slither of hope that there might be a minuscule part of him that didn't hate her—at least not *as* much.

Get real, Rose. Kane isn't the kind of man to equivocate.

She cringed as a hard hand clasped her upper arm. She relaxed as *he*—Master Bear—pressed against her side. Strangely, it felt like he offered her … what? Comfort? No, her mind must already be in subspace to believe that.

Freaking hell, why is it only him that affects me like this?

Her fear notwithstanding, she felt the flicker of arousal warming her loins as the heat that always scorched her skin when he touched her imbued throughout her body.

"I assume your chit-chat is over?" The ridicule was idiosyncratic in his biting tone, ostracizing Shane's concern over her.

"Kane, be warned, once you cross the line of consensual to abuse, there'll be no turning back for you and Rose."

"You're delusional, Shane. She single-handedly obliterated any chance of *turning back*, as you so eloquently said." His fingers tightened around her arm. "Let's go."

"Master Bear?"

Kane's hesitation was brief like he was considering ignoring her soft plea. "Yes, sub RL."

"Tucker ... how is he?"

"Happy. Very happy."

A relieved smile curved her lips upward briefly. "I'm glad." She bit her bottom lip before she voiced her biggest fear. "Does he ... does he hate me too?"

The sigh was as brittle and as soft as a bee's wings but it thrilled straight to Rose's heart. There had to be hope and for every little sign her sharpened senses picked up, she cherished it like a precious jewel inside her soul.

"You're his mother, he'll never hate you. You are his rock and that'll never change." She felt his breath against her cheek. "That, and *only* that, is your saving grace." He yanked her along with him up a couple of steps onto the platform. "Enough talking. It's time for your evaluation."

"Really? Or is this my execution?"

"You are such a perceptive woman." He tapped her arm. "Straighten, sub. A hunched over form annoys me."

"I can't. Please, Master—awww, fuck," she cried at the cruel snap, of what felt like his crop, cracking against her nipples.

"I don't like a sub back chatting. Do as you're told, or I'll put a hook in your ass and tie it to your hair to force your shoulders back."

Rose whimpered but did her best to straighten as much as the restricted chain clamping her nose and clit together allowed.

"That's a tad better. Don't lose that form again."

Rose trembled as she felt him circle her. She tilted her head but couldn't sense where he was.

"As I said, this is your mid-training evaluation to see how you've progressed so far. It's not going to be a walk in the park. The first part is to assess your ability to take corporal punishment. Starting with a paddle, strap, flogger, and then to the high end of impact tools, a crop, cane, and a whip. Each Master will use an assigned tool for a period of five minutes in whatever fashion he deems appropriate to test your skill. Any questions?"

"Why am I blindfolded?"

Kane was taken aback. It was the last question he'd expected.

"Because without your eyes, your other senses are heightened. You'll experience every hit, every sensation, and emotion more intensely. It'll either enhance your ability to tap into the training you've received so far or cause you to fall off the cart."

He tapped the clapper of his crop against her nipple, softly, teasingly. It completely unsettled Rose. She hadn't expected anything but pain from him.

"Which tool will you be using?"

The teasing taps stopped, only to be replaced by the hard edge flicking over her nipples, back and forth until they stood hard and throbbing.

"Let's see if I'm right about you, sub RL. If you can feel me amid the rest of the Masters, maybe, just maybe I'll be lenient with the following evaluation."

"Master Bear, I—"

"Enough talking. Brad, it's time to begin. Get her set up, please." He turned to the crowd gathered all around the platform, eagerly anticipating what they perceived to be an entertaining scene about to unfurl.

Rose couldn't stay the trembling that shook her body as she felt Doms Brad and Michael by her side.

"Sub RL, this is going to hurt like the bejesus. I'll hold onto your waist in case your legs give in while Dom Brad removes the clamps, okay?" Dom Michael rasped in her ear.

She slumped against him, grateful for the way they had been gentle and caring with her since the subs had finished the degrading sanitizing and bath.

"Thank you, Sir."

"Here," he pressed a piece of leather between her lips, "bite on this. Let's not give them the pleasure of hearing your pain."

Rose bit into the leather, tears forming in her eyes at their unexpected gesture of understanding. She couldn't help but wonder if it was an instruction from Master Fox.

"Ready?" She nodded as Dom Brad's voice penetrated her frayed mind.

Brad did his best to alleviate the pain by squeezing the area behind the clamp before he unscrewed it but to no avail. Rose's knees did buckle and only the hard grip of Michael's arms around her waist kept her upright. The wail of pain, muted by clenching her teeth on the strap, as the blood surged back into the abused vessels of her clit, seared through her mind. Brad immediately straightened and removed the one from her nose. Her eyes rolled back in their sockets as the blackness she was already enshrouded in, threatened to swallow her completely.

"Easy, my pet, breathe. Come on, sub RL, deep breath," Dom Michael crooned in her ears. She latched onto his deep voice, appreciating Dom Brad rubbing and stroking her nose and clit to soothe the stinging pain. Together they eased her back until she could stand on her own.

"Thank you," she croaked, still with a zing in her ears from the silent screams.

"Come, let's get you ready."

They led her to the center stage and cuffed her wrists to the chains and her legs to the O-rings welded into the floorboards. The sound of the pulley was the only warning of the chains lifting and stretching her onto her toes, leaving her naked and spread-eagled. Her body glistened under the harsh spotlight with a combination of sweat and oils with which she'd been prepared.

"Sub RL, this will be a continuous evaluation. There will be no breaks from one Master to the next. I have explained that this is your mid-training evaluation. Do you consent to the nature of it?"

Kane's disembodied voice raked over her nerves that had spiked once she was chained. Her teeth clattered as she became aware of the drone of mixed voices all around her. She had known he'd push her limits, hard, and should've expected it would be done in full view of the members. She forced her mind to stay in the moment and not wander off to the next evaluation. If he had been able to tap into her darkest desires, she might just come to hate him after tonight. It seeped through her heart that maybe that was exactly his intention.

"Sub RL, your answer, please."

"Yes, Master Bear, I consent to the evaluation."

"You have the right to use your safeword, even under these circumstances. Remind me what it is, sub."

"Just get freaking on with it," she snapped, finally reaching the end of her patience. "Every damn body knows what the safeword is."

"Now this is a rather unfortunate response, sub RL, and as per the rules of these evaluations, you have just failed your first test. Not to mention, invited punishment from the club members you have just insulted."

"I'm sorry, but it's ..." She bit back the apology. He'd tell her it was too late anyway. She heaved in a deep breath. "King, Master Bear. My safeword is King."

"Very well. Masters, are you ready? Dom Danton is the timekeeper, please react on his call immediately."

Rose felt the loss of his heat as he stepped away from her.

"Begin."

She braced herself, her muscles tensed and her hoarse cry fell from her lips as the sting of a studded paddle connected with her left ass cheek.

"Don't tense up, Rose. Relax and lean into each hit." Master Hawk's voice echoed in her mind as she recalled the training sessions with him.

She did her best and even managed to a certain degree, but it wasn't easy as the paddle continued to crack against the same spot over and over until it felt like her one cheek was doused in lava. She almost sighed in relief when the next strike connected on the opposite cheek, only to whimper as it too received the same treatment.

"Time."

"Thank god," she gasped. She sensed the next Master behind her, realizing just how acute her hearing suddenly became. She even heard the swish before the strap made contact with her inner thigh.

"Sweet jaysus!" she exclaimed at the searing pain that shot from point of impact to her brain, but before she could breathe through it, the next one fell and then the next. She could feel each individual strap of what had to be a split end leather taws as it connected with her skin. This Master made sure to spread the hits all over her inner and outer thighs and ended with a couple of harsh ones over her buttocks just before Dom Danton called time again.

Rose's breathing had increased as had the number of areas that burned and throbbed. Someone checked the cuffs at her ankles and wrist.

"How are you doing, sub RL?" Danton's deep voice rasping in her ear caused her to relax. She'd come to like him during her time in the cage under his care. He might appear rough and dark but he had a soft heart.

"I'm okay, Sir."

"Give me a color, sub." His voice darkened and Rose cursed. Another mistake.

"I'm green, Sir."

"Good." He stepped away. "Begin."

"Awwww! Fuck!" Rose screamed as the swish of the flogger barely registered before metal balls slammed against her labia and seared against the soft skin just inside her slit.

She puffed as she mentally endeavored to prepare herself for the next one. She didn't need to see to know what tool this Master used. Only one thing hurt as much—a metal ball flogger. It was shorter and therefore used from close proximity. She wailed as the next strikes from between her legs curled all the way around to the front and slapped against her clit.

She heard herself snorting in haggard breaths as she desperately tried to breathe through the pain. Another lash impacted hard and then they rained down in a blur, all over her pussy and without warning, her nipples.

"Jezuz! Oww fuck!"

If she hadn't been strung up, her knees would've buckled as more hits, this time from the front, slapped against her pussy and seared the sensitive skin of her anus.

"Time."

Rose struggled to breathe as she imagined she could feel the pain where every metal ball had landed. She didn't know how much longer she'd be able to endure, and by her count, there were still four Masters left. She was far from ready when Danton's voice echoed in her ears.

"Begin."

She had mentally prepared herself for a leather flogger and was completely blindsided when the searing lash of a whip cracked against her outer thigh and immediately the opposite one. It didn't have the impact of a long-tailed whip, it was too intense, too hard and made her jerk and thrash with every strike.

Her screams intensified as the lashes connected all around her body, curled around her waist to sting her stomach with the scorching kiss as bitingly sharp as lava. She lost the ability to concentrate, as every nerve ending sparked painfully with each strike and tensed in preparation for the next.

"Focus, sub. You can do better." Rose gasped as she heard the voice in her mind as clear as the crack of the whip against her skin. She felt him then, his heat emanating from his body, reaching out to her as he circled her body. *"Remember my warning in the past, sub. Do not disappoint me."*

Another strike. Rose screamed and the chains rattled as she jagged and twisted to avoid the next one.

"Stop, please Master Bear ... stop!" Rose sobbed and twitched in desperation as the one lash after the other rained against her back.

"You know better. Use it. Now!"

This time Rose obeyed, her mind completely frayed bare by the pain that scorched to her brain.

"KING! King-king-king," she shouted and ended mumbling it over and over, but Kane had stopped even before she'd opened her mouth.

"No," he stopped Danton when he reached up to uncuff her. "Rub soothing gel and arnica on the welts first."

Rose hung in the chains and whimpered pitifully as Danton gently rubbed the ointment all over her skin. She stilled when she felt his heat in front of her. A touch, against her chin, so soft and brief, she thought she imagined it.

"Good girl."

She couldn't have been more surprised to hear the quiet voice utter the word, but it broke through her defenses and she burst into tears. She had failed him and still he praised her.

"Hurry up, Danton," Kane snapped as he stood in front of Rose, feeling every raw sob tug at something deep inside him. Something that had died too long ago and the one thing he refused to give in to now.

He caught her in his arms once Danton unchained her. "Jenna, bring an energy drink to the aftercare booth, please." He carried her in stoic silence to the large Reception Hall of the dungeon and settled in a booth in the corner.

Rose couldn't stop the tears and with an annoyed sigh, Kane removed the blindfold.

"Enough, sub RL. You suffered through four harsh impact tools without a single tear. Why are you crying now?"

"Because I failed you."

"No, sub, if you hadn't used your safeword, you would've failed. Remember, even in a scene or during punishment, it's not about how much you can endure but knowing when you reached the end of your limits and then having the strength and presence of mind to end it. That's what submission is about, Rose. Giving someone the power over you and trusting them to take care of you but similarly to be strong and confident enough to take it away."

"Thank you."

Kane looked at her, studying her pale face. He noticed the dark circles and heavy bags under her eyes for the first time. He cursed softly. Evidence that she hadn't been sleeping. He frowned, realizing that it would be cruel to continue onto the second round under the circumstances. His lips thinned. Especially if he wanted her to suffer the full effect of her own dark desires. No, it'll have to wait, at least until she'd had a full night's sleep.

"Thank you for what?"

She glanced at him briefly, and her fingers trembled as she traced the buttons on his shirt.

"I heard you," she murmured, the disbelief of it was shallow in her voice. "In my mind, warning me, telling me to use my safeword."

Rose melted against him. His reassurance managed to soothe her tortured soul. Because of how he'd acted earlier, she would never have expected he'd offer her the caring side of Master Bear. She'd expected the worst and was prepared for it. Once again, he managed to surprise her. She was still mulling over his behavior in her mind when the stress and no sleep while locked in the cage caught up with her and she fell asleep, curled up on his lap.

Kane was startled at first to hear about her experience but knew he shouldn't be. She proved weeks before already that she had submitted to him as her real Dom. That was why she had been able to tap into his thoughts.

"Pity about your lies and deceit, Rose. It could've been good between us. Even better than before. Now … there's nothing left but emptiness and disappointment."

Chapter Twenty-One

"I'm sorry to interrupt your bonding with Tucker, Kane, but this is important."

Kane's face appeared on the monitor on the wall in the boardroom of BSE for the Skype call. He'd spent the past three days and nights at his house on Key Largo getting to know Tucker. Tucker had been happy to stay at home with either Danton or Evans as company, the couple of times he had to go to the island, including the previous night. It hadn't been a consideration to stay at Castle Sin after he'd put Rose to bed. He'd gone home to be with his son.

"I'm sure it is, Stone. You all look very serious. What's up?"

"There's been a security breach at the Florida County Recorder's Office." Stone didn't bother to hide the concern in his voice. "Someone obtained Be Secure's registration and shareholders list."

"Fucking hell. How did it happen? I thought their systems were impenetrable." Kane glanced to the side. "It's your turn to impress me with your culinary skills. Breakfast duty is yours, my boy. I won't be long."

"Are eggs and bacon your staple food?" Tucker's teasing voice floated to the men watching. "I mean big men like us ..."

"Exactly, my boy. You've got my genes, so lots of eggs and bacon."

"Just don't tell Mom. She's got this thing that a lot of fat is bad for me."

Kane chuckled. "I won't be long. Get started on the bacon."

"Righto, Captain."

Kane's smile depicted that of a proud father as he turned his attention back to the screen. "And? How did they do it?" He returned to the topic at hand.

"Violently," Shane said shortly. "Cut the poor department head's throat while strangling him with a wire apparently."

"That's fucked up. All our personal details are on those documents." Kane sat forward. "Do they know who did it?"

"No. The FBI sent over the CCTV footage that covers the hallways and entrance into the building. Based on the timestamp of the recordings versus time of death, the only thing they could pin down is that it was a huge man. He's a clever bastard. He made sure his back was to the cameras at all times." Hawk said.

"Why now? What triggered someone's desire to find out who owns Be Secure Enterprises?" Ace said as he studied the video clip Parker replayed for Kane's benefit.

"The only thing I can think of is that there's a mole in the FBI. It happened within hours of Alexa setting up the meeting yesterday morning to discuss money laundering involving the Chinese Triads." Stone frowned. "If that's the case, you and Tucker need to leave Key Largo immediately, Kane, and get your asses over here. They obtained our home addresses with the shareholders agreement but The Seven Keys Island isn't listed anywhere."

"You're right. I can't take the chance of my son getting hurt. I'll take my boat. That way we won't be caught out in the open. We're leaving in ten minutes."

"Parker, set up a perimeter watch via GeoEye on Kane's property. Warn him if there are any suspicious movement in the area."

"Will do, but it'll take about five minutes to zoom in on his place," Parker said as he opened the locator system.

"Is Savannah with you on the island, Hawk, or should I pick her up?"

"We stayed over last night, Kane, but thanks for asking. Now get your asses over here."

"Have any of you seen Rose this morning?" Kane asked in a quiet voice.

"I checked up on her before breakfast. She was still sleeping and I told them to leave her be," Shane said sipping his latte.

"Good. She didn't get much sleep in the dungeon."

"I'm curious," Stone interjected, "what made you decide not to continue with the scene you had planned?"

"She fell asleep during aftercare and I realized she was bone tired. I want her completely lucid and aware for that scene," Kane clipped out.

"In other words, you still intend to go through with it?" Shane looked at the monitor with a deep frown etched between his brows.

"Why wouldn't I?"

"I just thought ... never mind," Shane cut himself off and finished his coffee. "Better go check what that boy of yours is doing in the kitchen. It sounds like he's attempting to break every pot and pan you own."

Kane laughed and for the first time in years, he looked carefree and happy. "I guess you're right. We'll be there in thirty minutes. Oh, and Stone, let's give the trainees the day off. I want them all dressed properly—the subs as well. No skimpy outfits. Make sure all the dungeon entrances are locked. I'm not completely ready to have the BDSM talk with Tucker yet."

"This ought to be good. What exactly are you planning on telling him we do here?" Ace asked with a teasing smirk.

"Fuck if I know."

"Far be it for me to burst your bubble, old timer, but if your son managed to find the island, I'll bet you my Bugatti Veyron he already knows all about BDSM *and* that you're a kinky dad." Parker chuckled at the expression on Kane's face.

"Fuck off, pup. What do you know anyway?"

Kane cut the connection, muttering about know-it-all puppy cousins. He was still amazed at how cleverly Tucker had maneuvered Salvino and the headmaster to take him on a boating trip, purely to have a legitimate excuse to leave school. He'd planned his escape perfectly. While Salvino concentrated on maneuvering the boat out of the docks, he managed to jump onto a ferry leaving for Miami at the same time. He'd signed on for diving lessons once there but as soon as he had the gear, he quickly took off toward the island. According to him, he'd managed to lock onto Rose's cell phone location during that split second where the GeoEye satellite realigned around midnight. The only thing he hadn't bargained on was the underwater alarm sensors around The Seven Keys Island.

Kane shook his head.

"He's my son, okay. Just as dogmatic as his old man when it comes to doing something he has set his mind on."

He frowned as he realized the cacophony of clattering pots and pans had gone quiet. In fact, it was silent ... eerily silent.

"Tucker? Son?" he called as he walked down the hallway and into the great open room. "Fuck! Tucker!"

Kane's heart missed a beat and he went cold. He looked around. Pot and pans were scattered all over the kitchen.

"What the fuck?" He yanked out a meat cleaver that was stuck on the side of the bar counter. "Tucker!"

He ran onto the patio and looked around frantically. One of the patio chairs was knocked over and a piece of red material stuck to the armrest. He lifted it with a trembling hand. It was from the shirt Tucker was wearing. With a violent curse, Kane ran around the house and looked up and down the street. It was still early and therefore quiet. He circled the house, searched the beach before he turned over the house from top to bottom.

Tucker was gone.

The mess indicated that he hadn't gone willingly.

"Why the fuck didn't you shout out or call me, Tucker?" Kane's raw cry echoed through the house. The CCTV system had been disabled early morning in preparation for the upgrade he had planned to install today in and around the house. He stormed to the study to get his phone. He made a call to Shane as he ran upstairs to his bedroom to change.

"Hey, Kane, did you—"

"Get over here. Tucker has been taken."

Shane didn't ask any questions. "I'll be there in fifteen minutes."

"Keep this quiet, Shane. I don't want Rose to find out."

"Agreed."

Kane dressed in black combat gear and boots. He meticulously packed a duffel bag with weapons;

knives, guns, and Shuriken—ninja stars. He had just loaded his bag and a wooden crate into his Fountain 32 ThunderCat powerboat, docked at his private marina, when Shane arrived with Danton on his heels.

"Don't even bother," Shane said at Kane's sharp glare as he jumped into the boat. "This man has a sixth sense and by the time I got into the boat to leave The Seven Keys Island, he was already waiting for me."

"No one fucks with our boy," Danton grunted and settled in the back of the boat, ignoring Kane's exasperated glare.

"This is going to get ugly, Danton. I'm not ..." Kane heaved in a calming breath.

"Yeah, I fucking hope so. I've got enough explosives in my bag to blow up Key West. so ... what are you waiting for?"

"Guess I didn't need to load this crate then," Kane said dryly and started the engine.

"Where are we headed?" Shane asked as he settled next to Kane.

"Miami. Chan Ho's place."

"How do you know Tucker's there?" Danton leaned into the seat as Kane eased the boat away from the marina.

"A hunch. I also recognized the man in the CCTV footage you showed me this morning. One of the GeoEye shots Parker zoomed on last week when he showed us where Malik is hiding out, had him in the background. Same angle. I recognized his profile. It can't be a coincidence that Tucker is taken the day after the information about us is leaked."

Kane handed his iPad to Shane with the GeoEye program open. "Red dot marks the spot. Zoom in and find the best access point into the property and the closest marina or alcove where I can dock."

He concentrated to keep his mind blank, to focus on finding Tucker and getting him home safely. The drone of Shane and Danton's voices merged with the swish of the water as the powerboat slid soundlessly through the gentle waves.

"Right. The property is in Palmetto Bay in the Deering Estate," Shane said from beside him. He pointed to a slight alcove on the map. "This is the closest spot to dock, at the Deering Point People's Dock. It's not visible from any of the properties, so they won't detect us. The alternative is to dock a couple of yards past the dock under these brushes. Ho's house is this one, the closest to the dock. There are three entrances, the front door, back door, and a sliding door facing the ocean."

"So, we each take an entrance?" Kane slanted brief glances to the map as Shane explained.

"Depending where they are. Danton brought a heat detection sensor with. Once we establish how many people are inside the house, where they are and if the outside perimeter is clear, we can decide point of entry."

"There might be a problem," Danton said thoughtfully. "That Estate has security guards that do regular perimeter checks. We might have to wait until after their check is complete before we breach. It'll mean we can't dock at the Deering Point People's Dock."

"I agree. It'll be better if the boat is hidden under the shrubs and trees on the other side," Kane said as he keyed in the coordinates. "Twenty minutes. Get the gear ready. We're going in hot but fucking make sure you don't shoot at Tucker."

"And make every shot count, no stray bullets that can ricochet either," Danton interjected.

"That's our aim, Danton. They fucked with the wrong people this time." Shane dragged his and Kane's duffle bags closer and sat next to Danton. Silently, they began to check the weapons. Extra bullet clips, knives, and ninja stars were secured in the combat belts they'd be wearing.

"Boat's secure," Kane said as he yanked the tie-rope tight around the stump of a tree. He glanced to where he guesstimated Danton stood higher up on the incline. "Danton, can you see it from there?"

"No, the shrubs and trees are too dense."

Kane and Shane joined Danton and stood hidden amidst the shrubs bordering a large lawn leading up to a gray and white mansion a couple of yards further up. It was a quiet mid-morning. Nothing moved, other than the slight breeze. Kane cast his eyes upward as a rustling alerted him. The blue sky peeked from above their green camouflage. His heart thumped against his chest. He tried to calm himself but the anger and concern for his son was numbing.

"That's the house," Danton said as they peered around. He pointed to the left. "Our best access point is from that section of trees. It's closer to the house and at least it will give us adequate cover until we approach."

"It's at least an eighty-yard sprint to the property from there. We better be sure there's no one on that side of the house when we charge," Shane peered around for another possibility. "But Danton is right, that is the best point for approach."

Kane checked his watch. "It's ten-twenty-eight. If the security does regular perimeter checks, it can either be hourly or thirty-minute intervals. Let's wait five minutes. If they don't pitch, we move."

They settled in to wait. Danton took out the heat sensor unit and moved around as he scanned the property.

Kane's mind drifted to the moment his eyes had fallen on Tucker and the punch in his heart had told him that he was looking at his son, his flesh and blood. His fingers tingled as he recalled that first touch when he'd reverently reached out and traced his face, like he was scripting every line to memory.

His son. The most perfect feeling he had ever known had swept through him at that moment, the love that instantly settled in his heart had rocked him to his core. He had committed without hesitation that he would do anything in the world for him. He was his—his boy. Without any thought, he'd felt the connection, one that would never be broken—Tucker held Kane's soul in his heart, and his heart was forever Tucker's.

Kane had always loved and protected fiercely. For his own child, he would walk through the gates of hell to keep him safe. He had been given the most sacred gift, one that he had believed wasn't meant to be … not for him. They had just found each other and there were so many things he'd love to experience with Tucker. Explore new places together, be adventurous, and allow him to take risks but assuring him that his father would always be standing by to catch him if he fell. Most of all the love that had sucker punched him at first sight would grow and Kane knew he'd love him with every power he possessed.

His eyes grew darker, flashes of blue in their shallow depths glistened with malevolence in their sockets. No one was going to take his son from him and he wouldn't hesitate to kill those who threatened or hurt Tucker.

"Heads up. Security two clicks south heading our way," Danton warned as he joined them again. They huddled lower, covertly watching the guards chatting animatedly as they strolled closer, following the paved pathway. They passed less than three yards from where they were hiding and continued on to disappear minutes later between a row of trees.

"Heat sensor picks up six bodies. Two in a seated position to the back of the house, which I assume is the kitchen. Two seated in that room with the large bay windows to the right of the front door. The other two in a level lower." Danton turned the unit so Kane and Shane could see and pointed on the screen. "One is lying down and the other sitting a couple of feet from him. I assume it's Tucker and his guard."

"Must be a basement or tornado bunker," Kane mused as he scrutinized the surroundings. "No one on the outside perimeter?"

"Nope," Danton said looking around.

"What about the security sensors that Parker mentioned?" Kane squinted and pinpointed three from their location.

"Got it covered. I swiped a scrambler unit from Parker's arsenal. Once we move, it'll shut off the circuit and their monitors will be lovely blinking snow. It'll give us time to get inside before they realize something is amiss."

"Good job." Shane thumbed him on the shoulder.

"So, how do you wanna run this?" Danton asked as he kept the heat sensor pointed at the house.

Kane stared at the house, briefly considering what awaited them inside—his son and one of the cruelest crime leaders in the world. He would die protecting the one, but the other, he wouldn't blink when he killed him. Two opposing emotions, love and hate, there was a thin line between them as both were equally strong. This time, it was a line *they* decided to cross and for that, he'd have no mercy.

"We detour via the docks to the thicket closest to the house and approach from there. Let's move now."

They ran as one man, huddled over, back to the water's edge. It didn't take long to reach the thick bushes to the side of the house.

Kane glanced at the heat sensors on the screen. "They haven't moved. I think it's safe to assume that the two in the front are Chan Ho and Zikri Malik, which means the ones we need to eliminate first are the ones in the back." Kane scrutinized the windows as he patted the unit in his ear. "Check your coms. Echo, Charlie clear?"

"Echo clear," Danton said.

"Charlie clear," Shane confirmed.

"We go in low and fast." He pointed two fingers to the right side of the house. "I'll cover the front. Shane, you and Danton hit the back door. Do it quick and quiet. Give me a heads up when it's clear and you're moving to the front room." He gripped his Kahr P9 double-action semi-automatic in his right hand. "Arm up. Hit that scrambler, Danton. We move ... now!"

The three bodies moved quickly and stealthily. Kane reached the front door and slowly turned the handle. The door eased open. He flattened himself against the wall. Through the slight opening, he had a clear view down the hallway. He cringed at the echo in his ear of a door squeaking and a voice growling, "What the fuck?" Two soft pings popped in his ear coms.

"Back perimeter clear," Shane confirmed in a quiet voice. "Moving."

Kane eased the door open with his boot. It led into a large entrance hall with four arches. Danton and Shane appeared in the hallway and moved around the front of the staircase. Shane counted off his fingers. They moved on one, surprising the two men who were in the midst of an argument.

"Who the fuck are you?" Chan Ho exclaimed as he jumped up.

"You're not much of a leader if you don't even know the people you're fucking with, are you?" Kane taunted him.

Chan Ho's eyes narrowed as he noticed Zikri going pale and tried to shrink himself unnoticeable into the sofa.

"Yeah, and he's clearly not a movie fan either," Danton scoffed. "Otherwise he'd have recognized the men he'd been stealing from for years."

"Look, there must be some misunderstanding," Zikri hedged, holding out his hands beseechingly. He glanced toward the arched entry, obviously hoping for the guards to arrive.

"They're not coming. They're probably already burning in hell," Shane mocked him.

"What do you want?" Chan Ho sneered as Danton's words sunk in and realization struck.

"You have something of mine." Kane's lips barely moved.

Chan Ho crossed his arms over his chest. He smirked as he looked between the three men.

"I'm not scared of you."

"I don't suppose you are, but if you think we're here to negotiate, you're a bigger fool than you were to take his son from him," Shane taunted him openly.

"What are you trying to achieve?" Kane stared at his opponent unblinkingly.

"I have worked very hard to become the leader I am today and I'm not going to stand by and watch a bunch of *actors* destroy it," he snorted viciously. "Your interference is going to cost you. Involving the FBI and DOJ was a huge mistake, Sinclair."

"Ha, isn't this a crock of bullshit." Danton smirked.

"You used the same bunch of actors for years to launder money and enrich yourself, you fucktard." Shane took a threatening step closer.

"None of that matters," Kane said. "You made a mistake to take my son. You threatened him and placed his life in danger."

"Your son is fine!" Zikri exclaimed. "Go, look for yourself. He hasn't been hurt."

Kane didn't take his eyes from Chan Ho, who tried to move unobtrusively closer to him. He noticed the way his muscles bunched, how he shifted his legs and rolled onto the balls of his feet.

His eyes narrowed, it was a move he recognized, one that the undefeated Kung Fu champion always used before his final attack.

"Danton, get Tucker and Shane, keep your eyes on this little weasel," Kane said colloquially as he uncocked his gun and handed it to Shane. The smile he offered Chan Ho took him aback but only for a second.

He barked out a laugh. "Ah, your bravery is commendable, but this isn't a movie set and you obviously don't know who I am."

Kane snorted as he spread his legs, one in front of the other, and sunk his hips lower, firmly planting his feet. His arms remained hanging loose by his side. "A master in more than one of the ancient combat fighting skills, and the undefeatable champion of the Kung Fu World Championship since 2003. I know exactly who you are, you motherfucker."

Chan Ho was clearly shaken and not as confident as a moment before as he watched the familiar Krav Maga stance of the tall man in front of him. He was all muscle, and instinct warned him Kane Sinclair wasn't someone easily defeated.

Then Chan Ho moved, a blur of movement as he went airborne and aimed a mortal kick at Kane's head. Only, he moved in that split second before his lethal foot connected. One moment he was flying through the air and the next a brutal palm accurately punched him where his breastbone ended. He slammed back against the wall from the force of the hit. He stumbled forward, struggling to breathe as pain blinded him. Every breath he took felt excruciating. He clutched his chest.

"Yep, he just broke your breastbone, fucktard. Not so much of a champion now, are you?" Shane leaned against the arch as he laughed at the surprised Chan Ho.

"It's impossible," he teemed. "I'm unbeatable!"

"Go for it, motherfucker. I'm waiting." Kane had returned to the same position he was in before.

Chan Ho simmered. He closed his eyes and forced himself to push the pain to the back of his mind.

"Ahhhhheee!" He pulled out of the brief meditation with a yell at the same time as he charged Kane in a flurry of kicks and palm slashes.

Kane deflected each one, seemingly without any effort. Chan Ho continued to attack, laughing in glee as he managed to land a few kicks and hits that caused Kane to stumble. Frustration began to eat at him as nothing he did seemed to faze the American. He wanted to wipe the smile from his face but he couldn't get close enough. He was getting tired, the pain throbbing in his chest drained his strength.

A sudden gush of pain jolted through Chan Ho's body. His breath wheezed from his chest as he clutched his aching stomach. His arms lost tension and his legs began to tremble. The fucking bastard was so quick, he never saw the flick of his leg, only the impact that felt like everything inside him burst open. He willed his legs not to crumble as he retreated, feeling more bruised and winded than ever before.

"Come on, Ho, is that the best you've got?" Kane taunted him, circling him on the balls of his feet.

His eyes flickered to the knives and stars in Kane's combat belt. It was time to end it. No one could beat him in a knife fight. The next move came fast and furious as he did a flying kick at Kane's head but twisted his body at the last moment to sweep his legs from under him. As Kane went down, he pulled out one of the knives.

"Aahheee!" he screamed and turned to bury the blade in his heart. "Fuck!" he sneered as Kane was already on his feet.

Chan Ho wasn't scared of anything, especially as he had an army of Triad Soldiers to protect him, but the death threatening smile on his opponent's face scared the shit out of him. He looked around frantically at Zikri. "Where the fuck is Li?"

"How the shit should I know?" Zikri puffed, his eyes fearful. If Chan Ho lost the fight, he was screwed. He wasn't a fighter, but he had no intention of going to jail.

"Ah, now it's gonna get interesting," Shane said with a smile.

"This is becoming boring," Kane snapped.

Chan Ho once again didn't see it coming as the devastating kick came out of nowhere, swept up and powered by Kane's tightly coiled torso. It exploded at the end of his boots across the front of Chan Ho's face.

"Holy crap! Wow! Yeah, Dad!"

Kane's head snapped around at Tucker's excited voice. His gaze thoroughly examined his body but couldn't find any signs of him being hurt.

"Get him out of here," Kane snapped as he returned his attention to Chan Ho.

"Hell no, I'm not going anywhere. I wanna see this. Did you see that kick, Uncle Shane? Wow … just wow!"

Kane did his best to shut out his son's excitement as he stared at Chan Ho, twisting around on the floor, his hands covering his face. Blood spurted from his severed upper lip and broken nose. He yanked him to his feet with a hand fisting his collar and slammed him against the wall.

"You should never have taken my son, Ho."

"I'm sorry, I only tried to protect my interests," he wailed.

"Wrong fucking answer, you asshole," Shane snapped.

Chan Ho furiously blinked, desperate to see through the blood that flooded his eyes. Fear crawled through him in that moment as his gaze locked with eyes the color of death, a darkening blackness swirling with gray. It was a vow of hell winking at him.

"You're an actor, not a killer." Chan Ho cackled out a gleeful laugh. He might have lost the fight, but he had too many contacts to keep him in jail, even in America. "I'll be out of jail in a blink and then—"

"It's actually painful to listen to this prick, isn't it Kane?" Shane said conversationally.

Kane's head snapped around. He growled as he noticed Tucker watching the fight with an animated expression.

"Get Tucker out of here, Shane. Now!"

"Yeah, your dad is right, my boy. It's not something you should witness." Shane pushed away from the wall.

"Dad! Watch out!"

"Fucking coward!" Kane roared as white-hot pain seared through his side. He panted as the thin razor-sharp knife that Chan Ho had still been clutching in his hand tore through skin and flesh in his side. It would've been a killing wound but as

Kane twisted around at Tucker's warning, it missed its mark.

He slammed Chan Ho back against the wall, holding him by the scruff of his shirt.

Chan Ho struggled as he stared into Kane's eyes, meeting the look of death for the first time in his life. He struggled violently and screamed at Zikri, "Don't just sit there. Help me!"

Zikri didn't respond, he was planted in his chair by fear as he watched Kane unstrap a shining, carbon stainless steel knife from his arm.

"Nooo!" Chan Ho shrieked, doing his best to escape the muscled arm securing him to the wall. He panted painfully as he felt the knife point press against his flesh. "You can't do this!" His breath struggled from his lips as the tip of the blade sliced through skin, muscle, and sinew with calculated slowness.

"Ugh ... Nooo," he puffed out a scream as it felt like his insides were ripped apart when Kane twisted the knife and forced it deeper. "Help me," he gasped frantically reaching a hand out to Zikri.

Kane felt nothing as he watched the fear and pain play an act of death in Chan Ho's eyes. No empathy, no guilt or remorse as he turned his hand viciously a final time.

"I protect what is mine and I have no mercy for motherfuckers like you. You stole my son, you threatened his life, and you scared him," he growled. With brute strength, he thrust the knife all the way into his body, ripping, slicing, and tearing away at his flesh.

Kane stepped back as he pulled out the blade, watching impassively as the mighty leader of the Sun Lee Fong Triads sank to his knees. His face twisted in a grotesque mask of pain as he spasmed and jerked on the floor.

"For that, you will die in your own blood."

"Hey! Where do you think you're going?" Tucker didn't hesitate and with amazing agility he did a flying kick from a standing position, snapping Zikri's head to the side and followed through with the other leg in a devastating kick to his stomach. He went down like a log.

"Holy crap, just look at our boy," Danton said as he arrived, looking bloody and battered after a brutal fight with the huge Sumo wrestler, Li. "If I ever doubted you're Kane's son, that kick just clinched it."

"Where did you learn to fight like that?" Kane asked with a dark frown. The last thing he'd wanted was Tucker to witness this brutal side of him.

"Mom insisted I learn to protect myself. I don't know why but she was always concerned that I might be in danger." His chest puffed up. "I've got a junior black belt in Krav Maga." He stood tall as he looked at Kane. "For the record, Dad ... I wasn't scared."

"Well ... whaddya know? Like father like son." Danton smiled at Tucker.

"Dad!" Tucker screamed and stormed forward to push his shoulder under Kane's arm as he stumbled and went down on his knee. "He's bleeding! Uncle Shane, do something!"

"That cut is deep and you've lost too much blood already." Shane looked at Danton. "All set?"

"Yep, ready to rock and roll."

The powerboat was already heading toward Miami harbor to get Kane to a hospital when an explosion shuddered through the atmosphere.

"Yeah, motherfucker, you messed with the wrong Sinclair."

Chapter Twenty-Two

"Tucker! Are you okay?" Rose stormed into the hospital room and aimed directly at her son standing at the end of the bed. She hugged him tight as tears flowed unchecked over her cheeks.

"Mom! Let go. I'm fine," he mumbled against her shoulder.

She released him, but her hands trembled as she touched his face, his arms, and back to his face to ensure he wasn't hurt.

"I've never been so scared in my life when I heard you'd been kidnapped."

"Mom, relax. As you can see, I don't even have a bruise. Besides, you had no need to worry. Dad already saved me by the time you heard the news."

"That's completely beside the point. God, Tucker, I don't know what I would have done if something had happened to you." Fresh tears filled her eyes.

"Ah, no Mom, please don't cry. I hate it when you cry."

Rose was startled as she looked at him. "I never cry."

"You do, all the time in your sleep."

She had no response to that and she couldn't even deny it. She woke up many times crying in the middle of the night. She just never knew he'd heard it.

Her gaze was drawn to the big man lying in the hospital bed, watching the reunion between mother and son with a closed expression. It sparked Rose's irritation that even under the circumstances he presented a mask of indifference to the world.

"And you!" She pointed a stiff finger at Kane, finally throwing caution to the wind as yet another fear slayed her bare. If she had to lose him again ... it didn't bear thinking of.

"Me?" The response accompanied that libido sparking eyebrow crawl.

"Yes, you! What were you thinking chasing after a goddamn Chinese Triad leader? Don't you have any common sense?" She threw her arms in the air and turned in a circle until she faced him again. "Tell me, Kane Rothman, why do we have police officers? FBI agents? DOJ agents? Good lord! Name any letter of the alphabet and America has agents that go along with it." She glared at him, fists on her hips, and her foot tapping on the floor.

Kane glanced at Tucker, not bothering to hide his mirth. "Is she always this melodramatic?"

Tucker rolled his eyes. "You ain't seen nothin' yet."

"I am so glad the two of you find this amusing." Her eyes narrowed on Kane. "I'm waiting."

"For what? Oh ... that wasn't a rhetorical question? You actually expect me to answer it?"

"Kane Rothman, you have one—"

"Rothman? You had a child together, Rose. How is it that you don't know Kane's real name?"

Peyton asked as she and Stone walked into the room.

"Fuck," Kane muttered.

Rose looked at Peyton and then at Stone, completely ignoring Kane. "What is she talking about?"

"Rothman is our acting name. We chose to keep our identities private to ensure we have a life we can live without the paparazzi knocking on our doors or camping out on our lawns." Stone glanced briefly at Kane who lay back and stared at the ceiling, waiting for the explosion.

"So, Rothman isn't your real name. Pray tell, who are you then?" Her voice could freeze over the entire North Atlantic Ocean.

"Sinclair," Kane said quietly.

Rose turned to face him. She stared at him for a long time, battling with the hurt that filled every chamber in her heart.

"Rose," Kane began, expecting her to rip into him. When she did speak, it was in a husky voice, filled with so much pain and desolation, it tore through his heart. He started, surprised at the emotions he felt ... for the first time since the explosion.

"You asked me to marry you that night. You gave me an engagement ring. It was all a lie, wasn't it? You never intended to honor that promise you made ..." Tears filled her eyes, but she stubbornly forced them back. "That's why you never told me who you really were. You never, *never* trusted me. You found me guilty of so many things, all without giving me a chance to explain. You treated me like shit while you ... God, you're such a bastard."

"Rose, that's not what—"

"Fuck you, Kane *Sinclair*. I hope you—"

"Mom!"

Rose heaved in a deep breath at the reproach in her son's voice. She looked at him, sadness overwhelmed her as she noticed the shock in his eyes at war with grief that what he had just found might be taken away from him. His father. She reached out to cup his cheek with a trembling hand.

"I love you, Tucker, more than life itself. I'll never keep your father from you, but I can't ... I can't be here ... I need to leave."

She pivoted and ran out the door with the sound of Tucker's confused voice calling after her, ringing in her ears.

"Stone, stop her. She can't leave."

"I can't force her to—"

"You fucking stop her or I'm getting out of this bed. Lock her in my apartment if you have to but keep her on The Seven Keys until I return."

"Okay, but I'll have you know this is … Jesus, get back in bed, I'm going," Stone snapped as Kane struggled to get off the bed. He sprinted after Rose.

"Well, it seems I was right. There *is* a story here." Peyton stared at Kane. "Maybe I should start digging to get to the truth, seeing as you're too hardheaded to give her a chance to explain."

"Keep your nose out of my business, little snip. I'll handle this my way."

"Yeah, like that puts my mind to rest any." She smiled broadly as she strutted in front of the bed with a twinkle in her eye. "See, here's the thing. You," and she pointed at his head, moving her finger up and down his body, "are stuck in that bed for a couple of days, so," she wiggled her shoulders at him, "you can't stop me."

With that, she trotted toward the door and with a "Toodles," over her shoulder, she disappeared down the hallway, ignoring Kane's roar, "Peyton, get your ass back here!"

"Dad? Is it true? Did you just ... string Mom along? Like one of your groupies?" Tucker couldn't hide his upset.

"No, Tucker. I loved your mother, so much that I haven't been able to move on after ..."

"Tell me! What happened? Why didn't you marry her?"

"Son, it's a complicated story. One I don't even know half of. Hell, I know shit." Kane sighed heavily. "I promise you, I will sort this out and I will tell you everything, but first ... I need to fix things with your mother."

"When?"

"As soon as I get out of the hospital."

"Ready to go, Champ?" Shane asked from the doorway.

"I guess." Tucker looked at Kane. "She can't be alone, Dad. I need to be with her. She needs to know that I still love her as much as always, that you haven't taken her place in my heart ... that you're in there alongside her. Please, I hate seeing my mom so unhappy."

"I agree." Kane looked at Shane. "Did Stone find her?"

"Yes, and I have to tell you, she's not happy. I just came to check if you were still okay after all the curses she'd placed on your head as he bundled her into his truck."

"Good. She'll be in my apartment. Take Tucker to her, and you, young man, promise me that you won't go wandering through the castle on your own."

Tucker was too eager to get to Rose and readily agreed. Kane watched him go with a thoughtful expression on his face.

"I fucked up. I loved her and I should've asked first what had happened, rather than allow the years of grief to burst out in a rage of distrust."

But Kane knew that even in retrospect, he wouldn't have acted any differently. There might have been a reason for what she'd done but keeping his son from him, it was the one thing that hurt him the most.

"She knew how badly I wanted children. She knew and still, she denied me sixteen years of my only son's life."

Faced with the emptiness that had been his companion for so long, Kane honestly didn't know if he had it in him to forgive her for that.

"Not even for Tucker's sake."

Two weeks later ...

"Tell me, Rose, what is the Dominant's role?"

Once again, Rose stood in the spotlight on stage, naked, with her hands cuffed behind her back. This time, she quivered with anger. Kane had kept her locked in his apartment for two weeks. One of which he had been present at Castle Sin after his discharge from hospital, but not once had he bothered to come to her. He ignored her existence and made her feel even more inconsequential in his life.

She was tempted to sass him but decided against it. The heavy beat of Van Halen in the background, mingling with the deep voices of members, meant all eyes were on her ... again.

She gave his question brief consideration and quickly recalled, "To give the submissive what she needs, Master Bear."

"Do subs readily admit to their needs, sub RL?"

"I suppose it depends on how dark their needs are, Master Bear."

"Elaborate."

"Mostly subs believe they know what they want, but it's not what they truly need to experience; those deep, dark and secret desires we only dream about."

"Why is that?"

"I don't understand?"

"Why are you scared of admitting to your deep, dark and secret desires, sub RL?"

Rose licked her lips and shifted her weight from one foot to the other. Strangely, she wasn't overly concerned about being naked in front of all the strange eyes. Maybe Kane had managed to instill at least that in her subconscious. She had no right to criticize that which belonged to them.

"Focus!"

"Yes, Master Bear." She took a deep breath before she answered his question. "I keep mine buried because ... I'm scared."

"Of what?"

"Of getting hurt," she lilted softly. "Of feeling cheap and like ... a whore."

Rose held her breath as she sensed Kane circling her. Her skin tingled in the wake of feeling his gaze on her nakedness.

"Being called a whore or a slut during a Dom/sub scenario, Rose is different than in the actual definition of the word. In line with that, has anyone ever been called a whore or a slut in any of these dungeons?"

Rose tilted her head as his voice now came from behind her. She dragged in a deep breath.

"Other than you not so long ago ... not that I know of, Master Bear."

Kane didn't immediately respond. He cast his mind back and cursed silently as the times he'd called her a slut in a derogatory way flared to the surface.

"The circumstances were different." His voice lowered. "Ban the thought of a whore from your mind."

Rose frowned as his voice sounded from in front of her. It was disconcerting to be in the dark, not knowing what to expect or where she was and who were all watching her.

"The nature of this scene for your evaluation is very advanced. You may find it impossible to safeword if you want out."

Rose felt a trickle of fear mixed with excitement course through her. She recalled what Shane had said at her previous evaluation. She trembled as the memory raised like a serpent from the deep sea. Kane knew what her darkest desires were. Was this it? Did he truly plan to give her the one thing she'd secretly been yearning to experience no matter how debilitating it could be for her?

There was a reason it was a secret. She would never have requested such a scene with any Dom, not even Master Bear. She began to shiver.

His warm hand palmed her cheek. She instinctively leaned into his touch.

"I know I've been malevolent towards you since Tucker arrived, Rose, but in the dungeon, right here and now ... do you trust me as a Dominant, your Master?"

His familiar dulcet-toned voice wrapped itself around her senses and overwhelmed her defenses, coaxing her submissive persona to immediate obedience.

"I acted harshly and out of character and for that I apologize."

She listened to his soft, cajoling tone. She could imagine his eyes smoldering with warmth and understanding that always managed to wrap her soul in a benevolence; that assuaged all her fears.

"Apology accepted, Master Bear."

"This scene is going to push every limit you have while at the same time, it'll bring you the dark excitement you crave. Do you wish to continue, little dove? Do you trust me enough to give you the darkest of your desires and ensure that you're not hurt?"

Rose still considered her response when her head bobbed up and down in courageous consent.

"No, sub RL, say it out loud so everyone can hear."

"Yes, Master Bear, I wish to continue. I trust you to take care of me during the scene," she said in a silvery voice, silently praying that she'd be able to endure what was coming and not disappoint Kane … or herself for that matter.

"Come." Kane uncuffed her wrists and led her to a padded table. "Lay back." He pressed a soft round object in her hand. "This is a red stop sign. As I said, you might not be able to speak when the scene reaches its peak. Dropping the sign means you're safewording and the scene ends immediately. Do you understand, sub RL?"

"Yes, Master Bear."

"Good, stretch out your hands, please."

Rose complied and forced herself to relax as he cuffed her hands to the sides of the table beside her ears. His heat so close managed to ease her fears. His fingers traced her chin and the straightness of her nose. "So beautiful." His voice sounded sad, but before she could investigate it further, his fingers wrapped around her throat.

She gulped a breath. *Oh, sweet holy shit, he does know!*

His fingers stroked the softness of her skin tenderly. "Although this is something deep inside you that needs to be explored, it's still important to concentrate on what you've been taught. Remember the volleyball game?"

"Yes, Master Bear." Rose's skin sizzled everywhere his fingers lingered.

"In this scene, you'll have many sensations and emotions to deal with and therefore I'm giving you a goal to aim for through it all. Have you guessed what's about to happen, Rose?"

"I ... think part of it is asphyxiation," she said hesitantly. He had taught her the pleasure of submitting to a firm hold around her throat. It had always been a desire for her to be pushed a little further.

"Yes, and therefore focus is of the utmost importance in this scene, my pet and I need you to concentrate. Your goal is to keep breathing in and out, no matter what happens in between. Do you understand?"

"I do, Master Bear."

"Let's practice. On counts of five, I want you to breathe in and out. Come, do it for me."

Rose felt the quiver of excitement rising higher inside her as she breathed in and out, counting in her head at the same time.

"Good girl."

Rose lifted her head as his voice came from afar.

"Oh!" she gulped as suddenly his hard hands closed around her hips and he pulled her body toward him until the table cut into her ass cheeks and her legs dangled over the edge. Her arms were now stretched above her.

"Focus! Remember, no matter the restriction, your goal is to breathe, on the count of five and don't stop." His voice deepened in a dark warning. Rose gasped in a breath and counted it out in her mind, her chest rattling with nervousness. His hand warmed her skin as he rested it between her breasts. He drew small circles on her skin that managed to calm her.

"Easy, little dove, breathe in ... good," his smooth voice edged darkly. "And out."

Rose concentrated on his voice and continued to follow his directions, sighing as he brushed his hands over her breasts and gave them a gentle squeeze. She moaned as he palmed her nipples, her breathing smooth and relaxed as she settled into the breathing rhythm. Her breath hitched as he traced his hands over her stomach, to follow the rounded curves of her thighs to her feet.

"Ahh," she groaned as he lifted her foot and kissed the inside of her knee as he gently guided her leg up and to the side. He rubbed the arch of her foot, while massaging her calve. "Ohh!" Rose gulped in a breath as she felt another hand brushing over her knee. It couldn't be Kane's as both his were tracing the inside of her thigh.

Of freaking hell! This is it. He's going to make me ... fuck-fuck-fuck!

She cried out as a crack sounded in her ears before the sting on her nipples registered.

"Stop breathing again and I'll extend this scene by ten minutes every time. Do not forget, sub RL, this is part of your evaluation. Breathing is your ultimate goal. Understood?"

"Yes, Master Bear," she squealed as the second pair of hands pulled her leg up to her waist and teased the soft skin of her inner thighs, spreading her wide open to the hungry eyes of the crowd.

Rose had never been in a threesome and suddenly the prospect of exactly what lay ahead slammed home. Yes, it had always been her secret desire to be at the mercy of many, touched and fucked until she lost count. Now that it was about to become a reality, she was fast losing courage. She opened her mouth to call out to Kane.

"Oh ... mmm," she moaned as a third pair of hands cupped her breasts, to tease her nipples with pinches and tugs at the same time as the other two meandered to her core and playfully dipped their fingers inside her slit, rubbed her clit and very quickly made her forget to breathe.

Kane was quick to remind her with a sharp slap on her thigh. She chucked in a breath and did her utmost to concentrate and settled back into a rhythm of five counts.

"You just gained another ten minutes, sub RL."

Rose stiffened, very aware of the teasing and arousing hands all over her body, but she was frighteningly cognizant of the fact that Kane's voice had come from a distance. He wasn't one of the men caressing her anymore.

God! He's left me alone with them. The wail inside her mind assisted to further unsettle her. He had left her at the mercy of others. For all she knew, strangers even. Whereas before she'd been keen to continue, to push her boundaries, relaxed in the knowledge that he was taking part, suddenly, everything inside her screamed at her to end it. The protest formed in her mind, she opened her mouth when suddenly the entire scene shifted.

"Fuck! Oh shit, oh shit," she cried out as her body became the feeding ground of ravenous mouths and lips latching onto her. Her left nipple suffered the nibbling and gnawing of sharp teeth biting the hardened nub while the other was drawn deep into a hot mouth and sucked on vigorously.

Rose struggled to keep breathing on the count and as she battled to keep the rhythm, she realized there were an equal number of mouths paying homage to her body. They knew exactly how to arouse and she arched helplessly into it as they rubbed, teased, licked, and sucked at leisure.

All thought to end it, completely forgotten.

Her gasps followed as they boldly spread her body open, leaving her pussy on show to all that stood watching. Her body wasn't hers anymore, they took over and molded every sensation to their will, leaving her vulnerable and overwhelmed.

"Stop," she moaned as she felt her body tremble violently under their onslaught, suddenly scared that she'd bit off more than she could chew.

She gasped as Kane's deep baritone sounded next to her face. "I love that word. Stop. A single syllable." His voice darkened warningly. "You know it means nothing in here. You can scream, beg, and plead and that won't matter. What will, Rose?"

"S-safeword, king or I have to drop the stop sign," she managed to gasp as it felt like she had become the victim of an octopus, sucking on every nub and erogenous zone of her body.

"Remember that but until you do, I'm warning you, do not stop breathing again."

Rose should've known better, and maybe she did, knowing nothing would come of shouting out stop, except it had brought Kane closer and gave her a breather. She was mortified at how aroused she was. She was wet and could already feel the embarrassing cold patch under her ass as she moved restlessly on the table. Her legs were caught once more in two pairs of hands and pulled all the way up beside her waist, leaving her spread open for everyone to see how swollen she was, maybe even notice how her pussy twitched uncontrollably.

"One more thing, sub RL, in case you forgot, you're not allowed to come until I tell you to."

Rose almost spat a curse at him as the play intensified, a tongue slipped deep inside her pussy and sucked, hard, while fingers strummed her clit and two mouths vied for a variety of sensations on her breasts. She opened her mouth to beg for permission to come as the coil inside her cranked up to snapping point when teeth clamped around three nubs, bit into them hard and shook viciously.

"Ohshitohshitohshit," she screamed as spasm after spasm shuddered through her. She got caught in a rogue wave that catapulted her so high that every muscle in her body twitched uncontrollably. She gasped, having lost the ability to breathe.

"Disappointing, little dove," Kane grunted.

Rose barely heard him, completely caught in the spell of the mouth feasting on her pussy while the other lips fluttered over her skin, leaving her trembling and too soon teetering on the edge once more.

'I can't ... it's too much. I can't ... breathe," she gulped as the hands shifted again, clamping her legs against her waist, lips curled around her nipples, a hard cock probed at the entrance of her pussy. She struggled, suddenly unsure she wished to continue, especially as she had no idea who it was.

"Easy, my pet," Kane's voice soothed her, as did the warm pressure of his fingers folding around her throat. "It's time, little dove. Remember what I said about the ball, Rose." He breathed against her lips and kissed her briefly. "Now ... hold your breath and keep it until I tell you to release."

Rose instinctively obeyed and dragged in a deep breath at the same time as a hard condom covered cock thrust hilt deep inside her. Her hips lifted, she inched closer to the edge as he began to plunge in a lazy rhythm.

The pressure of his fingers tightening around her throat yanked her back, and on a moan in her mind, she felt the orgasm ebb into the distance. She felt on the verge of exploding, in her mind as everything began to swim.

"Release."

Her nerves sparked to life as she responded to his command and puffed out her breath. The cock pounded harder, lips sucked and tugged on her nipples, yet another toggled her clit with an errant finger. She was at the mercy of strangers, that played her body like a musical instrument as one cock was replaced by another and another until she lost count. Her body shuddered, leaving her wriggling and writhing in shameless surrender to their unspoken commands.

Kane's voice controlling her breathing and the pressure of his hand around her throat was the only light in the dark world that surrounded her. A guiding light in a tumultuous storm that threatened to throw her headfirst into the deepest bottomless pit as she reveled in the most debaucherously act imaginable.

Her nipples burned from all the sucking, biting, and pulling. Her clit was swollen and sensitive and still, there was no end, no gruff order for her to come. This was what she'd wanted but it was so much more, so perverted and wrong that she shuddered in shame as her body kept begging for more. She blindly followed her Master's orders to hold her breath until her lungs burned and her head threatened to burst. It became insouciant of the lust that drove her as she canted her hips into the cocks plundering her body, the worst kind of perversion.

"Oh lord ... more! I need more!" she heard the croak echo in her ears, mortified to realize it was her own voice begging and pleading to drown her in an act of unexpurgated lust.

She thrashed as the tension of the lips gnawing on her nipples increased as yet another spent cock slipped from her pussy. Lips locked on her clit and sucked, then gnawed on it in tandem with those at her breasts.

"God! Stop. Owww ... Fuck it hurts ... it's ohshitohshit," she moaned as heat flushed her body with flashes of pain from three different directions. Every nub was over sensitized, painfully aroused and still ... needy.

"Hold your breath." Rose obeyed the harsh order but almost lost it as a cock slammed inside her so hard, she shifted higher on the bed. Her breath puffed from her lips. "Breathe, sub," Kane guttered above her as his hand closed around her throat and squeezed, gently this time. She stilled, and for the first time, felt the cock pulse inside her. It was him, Master Bear. Her head began to swim as he pulled back and pounded into her. She lost all sense of control as sensations melted into one, flaying helplessly in the growing crescendo that he now held in the palm of his hand.

She felt like she was floating in outer space, her mind had shut off, but responded automatically to his commands to breathe and release as he powered into her.

Then the game shifted once again. His fingers tightened around her neck as he pulled out and hands turned her so that her hips were sideways. She whimpered. Kane's fingers tightened and then he slammed back inside her.

"Hold," he ordered. She chucked in her breath only to release it on a scream as another cock plunge hilt deep into her anus. His fingers tightened again, his voice grated, "I said hold!"

Rose obeyed, struck blind by the cocks pounding her in time with her breathing. Kane's fingers tightened to the point of choking her but she was too caught up in the moment to care, all the while edging closer to exploding. The friction of the two cocks as they fucked her turned her brain into a mindless toll, spinning out of control. Sensations she'd never known existed pulsed through her.

Kane's fingers tightened; she didn't fight it, instead, she exulted in it as her back bowed against the hips slapping against hers. He knew exactly when to release the pressure, when to tighten. The blood rushed through her head, leaving her lightheaded; her fingers squeezed the stop sign in her hand as the thundering wave crashed just out of reach.

She teetered on the edge, thrashing against the fucking cocks, so close, she could feel the heat rush over her and then ... he took it away.

She cried out her frustration, not because they still fucked her like wild stallions eager to mate, but because he denied her the pressure of his hand around her throat. She heaved in desperate breaths with aching lungs, her body now completely spiraling out of control.

"Come, little dove. Show me how hard you can come."

His raw voice in her ear was the conduit needed, that she'd been waiting for. Her body solidified, they pounded and she shattered, completely at the mercy of her pussy clenching as spasms wracked her body. She tried to breathe, to rise above the wave crashing toward her but as Kane grunted his orgasm into her, his heat was the final spark to trigger another violent climax at the same time as the cock in her ass ejaculated.

Rose lost the battle as she gave in to the dark void of unconsciousness swallowing her whole.

Chapter Twenty-Three

Rose woke to the bright rays of the sun through the window. She kept her eyes closed and stretched lazily, only to stiffen at the muscles screaming in protest.

"Oh lord," she moaned as her hands moved to the swollen tenderness of her pussy. Everything came flashing back, like a movie on replay. She buried her face in the pillow. How was she ever going to face anyone again? She could only imagine what the other trainees and the Masters must think of her.

She stiffened as warm hands stretched her legs out and gently began to massage the knotted muscles in her calves. When they gentled the stiff ones on the inside of her thighs, she dared to peek through her fingers.

"About time you woke up," Kane murmured softly as he continued to do magic with his fingers on her straining legs.

"What time is it?" She groggily turned her head to stare out of the window. The sun was already midway to noon. "Goodness. I can't even remember falling asleep last night." She glanced around. "Certainly not in your bed." Rose was beyond confused. Ending up in Kane's bed was the last thing she'd expected.

"You didn't fall asleep, you passed out."

Kane chuckled at the blood red blush that flushed her cheeks.

"I feel so ashamed. I don't know how I'll ever be able to show my face outside this room again."

He continued to massage her legs. "There's no reason to feel that way, Rose. In Castle Sin, scenes such as yours aren't unusual. It forms an important part of the training; to push trainees past their comfort zone. Through it all, they learn to trust in the power of their submission to submit to something they either fear or believe is perverted." He glanced at her. "Tell me how it made you feel."

Rose gave his question deep thought as she cast her mind back to the previous night. It was difficult to filter through and separate the myriad of sensations that she had drowned in, from the emotions that had rallied for attention.

"One thing I do know, is that I have never before felt as vulnerable or overwhelmed. Not necessarily because I was blindfolded and not knowing who it was who touched or fucked me but because of how it made me feel. Of the sensation that completely blindsided me. There were so many all at once that I couldn't comprehend what who did to cause which one. It was ... frightening, exhilarating, and arousing. I can't remember that I've ever been engulfed in so much lust raging through my entire body."

She blinked at him as she licked her lips. A shy smile curved her lips in a pout. "The worst of it was ... no matter how many times and how many different cocks fucked me, there was a point that I wanted more, my body screamed for more. Good god, how perverted is that?" She covered her cheeks with her hands.

"There's nothing perverted about acknowledging the desires of your body, Rose. Freeing your mind from the shackles of a conservative community is what the BDSM lifestyle is all about. To embrace needs that spark your desires and to have the freedom to explore the needs that drives those desires." He watched her quietly. "Is there more?"

Rose pushed into a sitting position and leaned against the headboard. "I'm not sure exactly how to express it, but there was a point where I felt empowered. You know … when I listened to the Doms grunt and groan as they fucked me, the way they caressed me, it felt as if they reacted to the demands of my body, the direction of what my movements guided them to feel. Although I was cuffed and at the mercy of so many hands, lips, and cocks at the same time, I felt all powerful."

"Bravo, little dove. You just passed your evaluation with flying colors. That's what I wanted you to realize by choosing that specific need of yours. That submission gives *you* the power. You give it and you can take it away just as easily. If you only know how everyone involved in that scene looked at you, with such awe and reverence, unable to control the lust you evoked in them ... ah, sweet baby, you'd be astounded at the effect you had on us all."

"On you ... too?" Rose latched onto the one word that gave the entire experience more meaning. That he too, had been completely invested in the scene.

"More so than any of the others," he admitted in a gruff voice. His eyes locked with hers.

"Watching you last night and experiencing your darkest desire with you, made me realize just how much of an idiot I've been. I allowed the demon inside me to guide the way I treated you, and for that, I am eternally sorry." He placed his fingers over her lips as she attempted to talk. "No matter the justification I had, there are other ways to resolve it without allowing my emotions to take over."

Kane sighed heavily. "I told myself I don't want to know; that whatever the reason, you still deceived me. It's not working. It's eating away at me, Rose. I need to know what drove you to throw away the love I offered, the life we had dreamed of together … for keeping my son from me all these years."

Rose wrung her hands together as she struggled to put her thoughts together. Kane closed his hands over hers and squeezed gently.

"Relax, Rose, and take your time. I promise I'm not going to explode again. Having Tucker in my life is too important to fuck it up again."

"I need you to know that whatever happens between us, I'll never keep him from you again." Tears filled her eyes. "Even if it means he prefers living with you, I'll step back and give the two of you the time I've denied you for so long."

"That means more to me than you'll ever know." He brushed his hand over her cheek. "Tell me, Rose."

Rose dragged in a straggling breath and then the entire sordid tale fell from her lips. Kane listened without interrupting her. His body solidifying as she named Roy Summers as the main instigator with Leon Salvino as the mastermind behind it all.

"I initially refused, but Roy kept showing me clips of you during filming. It made me realize how in your element you were, how happy you looked, and how amazingly talented you were. I couldn't take that away from you. I didn't want to be the one to make you look back years later and regret walking away from something you loved so much. I feared you might blame me … I tried so hard that week to change your mind. To try and make you see you could continue acting, that it wouldn't affect my feelings for you, that we'd make it work and be happy."

"That's what the arguments were all about that entire week? You tried to find an alternative to giving in to Roy and Leon's fucked up plan to make you disappear?"

"Yes, I loved you with all my heart and thinking of never seeing you again … it broke me." Rose looked down and realized Kane still clasped her hands. She unfurled hers and tentatively folded one around his and used the other to caress the top one. She relaxed when he didn't pull away.

"Why didn't you just walk away, Rose? A bomb explosion? For God's sake! Why go to such an extreme?"

"I asked them the same question. They were adamant that disappearing wouldn't be enough. That you wouldn't allow me to walk out on us. They said if you believed I was dead that ... acting would give you focus again."

"They were right. Working long hours and falling into bed dead on my feet was the only way I managed to get through each day ... especially that first year while my hands were healing."

Rose looked startled. "Your hands?"

Kane turned his hands over. "Oh, my god!" she exclaimed as she traced the uneven surface of the skin on the inside of his fingers.

He smiled wryly. "At least the burns weren't as deep and bad as yours. It took many skin grafts to fix my palms but my fingers suffered structural damage and as you can see ... I have no fingerprints."

"How ... what did you do?" Rose had gone pasty at the thought that Kane could've died trying to get to her.

"I was just about to dive into the ocean when the explosion ripped through the air. At first, I couldn't believe my eyes and then I ran. As I approached, I could hear your horrific and terrified screams. I tried to get the sliding doors open but the aluminum had melted shut and the windows were all shatterproof. I couldn't break them. I refused to give up and kept trying ... I didn't even feel the pain of the burns. I just had to get to you. When your screams stopped ... the world around me turned black. Something inside me died in the fire that night. I've never been able to get it back. No matter how hard I tried."

Rose lifted his hands and kissed his fingers, tears wetting his skin. He pulled his one hand from hers and tilted back her chin. "Don't cry for me, Rose. It's in the past and maybe now the nightmares will stop."

"You still have nightmares?"

"More than I care to remember and it's always the same. I wake up clawing at the bed in a desperate attempt to open the door and end up … sobbing when your screams die in my ears."

"I'm so sorry. I … if only I hadn't listened to them. I should've trusted in you. In the decision you made for your life. They had … we had no right to manipulate you into making you believe I had died."

"You almost did, didn't you? What went wrong?"

Rose dragged in a stuttering sigh. "I have thought about it so many times over the years and I always wondered … when I phoned Roy to tell him it was time, he told me I had ten minutes. In other words, to get through the hatch he'd secretly installed in the closet into the underground tunnel to get away. But I had just finished dressing when the bomb exploded. Eight minutes early. I honestly think they never intended me to escape. I … maybe I'm wrong, but I couldn't help thinking they wanted me to die in that explosion. I remember Mom telling me how angry and shocked Roy was when she contacted him to tell him in which hospital I was. That's why I changed my name again. I didn't trust them, not around me, and definitely not around Tucker."

"Tucker," Kane rolled the name on his tongue. Rose's hands tightened around his.

"I am eternally sorry for keeping him from you, but ... I didn't know what to do in the first years. I knew I couldn't approach you. For one, I was terrified of Roy and Leon, and ... I had become a different person and I guess over the years I convinced myself it was for the best. For all of us if you never knew about him."

"That was the biggest mistake you made in all this, Rose." His gaze pierced through hers. "And the one thing I honestly don't know if I'll ever be able to forgive you for."

"I know." Rose took a giant leap of faith. "This might mean nothing to you but I need to say it. I never stopped loving you. You have always been in my heart, my protector and guiding light during bad and good times. I always thought how you would respond when Tucker asked difficult questions." A brief smile touched her lips. "He is so much like you. He's got all your good qualities and unfortunately some of the not so good, but I thanked the Lord every day of my life that I had a piece of you to touch, to hold, and to love."

"Rose—"

This time her fingers on his lips silenced him. "I have tried—so hard—over the years to move on but I couldn't. You were always there when I believed I found a man I could come to love. Eventually, I gave up, knowing that no one could ever replace the love I had ... and still have for you."

Rose pulled her hands from his and slipped from the bed. She smiled gently, her eyes glistening with tears and the love she didn't bother to hide from him.

"I'll go and pack my things. I know I've overstayed my welcome. It's school holidays, so if Tucker wishes to stay with you, I won't stop him and if ..." she swallowed hard, "if he chooses to move here and live with you in Key Largo, I'll accept that too. All I ask is that you please, *please* never keep him from me. I don't think I'll survive if I never see him again."

Kane didn't move, but his eyes followed Rose as she looked around and with an apologetic smile picked up the white shirt he'd worn the previous night and slipped it on. With a final yearning look in her eyes, she turned and ran out of the room.

The sunshine seemed dimmer and the future bleak in the emptiness that she left behind. With a heavy sigh, Kane got up and stood under the shower until his skin started to wrinkle.

"Stop moping over it, Sinclair. At least now you know the truth and you can let go of the bitterness inside you. Don't forget that you have the brightest sunray in your life—your son."

He got dressed and for the first time in years, he didn't feel the dark cloud of loss hang over his head as he walked into the kitchen.

"Hey, Dad. About time you woke up." Kane smiled at him, realizing he'd used that exact phrase earlier on Rose.

"Tucker? What are you doing here?"

He shrugged in response but chewed on his lip. Kane detected a sadness in his eyes that he tried his hardest to hide.

"What's bothering you, son?"

"Mom said she's leaving today." He looked around as he furiously blinked to keep the tears at bay. "I had hoped you and I would have more time together."

"You don't need to go yet, Tucker."

"Yes, I do. I need to be there for her. Mom isn't as strong as she makes everyone believe."

"What do you mean?"

"I don't know what happened all those years ago, but I do know that it has haunted Mom all her life. I can't tell you how many times I woke up to her screams of terror when she had nightmares or other nights, listening to her cry herself to sleep. The worst of it was that I could do nothing to help her. All I knew was that she was hurting, all the time, and it never stopped. I know this might sound bad but when she decided to move to Miami and gave me the choice to be a day student or go to boarding school, I jumped at the chance. I had hoped it would help her heal if she went away." He shook his head sadly. "But she never did. When she came home for school holidays or took me on vacation, the nightmares still happened, she still cried herself to sleep."

He shifted uncomfortably in his seat. "I had hoped ..." he glanced at Kane, "you know ... that you and her ... that maybe you still loved her and we could be a family. Then she'd lose that sadness in her eyes and she'd be happy. Don't you think she deserves to be happy, Dad? And you, me ... all of us?"

"Tucker, I ..."

Kane stared at the hopeful expression on his son's face. His words echoed in his mind. Rose had suffered just as much, if not more than he had over the years. Yes, she had made a mistake to be conned into believing those two motherfuckers. Although she looked different, he knew her, deep down she was still the same woman, Narine Bosch, *his* Narine, the woman he'd sworn to love until the day he died.

Try as he might, he still couldn't get over Tucker, that she'd kept his existence from him.

"She came here because of me. I begged her to find a way to tell you about me because I wanted to meet you, to have you in my life. She didn't have to do that but she was willing to face your wrath to make up for the wrong she did in never telling you about me."

Tucker smiled wryly and, in that moment, Kane saw himself in his expression.

"I know this sounds cheesy and my friends will piss themselves laughing when they hear me now." He shrugged it off and turned serious again. "Whatever she did to hurt you, Dad, I don't think she had a choice. Not telling you about me ... I'm here now. I am your son and we have the rest of our lives to make up for lost time. The moment I saw you, I loved you, Dad. You're the kind of man I want to be one day." His voice thickened. "I'd like to think it'll be the kind of man who can open his heart to forgive and to love again."

Tears trickled over Tucker's cheeks but he didn't look away.

"You are wise beyond your years, my son. I do love you and I'll move heaven and earth to make you happy." He brushed the tears from Tucker's cheeks, unperturbed that his own were also wet. He smiled and jumped from the barstool.

"Where are you going?" Tucker shouted after him as he stomped out of the kitchen and back to the bedroom. Kane didn't respond but returned within minutes, a determined expression on his face.

"Dad? What's happening?"

"It's time *I* make right a wrong. You better tag along. I might just need your suave persuasion skills to save the day."

Rose did her best not to snap at Cora and Diana who refused to let her be and wallow in peace as she packed her bags.

"I don't understand. Last night Master Bear still did a mid-training evaluation, a fucking hot one, so much so it's the talk of the castle this morning," Cora yanked the top Rose was folding out of her hand. "Come on, Rose! Talk to us. You passed your evaluation with flying colors. Why are you leaving? Why now?"

"It's complicated, and no, I don't want to talk about it."

"It'll be remiss of me not to tell you that talking is the best cure for a broken heart, Rose." Diana took the top from Cora and folding it neatly, added it to the pile in the suitcase on the bed.

"I appreciate your concern, but I'll be—"

The women started at the shrill siren renting the mid-morning air like a butcher's cleaver on a carcass. It was a violence to the calm that had been before.

"Is that a perimeter breach alarm or the siren to call everyone to the Gathering Hall?" Cora said as she rushed to the door to peep outside. "I never know the difference between the two. I guess we better go and see."

"I need to finish packing." Rose continued folding her clothes.

"One never ignores an alarm. For all we know there's a fire in the castle," Diane said as she caught Rose's hand and dragged her along.

"I'm sure we would have smelled smoke if that's the case," Rose muttered but had no choice but to go along as they all but dragged her down the stairs.

They found everyone in the Gathering Hall, looking around in confusion.

"Hey Mom, are you finished packing?" Tucker put his arm around her and smiled at her. He looked like a cat that had just received a bowl of cream.

"Almost." She looked at him and realized that he was already as tall as her. She patted him on his head. "When did you grow so tall? One of these days I'll have to look up at you."

"Yep, as they say, time doesn't stand still and neither do the Sinclairs."

Rose laughed. "Oh, really? Exactly who are the they you're referring to?"

He bumped his fist against his chest. "Us, the Sinclairs."

Rose was too delighted at how happy he was to feel affronted that he referred to himself as a Sinclair.

"Come, let's go to the front. I wanna see what the fuss is all about."

"No, Tucker," Rose bore back but he was too strong and tugged her along with him as he weaved his way through the people standing around. "I prefer to stay in the back. Tucker, let me ..."

Rose stumbled to a halt and she stared wide eyed at the most unexpected view as the people separated a path to allow them through. It took a second or two for her fried mind to register what she was looking at and even though it was right before her, larger than life, she struggled to comprehend the reality of it.

"What is this?" she croaked, clamping her hands together to settle the trembling that started from deep within.

"Go, Mom, he's waiting for you." Tucker prodded her with a push from behind.

"Don't ..." she glared at him over her shoulder as she stumbled forward, "push me!"

Tucker just smiled broadly and urged her on with waving hands. "Go!"

Rose turned forward and took a few tentative steps closer. It seemed unreal, especially in lieu of the discussion they had earlier but it wasn't. It couldn't be because there he was ... the mighty Master Bear, on his one knee, holding out a red rose. His eyes ... *oh lord, his eyes!* She became lost in them. In those warm earthy hues, he offered his soul, openly and with the kind of beauty that expanded the moment into a personal eternity, a heaven she could only dream to be a part of.

"A man is only as good as the mistakes he admits he made. More than that, my ... *our* amazing son taught me that a man who strives to correct them, to know when to forgive and to forget is the kind of man he wishes to become."

Rose could barely see him through the tears that blinded her. To hear him call Tucker their son with so much love in his voice, filled her heart with more joy than she had ever felt.

"I am so proud of the son you honored me with, Rose, for the upbringing that you gave him and taught him all the values and love that made him such a wonderful young man. It's a gift I'll treasure inside my heart forever."

"Mom! Go closer," Tucker urged her from behind and gave her another little push.

This time, she didn't need it and found herself in front of Kane. He caught her hand and placed a warm kiss in her palm.

"I loved you with everything in me all those years ago. It's a love that never faded. A love that wouldn't let me forget or allow me to move on. I now know why. The Universe had destined us to be as one. We are fated to be, and contrary to what Shane might say about me, I'm not a fool."

The people chittered in mirth. Shane smiled with a happiness he couldn't hide.

"Only a fool would allow a woman of such beauty and grace, honor, integrity, and love to slip through his fingers. I love you, Rose Lovett, so much it hurts thinking of you at times. Yes, baby, you, the woman that you are now. I see the one you were in you, in the naughty glint in your eye, in the way you smile or pout your lips when you're annoyed. I love all of that, but I adore you, Rose, the woman you have become through pain and suffering, all of it, you did for me. For that, my love, you are the most precious gift destiny could have placed on my path."

He gave her his naughty boy smile and held out the rose. She was still too overwhelmed to do anything but take it. He dug a square black box out of his pocket, opened it and stared at it for long moments before he held it out to her.

"I gave you this ring once and with it my commitment that I'll love you until my dying breath.

That hasn't changed. Rose Lovett, I'm asking you once again ... no, I'm begging you to be my savior ... will you marry me?"

Rose gasped as her eyes dropped to the ring he held out to her. The tears flowed freely as she covered her mouth in awe. She blinked at him, a beatific smile eroded the years of bitterness.

"It's my ring! You found my ring! Oh. god, Kane ... how ..." She heaved in a deep breath to calm herself as she looked into his eyes. "I told you earlier, you've been my saving grace throughout the years. You've lived inside my heart and soothed my soul all along. I love you, Kane Sinclair, for the man you were then and for the man you are now, the father of my ... *our* son and the only keeper of my heart." She brushed her fingers over his lips. "Yes, a thousand times, yes. I'll marry you."

Kane got to his feet, grumbling. "Goddamn, Tucker, this is the last time I listen to you. On my knees for goodness sake, at my age. They're fucking killing me."

Everyone burst out laughing as he caught Rose in his arms. She cupped his face and stared at him with glistening eyes. "There is one condition."

Kane stiffened but refused to allow past beliefs blacken the day. "Only one?"

"For now," she giggled as he cast a dark look at her.

"I'm listening, my love."

"I waited long enough. A seventeen-year engagement is a lifetime. I want to get married soon."

"Exactly what I was gonna say," Kane murmured as his head lowered and caught her lips in a passionate kiss.

"Whoa, Dad, that's more like it ... and something you have to teach me!"

Epilogue

Three weeks later ...

North Pacific Ocean, fifty miles off the coast of the Hawaiian Island, Oahu ...

The engine of the Fountain 32 ThunderCat powerboat purred like a content tiger as it slowly rocked to a halt. Kane cut the engine and looked around.

"Perfect day for a dip in the ocean, don't you agree, Shane?"

"Indeed. The tranquility of the water is so calming this time of day."

"This has gone beyond being funny, Kane. You said you wanted to check the location for the scene where Stone and Hawk are killed off in the movie. Not that I understand why you insisted we meet you in Hawaii while on honeymoon. The scene is only filmed next month." Leon Salvino glanced around. An uneasy feeling rippled down his spine. They were in the middle of the ocean. There was nothing in sight, except the ocean. "Besides, this isn't the location." He struggled violently against the ropes. "And why the fuck are we tied up?"

"Just keeping it real, Leon," Kane said dryly.

"You're trying to scare us, and however entertaining this is, it isn't funny. You're acting like fucking vigilantes." Roy's voice sounded thin and wary, belying the confidence he tried to relay.

"Don't you always find remarks like that entertaining, Kane?" Shane glanced at the two trussed up men on the back seat of the boat. "Comfy?"

"Fuck you!" Leon sneered. He struggled, but as they were hogtied, it was a fruitless effort.

"Thank you, but I prefer someone a little more feminine than you." Shane tapped his chin as he regarded them with a serious expression. "You know, Kane, maybe we were a little hasty. It might just be more rewarding to ensure the two of them become the bitches for all inmates in prison."

"For all we know, they might just end up liking getting fucked in the ass, so no, forget it." Kane's chilled gaze glimmered as he stared at them. "Let's get this over with. I've wasted enough of my time on these useless pieces of shit."

Leon cracked out a laugh. "What are you gonna do? Leave us in the middle of the ocean? Brilliant plan, Sinclair. We both happen to be excellent swimmers. It might take us a while but we'll reach land soon enough."

Kane and Shane smirked.

"They don't seem to get it."

"They sure don't."

"Look, Kane, this has gone far enough," Roy said. "We fucked up but Narine was never supposed to get hurt. I don't know how the bomb went off early but it happened. If I could go back—"

"But you can't. You took something away from both of us that we'll never get back."

"You found each other again!" Roy wailed.

"The seventeen years we lost can never be recovered and for that, you'll pay dearly. You stole from us, from Marvel, and from the fans using dirty money that gave the fucking criminals the opportunity to kill more people with their drug and sex trafficking."

"The fact that we're here listening to your veiled threats, means you have no proof, otherwise you would've had us locked up. You're not the judge and jury, Kane. If, and it's a big if, we're to be prosecuted, it'll be done in the legal justice system."

"Still doesn't get it, do they?"

"They sure don't."

"Fuck you both! Take us back to the island. This little excursion of yours has gone on long enough," Leon demanded.

"Did you happen to hear about the unfortunate death of the Triad leader, Chan Ho and his money laundering cohort, Zikri Malik?" Kane opened a bottle of cold beer and took a long sip.

The two men went quiet. They glanced at each other.

"Yeah, apparently there was a gas explosion."

"Hm ... were you aware that they kidnapped my son to try and convince us not to inform the FBI and DOJ of their money laundering in the U.S.?"

Both went deathly pale.

"I see that they do, Kane." Shane caught the beer he tossed at him.

Kane placed a sneakered foot on the seat and leaned forward on his knee. "See, they made a mistake doing that. The Sinclairs protect their own, violently, if need be."

"Y-you blew up the house?" Roy stared at them, fear arriving in his eyes for the first time. "With them inside?"

Kane straightened, his eyes turned glacial. The smile he offered promised the kind of retribution they didn't care to consider.

"Zikri Malik, who you had a very lucrative relationship with, isn't that true?"

They sputtered their denial, trying to bear back as Shane stepped closer. He smirked. "Relax, I just need to get the cooler box."

"The DOJ and the FBI have enough intel to unravel the Chinese Triads in the U.S. Hopefully, get rid of their U.S. vein completely. Oh, in case you were wondering about your offshore accounts ... don't. They've been shall we say ... closed." Kane smirked mockingly.

"What the fuck are you talking about?" Leon's face turned red with anger.

"Don't worry about it too much, though. It's being put to good use to develop halfway homes for sex trafficking victims." Shane interjected.

"You had no right to do that!" Leon exploded.

"Now, isn't that calling the kettle black?" Kane said colloquially as he lowered the binoculars he'd been looking through. "Perfect, I see our feeding ground has drawn many eager participants."

"Indeed. Let's hope they don't have refined tastes because scum like this would probably leave a bad aftertaste." Shane grunted as he opened the cooler box.

"What is that? What the fuck is that?" Roy screamed as he tried to lift himself to look inside.

"I'm going to give you one opportunity to redeem yourself and perhaps change our mind of the outcome of this excursion as you put it." Kane folded his arms over his chest. "Was the bomb intentionally detonated early to kill Narine?"

Roy glanced at Leon, who gave him a dirty look.

"Fuck you, Kane. Roy already explained what happened."

"Indeed, he did. Pity I don't believe him." He unsheathed the knife from his belt. "We're wasting time. Let's see if they're good swimmers like Salvino claims."

Kane cut through the rope behind their backs and the ones around their ankles. Shane hauled them to their feet. Seconds later their bodies hit the water when Shane and Kane lifted them bodily and threw them overboard.

"You motherfuckers," Leon surfaced, sputtering and cursing. "You're gonna pay for this."

Kane and Shane laughed, leisurely finishing their beers. Kane nodded toward the left. "They seem a little agitated, don't you think?"

"Yeah, perhaps they smelled the stink of these bastards."

Roy and Leon's heads snapped in the direction they were looking.

"No, you can't be serious," Roy all but sobbed as he identified the frightening sight of what appeared to be twenty or thirty sharks circling in the distance. Leon had turned into a statue, his gaze riveted on the fins that seemed to be edging closer.

"What do you want from us," he managed in a hoarse croak.

"Really? You need me to repeat the question?"

"Kane, you have to be reasonable. We were desperate. We couldn't afford to lose you at the time. You and Shane were what made the Space Riders," Roy keened in a high-pitched voice, desperately trying to reach the boat.

"It really is laughable that they still don't get it."

"It certainly is."

"Yes! Yes! There I said it. I admit it all. The bomb was detonated early. She wasn't supposed to survive, but now that you've found each other again, I'm glad she did. I truly am." Leon joined Roy in his frantic dash toward the boat as he realized it hadn't been his imagination. The sharks were slowly swimming closer. "Now get us out of here, for fuck's sake!"

Kane laughed evilly. "They still don't get it, do they?"

"They sure don't."

"Kane, I beg you, please. I don't want to die. I'm too young and not … not like this," Roy sobbed pitifully.

"See, I don't give a shit about whether you want to die or not. You intended to kill the woman I loved and planned to marry. For that, you are hereby sentenced to death."

"You have no right! Fuck, why are they coming closer?" Leon shrieked.

"Might be the slice I made on your ankles when I cut you loose," Kane said conversationally.

"Or it might be the tantalizing smell of all this fresh meat and blood," Shane said and with a mighty heave emptied the cooler box filled with raw meat and blood over the two men frantically trying to reach the boat.

"NOOO!"

"Jesus! Help us!"

Their wails carried over the emptiness surrounding them as Kane started the boat and eased it a few yards away.

"Another beer?"

"Don't mind if I do."

The smell of the fresh blood turned the lazy approach of the great white sharks, known for infesting these waters, into a sonic dash to feed.

Kane and Shane watched impassively as the sharks reached their target and tore at the men. Their pitiful screams were cut short within seconds. It was over within minutes, and soon, the swirling water returned to its usual calm.

The only sign of the carnage that took place was the red stain in the beauty of the otherwise turquoise hue of the ocean.

"That was too quick," Kane sneered as he finished his beer in one gulp. "They should've suffered longer."

"I agree but they're exactly where they belong once they get expelled in the excrement of the sharks, at the bottom of the ocean, where they'll follow the same path over and over, courtesy of the seabed dwellers."

Shane slapped Kane on the back. "Let's get back. I'm sure your bride is eager to continue your honeymoon."

The warmth at the thought of his lovely wife cleared his mind of thoughts of violence and death to be replaced by visions of her beauty on their wedding day.

Finally, she was his. His wife.

"Not as eager as I, Shane. Never as eager as I."

The End

Excerpt: Ace

CHAPTER ONE

Something was wrong. Ace could feel his body shake but the ground didn't move and neither did he.

"Shit." He could hear the rawness of his voice in his ears. "What the hell is that sound? It sounds like metal on metal. Something or someone is scraping?"

He looked around. He stood on a dirt road, where, he had no idea. The strangest feeling overcame him. Like his body was upside-down, tumbling over.

"Fuck … it hurts!" Pain exploded in his mind. He blinked and suddenly there was nothing. No daylight, no meadow or river ... everything he had woken up to was gone. He felt cold and different as he struggled to move. To put one foot in front of the other. His legs were weak. He felt like a toddler ... no, there was too much pain radiating around his skull to move.

"What the fuck is happening to me?" he shouted but a croak was the only thing that escaped his dry lips. He heaved in a deep breath and gagged as a strange odor filled his nostrils. So strong, he could taste the vileness in his mouth. He tried to place it but the only familiar scent he could detect was rotten food and dampness. The other, the stronger prurient odor didn't feel natural as fumes filled his lungs, his stomach. Every muscle in his gut contracted with a violent surge. A thin liquid passed his lips in a spray ... and then everything stopped.

Darkness engulfed him. He couldn't see. He couldn't hear.

"Maybe I'm dead. Yeah, that must be it. I feel ... dead."

"Not yet, Ace, but if we don't get you out of here quickly, you just might be."

Ace forced his eyes open. His eyelids fluttered as he squinted against the light shining in his eyes. Not that it was a bright light, but it felt that way.

"Stone?"

"Yeah, cuz, it's me. Hawk, Kane and Shane are also here."

Ace cried out as Stone attempted to lift him from the floor.

"Fuck that hurts," he groaned, clutching his shoulder.

"Good God, Ace. What the fuck did they do to you? You look like shit." Stone tentatively examined his limbs. He frowned in concern at the purple bruises that covered Ace's entire upper body. He prayed he didn't have any internal injuries which could be exacerbated by sudden movement. "Your shoulder is dislocated."

"Pop it."

"It's gonna hurt like fuck."

"Everything hurts like fuck. Just ... AWWW! Jesus!" Ace screamed and then clenched his teeth as Stone popped his shoulder back in place. "You could've fucking warned me."

"I could've but this way I didn't have to try and figure out whether to pop on three or after three."

"Fuck off," Ace grunted as Stone taunted his habit to say, "Go on three."

"Let's go. We have a small window to get back to the pick-up spot. Danton is circling the chopper just out of sight." Stone pushed his shoulder under Ace's arm and dragged him upright. "Can you walk?"

"I think I have a sprained ankle but I'll run if I have to. Just get me the fuck out of here."

"What's the hold-up. Hawk detected a vehicle approaching. We need to move. Now." Kane cursed as he noticed Ace's condition. "Bastards did a real job on you." He grabbed hold of him on the other side and between him and Stone, they half-lifted, half-carried him out of the dungeon-like basement and up the stairs.

Ace had been held hostage for three weeks in a rebel compound a couple of miles north of El Salvador in Cuba. From what Parker, IT guru and brother of Stone Sinclair, primary owner of Be Secure Enterprises, could establish, the rebels had associations with the Chinese Triads. The Sun Lee

Fong Triads were after the Sinclairs' blood, ever since the death of their leader, Chan Ho. He had been killed by Kane for kidnapping his son, Tucker two months prior. Ace had been the bait to lure the rest of the cousins into a trap and kill them off. Unfortunately for the rebels, they had no idea how resilient the Sinclair cousins were.

"Evac route has changed," Hawk said as he and Shane came running toward them. "Good to see you, Ace."

"Likewise, but can we leave the niceties and get the hell out of here?"

"Grumpy as always, I see," Shane said as he peered outside. "Two vehicles are approaching. We need to leave through the back and then circle around to get to the pickup point."

"We better hustle. They're here." Hawk took the lead with Shane following behind Stone and Kane carrying Ace, who seemed to be getting weaker by the moment.

"Stone, you've got less than two minutes to clear that building. They've split up and one group is going around the back." Parker's voice echoed in their ear coms.

"Move!" Stone barked as they sped up. "We fucking lost our advantage."

"Prepare for a shootout. They're armed to the teeth," Parker's warning came as they exited the back door. "Move straight forward into the bushes. They're too close to go around to the side. You have to get out of sight!"

Hawk didn't hesitate and ran ahead, keeping vigilant to ensure Stone and Kane were secured as they labored on with their load. They reached the cover of the bushes just as four men rounded the corner. They hunched down, silently watching the men scan the surroundings.

"Zhang Yong is paranoid. There's fucking no one here." The biggest of the men grumbled as he lit a cigar and puffed on it. He pushed the AK47 that hung on a sling to the back of his hip. "This is a waste of time. Those Americans aren't coming for their man. We should just kill the bastard."

A loud commotion and shouting from the inside of the compound alerted the four men.

"Let's move," Stone whispered. They carefully edged backwards, keeping their eyes on the men as they opened the back door that the Sinclairs had just exited.

"Escaped! The prisoner is gone!" A furious voice shouted from inside.

"Now, run!" Hawk said as they broke into a sprint as soon as they were out of sight behind a row of thick bushes, the sound of the burly man's voice following them through the thicket.

"What the fuck? How?"

"I told you they'll come for him. You fuck! Find them!"

"How far to the rendezvous point?" Kane asked with the voices growing fainter behind them.

"One klick, give or take," Shane said.

"Hang in there, Ace. I know you're in pain but we can't afford to slow down," Stone said as he tightened his grip around Ace's waist. He was becoming steadily heavier the further they went. Stone suspected he was losing the battle against consciousness. He kept his Fitty at the ready. They were each armed with M2 .50 caliber machine guns.

It was lightweight and easy to handle, especially in a situation like this, where they were on the backfoot.

"We need to push faster. I can hear them searching the bushes behind us." Hawk tapped his ear com. "Danton, were coming in hot. Expect IDF. They're on our tails. Eight minutes to rendezvous."

"Roger that. We've got you covered."

"Push it! They'll be alerted when the bird approaches and chase us down with their Jeeps. We'll be sitting ducks in that eighty-yard dash toward the helo." Shane urged as him and Hawk shadowed the three men struggling to speed up.

"I've got them! Over here! They're just ahead of us." A voice shouted from behind them.

"Fuck! Danton, you have to get as close as you can to the edge of the trees or we're fucking toast," Hawk shouted into the com as they ran. The sound of the chopper overhead offered some relief as they charged ahead.

"Keep going. Don't stop at the edge of the trees. We're gonna hit that bird flying," Shane graveled loudly, cognizant of the increasingly loud noise of running feet hitting the ground not too far behind them.

"Bird down. Get in. Move! Move!" Danton screamed as the chopping sound of AK47 rifles accompanied the bodies appearing from the edge of the trees. "Zeke, give them cover."

Zeke moved the locking arm of the M240H 7.62mm machine gun and aimed at the tree line. His hand folded around the spade grip as he fed the bullets from a 200rd box on the side of the mount. He squeezed the butterfly trigger.

"Take that, motherfuckers!"

The folly of bullets was enough to scare their pursuers to fall back and hide. It gave the four men the gap they needed to get Ace on board before they jumped into the chopper.

"Go! Get us the fuck out of here," Hawk shouted above the sound of the automatic chopper gun and cursed as a couple of bullets from the tree line slammed into the steel frame.

"Ugh!"

"Stone!" Kane's raw shout echocd over the ear coms. He went on his knees next to Stone who had been flung backward as he got hit and rolled over, lying prone on his stomach. A darkening pool of blood spread out over the floor.

"He's been shot." Kane said as he gently turned him over. "Jesus!" Kane yanked off his jacket and frantically pressed it over the gaping wound in Stone's chest. "Danton, you better get this fucking chopper to the closest hospital and fast."

"Someone talk to me! What happened to my brother?" Parker's voice raised in alarm over the ear coms.

"Stay calm, Parker. We're getting him to a hospital." Hawk's deep voice graveled through the cap of the chopper.

"How bad is it?" Parker asked in a strained voice.

Kane didn't immediately answer. His concerned gaze met Shane's who covered his eyes as he shook his head. As the two oldest of the cousins, they were the ones who did everything in their power to protect their family. It was the first time that one of their own got hurt during a rescue operation. Kane heaved in a deep breath. His voice sounded brittle.

"It's bad, Parker. Very bad."

Find Castle Sin series here: Castle Sin Series

More Books by Linzi Basset

Castle Sin Series
Stone – Book 1
Hawk – Book 2
Kane – Book 3

Club Devil's Cove Series
His Devil's Desire – Book 1
His Devil's Heat – Book 2
His Devil's Wish – Book 3
His Devil's Mercy – Book 4
His Devil's Chains – Book 5
His Devil's Fire – Book 6
Her Devil's Kiss – Book 7
His Devil's Rage – Book 8

Club Wicked Cove Series
Desperation: Ceejay's Absolution–Book 1
Desperation: Colt's Acquittal – Book 2
Exploration: Nolan's Regret – Book 3
Merciful: Seth's Revenge – Book 4
Claimed: Parnell's Gift – Book 5
Decadent: Kent's Desire – Book 6

Club Alpha Cove Series
His FBI Sub – Book 1
His Ice Baby Sub – Book 2
His Vanilla Sub – Book 3

His Fiery Sub – Book 4
His Sassy Sub – Book 5
Their Bold Sub – Book 6
His Brazen Sub – Book 7
His Defiant Sub – Book 8
His Forever Sub – Book 9
His Cherished Sub – Book 10
For Amy – Their Beloved Sub – Book 11

Dark Desire Novels
Enforcer – Book 1

Their Sub Novella Series
No Option – Book 1
Done For – Book 2
For This – Book 3
Their Sub Series Boxset

Their Command Series
Say Yes – Book 1
Say Please – Book 2
Say Now – Book 3
Their Command Series Boxset

Paranormal Books
The Flame Dragon King - Metallic Dragons #1
Slade: The First Touch
Azriel: Angel of Destruction

Romance Suspense

The Bride Series
Claimed Bride – Book 1
Captured Bride – Book 2
Chosen Bride – Book 3
Charmed Bride – Book 4

Caught Series
Caught in Between
Caught in His Web

The Tycoon Series
The Tycoon and His Honey Pot
The Tycoon's Blondie
The Tycoon's Mechanic

Standalone Titles
Her Prada Cowboy
Never Leave Me, Baby
Now is Our Time
The Wildcat that Tamed the Tycoon
The Poet's Lover
Sarah: The Life of Me

Naughty Christmas Story
Her Santa Dom
Master Santa

Box set
A Santa to Love – with Isabel James
Christmas Delights – with Isabel James

Linzi Basset

Books Co-Written as Isabel James

Zane Gorden Novels
Truth Untold

The Crow's Nest
A journey of discovery on the White Pearl

Christmas Novella
Santa's Kiss
Santa's Whip

Box set
A Santa to Love – with Linzi Basset
Christmas Delight – with Linzi Basset

Poetry Bundle by Linzi Basset & James Calderaro

Love Unbound - Poems of the Heart

About the Author

"Isn't it a universal truth that it's our singular experiences and passion, for whatever thing or things, which molds us all into the individuals we become? Whether it's hidden in the depths of our soul or exposed for all to see?"

Linzi Basset is a South African born animal rights supporter with a poet's heart, and she is also a bestselling fiction writer of suspense-filled romance erotica books; who as the latter, refuses to be bound to any one sub-genre. She prefers instead to stretch herself as a storyteller which has resulted in her researching and writing historical and even paranormal themed works.

Her initial offering: Club Alpha Cove, a BDSM club suspense series released back in 2015, reached Amazon's Bestseller list, and she has been on those lists ever since. Labelling her as prolific is a gross understatement as just a few short years later she has now been published over fifty times; a total which excludes the other published works of her alter ego: Isabel James who co-authors.

"I write from the inside out. My stories are both inside me and a part of me, so it can be either pleasurable to release them or painful to carve them out. I live every moment of every story I write. So, if you're looking for spicy and suspenseful, I'm your girl ... woman ... writer ... you know what I mean!"

Linzi believes that by telling stories in her own voice, she can better share with her readers the essence of her being: her passionate nature; her motivations; and her wildest fantasies. She feels every touch as she writes, every kiss, every harsh word uttered, and this to her is the key to a never-ending love of writing.

Ultimately, all books by Linzi Basset are about passion. To her, passion is the driving force of all emotion; whether it be lust, desire, hate, trust, or love. This is the underlying message contained in her books. Her advice: "Believe in the passions driving your desires; live them; enjoy them; and allow them to bring you happiness."

Stalk Linzi Basset

If you'd like to look me up, please follow any of these links.

While you're enjoying some of my articles, interviews and poems on my website, why not subscribe to my Newsletter and be the first to know about new releases and win free books.

Linzi Basset's Website and Isabel James' Website
Linzi Basset Twitter and Isabel James Twitter:
Friend Linzi on Facebook or Friend Isabel James on Facebook
Linzi's Facebook Author Page and Isabel James' Facebook Author Page
Linzi on Amazon and Isabel James on Amazon
Linzi All Author-Page and Isabel James All Author Page
LinkedIn
Instagram
Goodreads
BookBub
YouTube
Pinterest
MEWE:
Linzi's Lair on MEWE

Like my Facebook pages:
Linzi's Poetry Page

Club Wicked Cove
Club Alpha Cove
Club Devil's Cove
Castle Sin Series

AND, don't forget to join my fan group, Linzi's Luscious Lair, for loads of fun!

Don't be shy, pay me a visit, anytime!

Printed in Great Britain
by Amazon

65889098R00332